CRITICAL ACCLAIM FOR

Sailing

"The achingly honest pictures presented here of courage and cowardice, gritty rage and soft denials, make for an absorbing, uplifting, and genuinely satisfying book."

—*Boston Phoenix*

"In passages of lyric beauty and emotional resonance, Kenney makes sailing a metaphor for life. . . . This is a powerful testament of the power of love to transcend tragedy, written with uncompromising honesty and insight."

—*Publishers Weekly*

"Kenney works a miracle in *Sailing*. . . . She has written a love story that . . . ends by being a work of unusual substance and power."

—*San Francisco Chronicle*

"Her novel can rightly take its place on the bookshelf next to those works, such as Tolstoy's *The Death of Ivan Ilyich*, that detail illness's effects on the human body and spirit. But *Sailing* can as easily be shelved with those volumes that demonstrate the indomitability and triumph of love."

—*Milwaukee Journal*

"It's a wrenchingly unforgettable story. . . . It has much to say about the often shaken but ultimately unbreakable human spirit."

—*Christian Science Monitor*

D0829862

CONTEMPORARY AMERICAN FICTION

SAILING

Susan Kenney won the first annual "New Voices Literary Award" from the Quality Paperback Book Club for *In Another Country*. She won the 1982 O. Henry Award for her short story, "Facing Front." She is also the author of two mysteries, *Graves in Academe* and *Garden of Malice*. She teaches creative writing at Colby College.

Sailing

Susan Kenney

Penguin Books

PENGUIN BOOKS
Published by the Penguin Group
Viking Penguin Inc., 40 West 23rd Street, New York, New York 10010, U.S.A.
Penguin Books Ltd, 27 Wrights Lane, London W8 5TZ, England
Penguin Books Australia Ltd, Ringwood, Victoria, Australia
Penguin Books Canada Ltd, 2801 John Street, Markham, Ontario, Canada L3R 1B4
Penguin Books (N.Z.) Ltd, 182-190 Wairau Road, Auckland 10, New Zealand

Penguin Books Ltd, Registered Offices:
Harmondsworth, Middlesex, England

First published in the United States of America by Viking Penguin Inc. 1988
Published in Penguin Books 1989

1 3 5 7 9 10 8 6 4 2

Copyright © Susan Kenney, 1988
All rights reserved

Portions of this book first appeared in *The Hudson Review* as "Sailing" and
"In Case You Don't Come Back" and in *Ladies' Home Journal* as "Nativity."

Grateful acknowledgment is made for permission to reprint an extract from
"The Dry Salvages" from *Four Quartets* by T. S. Eliot. Copyright 1943 by T. S. Eliot,
renewed 1971 by Esme Valerie Eliot. Reprinted by permission of
Harcourt Brace Jovanovich, Inc. and Faber and Faber Ltd.

LIBRARY OF CONGRESS CATALOGING IN PUBLICATION DATA
Kenney, Susan, 1941–
Sailing.
(Contemporary American fiction)
I. Title.   II. Series.
[PS3561.E445S25 1989]   813'.54   88–28957
ISBN 0 14 00.9333 8 (pbk.)

Printed in the United States of America
Set in Sabon
Designed by Quinten Welsh

Except in the United States of America, this book is sold subject to
the condition that it shall not, by way of trade or otherwise, be lent,
re-sold, hired out, or otherwise circulated without the publisher's prior
consent in any form of binding or cover other than that in which it is
published and without a similar condition including this
condition being imposed on the subsequent purchaser.

This book is dedicated to
my son   my daughter
James McIlvaine Kenney   Anne Morrow Kenney
and in honor
of their namesakes
James Morrow McIlvaine   Anne Morrow Lindbergh
with my love

The sea howl
And the sea yelp, are different voices
Often together heard: the whine in the rigging,
The menace and caress of wave that breaks on water,
The distant rote in the granite teeth,
And the wailing warning from the approaching headland
Are all sea voices, and the heaving groaner
Rounded homewards, and the seagull:
And under the oppression of the silent fog
The tolling bell
Measures time not our time, rung by the unhurried
Ground swell, a time
Older than the time of chronometers, older
Than time counted by anxious worried women
Lying awake, calculating the future,
Trying to unweave, unwind, unravel
And piece together the past and the future,
Between midnight and dawn, when the past is all deception,
The future futureless, before the morning watch
When time stops and time is never ending;
And the ground swell, that is and was from the beginning,
Clangs
The bell.

T. S. Eliot,
from "The Dry Salvages"

Contents

PART

I

I

Sailing

The Indian Cove boatyard takes up almost the whole wharf, with its floating dock and boat slips, its lobster shack, its chandlery and sail loft, the boat brokerage office around the back. The graveled drive edges over the hill toward the water, but Phil parks the car behind the office and he and Sara walk down to the dock. It's warm for late October; even so he wears corduroy pants and a crewneck sweater over a flannel shirt, a down vest over that. He's felt slightly cold ever since they sent him home from the hospital last month, something to do with altered metabolism, the doctors say, or maybe it's just the loss of weight. Skinny people seem to feel the cold more. He's not skinny, at least not yet, but he does get cold.

The air is so warm now it's hard to believe it's no longer mid-summer. But all around them as they've driven from yard to yard looking at boats, the trees have been flagged with autumn colors, the leaves so bright they seem to flicker and change before his eyes and he feels pulled along by the pressure of their turning. He has found that if he stares closely enough he can freeze that burning look into an image as still and permanent as a painting done on glass. As he stares now across the bay at the surrounding hills and islands, the landscape takes on that flatness, that brittle luminous clarity of detail. He blinks. The sharpness dissolves; the truth is, the foliage is already past its peak. The scarlet maples are mere remnants, the colors have faded, so that far away the land on the horizon lies curled around the water like a rusty chain.

He senses a movement next to him, a stirring of the air. Sara has walked off and is pacing up and down the wharf, hands stuffed into the pockets of her jeans, looking down at the sailboats bobbing in their slips. It's a couple of hours past low tide, but the boats are still a good five feet below the dock. Phil watches her as she comes back toward him, feeling more removed from her than he is in actual distance; this is the way it's been ever since he got out of the hospital more than a month ago.

He walks down the hall toward the long Chippendale mirror, peering at his reflection, half-expecting it to disappear. The mirror is old and makes him look more blue and fragile than he really is. The truth is, he looks no different now, a little thinner perhaps, but really very much the same. He has lost no weight to speak of, only five pounds or so, is still strong, but there is a pallor to his complexion, as though someone had powdered his face with chalk and then blown all but a bare residue away. He feels this paleness as a thin layer of ice water just beneath his skin.

He is still examining himself in the mirror when he sees Sara come and stand behind him. As his reflection's eyes catch hers he says casually, lightly, "Now I ask you, do I look like a dying man?"

Sara blinks, goes ghostly pale herself. Before she turns away she says quite calmly, her voice as precise and level as the glass, "No, as a matter of fact you don't." But he is sorry that he asked.

Sara walks down onto the dock and stands next to him, looking at him with an air of expectancy, as if to say, "Now what?" This is the third time they've been to this particular boatyard in the past month, because Phil has seen a boat here that he likes more than any of the others they have looked at this fall. It's one of the boatyard's charter fleet, a twenty-odd-feet long full-keel fiberglass

4

sloop with a small cabin and lots of wood trim, fairly new sails including a big deck-sweeping genoa, and an outboard motor in a well in the aft compartment. Phil likes the idea of the full keel, the sleek look of the upswept stern, the quaint extravagance of the cabin, even though he can't imagine ever using it; the idea of sleeping in anything that narrow and confined gives him the creeps.

The boat is a little bigger than they had in mind—also older, twenty years old, in fact—but in very good condition. "A real classic, Alberg design, don't build 'em like that anymore," the used-boat broker told them the last time they were here. "Hey, man, this boat will take you anywhere you want to go." A real bargain, too: the yard is going out of the charter business, so they've put all the rental boats up for sale. Big as it is, the broker was careful to point out, it only draws three and a half feet. "Fix yourself up with a heavy-duty trailer, you can haul her right home and sail her in one of those big lakes," he told them. The boat is sitting in the water below them right now. Phil can see it tugging at its mooring lines, moving up and down with the swell.

"What do you want to do?" Sara asks.

Phil shrugs. "I thought we could just walk around, look at the boats, talk to the broker, do what we always do . . ."

Sara turns away. After a moment she says over her shoulder, "I don't see why you want to keep looking at boats all the time if you think we can't buy one."

For an instant Sara reminds him of the boat, tugging at the lines, impatient to get on with it. Phil feels no need to get on with anything; he is perfectly content to stay as he is. "I like to look at boats," he answers. "I love boats. Besides, it's not so much the boats themselves as the idea of boats. You know that."

Sara shakes her head slightly, but she does know, Phil is certain of that. After all, she is the real sailor. It was her tales of sailing in her youth—Comets, Lightnings, Bantams, Stars, white flags rampant across a field of blue—that had gotten him started on this so late in life in the first place. He hadn't learned to sail until after that bloody mess of an operation that almost killed him two years ago, at Sara's suggestion, in a boat borrowed from friends. It had come upon him as something of a revelation, and his only regret was that he had waited until he was thirty-five years old even to try. They had been looking for a boat of their own before he got sick again, and they are still looking, more as a way to pass the time than anything else. It is not so much the boat itself, or even sailing, as the idea of it. There is something so complex yet pure about the relation of wind and sail, so absorbing about the need to balance conflicting forces, that he finds sailing is all he thinks about, or tries to, and it is more than just a way to pass the time. Who had ever thought to harness the wind with little more than a bedsheet, two sticks, and twenty yards of rope? His sailing manuals have little to say about this, other than that it was inevitable that the earliest seafarers should find a way to use the free power of the wind. That seems obvious enough. But who were those early seafarers? Aborigines? Indians? Phil imagines a birch-bark canoe, a buffalo skin hoisted on a spear, a lone Indian with feathers in his hair being blown before the wind down Gitchee-Gumee, down the shining Big-Sea Water. But he knows this is wrong; it was not the Indians but the grave Tyrians—Phoenicians—who first ventured into open ocean under sail, or so the story goes. Still, as he looks out across the water he sees the sailboats making a temporary encampment in light air, their sails like wigwams against the ragged trees.

"Besides," he says by way of conversation, "it's too late in the season to buy a sailboat. We'd never use it."

There is a slight pause. Finally Sara says, "We could buy it for next year."

This is the sticking point, of course; everything always comes back to this, the question of next year. Phil says nothing, hoping she will drop it, sorry he even brought it up. But she goes on.

"We've spent all this time looking, and we know what we want, so why don't we just buy it? We've got the money. We can trail it home, store it over the winter, and put it in the lake next spring." She gestures at the boat below them, the *Loon*. All the charter boats have bird names stenciled on their transoms: *Osprey*, *Eagle*, *Tern*, *Teal*, *Loon*, *Petrel*. Phil glances down at the *Loon*. He likes it well enough, but he'd just as soon go right on looking. Sara likes to have things settled, nothing left up in the air. Phil is sympathetic to her need for certainty, her impatience; he just doesn't share it.

"That way we'll have it," she persists. "We won't have to waste time looking next spring. We can start right in at the beginning of the season."

Phil sighs. It is clear she is not going to drop it. He does not want to be cruel, but there are times when he wishes she would get over these dogged forays into the future. They make him uncomfortable. "I may not be here next spring," he says. He hears her quick intake of breath.

"Don't say that."

"Why not? You know it's true."

"You don't know that. Nobody knows that."

"It doesn't really matter," Phil says. "I just don't think it's worth the risk. What are you going to do with it if I'm not here?"

"Sail it myself," she says sharply and walks away. Behind him he can hear the gravel crunching, but he does not turn to see where she is going. He steps to the edge of the dock and looks down, sees far below a shadow of himself only a little darker than the murky, oil-slicked water, undulating strangely with the moving tide.

When Sara returns to the dock she has Wally Perkins, the yacht broker, in tow. "Hi. How's things? Your wife says you two might be interested in going sailing. The *Loon*'s available, if you want to take her out. We're pulling all the boats out first of the week, so now's your chance. No charge. I'll even throw in the gas for the outboard."

Phil hesitates, looks from one to the other. He hasn't thought about actually going sailing, it's so late in the season.

"How long have you got?"

Phil blinks, stares at him.

"Most of the day," Sara answers quickly. "I told the baby-sitter we'd be back by the kids' bedtime. It's about a three-hour drive, if we leave by five . . ."

"Oh, that's plenty of time," Wally says. "You can get a real feel for a boat in an afternoon. No problem."

Sara and Wally Perkins stand on either side of him, waiting for him to decide. Phil looks at Sara. This is her idea. Still, he understands it as a gesture, an alternative to looking that isn't buying, in fact a compromise. It's a nice day, the air is warm, and they have lots of time. He smiles to himself, then nods.

"Sure, why not?" he says. "What have we got to lose?"

Lying in his hospital bed, he cannot see all the way down the corridor, but Sara can. He sees her stiffen. "Here he comes," she says quietly, her fork resting in the macaroni and cheese she is supposed to be eating for lunch. Phil lies back against the pillows, a layer of ice water spreading under his skin. The arteriogram was done on Wednesday; it's past noon on Thursday now and still they haven't heard. He has told Sara that this means bad news; good news travels fast in a hospital and no news is bad news, but Sara, meliorist as always, has insisted that the doctor is very busy, that they finished the test late, that it is all very complicated, that it doesn't mean a thing; at worst it means a puzzle. But Phil knows what it means. He watches Sara lift her fork to her mouth, glad that she is eating. He hasn't felt much like eating lately himself. First it was all the tests, and now the hospital food seems to turn his stomach. Maybe he's just gotten out of the habit of eating. When he gets home, Sara says, she will feed him up.

Now he can see the doctor coming toward his room. He certainly looks grim enough, Phil thinks, his brow furrowed, his mouth drawn up in a tight pucker of what could be either disgust or resignation. He's as pale as Phil feels. His hands are behind his back as he walks along, but as he comes through the door he brings them forward, holding Phil's chart in one hand. He pulls up a chair, sits down, flips open the chart, and studies it. Oh, hell, Phil thinks. He doesn't know a thing. The doctor looks up, nods at Sara, then fixes his eyes on Phil.

"Hi, Phil. How're you feeling?"

"Fine." It's a lie, of course, he has a headache, his nose is stuffed up, and his stomach is bothering him. But one of the rituals of hospital behavior is that you don't complain.

"Good," the doctor says, and looks back down at the chart, flipping over pages again. Phil glances at Sara, who is chewing macaroni and cheese in slow motion, as though she's forgotten what she's doing. Her eyes are riveted on the chart, and Phil knows that she is busy trying to read it upside down, an old trick of hers. But the doctor is flipping the pages over too fast, not even looking at them himself. He knows what's there. Finally Sara swallows, and pushes the fork around in the small casserole, but does not take another mouthful.

"Hey, Sam," she says. "How come you always show up at lunchtime?"

Sam's face creases into a smile; for a moment he looks like an amiable troll. "Is it any good?" he asks, peering over at Sara's dish.

"I couldn't tell you," Sara says, and puts her fork down. She waits, watching Sam's face, sitting on the end of Phil's bed with her hands folded in her lap, looking, Phil thinks in admiration, perfectly composed.

"Well," Sam says, and shuffles the chart once more. Then he shuts the hinged cover with a snap, crosses his legs, folds his hands casually, and stares out the window. He takes a deep breath. Here we go, thinks Phil. "The arteriogram demonstrates conclusively a large mass, presumably tumor, in the right retroperitoneal space, surrounding the kidney. That's what's causing your extreme high blood pressure, which is what caused those bad headaches, nausea, dizziness, all those other symptoms. The reason I'm late," he inclines his head at Sara, "is that I've been on the phone to Lahey, the head kidney man at Mass General. We talked quite a long time about you, Phil." Sam darts a look at Phil, clears his throat, and sits in silence.

Phil lies back against the pillows, feeling suddenly exhausted. His mouth is dry and he is short of breath. Side effects of the drugs, he thinks, looking up at the ceiling. He concentrates on slowing down his breathing, the pounding of his heart.

"And?" Sara asks.

Sam shifts in the chair. "His conclusion is that whatever can be done can be done here."

Phil feels relieved. He won't have to leave home, go to another hospital for more tests, not see Sara and the kids every day. Maybe he can go home soon, spend some time outside while the weather is still nice, see if he can borrow the Lanes's boat again, and do a little sailing. Maybe he can even go back to work.

"What's that?" Sara asks. "What can be done here?"

Sam clears his throat again; he must have a cold too, Phil thinks, poor bastard.

"That's what I want to discuss with you. The options." He glances at Phil. "You've taken medical leave, haven't you?" Phil shakes his head. "AWOL, huh? Well, you better do that. The college will just have to do without you for a while." Phil nods, resigned. He hadn't wanted to stop work in the first place, but things got out of hand, and now he's stuck with it. Still it's probably better to step out early in the semester, before they all get too used to having him around.

"Then what?" Sara asks. "More surgery?"

Oh my God, Phil thinks. Not another operation; the last one damn near killed me. I'm not doing that again. He shuts his eyes tight, wishing he were somewhere else. Sam's and Sara's voices echo, then grow smaller, as if they were leaving the room, but when he opens his eyes a slit he can see that they are still sitting right where they were.

"It's clearly inoperable," Sam says. "That means . . ."

"Why?" Sara interrupts him. "Why can't you operate?"

Sam shuts his eyes, then opens them. "The mass is too large, and spread all over the retroperitoneum," he says, as if this were perfectly self-evident.

But Sara doesn't give up. "Didn't you say it was on the right side?"

"Right, left, left, right," Sam says crossly. "What difference does it make? It's all over him." Phil opens his eyes wide, sees Sam wave his hand dismissively at Sara, as though she were a pesky insect. He's getting impatient, wants to get this whole thing over with. Phil thinks how much alike Sam and Sara are, a matched pair of bulldogs on either end of a rag. Sara wants to know everything, and she wants to know it now. Sam wants to get out of here. Sara, inexplicably, is stuffing forkfuls of macaroni into her mouth, chewing and swallowing. The thought makes him sick; he can't believe she's still eating. Then he is overtaken by an awful thought; he sits up and leans forward on one elbow, addressing Sam.

"Not chemotherapy?"

Sam glances at him, startled. His eyelids flutter closed and he dips his head, but Phil can't tell whether the movement means agreement or dissent.

"Chemotherapy and radiation have been demonstrated to have no effect on this kind of tumor," Sam says.

Phil lies back, once again relieved. No chemo, no radiation, no operation. No getting sick, no losing his hair. David and Linnie will not have to watch his retching, vomiting, getting bald. But Sara's voice breaks in on his relief.

"What kind of tumor? Couldn't it be something else?"

Phil can't understand why she is so persistent. What more is there to know? His mind is swaddled in a kind of pleasant fog, his grandmother's crazy-quilt stuffed into all the nooks and crannies that were echoing so strangely a few minutes ago. He feels sleepy. He wishes Sam would leave, that Sara would let him go.

Sam's voice drones on. "Same as before. Renal cell carcinoma. Metastatic kidney cancer. It's not good, Sara." His patience is elaborate now, his politeness palpable. Phil can feel it stretched thin, twanging in the air.

"That's not what Sloan-Kettering said."

Sam rolls his eyes to the ceiling. "It's the diagnosis of record," he says.

"They said it was some sort of ganglioma. Not renal cell," Sara says doggedly. Phil can hear the desperation edging into her voice. That was over two years ago, that other opinion. Still, he's got to hand it to her, remembering all that stuff, keeping it in her head all this time. He feels sorry for her, left holding the bag like this. He feels as though he has behaved badly, let everybody down.

"It doesn't matter," Sam says curtly, standing up. "It's all the same, six of one, half-a-dozen of the other." He tucks Phil's chart under his arm. "Any more questions?" He looks at Phil, carefully avoiding Sara.

"Yes, I've got a question," Sara says clearly. "If it's not surgery, and it's not radiation or chemotherapy, then just what the hell is it that can be done here?"

Sam pauses in the doorway, his face inscrutable. There is a long silence. Then he looks directly at Phil.

"If it were me, I would do nothing," he says, turns abruptly and walks away.

They both stare after him for a moment, then Sara flings down her fork and jumps up, runs out the door and down the hall. It isn't until she returns a few moments later, saying through the doorway, "I'll be right back, I've got to talk to Sam," that he realizes he thought she'd run away.

The sailboat's wake leaves a corridor of calm behind them as the wind pulls them forward. Not a lot of wind, just enough. Phil leans back against the cockpit coaming, elbows resting on the deck, watching Sara at the helm. He smiles at her. "How does it feel?" he asks.

"Fine," she answers, stooping slightly to peer under the boom, checking the set of the jib. The near feather is fluttering wildly. Phil pulls the jib sheet in. The feathers flutter, then lie flat against the sail as though they had been pasted on. "It's a great day for sailing. Who wants to look at boats when you can sail one?" She pulls the mainsheet in slightly so that both sails are close-hauled, their curves parallel. The boat heels slightly. Phil moves to windward, sits next to her. They sit for a while, not talking. Phil's arm lies along the coaming, just touching her back, so that she can lean against it if she wants, the way the sail leans against the air behind it.

He looks up to where the mast prods the sky in small half-circles. The sky goes on forever, uniform, clear, vast. Far up, very small, a red kite flutters and swings against the air, scooting back and forth, captive on its string. No, too far out, Phil thinks; it must be loose, blowing out to sea. As he watches, it loses the wind, begins to fall, slowly drifting down a zigzag path. Phil stares up at it, mesmerized by the precision and predictability of its movement, the balance of conflicting forces. Back and forth, back and forth, a fast swoop, then slow recovery, friction overcoming gravity, each time a little lower down. He feels himself drawn up, and for a moment he is riding the kite, high above, looking at himself and Sara in the sailboat. He sees the white triangle from above, as bright and angular as a gull's wing. But he is also in the boat, watching the kite's red diamond swoop closer, falling toward them, bringing him with it. He nudges Sara. "Look," he says. "A lost kite."

Sara glances upward. "That's not a kite," she says casually. "That's a red maple leaf."

With an odd jerk, Phil's sense of size and distance contracts. It is indeed a leaf. Phil watches it flutter past, fall into the water and float there. The scalded, curled-up edges catch the wind, and the leaf skims away. The wind is coming up. Phil can see it on the water, roughened patches of darker blue scattered here and there, moving closer. "Look out," he says. "Here comes a puff."

Sara pushes the tiller away slightly, reaches over to release the mainsheet, but it's too late; the boat leans, then heels sharply as wind gusts into the sails. Like a giant hand the wind presses the sails down toward the water, then just as abruptly lets them up. The boat tilts wildly. Water rushes up and foams along the rail. Suddenly the deck is perpendicular, and they are standing nearly upright, their feet braced against the opposite seat. A second wave sluices over the rail. Sara hangs onto the tiller for a moment longer, then says, "Here, you take it," as she turns and claws her way onto the deck, instinctively throwing her weight out over the rail to bring the boat back down, even though with a full-keel boat this size it won't do any good.

Phil grabs the flailing tiller. The *Loon* is wallowing, trying to round up into the wind, the sails banging and snapping. He's just as glad they decided not to fly the genoa, this boat is so responsive to the wind. He takes the mainsheet from Sara, eases off slightly, lets the main out, then holds the tack, studying the telltales, adjusting and correcting until once more the feathers lie flat against the sail. The boat heels over smoothly, not too far, and runs through the waves. The water foams and hisses as the boat pushes it aside.

"I couldn't hold it," Sara says from the deck above him.

"That's all right," Phil says absently, already caught up in the business of sailing. He looks backward over his shoulder and without turning his head adjusts the tiller so they are on a beam reach. The boat seems to lift up and leap ahead. "That's it," he says. "That's perfect."

He's talking to Spencer, the head man at Boston Institute for Cancer Research and Treatment. Sara is hovering somewhere in the background. It was her idea to call, to try and find out what's taking so long. It's been almost a month since Phil got out of the local hospital, more than that since all his records were sent down. There are some things he would rather not know right now, but Sara is insistent, insisting they should know whatever there is to know, even if it's nothing.

"Ah, yes. Mr . . . Ah. Why yes. What can I do for you?" He's very courteous, with a small, neat, finicky voice. Phil wonders what he looks like in real life, if he is a small, neat, finicky person.

"I called to see if you knew anything yet." Already he feels at a disadvantage. The Institute gets hundreds of referrals every month; probably Spencer doesn't even know who he is. He hears the sound of papers being shuffled on the other end.

"Ah yes. Here we are. Well, as a matter of fact, things are getting on quite nicely. We've sent your slides all over the city. Interesting case." Phil imagines a fleet of taxicabs with his slides and X-rays riding in the back seat crisscrossing the streets of Boston. "We've got a pretty good idea," Spencer goes on, "but we're still waiting for a definitive answer. One more country to be heard from."

Oh, Christ, another country? Phil thinks, then realizes Spencer is speaking metaphorically. At least he hopes he is. Anyway, as far as Phil's concerned it's all in another country. He feels strangely breathless. Sara is standing at his side, looking anxious.

"Ask him," she urges. "Ask him."

"Do you have any better idea what it might be?"

"Well. We have to use special dyes, a very complicated procedure, but yes, most of the reports have come back. Yes, here it is. Probably paraganglioma or pheochromocytoma. It's quite rare. A difficult diagnosis."

"Para-gang-glioma," Phil repeats. The word means nothing to him. He can't even pronounce the other one.

"Not renal cell?" Sara says, grabbing on to his arm. "Ask him to spell it." He doesn't understand why she gets so excited. They are only words.

"Not renal cell carcinoma?" he repeats to Spencer.

"No, oh no. Who told you that?"

"It's something different," he says to Sara.

"I beg your pardon?" Spencer's polite voice says faintly over the line. Sara has turned away. Phil cannot see her face.

"I'm sorry. I was talking to my wife. We were told up here that it was renal cell carcinoma."

"Oh, I see. No, it looks like paraganglioma all right." There is a silence; the phone hums. "Did you have any other questions?" Spencer asks finally.

"Ask him what they're planning to do," Sara says.

"What's going to be done? I mean, can you give us an idea of what's going to happen next, when they're . . . when you're . . ."

"Yes, well." The voice seems to shrink and fade inside the telephone. "I think we'd better get you down here for a consultation, anyway. Possibly, no, make it probably, an operation, but we can't tell at this point. We'll need more tests. But we'll definitely want to see you. And your wife, of course."

"How long," Sara says. "Find out how long."

"When?"

"Ah well. I think we might as well wait until the last report is in." He sounds so tentative. Phil wonders briefly if he is being evasive. But then the voice comes on much louder. Maybe it's the connection. "Quite probably right after the weekend," Spencer says. "As soon as we get a free bed. Then we'll want to get more pictures of that left side . . ."

"Left?" Phil asks. "Why the left?"

There is a puzzled silence. "That's where the tumor is." Pause. "Isn't it?"

Phil holds the phone away from his ear, stares at it. Sara comes back and stands close to him.

"I thought it was on the right," Phil says finally. "That's what they told us up here."

"Oh, well, that could be. But we'll find out," Spencer says cheerfully. "Don't worry, we'll get it sorted out. You'll be hearing from us. Goodbye now." He breaks the connection, leaving Phil holding the empty phone.

He turns to Sara, shaking his head.

"I give up," he says.

Sailing is not so much a science as an art, and thus demands complete attention, Phil thinks, turning his head now toward the mainsail to check the luff, now toward the water to look for cat's-paws, feeling the steady pressure of the tiller under his hand. There are so many variables, wind strength and direction, tide changes, rocks and shoals, so much to watch for. And then there are matters of discretion, whether to sail closer to the wind to gain distance at the expense of speed, or to lay off to gain the fastest point of sail. In sailing you don't always get exactly where you meant to go. It is a question of balancing forces that are constantly changing, possibilities that continually transmute. Still there is that moment always hoped for, when everything conjoins and the boat leaps forward, creating its own wind, apparent wind exceeding true wind, drawing the boat onward. Looking at his own tautened sail, he wonders who ever imagined that wind blowing sideways would make a boat go forward, that the fastest point of sail is a beam reach, the wind at your back blowing over the rail, the sails almost perpendicular to the direction of the wind.

"Aren't you hungry?" Sara asks, breaking into his concentration. He looks at his watch. They have been sailing for almost three hours, threading their way in and out among the coastal islands as far as the mouth of the main bay. It's long past lunchtime, but Phil shakes his head, twitches the mainsheet, adjusts the tiller. He's not thinking about lunch. The boat's speed increases almost imperceptibly. Ah, good, he thinks. He pulls the sail in more; they are sailing close-hauled, to gain distance to windward. But not at the expense of speed.

"We should start thinking about getting back," Sara says after a while. "Even if we're not hungry, it's still a long drive home."

Phil nods absently, watching the configuration of the sail, the arrow line of telltale pointing out the wind direction. "I could stay out here forever," he says without thinking.

Without even looking at her he can feel her stiffen, feels it almost as a change in wind direction, her sense of outrage at the lack of forever, or even next year. He wishes he had said something else.

"Be that as it may," Sara says calmly, "I think we should be getting back while there's still wind. Who wants to chug all the way in with that disgusting thing?" she finishes, gesturing toward where the clunky old engine hangs down through its well inside the stern compartment. Phil has forgotten it existed, but there it is, their insurance against the failure of the wind. No, they would not want to go back that way, with all the noise and smell and commotion.

"All right," he says, and pushes the tiller across the coaming. The boat begins to swing around, then stalls, its sail flapping aimlessly, as limp and fragile as a closed eyelid. The water has lost its ruffled quality, and between them and the shoreline the surface lies as flat and slippery-looking as a pool of oil. The boat coasts for a few feet, then settles back into the water like a roosting bird. The wind has simply blown itself away.

"Well, how do you like that?" Phil says, leaning back against the deck. The tiller nudges his hand, and he slaps it away. "Wouldn't you know? You can't trust anybody." He looks back toward where they came from; they must be at least three miles out. He can't even make out the boatyard from here. "Isn't this just our luck?" He hasn't meant to sound so resentful, but the annoyance wells up from someplace deep inside and surprises even him. He stares around at the surface of the water, looking for any sign of wind.

There is a silence. Then Sara says, "Do you want to talk about it now?"

"Shhh," Phil mouths, shaking his head and waving her to silence. Not twenty feet away a black faucet has appeared above the surface of the water. Sara looks bewildered; he puts a hand on her head and directs her gaze toward the loon. The faucet-like head swivels, showing a white neck patch, flashes a startled red eye at them, then with a quick looping dive shoots away under the water, a dark torpedo speeding out of range. Birdmarines, his son calls them. Often they float with their bodies almost submerged, only their heads and necks showing, turning silently, intelligently, like periscopes, precise, mechanical.

"I didn't know they came out this far," Sara whispers, her head swiveling in an odd imitation of the bird. "Where is it?" Silently they watch the smooth surface for the loon's reappearance. Phil is grateful for the distraction. The sails hang loosely, the boom sways back and forth in the slight swell, and the only sound is the clink of halyards swinging against the mast. Phil misses the sound of the wind; the air seems empty now.

The loon does not reappear. Sara stands up, her hand shielding her eyes, and looks all around. "Do you suppose we frightened it?" she asks, her attention focused on the loon, or lack of it. Phil can't take his eyes off her now; he stares at her, seeing her anxious for once about something else but him, the intensity of her concern. He knows that she is willing the loon to reappear, drawing it toward the surface with her vigil. Then he realizes that he is holding his breath, watching her. Carefully he lets it out, not wanting to startle her. He jumps as he hears overhead the sudden raucous cheer of gulls, sees them flung across the sky like so many bits of torn-up paper. They wheel and turn, jeering, squabbling. He wonders if the loon can hear them. A few white feathers float down, settle on the water and seem to stick, motionless, in a pool of tar. The silence lengthens, and Sara does not move.

"Don't worry," he says at last. "They can stay down as long as fifteen minutes."

She turns and looks at him, bemused. "How do you know that?"

Phil shrugs. "I read it in an article. Loons are an endangered species."

"Well, this one isn't," Sara says, pointing behind him. Far away the black crescent head sticks up above the surface, flicks around, spots them, and quickly sinks out of sight again. Another disembodied head appears, or is it the same one? No, there are two; Phil has read that they travel in pairs, and usually mate for life. For several minutes he and Sara watch the loons work their way in and out under the still water, relieved of the necessity to talk. They just sit, listening to the halyards clank like cowbells. The water is as still as glass. Phil looks up into the shrouds, sees the telltales hanging limp and motionless. He reads this as defeat, stands up, lifts the cover of the engine compartment and reaches for the starter handle of the motor.

"Phil, wait." Sara's voice startles him. "Can't we talk a minute before you start that thing?" Even without looking he knows she is regarding him across the cockpit; he feels like a skewered butterfly. He knows what she is leading up to, and he feels the resistance stiffening, pressing upward. She wants to talk, but what good does talking do? What is there to say? He turns, stares past her to study the meager motion of the telltale on the shroud. The little bit of thread twitches, then falls limp again. There is no hope of wind. There is no escape, though talking is the last thing he wants to do.

"Phil, we've got to talk sometime. You may be leaving in three days." Her voice goes on, relentless, to its real point. "If we bought the boat then we wouldn't have to keep borrowing. You could sail it any time you wanted and not worry. And we would have it . . ." She does not say the words "for next year"; she will not make that mistake again. "It'll give you something to think about when you're down in Boston. Something to look forward to."

Phil finally looks at her; he knows she feels his silence as a rebuke. She looks so pretty, sitting there with her cheeks reddened by the wind, her hair all blown around in wisps, a fuzzy halo around her face, her hands clasped in her lap. She is staring at him earnestly, intently, and suddenly he recalls all the stories she has told him about her father sailing in an old crock of a boat those summers on the lake where she grew up, her father gay and smiling in the pictures, dead long before Phil met her. He realizes in this instant that if they buy this boat and sail it on the lake near them Sara will have recreated nearly all the elements of her childhood and early youth. He knows that this is not her motive, that she is not even aware of it, but he feels this knowledge as his own guilt, thinking of her father dead so young, the loss he knows she still feels so acutely, and accepts the knowledge, standing helpless in the rocking boat, that this is the worst thing he could have done to her, this dying of his own.

"I don't want to talk," he says, as gently as he can. "I just want to sail."

"I know that," she says and starts to cry.

He starts to reach out for her, but hesitates; there is really nothing he can do for her, not now. Instead he reaches for the starter cord. He grabs hold, cocks his shoulder, is about to yank when he feels Sara's hand on his arm. He turns, and she points wordlessly at the horizon. He hears, inside the silence, a regular lapping noise, gurgling, percolating as though the boat were moving. Little ripples appear along the surface of the water. But when he glances quickly at the shrouds the thread is limp.

"The tide is turning," Sara says. "That means there'll be wind."

"Oh, sure," Phil snorts. "Wind from where?" He waves her off and leans toward the engine. "That's an old salt's tale."

"It's true," Sara insists. "Something about the movement of great masses of water all at once. Stirs up the air. The wind dies down, then comes back from the opposite direction. I read it in one of your books." She sticks a wet finger up, sitting there almost primly, like a schoolteacher making one last point to an unruly class. "You just wait, we'll be able to run all the way back."

"So now you can predict the future," Phil says, smiling at her prim certainty.

"You bet," she says.

Sure enough, standing upright in the cockpit, Phil feels a slight wind grope across his face, pluck at his hair. He squints across the water, sees far off tiny ripples starting as the wind frays the water into little raveled skeins of white. The sea resembles a worn and crumpled garment someone has spread out and tried to smooth. As he watches, it buckles, flaps, then frays to foam, changing color as a line of darker blue flies toward them.

"Here it comes!" Phil barely has time to shout, as he sits down and grabs for the tiller and the mainsheet. Suddenly the wind is all around them, waves splashing against the hull, shooting up like whitewater. Farther away, the surface breaks as though it were flowing over a series of obstructions, but there are no rocks or shoals out here; it is the wind driving the water back against the tide. The wind frets the chop to miniature fountains, and blows their spray to smithereens. Phil heads the boat around, and the wind knocks them forward, swings the main far out to one side. The jib whips back and forth around the forestay. Sara grabs a long wooden pole from down below, leaps up on deck, moves forward swiftly. She captures the flailing jib, inserts the end of the pole, angles the pole into the mast and stretches the sail out the side opposite the main. "Hey, what are you doing?" Phil shouts, impressed by her agility.

"Setting the jib for wing and wing," she answers breathlessly, hopping back down into the cockpit with a jib sheet in her hand. The boat moves forward, gaining speed, scooting along over the waves. Now they are sailing and there is no more time to talk.

There is something so complex yet pure about the relation of wind and sail, Phil thinks, as he stands on the dock watching the yardman strip down the *Loon* and tie it to. Sara is standing next to him, and he can tell that she is not watching the boats. He hears a motor start up and looks out through the multitude of bobbing masts to where one is moving, a sailboat gliding through the channel in the chop, its sails fluttering. Someone starting out even this late in the day. Phil wishes he were with him. But it is almost time to start for home. He feels rather than sees Sara contemplating him. She reaches up and puts a hand against his cheek. It feels like a patch of sunlight warm across his skin.

"You look wonderful, you know. Your color's better, not so chalky. This is good for you," she says.

All around him the yellow birch leaves turn to the hardness of brass and rattle in the wind. He looks at Sara, silhouetted against the leaves, her yellow windbreaker the same color, her face ruddy and hopeful from the sun and wind, the long day's sail. It is a matter of balancing conflicting forces. He looks all around him, at the trees, the masts, the sea, the sky, pale and fathomless overhead. The wind blows, the landscape moves, but it does not stare back. Hard, indifferent, the leaves of brass, of copper, of bronze, the vast unbroken mirror of the sky, the water shards of broken glass glittering in the sun, have nothing more to say to him, nothing at all. He feels this silence hardening inside him. Sailing close-hauled means gaining distance, sometimes at the expense of speed. Even in sailing, you can't always get exactly where you want to go.

"I wish that I had died during that first operation," he says. "Then you would be used to it by now."

Sara stares at him for an instant, then turns and runs, the wind behind her spinning hard discs of leaves across her path. He watches as she runs down the dock, across the wharf, up the little graveled drive and out of sight, going nowhere, anywhere, Phil thinks, as long as it's away.

When she comes back, he is still standing on the dock, staring out across the bay. Sara stands close to him, slides her hand between his arm and side. He doesn't speak, doesn't look at her. After a while she withdraws her arm, and they stand side by side, not touching, staring at the water. The wind is gentler now, the waves no longer frayed with white.

"I bought the boat," Sara says finally.

Phil nods. It is not sailing so much as the idea of sailing, not boats, but the idea of boats. He looks at Sara curiously, as if from far away. He wonders if she has acted out of knowledge, faith, or sheer bravado. He wonders what, if anything, she knows, and how she knows it. But then it hardly matters; she has already said that she will sail it herself. Life will go on without him after all.

Across the bay the sunlight falls obliquely on the water, turning the ripples into tiny bright dagger points of light, and for a moment, as he watches, each one becomes a minute triangle of sail, dashing one after another, hundreds of sails dancing, scooting, rushing persistently across his line of sight. But then his vision clears, and once again he sees only ripples touched with light. Far down the bay another triangle of sail, real this time, heads up into the wind, shivers momentarily, then tightens to a plume. Standing there, Phil sees his whole life compassed in this passage of one feathered sail across a sea of jagged glass.

"You can always sail it yourself," he says.

"You'll be here," Sara answers.

22

2

Where You Want to Go

"...*here*," echoes faintly, a mere whisper, and as Phil looks behind him, he sees he is in some sort of tunnel made of corrugated metal, ribbed like the inside of a vacuum cleaner hose. It sounds like a vacuum cleaner, too; he seems to be surrounded by a loud continuous roaring, sucking noise, the steady noise of fans pulling the air in one side and down under the river and out the other side, an unimaginable idea to begin with, but there you are, or rather here he is, also on his way, he hopes, out the other side.

Up ahead and around a slight curve he can see the pale shimmer of what he takes to be daylight; the end of the tunnel can't be too much farther, which is a good thing, because he's pretty much out of breath, his chest feels tight, and there's a stabbing pain in his right side. It even smells like the car tunnel, that mixture of exhaust and disinfectant and musty used air that always used to remind him of ether and make him carsick as a kid passing through, even with the windows shut. He feels as though he might get sick right now, so he quickens his pace toward the faint glow. If this is the tunnel he thinks it is, it's only a few blocks from his old New Jersey neighborhood.

He shivers in his lightweight shirt and trousers; he hopes it will be warmer outside the tunnel. The pale lozenge is widening, at its center a scorching whiteness that dazzles his eyes so that the figure he sees coming toward him is nothing but a dark silhouette, beckoning. The figure is familiar; he feels as though he's seen him before, but he hesitates, stops and squints, trying to filter out the bright daggers of light. It's not that he's afraid, just cautious, after all this isn't the best place to be whether it's broad daylight or not, even if you're six-three and two-hundred, or were when you started. Yet there's something about the rolling walk, the set of the head, the hand beckoning . . .

Suddenly the thick air turns turbulent, the roar increasing, rolling over him like surf, and he hears the deafening noise of a shock wave throbbing through the narrow tunnel, a tidal wave of air, leaving no room for him. He looks around in panic, knows he'll never make it out, but just ahead the figure stands half-obscured, motioning from a door-sized opening in the ribbed wall. With one leap he makes it inside the smaller passage just as the semi roars by, sucking the air along with it, cleaner air washing over him, fresh and cold, as out of breath he follows his companion up the winding concrete incline of the smaller tunnel, a ribbed conduit slightly higher than his head, then up two flights of steps onto the street.

He was wrong; it's dark out. The streetlights are lit, and as if that weren't enough, all those funny stunted trees with the peeling bark lining the street between the sidewalk and the curb are strung with Christmas lights, and he can see Uncle Danny's face quite clearly now, smiling at him, nodding a welcome, as if to say, Here we are again, back on the same old street, but just as he's about to say how surprised and glad he is to see him again after all these years, Uncle Danny jerks his head *Come on, this way*, and Phil hurries to catch up with him, just as he remembers doing as a boy in short pants, coming home from Catholic school at the same time Uncle Danny got off his shift at the docks. It's funny, he thinks, walking along the sidewalk next to Uncle Danny, looking at the row-houses stretching off in the distance as far as he can see, the snow piled up in petrified gray waves, how things look the same, not smaller as they so often do when you come back as an adult to a place you spent time in as a child, but here everything is exactly as he remembers it, on such a scale that he almost feels small again, but he's not, because there's Uncle Danny rolling along next to him in his workshirt and heavy pea jacket, dapper as ever, no older than the last time Phil saw him, but half a head shorter than Phil is now.

"Where are we going?" he starts to ask, but it's too late, because Uncle Danny is turning in at the iron gate of a house Phil doesn't recognize. Even though he's freezing now in just his shirt, he hangs back, but Uncle Danny turns and smiles reassuringly, so Phil takes a deep breath and marches right in behind him into a narrow hallway with stairs up one side, several doors along the other.

Uncle Danny opens the first door and Phil squeezes past, expecting Uncle Danny to follow him, hears instead the door closing quietly behind him, no Uncle Danny, the room empty except for a couple of easy chairs drawn up to the fireplace and a huge Christmas tree plastered with all kinds of decorations, encapsulated in a web of tiny lights like distant stars, mere pinpoints blinking on and off, occupying the space in front of the big bay window. A stocky, white-haired old man is standing on a stepladder with his back to him, hanging yet more Christmas balls on the already crowded tree. The old man backs down the ladder, the tree sways, and several ornaments drop off into the swirl of angel hair artistically arranged to cover the base. "Whoa there!" the old man remarks as he one-hands a big iridescent glass ball, carefully reattaches it just as another smaller ball with white flocked lettering rolls down a branch and hits the floor with a pop, explodes into glittering smithereens. He shrugs, and backs down the ladder. "Sometimes they're just too many for me," he says as he turns around. He stretches out a hand. "How're you doing, Phil?"

Phil just nods as he shakes the hand, racking his brains trying to place the old man, but he knows he's never laid eyes on him before, even if he does know Phil by name. Uncle Danny's brought him to the wrong house, only this old bird hasn't figured it out yet.

Not that he doesn't have his hands full already, because the ornaments—all kinds of them, not just glass balls of various shapes and sizes, but animals and birds, figures, every type of decoration Phil can think of—are dropping off the tree one after another like too-ripe apples, and the old man scurries around the bottom of the tree after them, trying to put them back as fast as they fall off. Some of them break, and some of them just roll around on the big wad of angel hair underneath. "Here, let me help you," Phil says politely, reaching past the old man to catch another ornament on its way down. It bounces right out of his hand, hits the floor and rolls toward what looks like a capped drain near the wall, and as Phil bends over, wondering what a sewer drain is doing in the living room, he hears a faint hum or whistling noise, but before he can pick up the glass ball the old man grabs it, juggles it for a second, and sticks it back on the tree.

"That's okay, Phil," he says. "They're always falling off like that. Some I catch and some I don't, but I'm the only one who can put them back; nobody else knows where everything goes. But never mind that now. Have a seat." He smiles at Phil and gestures toward one of the chairs, a kindly, older man of indiscriminate age with a round, benign-looking face, white hair combed to one side, a neatly clipped mustache, worn V-neck camel's hair cardigan sweater and shirt buttoned right up to the neck, no tie, baggy pants and carpet slippers. "I understand you haven't been feeling too well lately."

Oh, shit, Phil thinks. Another doctor. Resigned, he sits down in the chair, leans back, and Bam! the chair seems to collapse underneath him; his head goes back, his legs fly up and the next thing he knows he's stretched right out staring up at the ceiling; it's not an easy chair, it's a recliner like the one his grandfather used to sit in. As he's struggling to regain a sitting position, he hears the old man says, "It's okay, Phil, just sit back and relax. All you have to do is think of the moment in your life when you were the most purely happy."

Oh great, not just a doctor, a shrink. "Excuse me?" Phil says in a neutral tone just short of withering, wanting to let this guy know he thinks this whole thing is a bad idea.

"I want you to pick the moment in your life when you were

happiest," the old man repeats slowly, enunciating carefully in case Phil needs to read his lips.

Phil just stares. "What for?"

"Because you're going to spend eternity in that moment, and I want you to have your chance to pick where you want to go."

Phil watches dumbfounded as the old man turns back to the tree, casually shoots out a hand and fields a small ornament slithering down a lower branch, replaces it higher up. Phil can just barely make out some lettering on the ball. It's someone's name, and then he realizes that all the decorations, too many to count, have names on them, like the ones he used to make in grade school with glue and glitter. Uh-huh. He gets it now; this is some sort of hospital or loony bin. Okay, that's it, he thinks, I'm leaving. "No, thanks," he says to the old man. "I've got to go." He starts to get up off the chair, feels himself pressed back, held down.

"I'm sorry, but you can't leave yet," the old man says as Phil tries to disengage himself from the nearly horizontal chair. He hikes his baggy trousers and sits down in the other chair, crosses a leg and looks sadly at Phil. "Don't you know me, son?"

Oh, Christ, Phil thinks. The guy's not a doctor or a shrink; he's a priest. "Sure, Father," he says obediently. "I'm sorry." And even though he hasn't crossed himself in over twenty years, his first two fingers twitch and his right hand rises involuntarily toward his forehead.

"Well, it doesn't really matter," the old man says with a resigned smile, as if he knows Phil is just humoring him. The sound of the ornaments plopping off the tree one after another distracts Phil, and he motions toward the tree.

"Don't you . . . I mean, won't they . . .?"

"They'll be all right as long as they don't fall off the floor and roll down the tube. Of course the ones that smash themselves I can't do much about, but then . . ." He shrugs. "Back to you. Got that moment yet? How about when you were a kid? Your first baseball hit? Summers at the beach? Maybe Christmas?"

Phil doesn't answer. How much does this guy know about him, anyway? He shakes his head, not wanting to be rude. "I can't remember . . . my head . . ."

"Memory lapse?" The old man stands up briskly, shaking his pant legs down. "No problem; I can help you out on that." Phil watches as he pads over to a side window and pulls the shade all the way down like a movie screen, hits a switch on the wall next to Phil's chair. The lights go out, leaving only the wavering ruddy glow of the fire, the starry pinpoints of the Christmas tree lights. Behind him Phil hears the click and whirr of a movie projector. A bright cone of light shoots out, hits the screen and turns into an oblong, then begins to flicker. Phil hears a slap and the cry of a newborn, and looks up startled at a red and bloody infant hanging upside down and squalling across the screen. What the hell is this? he thinks in disgust, home movies?

The old man hands him something that looks like a pack of cards, except it has wires coming out of it, a lot of them; they curl around Phil's arm, slither down his leg onto the floor, and disappear into the wall behind the chair. He looks at the object in his hand in disgust; he hates things with wires, especially if they have buttons on them.

"I know it's not exactly state of the art, what with the wires and all," his host says apologetically. "I've got the more recent ones on videotape, but for folks your age the old sixteen-millimeter still has to do. Oh, well," he shrugs. "Beats cave paintings, right?" Chuckling, he points to the row of buttons. "This is the play button, that's the fast-forward, this one's slow-motion, and this is the pause button for when you want to stop the action. There's no reverse, so you'll have to be a little careful not to go past the moment you want, because you can't go back. Just let me know when you come to it: I've got to see to the tree for a bit. No hurry." He bustles off into the dimness.

What is this? Phil thinks in annoyance, wrapping a hand around the control box. To his dismay the figures on the screen do a fast fandango, jiggle and bounce, the sound blurs into static, and behind him the projector whines in high gear. *Take your thumb off the button, dummy*, he tells himself, pops his thumb up, and there he is, six years old or so, standing in front of a gray stone wall or building, glowering resentfully at the camera, chin down, belly sticking out, feet scuffing the grass. Oh, God, he thinks, it *is* home movies. Mine.

His own boyish face glowers at him from the window shade. What bullshit, he thinks; this old fart can't be serious. He puts the control box aside and tries to get up, only to find something is still holding him down. It's as though he's belted in, but in an instant of bewildered paralysis he realizes he can't tell whether it's an inner or an outer constraint. What if the old guy *is* serious? If he quits now, and it's all really true about eternity and this perfect-moment business, will he have to take potluck?

Oh hell, he thinks, subsiding in his chair, why not? He's here now, might as well humor the old windbag. Besides, you can't be too careful. He smiles at the sudden memory of Sara, with that loony negotiable WASP agnosticism of hers, showing up in ICU with a priest in tow when he was in such rough shape after the first operation; "Sure it's all a crock," she said later, when they knew he was going to make it after all, "but you can't be too careful." Of course the guy was only Episcopal, still it's the thought that counts; Sara in that half-assed, scatty way of hers, never leaving anything to chance.

But he's neglecting the business at hand. Out of the corner of his eye he sees the big tree blinking on and off. Okay, why not start with Christmas? Even though he hates it now—all the fanfare and materialism obliterating the purely religious occasion, buy this, buy that, so much invested in this sham holiday, always haunted by the suspicion that nobody has ever really liked the presents he's given them, just as he has never seemed able to appreciate the ones he's been given as much as he should have—he thinks of David and Linnie, still young enough to find joy in anticipation alone, the possibility of satisfaction; how excited they get at the mere thought of Christmas, Linnie at eight not much older than that first image of himself, David at eleven still doggedly believing in Santa Claus; how happy they both seem, at least in that instant of discovering the marvelous, unexpected, perfect new toy, just an instant, true, but that's all he needs, and if he could find such a moment for himself . . .

He fumbles over the buttons, carefully depressing the one marked Play, and watches as the figures of his father, mother, younger sisters, uncles, aunts, cousins, both sets of grandparents, dance around their daily business until the meager New Jersey snow starts to fall, the tree comes out, the lights go on—only the lights, because Santa does the rest on Christmas Eve—the big illuminated reindeer head grinning over the front stoop, the loudspeakers playing "Rudolph the Red-Nosed Reindeer," "Sleighbells Ring, Are You Listening," and all those other goofy nonreligious carols, he feels himself smile, because it's their first Christmas in their new house in the suburbs, it's been snowing all week, piled high on the roof and in the road, a real white Christmas for a change just like in the movies, and everything is going to be perfect. He's lying in bed, in his as-yet-unfinished room in the attic under the eaves, staring up at the rafters in the dark, too excited to sleep. It's past midnight, and suddenly outside the window he hears a rhythmic jingling noise that can only be Santa's sleighbells, coming closer, then a series of muffled thumps coming from the roof, a rustling as Santa squeezes through the casement window (no fireplace in this house—too dirty), muted noises from downstairs, the crinkle of paper, a hum and a whirring, clicking noise, and he can't stand it anymore; he knows this time he's finally done it, stayed awake long enough to catch Santa in the act, and he creeps out of bed, along the floor, crouches on the top stair, peers through the railing, sees what is making the clicking whirring noise. He gasps and claps his hands, for under the tree, now fully decorated with ornaments of shiny glass, more than he can count, the Lionel train is circling round and round a track that snakes it way through piles of presents, just what he always wanted, and, overjoyed, he starts to laugh, then sees his parents' angry faces turned to look up at him, mouthing the words, "Get back upstairs to bed this minute, you bad boy, do you want to spoil everything? If you dare tell your sisters no more presents for you ever!" and he jumps up and scurries back to bed, hides under the blankets, thinking that it doesn't matter, there is still the train: his train.

He doesn't need to watch it all, he remembers. Sure enough, next morning it's still there, with other presents that don't matter, some socks, a shirt, a sweater, things he needs and opens dutifully, puts aside one after another, never taking his eyes off it, the long-anticipated moment . . .

"No, little Phil!" his father yells. "Don't pull that wire! Oh, Jesus, now you've done it!" as the sting of the electric shock numbs his arm, the engine shoots blue sparks, the cars screech to a frozen halt, a buzz and a plume of acrid smoke spiraling upward from the transformer; the train set is wrecked, he's broken it, though later, when they can afford the repairs required by the short circuit, it will be fixed, and each Christmas thereafter the train will come out, but it will be his father who puts it together, and runs it, until he is much older and can handle it himself, but of course by then he doesn't care, knowing by then also that the sleighbells were no more than the sound of tire chains, and the thumps and thuds were made by snow sliding off the roof, snow that now lies petrified and soot-encrusted along the roads and sidewalks of the crowded housing development in which they live.

So much for Christmas, no wonder he still hates it, he thinks as the reel runs on; so what's next? Ah, he might have guessed; here he is in his Little League uniform, grinning his fool head off, baseball bat cocked. Time to play ball. Here we go; he recognizes this field, this occasion. Not his first hit, but his first home run.

He sits back, letting the projector hum on, sees the pitcher wind up, his enemy, the little turd, two strikeouts in a row, sets his teeth and licks his lip, so nervous but not wanting it to show, his whole family watching, keeps his eye on the ball as it spins toward him and feels the sudden rush, *yes!* the wooden bat exploding SPLAT! against the ball, the warm stinging vibrations down his arms and sides and zinging right into his crotch as he drops the bat and watches the ball turn to a dot hurtling toward but not quite over the backfield fence, and his father yelling "Run, you knucklehead! *RUN!*" so he runs and runs, his loose dick bouncing up and down inside his baseball pants until to his surprise he feels it stiffen up like a toy pistol and finally understands why real players always wear their jocks, and the crowd is crazy, his father screaming, his mother, his sisters cheering, he hears them as he pounds around the bases, nothing like it ever before, so good he's dizzy with it, yet knows by the time he chugs into third base, out of breath, his feet dragging, his dick limp, knows in his twelve-year-old heart of hearts that it's already over, that there will never be anything like it again.

"Hey, wait a minute!" he yells, suddenly realizing the trick to this whole enterprise; he's been so engrossed in reliving the magic moment he forgot to freeze the frame at that perfect instant, and it's gone. Shit, he thinks, and slams his hand against the arm of the chair.

The images bounce; the control box makes a buzzing sound, then starts to beep. Phil breaks into a sweat as he sits there helplessly with the box clutched in his hand; now he's done it, broken the damned machine.

"Take your time," the voice says mildly out of the darkness. "There's no rush. It's still intact."

What is? Phil wonders grumpily. His past? The machine? The control box? Then the beeping stops. "Don't worry, it can be any time, right up to the present," the voice continues. "What about high school, your first kiss maybe?"

Hell, given a choice, Phil thinks, as long as we're talking sex, it's not the first kiss I'd pick. Damn! If he could just remember more, everything in sequence beforehand, then maybe things wouldn't sneak up on him. Letting the control box rest quietly in his hand, he sees that the images on the screen have subsided once more into pedestrian narrative. If this is his whole life recorded here (which of course it can't be—even his dad, the inveterate photographer, had to take *some* time off), this could take forever. Well, years, anyway.

Why screw around? he thinks. Or rather, why not? Let's get to it. He presses his thumb down hard on fast-forward and leaves it there, the projector behind him humming into a crescendo as it spins right through his sweaty adolescence, into college and out the other side, lets up a little as he recognizes those outrageous fake Gothic spires high above the long skinny lake in upstate New York, slows to a careful crawl as he hits the first week of graduate school, cautious because he's still not sure he can make this thing

go where he wants and he doesn't want to miss where he's going
this time.

And here they are, he and Sara, walking along together after
Victorian Lit class to the student union to get the ritual cup of
coffee, which she's already informed him she doesn't drink after
twelve noon because it keeps her awake all night, which he has
informed her in turn is a head job for sure, to which she replies
with some asperity that it certainly is not, at least with her, and
is now lecturing him on the effects of caffeine, empirically proven
in generations of her family, all of them made hyper by things they
didn't even know had caffeine in them, like chocolate cake and
headache pills and Pepsi, and it's all he can do not to laugh,
glancing down at her serious, round face with the downturned,
slightly sad-looking eyes, the full, slightly awry mouth jabbering
away, her angular arms folded like a grasshopper's around the
spiral notebook and a copy of *The Mill on the Floss*, so intent she
might as well be carrying on about some momentous discovery or
insight into the text, thinking that it's those arms that interest him,
the first thing about her he noticed, a long skinny arm raised in
the row ahead of him, remembers thinking it was the skinniest
arm he'd ever seen, remembers his shock when he heard her say
politely but firmly to the distinguished professor, "Could you please
speak up? We can't hear you in the back of the room." Jesus, even
he was embarrassed, as one of the ones co-opted in the back of
the room who couldn't hear. But the distinguished professor merely
nodded and spoke up. The skinny arm went down.

He couldn't get that arm out of his mind. There was something
about the grace of it, slightly tan, bare to the shoulder in those
days of Indian summer, tapering to the slender wrist, the small,
pointed fingers fragile as a curled leaf, swooping up, waving casually yet confidently, nothing tentative about her, so that he ad-
mired the smooth confidence of that arm, and the background he
could have guessed and in fact soon learned had produced it, an
old established upstate New York family—WASP of course, what
else?—not rich but comfortable, Phi Beta Kappa from some enormous, world-renowned midwestern university, here on a national

scholarship, a free ride for a year on brains alone, something he'd never even dreamed of as he struggled along with uneven grades from his tiny, obscure men's college, a heavy construction job each summer to finance what he suspects his parents, his father particularly, consider a really perverse choice of vocation as a college English professor. To be the first college graduate in the family is one thing, to make it your career is something else—"Okay, son," he can hear his puzzled dad saying, "I can accept your not wanting to be a priest, but wouldn't you really rather be a lawyer, go into business, maybe advertising . . .?" A situation this girl here, chattering on about Midol and Dr. Pepper and chocolate brownies, will never understand.

Yet even though he suspects a certain flakiness, prefers tall, rangy, sharp-nosed, aristocratic blondes who don't talk much, and she's short (well, not that short, her head is bobbing along about at chin level, say five-six) and brown-haired, and snub-nosed, always talking a blue streak, there's something about her that attracts (certainly not her body, nice legs and ass, but mostly even skinnier than her arms); perhaps it's simply that she's unlike anyone else he's ever met, and he wants to get to know her better.

Starting with her name. His friends Jane and Mack come down the path on their way to the student union, Mack a Harvard graduate enrolled in the business school, recently married to his high school sweetheart Jane, who is fresh out of nursing school and busy supporting Mack with her job as public-health nurse, meeting Mack for lunch still wearing her cap like one of those folded paper boats and her regulation navy blue cape.

So of course he does the polite thing and starts to introduce her to them, "This is my friend . . ." then realizing he isn't quite sure, decides to fake it: ". . . Sheila Galahad."

"No, I'm not," she says quicker than dammit, looking up at him with an amused expression on her face. "I mean, I'm your friend, but that's not my name."

He stares at her; he can't believe that she would say so right here, right now and embarrass him like this. "Excuse me?" he says with elaborate politeness.

"Sure," she says, taking it literally. She turns to Mack and Jane.

"My strength may be as the strength of ten, but my name isn't Galahad, or Sheila for that matter. It's Sara Gilead. Hi." She extends her hand to Jane, to Mack, and then with some irony, to him.

He wants to die. Why couldn't she have let him get away with it and told him later, privately? He vows never to go near her again, knowing that this directness bordering on tactless arrogance is something he can do without. Yet she seems to be everywhere he looks: in all his classes, walking down the same paths he's taking, rustling her books and papers in the graduate student common room, bumping into him in the stacks, in all these places; in all his thoughts.

She goes drinking with him and Mack and Fred and Howie— after all she's one of the guys, isn't she?—just another graduate student in English (though later she will defect and take up art history, studio art, then sculpture, her true calling; still she will finish her degree in English because, as she explains, she started it, and it doesn't hurt to have a trade). They are both assigned this god-awful paper on some obscure seventh-century Irish monk who wrote a travelogue, and after sharing the one text on him the library owns, they go out, just the two of them, to a different hangout, and he watches in disbelief as she orders a butterscotch sundae and consumes it along with the Ballantine Ale he's bought her.

"Why are you looking at me funny?" she asks.

"I can't believe you're doing that," he answers, shivering as a wave of nausea passes over him.

"Why not?" she says nonchalantly, twirling the last bit of gooey sauce out of the metal dish. "It all ends up the same place anyway."

"It's a matter of taste," he says austerely.

She looks at him skeptically over the rim of her beer glass. "You're one of those people who eats the stuff on your plate one thing at a time, aren't you? A purist."

"Of course," he replies solemnly, and they both start to laugh, because, of course, it's true.

One of those people. In the library elevator, riding down from the tenth-floor communal study room, she says she doesn't understand why John Henry Cardinal Newman did it.

Susan Kenney

"Did what?" he asks.

"Converted to Catholicism," she answers. "I mean he was already Anglican, that's practically the same thing, and all that agonizing..." She shrugs. "He could have saved himself the trouble."

He looks down at her to see if she's putting him on, but she's genuinely bewildered, her round, ingenuous face puckered with perplexity. She really doesn't get it. "Once you've been to Rome..." he murmurs distantly, then watches as it dawns on her.

"You mean you're Catholic?" she says as if it's just occurred to her that the world is populated by something other than Episcopalians. Or maybe he's imagining it, and it's really just that direct, no-nonsense tone of hers. When he nods, she looks at him as though he has two heads. The elevator door opens, waits a minute as they stare at each other, then whooshes shut. It does this for seven consecutive floors. Where is everybody? Phil wonders, wishing someone else would get on, but no one does. Any second now he expects her to say, Funny, you don't look Catholic. She keeps staring at him, trying to work it out. "I thought Boyd was an English name," she says finally.

"It's Irish," he answers.

"You don't look Irish," she says, squinting at him skeptically. "You're too dark."

"I take after my Italian grandfather," he says, not daring to look at her now, because he doesn't know whether to laugh or cry or thump the wall.

"You don't look Italian, either," she persists. "You're too tall."

They're in the elevator, she's looking him up and down, and suddenly he feels his groin getting warm and loose and twitchy. What he really wants to do is pick her up and kiss her, hold her to him; shut her up once and for all. Instead he drops his arms, holds his notebooks casually in front of his crotch like an apron so she won't see his fly start to bulge, and says with dignity, "And what do you think I look like? A Belgian Methodist?"

She doesn't miss a beat. "Byzantine," she says mildly. "You look just like one of those monks at Theodora's wedding, especially without your glasses."

Just then the doors flap open, other students crush in, pushing

36

them together. He's speechless, staring down at her, feeling the slender body pressed against him, all hipbones and knees and elbows, the thought that she's noticed him, thought about the way he looks, even without his glasses. "It's those big brown eyes and that one long eyebrow growing across your forehead," she whispers, crammed in next to him, sketching a fuzzy, scalloped line in the air with her pointy little index finger, and nudging him with a sharp elbow in the ribs so hard he winces, and his prick throbs warmly inside his pants.

As they leave the elevator to go their separate ways, she calls to him, "I'll show you a picture sometime."

Yeah, right, he says to himself, thinking what horseshit, what does she know about Byzantine monks, Theodora's wedding, Constantinople. He suspects it's all a bluff, mere rattling on: he wonders what, if anything, she actually knows, and how she knows it.

But the next day she turns up with a small print of a mosaic from a church in Ravenna, in a black dime-store frame. "There you are," she says, pointing. And sure enough, there is his likeness in the face of a Byzantine monk. "You can keep it," she says. "A present from me." He takes it back to his rented room and props it on his dresser.

"So what kind of name is Gilead?" he asks her over coffee, thinking he'll give her a hard time for a minute or two, just to get even. "Hebrew, maybe? As in: 'Is there no balm in Gilead?' " He leers salaciously, but she's not even looking at him.

"Scottish," she says absently, nursing her hot chocolate.

"Doesn't sound Scottish," he remarks innocently.

"It's Scottish all right," she says, not noticing his irony, her mind obviously on something else, as it often seems to be. "The name was corrupted when my ancestors came to America."

"Corrupted by what?" he says in disbelief, thinking of his immigrant Italian grandparents, given by mistake on Ellis Island the name of their town, not their family, his grandfather's father born Boyle in County Kilkenny, transmuted to Boyd in Albany because he could barely scrawl his name. Surely only penniless peasants such as these suffered the indignity of having their names changed

Susan Kenney

from what they should be, never the likes of her, "That's not my name," snapped out quicker than dammit, and don't you forget it.

"I thought it was only immigrants that happened to," he says.

She nods. "It was MacGilliaghed. Son of the servant of Ed. When they came to this country, nobody could spell it, so it got changed to Gilead." She looks up and smiles, propping her sharp elbows on the tabletop. "After all, they were immigrants too."

"Oh, right," he snorts, tilting himself himself back from the table with both arms, thinking, who needs this condescending bullshit? " 'My ancestors were immigrants too,' " he mimics. "Where do I get off? Like on the *Mayflower*, that kind of immigrant?"

"Nope," she says in all seriousness, "seventeen fifteen, after the First Jacobite Rebellion. They were on the wrong side."

"Oh, I see," he says with the elaborate patience that's getting to be a tic when he's around her. "Son of the servant of Ed, huh? Ed who?" he remarks dryly, thinking that'll shut her up.

"Oh, you know," she says with a straight face. She is nothing if not persistent, and she has all the answers, or thinks she has. "Could be any of those tenth-century upstart Anglo-Saxon warlords: Eadgil, Edwith, Edread, Edwin . . ."

My God, he thinks, feeling himself beginning to crack up. Doesn't she ever give up? Isn't there anything she can't expound upon at length, either because she knows all about it, or, as he is beginning to suspect, is making it up as she goes along?

"I give! I give!" he howls, and plopping his chair back down on all four legs, rests his head on his arms and laughs until the tears come. He hears her laughing merrily too.

And maybe that's it, after all, he reflects later, the real attraction, that she makes him laugh and feel happy, sometimes on purpose, sometimes unexpectedly, just by being herself, and after all those solemn years spent in relentless dogged pursuit of an idea of success or perfection he is no longer even certain is his own yet still pursues, it feels so good to laugh.

And it's a good thing, too, because he can tell from her sometimes distant, even distracted manner when she's with him that she doesn't want to get involved, though he's not sure why. So

38

they continue as friends, studying together, going drinking with the guys or, more often now, alone together in the little old bashed-up sports car he bought with what was left of this summer's construction money (even though she's told him she considers sports cars insincere, she seems perfectly happy to ride around in this one, particularly with the top down) until the stunned moment, after they've put in a long night in the library studying for midterms, and have strolled out into the deserted stacks to take a break, standing in front of a musty stack of unused books, suddenly they are in each others' arms kissing so passionately it makes him dizzy.

He drives her home and they kiss for a while in the front seat of the car; there is no back seat. She can't invite him in, she says; the little old lady who lives downstairs might hear them, and in fact at that moment a small, gray-haired person does pop her head out the door to see who's there with a cheerful "Hi, there dearie, just checking to make sure you're all right." He drives away with his heart thumping, his head whirling, a shit-eating grin on his face. It's not until much later, as he lies awake in his narrow bed in the rooming house, that he realizes he's in trouble. He's not her kind; she isn't his, they are too opposite, too different, not just their backgrounds and religion, but the way they look at life. She has big plans for herself, has even told him she doesn't want to get married until she's at least thirty, if ever, certainly not until after she's established in her career.

But what the hell. For now he decides to enjoy the illusion that they belong together, their burgeoning private romance carefully hidden from the others, who probe and pry, their persistent curiosity making the two of them co-conspirators in confounding the spies. She doesn't care who knows, she says at one point. That may be all right for her—she seems to have this private opaque core at the center of her being that no one else can penetrate. He on the other hand sometimes feels as though his flesh were made of air, so that if he's not careful people will look right through him and out the other side. It's one more difference between them.

In bleak moments he keeps coming back to this. Doomed; hopeless; it will never work, he knows this, broods on it, their differences so pronounced, not just the obvious ones of class and background and upbringing, but of temperament; his pessimism, her optimism, her self-confidence bordering on the cavalier ("But do you really *know* anything?" he blurts sometimes in exasperated disbelief at the randomness of the information she spouts with such prim certainty); his habitually humble opinion of himself accentuated by the seriousness of his intent; his devotion to abstract principles, her pragmatism. "I have my principles," he jokes, "but I can be had." He is about to add, so why don't you have me? when with a gravity he sees so seldom it surprises him, she shakes her head.

"No, you can't," she says solemnly. "Not you. That's what I love about you; your sea-green incorruptibility." Never mind that she's quoting a phrase from the Carlyle they've just read in Victorian, he's so stunned by her use of the word "love," however casual and inadvertent (he's sure it's just a manner of speaking, really: they are, technically, still just friends), that he vows to go on with this strange relationship of theirs as long as it—or he—lasts.

And while it lasts it's great. Faced with the persistent and unseemly curiosity of their graduate school cohorts about all the time they are spending together, they invent increasingly ingenious ways to outwit them. So no one will see his car outside her place, he parks it in the dorm lot across the gorge from her apartment and walks across the footbridge to pick her up. They meet in odd places, in grottoes in the Arboretum while the weather is still nice, in the bell tower stairwell of the undergraduate library when it rains.

One day it's cold and snowing, too raw to meet outside, and everyone's crammed into the graduate student study room in the library. As she goes by she casually drops a call slip next to his elbow, as though it were something he'd asked for. The slip's filled out, not with the PR or PS call numbers of their discipline, but with numbers he didn't even know existed: VK 1259 H65 C2. The title is illegible, and oddly, the time blank is filled in, too; usually the librarians do that only when they give you the book. He looks up at her, puzzled. Her lips form the words Meet me, and she grins. So he searches through the stacks in the bowels of

Sailing

the library, all the way behind the freight elevator well, and there she is, waiting for him. She stretches up her arms, and as he backs her against the stacks, just before he bends his head to kiss her, he sees the titles on the shelves. *Graveyards of the Atlantic; Great Ship Disasters of the 19th Century; Hope Perished Last: Tales of Survival at Sea.* "What the hell is this?" he whispers.

"The most unused stack in the library," she murmurs into his chest. "Naval Science. Since they got rid of NROTC there isn't much call . . ."

He kisses her before she starts to laugh. After that, as winter sets in for good, they both look up obscure subjects in the card catalogue, in the study room pass each other slips with call numbers and a time on them—GV 1896 ZQ, Circuses and Carnivals, or CN-CR, Tomb Inscriptions and Public Heraldry. In these unfrequented stacks, and in front of yet more shelves of even mustier volumes, they embrace at length, groping and kissing and pressing against each other, until they know their mutual absences will have been noticed by now, emerge sweaty and disarranged, breathing heavily, hot and bothered, to straighten up and cool down as they walk down separate aisles, take separate elevators at a decent interval, and arrive innocently back at the study room by different doors, carrying piles of books they've hastily collected from the return cart.

He marvels at her sometimes, watching her surreptitiously after one of their hot and heavy sessions, how she can be so passionate and still remain somehow detached, so that no matter how involved in each other they seem to be (the whole building could come crashing down around them and he'd never know it), she always senses when someone else is around and breaks away as though there were an alarm in her head, takes down a book, or suddenly pulls back, listening to the elevator humming down the shaft, the faraway rustle of pages turning, is always vigilant, so he is jealous of that reserve, that part of her attention not fixed exclusively on him. He wonders what it would take *really* to get her going, to lose herself completely the way he does, dwells more and more on this disparity until it becomes not just an obsession but his mission, to make her give in.

41

During the last weeks of the first semester he moves his typewriter into her apartment on the pretext that his typing bothers the other residents of his boarding house, and writes all his marathon papers there, sitting in the bay window overlooking the gorge. During study breaks, they sit on the couch and pet and paw and kiss, but still she will not let him make love to her; the tiny bedroom is off-limits, the door always shut. Her reasons remain obscure to him; when she draws back during one particularly feverish session, he says bitterly, "How come I have my principles but I can be had, and you don't have any, but you can't?"

She gives him an inscrutable look, gets up, straightens her clothes and busies herself about the apartment without a word. Terrified he'll lose her, or what little of her he's got, still he can't bring himself to apologize, so he simply lets the matter drop, and they pick up where they left off.

He tries not to be too insistent, afraid if he presses her she will stop seeing him altogether, even on these peculiar and increasingly uncomfortable terms. So when he leaves her, either in the stacks or at her place, he goes back to his room and lies awake, trying to convince himself that half a loaf is better than none. And though the shark fin of reality—his need, her evasion—surfaces again and again in his mind, makes him moody, resentful, depressed, he tries to hide this from her, sees to it that they remain friends, because, he tells himself, they always have such a good time.

After a big February blizzard, coming upon her unexpectedly in the stacks, her head in a book, he nudges her. "Meet you on Libe slope at three?" She looks up, startled—it's not one of their appointed times—then smiles and nods. The snow, great drifts of it blown into the hill, and the two of them lifting up big chunks and hurling them at each other, he unable even at nearly twice her size to get the better of her, until finally he pushes her into a drift, grabs her ankles and dunks her head first down into a snowbank. He sees her face, ruddy, streaked with melting snow, snow in her hair and eyelashes, running over her temples like upside-down tears, laughing and howling "You big bully!" grabbing his leg and pulling on it until he collapses on top of her in a heap of snow.

"You give?"

Sailing

"No, no, I'll never give!" she croaks, breathless with laughter, struggling against him.

Suddenly silent, unhappy, he lets her up and walks away, seeing in this moment the whole pattern of their relationship; she will never give, not everything. There will always be that part reserved from him, that center he can't reach. She will always have things her way. So in the spring, just before exams, he decides to end it, while he still has some pride left.

Abruptly he stops seeing her, talking to her, sitting with her, ignores the call slips, her invitations, walks the other way when he sees her coming. The bewilderment, then hurt in her face is at first almost more than he can bear, knowing as he does the persistent sorrow in her life, her father's early death, her mother in and out of the mental institutions she blithely refers to as loony bins, the whole responsibility for her younger sister and brother on her shoulders; intellectually he understands all this, and how it contributes to the unwitting cruelty of her behavior, her need to equivocate, to hedge her bets, yet the time has come at last, as he knew it must, when he can't take it any longer. It's not just his physical want of her, he has dealt with that so long and could go on; it is his greediness, his urgent, importunate and unseemly need for her full attention, for *all* of her. It's hopeless, he tells himself, no future in it, she's only playing with him, he always knew this. It's time to get out while he still can, before she makes a total fool of him.

She does anyway. Exams are over and everyone is packing up to go. He's feeling rotten, hasn't been eating or sleeping well, has lost weight, he hasn't shaved since the beginning of exams, feels grubby and hungover, and as if that weren't bad enough, he's convinced he blew it out his ass on at least two of the finals. So much for the career in academia. So it's home to another summer of building houses in yet another swampy New Jersey subdivision, waiting to hear if he made the grade. He's returning his books to the circulation desk in the lobby of the library when out of the corner of his eye he sees her coming toward him. He wants to cut and run, but he can't; all these goddamned books have to be checked in by him in person, or else he'll get the bill. He's shuffling slips at the desk, head down, pretending not to notice, when he feels her small, light hand on his arm. "I just wanted to say good-bye," she says. "I thought at least we could part friends."

He turns toward her, blurts, "I love you."

She blinks. They stare at each other, surrounded by students jostling to get to the circulation counter, the card catalog, the reserve desk. He looks down at her face, so serious, so sad, so silent, and something breaks inside him. This once, just this once, she's stuck for an answer.

Not for long, of course. He follows her outside and they sit in his car, the little beat-up sports car she has declared is insincere, and talk at length this early summer afternoon. "I'm not ready for this," she says in a voice tight with anxiety, tears rolling down her cheeks. "I don't know what to do." She does not say she loves him.

Can they part friends? she wants to know, going their separate ways for a while, in his case back home to his parents' house for the summer, in hers, to her family's home on another long skinny lake not far from here. Yes, they will part friends, he agrees. He is still somehow tied to her, even against his will. He knows now he must see this out to the bitter end, and it is not in his power to end it; as long as she wants anything from him, he can't help himself. If she wants to be what she calls friends, they will be friends. Once again he resolves to go on as long as he can.

And so he drives her home, miles out of his way, but who cares?—sees the run-down, rambling old house where she grew up, her crazy mother skewering him like some exotic specimen with her eyes, the teenaged bratty siblings looking him over as if he were from Mars, sees the genteely reduced circumstances of their lives, submits to all this, not knowing if he will ever see her again, knowing if he does things will be just as they are now; intolerable.

Later, after a dinner of so-called steak so tough even a lion couldn't chew it and so raw it wouldn't want to, heading south on the turnpike in the dark, he contemplates crashing the little insincere sports car into a bridge abutment, putting himself out of his misery once and for all. Chalk it up as an accident; who would ever know he just decided to up and quit? Then he thinks of his family, his mother, his father and sisters, all the pain and sorrow his act of cowardice would cause them. Whatever his other faults, he's not a coward or a quitter. Thus refusing to add insult to injury, he resolves to go on even without hope, to see it through.

Well, this certainly sucks, Phil thinks, watching the little sports car roar down the highway, carrying him away from her, his heartache a pain in his gut even now so sharp it seems it must be physical, as though someone has laid him open with a knife. Whose idea of a good time is this?

He shifts restlessly in the uncomfortable chair, thinking he'll just call it quits right here. He's about to hit the pause button when the old guy's voice comes floating out of the gloom over there behind the tree. "Hang on just a little while longer and you'll be out of the woods. Don't quit on us now."

Oh, shit, Phil thinks, subsiding back into the lounge chair, he sounds just like my father. But the words are a prod: *"Don't quit on me now."* He takes a deep breath and turns his attention back to the screen.

. . . the more miles he puts between them, the more it begins to seem possible that he can, with some effort, get free. He's got three months before there's any possibility of his seeing her again; he can bury himself in the hard physical labor of construction work, sweat her out of his system, go back to the routine of his own life, and in the fall, return to school a free man. No matter that he finds his parents' house small and suffocating, their life too, the endless round of shopping, errands, visiting relatives either in their houses or their cemeteries, Sunday morning Mass and Wednesday evening Mass, Holy Days of Obligation, confession, all of which he refuses to take part in, horrifying everyone by this sign that he has fallen away. The first kid in the family to go to college to better himself, they mutter among themselves, and look what happens; why couldn't he have gone to Holy Cross or some other nice Jesuit school? He suspects his mother of secretly lighting candles for him.

Despite his resistance he feels like a boy again, his mother up at 5 A.M. making his breakfast, packing his lunch, ironing his construction clothes, his underwear, his shirts, his sheets, wondering out loud when he's going to get a haircut and is he thinking of growing a beard? The fact is, he's a mess, he misses her so much, so when the letter from the dean's office comes telling him that he's been recommended to fill an unexpected vacancy in the University summer program for gifted high school seniors, a job as a dorm counselor, room and board, a small stipend, unlimited use of the library, along with the second letter informing him he's been awarded a small scholarship for next year, he jumps at the chance, quits his job, packs his bags, kisses his tearful mom goodbye, and heads back up the highway.

His way, via friends at his old college he *must* visit, naturally leads through her hometown practically right past her door, and on the spur of the moment he stops at the rambling, run-down house just to say hello. Only her mother is home; Sara, she tells him, has gone to their camp ten miles up the lake at a place they call Carpenter's to get it ready for the summer. "It's right on your way," she tells him. "I'm sure Sara would love to see you."

She gives him elaborate directions, a wicked gleam in her eye, so that it occurs to him, speeding up the road that runs south along the long, narrow, ice-blue lake, that maybe when he gets there he'll find some other guy in residence, a little fact the mother failed to mention—"Oh, by the way she has company"—or maybe doesn't know. There's no phone, so he can't call ahead to warn her he's coming, but what the hell, he thinks perversely, what has he got to lose? So he roars on, top down, wind in his face, hair blown back, feeling good in spite of his apprehension about what he'll find, past the little one-room schoolhouse and left on the dirt road, keep bearing left, down the rutted camp road to the switchback ("The bobby-pin curve we call it," her mother chortled at him, winking slyly) that nearly takes the bottom out of his low-slung little car.

Wincing as the rear end fishtails through a hump of loose gravel, nearly throwing him into the ditch, he throttles down, rounds the bend onto the flat land of the point, and catches his first glimpse of the so-called camp—camp indeed, typical WASP understatement; you could stack three of his parents' houses in it—a three-story yellow frame house in late Victorian Cottage style, gingerbread all over the place, a big wraparound porch, the lake gleaming no more than a hundred feet away. And there she is, standing on the porch as though she were expecting him.

He follows her into the house, its paneled interior dark even with all the windows and doors open to air the place out. She takes him through the rooms downstairs, telling him a little about the place, how it was built for a woman named Lydia by her handyman Jake Hoose, a local legend and a man much younger, who then lived with her for many years, to the great shock of all the neighbors, the idea of anyone living in sin in those late Victorian days, tsk, tsk, shows him the intricate millwork molding, whorls and Greek keys and Celtic squares, different in every room, the narrow paneling imported from the Orient, floated up the lake on barges, cypress and mahogany and maple, the fancy built-in book-cases, fireplace mantel peaked and decorated like a giant cuckoo clock, cupboards paneled like the walls, invisible when closed, everything golden, heavy oak furniture to match, white wicker furniture on the porch, the works.

She leads him upstairs where the sun streams in all the windows and the lake is visible as they pass from room to room, each with its large, as-yet-unmade brass bed, fancy oak dresser and table, all bathed in golden light, dust sparkling in the air, the wooden panels glowing in colors of honey, cinnamon and wine, and there, in the furthest bedroom of four, as his eyes dazzle, she turns to him without a word, yet he knows even before he puts his arms around her, bends his face to kiss her, that something has changed, and his heart nearly stops, then leaps and pounds against his ribs so hard he nearly faints as he embraces her, knowing the time is now, and *here* . . .

. . . as the warm fullness swells in his groin, throbs and pulsates down, pressing outward, hard and tight to bursting now, and he is falling, falling, his mouth glued to hers, tongue probing into warm, slippery darkness, eyes squeezed shut, floating on softness, the peak of fullness thrusting, and she helps him to press in, initial resistance like a finger and thumb girdling it, then the warm surrounding softness stretching to a void how different from rubbing hands or towels or clothes, then no more thought, no division between his flesh and hers, dissolving into darkness, whirling space, and he is floating on successive waves that toss his body upward, contracting, row, row, pump, pump thrusting—now! again!—until the fullness is intolerable, and his consciousness a small bright pinpoint and he's dropping headfirst from a great height, the fullness zinging in his gut and then Pow! the light exploding into a wheel—POW! a pinwheel revolving around the darkness, an expanding rim of light, then everything goes black . . .

. . . and he is washed up on the beach, limp and panting, draped over her exhausted, a humming in his ears, rockets still popping like distant fireworks behind his eyes. He blinks, props himself up on trembling elbows, and looks at her with reverence, shaking his head in disbelief. "Why?" he asks. "Why now?"

"My strength may be as the strength of ten," she says, "but I guess my heart just isn't all that pure." She tightens the circle of her arms around his neck and pulls him down, massaging his back and shoulders and buttocks with fingers as small and light as willow leaves. "I missed you so much."

He feels her trembling under him and realizes she is chuckling quietly. He's about to be insulted, but eyes closed, head pressed back against the pillow, she looks so happy, cheeks pink, long brown hair flung over the pillowcase, over her face, strands caught in her mouth, so pretty, and smoothing the hair away her eyes, tugging it gently from her mouth, he begins to smile himself. He can't remember ever being so happy as he is at this moment . . .

"*Oh, shit!*" Phil yells, fumbling frantically for the pause button, trying to freeze the frame but already in despair because he knows it's just like the baseball hit and he should have known; it's over and he's missed it!

Flinging himself back, his finger pressing on the button a fraction too late—but a miss is as good as a mile—he pounds the arm of the chair in frustration. He's missed it, fucking missed it; he should have hit the switch. He wipes the sweat from his face and sighing, readjusts his position. "Should-have me no should-haves," he can almost hear Sara saying, and it's true there's no going back. Regret is useless, even self-indulgent, he thinks, as he wistfully contemplates the golden-aired room, the lake sparkling in all the windows, the bright brass bed and rumpled bedclothes—who made it up with sheets and pillows, anyway? all the other beds were stripped—the articles of clothing he has no recollection of removing either from himself or her, much less how they got all over the floor, his own bare backside center screen, prominently displayed.

"I missed it," he mutters to himself, is mildly surprised when the voice answers.

"Keep on going; there's plenty of good time left. Take my word for it."

Phil glares crossly in the direction of the Christmas tree, the old guy not visible at the moment, though he's always ready to put his oar in, that's clear. Plenty of good time left . . . like what? He can't remember offhand one other perfect moment in his life, and he has no idea where to go next, having passed by his best shot at bliss.

"Maybe you ought to reassess your idea of the perfect moment," the old guy says mildly, peering out from behind the tree. "Perfect is the enemy of good."

I guess *so*, Phil thinks, wondering if the old man is, after all, not a doctor, a shrink, or a priest, but some sort of wise guy. He picks up the control gadget and contemplates it. Certainly there is nothing perfect about this little system he's set up here. There you are, coming right up on the real possibility, your thumb poised right above the money, and it's now? not yet, *now*? wait not yet, NOW? not yet hold it NOW? then POW! and dotdotdot. You blew it. Gone.

Still, Phil thinks, maybe he has a point. He has to admit there is something indecorous about floating through all eternity humping for all you're worth. Is it really bliss, or—what was it exactly?—"the moment when you were most purely happy"—when you're so out of it with pinwheels and rockets and bombs bursting in your brain you can't tell your ass from your elbow, let alone the ass and elbow of the person you're with. Phil shivers, cold sucking at the pit of his stomach, the sudden gaping maw of fear, of loneliness, and knows he's answered his own question. He wants awareness, not just mere sensation, the bare ass pumping blindly, the crotch zinging at the good hit or the stumble at cliff's edge, it makes no difference; that's the point; whatever the cause, the sensation is the same. So who wants to spend eternity humping a person you don't even know is there, who in that moment of supreme sensual delight might as well be a sand dune or a wave, so that for all intents and purposes you're floating alone in the void? There must be more to life than this; a point in time where sensation and cognition combine to create the perfect moment of unalloyed but not unconscious bliss. There must be times like that, Phil thinks. He sighs, pressing down without much hope on the Play button. What else is there to do but keep on moving? So let the good times roll.

. . . "Why now?" he asks her again later, curious about her change of heart. They are out in the canoe, floating lazily around the point in the late afternoon sunlight, the water so calm and clear it's as though they're hanging in air above the pebbly bottom, fish passing beneath them oblivious of their flitting, cigar-shaped shadow, their heads two fuzzy haloed knobs at either end. "Why not before?"

"I told you already," she says simply. "I missed you."

It's not enough. He needs to know more. He wants to know if things have really changed. "I thought it was out of the question, you had other plans, didn't want to get involved, your career . . ."

She dips her hand in the water, stares down at the V-shaped wake. "I was just afraid, I guess."

"Of what?"

She shrugs. "Oh, I don't know. Of losing control, maybe. Of losing something. . . ." Her voice trails off. She looks up at him, smiling faintly, and shrugs again. "I just don't know."

"Don't worry," he says. "You'll be safe with me."

She nods, and looks away.

"I love you."

"I love you too," she answers.

He looks at her, leaning back on the canvas cushions she's arranged for herself in the bottom of the canoe, her head turned slightly away from him, staring off into the distance down the lake, and thinks she looks so pretty, sitting there with her cheeks reddened by the wind, her hair all blown around in wisps, a fuzzy aureole around her face, tries to fix this moment in his mind, this happiness he can't believe will last.

Here? he thinks now, thumb hovering over the Stop button, watching the two of them floating gently on the crystalline surface of the lake, but a voice says inside his head: Not yet. Keep on going; there's more. Hang on.

He has to be at school that night, and leaves not knowing when he will be back. "I'll be right here," she says. "We've rented it to my cousins; I'm staying with them."

When he can take time off from work he drives the thirty-five miles over winding country roads to see her, even if it's only for an hour or so before he has to be back at the dorm for curfew. By then her whole family has moved in, except, thank God, that dotty mother of hers. The cousins are all over, big ones and little ones, her sister Fran, brother Vic—short for Vickery, a WASP moniker if he ever heard one—in and out at irregular times (apparently no one in the family needs to work a steady job summers, even though she claims they're poor); still they manage to fit in a somewhat furtive love life between slammings of the porch door, the rush of running feet, kids tumbling up and down the stairs shrieking "Excuse me!" as announcement of their interruptions, rather than apology.

He finds her upstairs, changing into her bathing suit, and takes her hastily, pressed hard against the paneled wall and hip-high molding, so that her shoulder blades and soft sweet ass show the imprint of grooved cypress paneling and Greek keys. They walk the Indian path far along the bluff and make love there, in the pine needles. "Right here in front of God and everybody," he murmurs.

"Not everybody," she says, pulling him down. "They're all back at the house."

And so he is content with this apotheosis for a while, but finally cannot let well enough alone. He wants more. He wants legitimacy. He wants her to marry him.

It is as before. He suggests, importunes, begs, accuses. She resists.

"Why not? I thought you loved me."

"I do love you. I just don't want to get married. We're too young."

He disagrees. "Twenty-three isn't too young. Marry me."

"What difference does it make?" she wants to know. "I will marry you sometime, just not now. I need to wait. Please, Phil."

He panics, afraid of losing her, thinking that if they get married, he will have her forever. Still she resists. So he backs off, decides to say nothing for a while. After all, it worked before, didn't it? He can be patient, wait her out; meanwhile, he just loves to be with her whether they get to make love or not; she is so wise yet still so funny, with her ironic wit, the lighthearted irreverent comic vision he knows she's carved out of an earlier darkness he, with his sheltered, safe, pedestrian history, can't even begin to understand. More than anything, it seems, he just wants to be with her.

He gets a weekend off from fun and games with the high school gifted; they drive home to New Jersey so she can meet his parents. "A friend," he tells them, just a friend, thinking he'll have to let them down easy, the fact she's not a Catholic, never mind what she thinks of *them*. "Oh, look, she's pretty!" his younger sister screams as they drive up.

"Did you tell them I was a dog?" she asks as he turns off the engine. And now it is her turn to be looked at funny, with her long, straight, beatnik (in their eyes) hairstyle, her unbecoming, oddball clothes she buys because they don't need ironing, her abrupt offhand remarks and that direct air translated by his parents into rudeness, her shyness turning to coldness, their tight-lipped unspoken disapproval, and oh, Christ, he thinks, how did I get myself into this?

He sees any hope of happiness receding indefinitely, torn between his future and his past, miserable if he does, miserable if he doesn't.

It's the little dog that finally resolves it. His sister Gloria has brought home a foundling puppy from her college dorm, a collie mix, so young he still staggers on his back legs and gobbles strained baby food. They are all agog over it, but of course his mother refuses to give it house room, dogs such messy creatures, she doesn't want it pooping on her rug, and his little sister Weezy (named for his mother, Louise) has hysterics, so he steps in and says he'll take the puppy, after all he's rented an apartment in an old farmhouse for next year, lots of room for a dog to run, and he's wanted another one ever since they had to get rid of his part-Dalmatian Major after the dog turned vicious and attacked his mom. Besides, back at school they have a running joke about giving pets literary names; Howie had a beagle named Beowoof, Mack and Jane had a stray cat named Tom Jones, wouldn't it be hilarious to have a collie and name him after that eighteenth-century fool of a poet laureate Colley Cibber? It seems fated, a collie, or close enough, out of the blue.

The two of them drive back with the puppy Collie Cibber in a box in the tonneau behind the seat, but when he gets to his dorm he finds out what he should have thought of in the first place, no pets allowed. "No problem," she says, "I'll keep him for you," and drives off in his car with the puppy to Carpenter's, brings the car back the next day, stays over in Jane and Mack's empty apartment. They make love until three in the morning, and he has to get back into his dorm room through the window. Luckily his room is on the ground floor.

Now he visits both of them at the house by the lake, and when the time comes to go back to school, it becomes clear that the dog is now hers, as all dogs anywhere in her proximity will always become hers, regardless of whom they were intended for.

He raises the question of next year. She still hasn't given in on the marriage issue, has rented an apartment of her own. Feeling her beginning to slip from his grasp once more, he makes one last pitch, badgering her far into the night, finally, in spite of his better judgment, knowing he'll have to pay for it later, issuing the ultimatum. It's time to fish or cut bait. Shit or get off the pot. "I can't go on this way any longer," he says for absolutely the last time. "This is it. Marry me, or this time I'm leaving and never coming back."

"Who gets the dog?" she says, trying to joke.

His silence lets her know he's serious. She gives in wearily, so that he thinks he has not so much won her over as worn her out.

Years after she will tease him, "I married you for your doggie." But he doesn't laugh, because he knows that it's truer than he'd like to think.

Ha, here's the wedding, he thinks as the reel spins on. Not exactly one of your golden moments, but worth watching just for the laughs. Holding the box, he depresses the Fast-Forward slightly, so that the tempo speeds up, like Keystone Kops or Charlie Chaplin, all the figures gyrating madly like a bunch of penguins in front of and then inside the Gothic-style Episcopal church by the lake, her sister Fran the maid of honor, his high school buddy Nick the best man, her brother and Mack the only ushers, her mother either drunk as a skunk or fucking crazy (or both) the entire time, his parents frozen-faced, trying to make the best of it. He is reminded of the old home movie Sara has of her parents' wedding. Elegant, subdued, the silent read-my-lips kind, her father young and handsome, debonair, a man he would have liked to meet but dead now more than ten years, her mother crazy as a coot, even then with that wicked nutty gleam in her eye, a look he hopes he never sees in Sara's.

And there they stand, looking so young, even from the back, the priest—the minister, really—with sweat pouring down his face in the middle of November, her sister dropping his ring so that it bongs across the marble floor like a section of steel pipe, lands at the feet of Mack, who fields it neatly and passes it along to Nick as smoothly as if the whole thing had been rehearsed that way, pure vaudeville, the two of them are so broken up with laughter they barely get through the vows, and forget to kiss each other at the end. They walk down the aisle not daring to look at one another, but smiling and happy-looking, here at the beginning of their life together, her hand in his, the fingers as small and delicate as a bunch of birthday candles. He can almost feel them now. Was he happy? No, he was scared shitless, he remembers, sweating and shivering just the way he is now.

Meanwhile the film is speeding onward, the first small apartment, just the two of them, the dog and seven tons of books, notebooks and papers everywhere, the odd lump of clay because even then she liked to make things with her hands, model little faces and figures and stick them on top of the books. So many distractions, grad school, comprehensives, the dissertations, first his, then hers. She seems so frail emotionally, tense and nervous under the pressure of finishing her degree, sees a psychiatrist for a while to get her head straight—"I told him that I keep thinking something terrible is going to happen," she reports, and the shrink tells her that's not unusual in people whose fathers have died suddenly and young, but it doesn't mean that something will; there's nothing that says she has to repeat her parents' lives. After he takes the college teaching job and they buy the old house in the country, he feels the two of them growing closer, their life together happy enough . . .

But wait a minute, isn't this where I came in? Phil thinks, as the squalling, bloody infant appears on the screen again. "Something's happened to the film," he calls out. "It's starting over." But no, because there *he* is, calling his dad to tell him that David's just been born, his dad breaking down on the phone, rendering him speechless with surprise when he says tearfully, "I hope your son makes you as happy and proud as my son has made me." "My son," he thinks, why, that's me. Once again the moment of sheer happiness, but he does not stop the film, because there's Linnie yet to come, and he realizes now that he needs them all, Sara and David and Linnie, no happiness complete without all of them, but it all seems to be going by so fast, and he fumbles for the pause button so he can catch his breath, but something must be stuck, because the film keeps speeding onward.

He jiggles the box, then yanks on it, trying to get things to slow down, not only that it's beeping and humming again, and in his frenzy to slow it down he sets the chair off even further into its stretcher mode and he's flat on his back writhing around in it trying to get his feet back on the floor when he hears a voice order sternly: "Stop thrashing around like that! You'll yank out the wires. Just relax, Phil, relax."

Obeying the stern voice as if by reflex Phil goes limp, tries to relax, though it's pretty hard stretched out flat like this, with the wires all tangled up like strands of hair, her hair in his face, dragging over his arms, his legs, his chest . . . He looks up at the screen, and there they are, the two of them in the hospital operating room, it must be Linnie this time, everything happening so fast, but not so frightening because they've been through it before, know what's going on, having been through it once helps, he hears Sara say, her face white and intent and concentrated, her hand in his a bunch of birthday candles, the bloody water gushing out, hold it, don't go so fast, now, hold it, one more, there, his daughter so small, so perfect, he can't remember being so happy, a complete set, one of each, and Sara laughing at the doctor I told you she was a girl I knew it all the time so now you can predict the future you bet, but then the smell gets to him and the lights, the humming, beeping hospital noises, the smell of anesthesia mixed with disinfectant, the pain in his side so bad now that he can't hold Linnie any longer, nauseated he hands her back to the nurse, turns to leave . . .

. . . and finds himself in another hospital room only this time he's the one on the table, stretched out pale, choking, tubes and wires . . . "No! No!" and he begins to cry, tears streaming down his face, rocking himself up and down, back and forth in the hard flattened reclining chair, because it's too late, there's nothing left, no time since without pain and fear . . .

". . . *Here*, you take it!"

Phil grabs the flailing tiller, narrow bone in his hand. The boat is wallowing, the sails banging and snapping. He takes the main sheet from Sara, eases off slightly, lets the main out, then holds the tack, studying the telltales, adjusting and correcting until once more the feathers lie flat against the sail. The boat heels over smoothly, not too far, and runs through the waves. The water foams and hisses as the boat pushes it aside. "I couldn't hold it," Sara says from the deck above him. "That's all right," Phil says absently, already caught up in the business of sailing. He looks backward over his shoulder and without turning his head adjusts the tiller so they are on a beam reach. The boat seems to lift up and leap ahead. *"That's it,"* he says.

"That the one?" he hears the old guy asking.

"That's it, that's perfect," Phil murmurs as though in a dream, holding his thumb down firmly on the pause button. "If I can just hold it . . ."

. . . And the wind is building now, into a humming, now a roaring, sucking noise. *Hang on*, he hears her saying. *You're doing fine.* That's it that's perfect, before it's too late, the pinpoint of light already wheeling . . .

Still pressing down on pause as hard as he can, sweat pouring off him, he lies back exhausted. In sailing you don't always get exactly where you want to go. He turns his head, vision blurred, to see the old man reaching toward a little sailboat bobbing on a branch of the Christmas tree. The round drain in the floor is open, and the roaring, sucking noise he took to be the wind is coming out of there. He stares at it, realizing it's not a sewer pipe at all; it's a large vacuum tube like the ones they used to have in department stores like Macy's or Abraham and Straus, for sending the sales slips and money to the cashier. The hole yawns black, hissing and sucking.

"What's that?" he asks in horror.

"Eternity," the old man says. "The memory hole. But don't worry, it doesn't hurt. You'll never know the difference. You'll just be floating right along forever in your perfect moment."

With a flash of understanding that almost heaves him off the chair, Phil realizes who this old guy is. This is God he's talking to. When that little sailboat goes down that black hole in the floor, that's it; it will be over. He will be dead. And Sara, and the children, his parents . . .

"No, wait!" he shouts to God. "It's too soon!"

"You can't put it off forever," God says mildly. "Think of all the pain and suffering you're in for. You don't have to go back. You can quit right now."

"I've changed my mind," Phil gasps. "I want to keep on going as long as I can."

God dangles the little sailboat over the black hole, shaking his head thoughtfully. "You have to pick a moment."

"Then make it now!" Phil shouts in desperation, hoping to get one last glimpse of Sara. Maybe there will even be time to say goodbye. "Make it where I am now!" He tenses himself, eyes wide open, ready to be sucked down the memory hole, all his joys and sorrows, pleasure and pain intact, right up to the present moment, wherever that is.

"Good answer," he hears God say. "But that's okay. You don't have to choose just yet. I was just checking."

Phil stares at him in disbelief. "You're kidding."

"I never kid," God replies mildly as he replaces the sailboat. "See you another time."

. . . and the chair seems to lose its anchorage, floats up, rocking and pitching as he hangs on for dear life, a roaring in his ears, a splashing, a sucking gurgling noise. He feels his consciousness contracting to a pinpoint of light, blinking on and off, sucked toward the vacuum tube opening, the yawning hole . . .

And suddenly he's back in the ribbed conduit, this time in the prow of a boat with someone in the back, but he can't turn around to see, because the tunnel roof is getting lower and lower, pressing down on him, his chest, and he can't breathe. His throat constricts, and he starts to choke. "It's all right," he hears someone say calmly as though from very far away, the voice thin and small, like Sara's fingers. "Just lie back and relax, keep your head down; you're doing fine. It'll all be over soon."

He's holding a canoe paddle, but it turns to a tiller, and then disintegrates to little sticks, mere splinters the size of birthday candles, then to icicles that start to melt as, clutching them, he lies back down in the bottom of the boat, feet first in the prow, chilled and sweating, as the water swirls around him, tossing the boat from side to side, and the tunnel is shrinking, he can't see the end, only its ribbed corrugations bearing down, around and around him, like wires surrounding, binding him, lower and lower, smaller and smaller, round and round as in a whirlpool, and it occurs to him as he is revolving helplessly downward, sloshing from side to side, that God has tricked him and put him down the vacuum tube anyway. The sucking, wheezing noise is growing louder, merging with the sensation, the darkness growing as he swims up toward the surface, holding his breath, his lungs bursting, the pain a red-hot zipper . . .

Sailing

"Keep him under just a little longer! He's not good enough yet!" he hears his father yelling. "Come on, Phil, breathe! Breathe, Phil, breathe! You've got to breathe . . . !" And he's back in the cold ocean trying to learn to swim, his father shouting at him, and flailing and splashing desperately he tries to breathe, takes in a huge gulp of salt water that burns his windpipe, his lungs, and suddenly the ribbed vacuum cleaner hose isn't around him, it's inside him, down his throat, the pain, the burning as he tries to breathe against the hissing of the tube, the sucking, the wires holding him on the narrow beach where he's been flung, sand grating on him, in his hair, his throat, his eyeballs, the beach so narrow and so hard, the little creatures plucking at him and all he feels is pain . . . .

"Phil."

"Mr. Boyd."

He opens his eyes, blinks at the brightness of the lights, makes out two blurred figures standing next to his bed. A TV monitor beeps a fuzzy line like tinsel, flashes indistinct numbers on the screen. There are lines and tubes everywhere, a caterpillar's tent of tubes and lines, beeping, bubbling, the hiss of the respirator tube they've just pulled from his throat. He swallows convulsively and takes a long shuddering breath, shuts his eyes because it hurts so much. He feels Sara's slight fingers cold against his palm, with a great effort curls his own around them. "You're doing fine, Mr. Boyd, just fine," Ristine the surgeon drawls. "We got it all."

3

The Idea of Boats

This is it, Phil thinks as he rows the dinghy out to the *Loon*, swinging around on her temporary mooring in the light breeze that feathers the surface of the river. The sky is clear, the air is warm even for June, and he's sailing the boat from the marina up to Indian Cove by himself. Even though David's nearly thirteen and Linnie ten, Sara's still nervous about leaving the two kids alone all day, never mind overnight. Poor Sara, caught betwixt and between; all that first summer they had the boat she insisted on going with him, even after he was sure he could handle the boat alone. She said she just wanted to keep him company—she didn't seem interested in sailing the boat herself—but he knew it was because she was afraid something would happen to him. And then she was always anxious to get back after a few hours—still is. This annoys the hell out of Phil, who wants nothing more than to sail for as long as he can as often as he can.

The big breakthrough came at the end of last summer, when he was invited by his old teacher and former colleague Gus Worth, along with four other friends, on their annual bluewater cruise—one whole week spent roaring all over the bay in Gus's forty-three-foot one-off ketch *Endeavour*, downeast as far as Roque, tacking here and beating there in all kinds of conditions, fog, high seas, calms, glorious days. It was just a fluke, one of the crew members unexpectedly dropping out, so they had asked him to go. He had learned more about sailing in one week than in all four previous years of flitting around the local lakes and inlets in assorted big and little boats. He had come back much more confident, determined to master the art of ocean sailing. After that he sensed a slight relaxing of her vigilance, a greater willingness to let him go alone. He'd gone by himself a couple of times, not too far, but then it was the end of the season, and they had to pull the boat.

Now it's another summer, the boat's in, and he takes it as a good sign that Sara's more worried about the kids than she is about him. He can sail to his heart's content, all day if he wants, no pressure to get back for the kids, for dinner, for this or that distraction from all he really wants to do these long summer days: sail.

He hums softly as he ships his left oar, flings the bag with his lunch, his foul-weather gear, and his running stuff into the cockpit. After he's sailed the boat up to Indian Cove and picked up the mooring he'll change from his boat clothes into his shorts and jog the five miles back to the marina, where he's left the truck. He could bum a ride, but the running is a routine he's been following ever since the weather began to get nice in April. Considering what a wreck of a man he is—down to one (slightly damaged, but still working) kidney, a bum liver, and God knows what else shot thanks to that first bloody mess of an operation, two scars now as thick as schooner rigging winding all up his belly and across his ribs—he's feeling pretty good. Better than ever, in fact, only the checkups—"necessary inconveniences" Ristine called them— every six months to remind him how bad things were before. No big deal really; he's come to think of them not so much as inconveniences but as waves to be breasted, like the ones that used to hit the beach at the Jersey shore during a storm, breakers to be gotten up and over, one after another, coming farther and farther apart as the storm subsided—every three months that first year, now every six, then once a year, until the magic number five—

and the sea is calm once more and he's declared officially cured. After this winter he'll have to go only once a year. Three years from now he'll be home free.

Sara was right; having the boat to think about while he was recovering from the operation was a good thing after all, a focus for his thoughts, something to look forward to after all those months of thinking he was a dying man. And miracle of miracles—which of course he doesn't believe in—here he is.

All things considered, he's glad they bought the boat, he thinks as he listens to the water slopping against the boat's hull, looks up at the mast with its cross-shaped pattern of spreaders gently revolving against the incandescent blue of the sky. The weather has been good this whole week he's spent doing all the last-minute things to get the *Loon* ready to go, scraping and painting the bottom, picking up the engine from storage, stepping the mast and putting all the gear back on board. He's already had a shakedown cruise with Cap Hawley, an expert sailor and well-known local navigator, always in demand for the big races, out to the islands and back, Manana and Monhegan, Camden and Castine. Last night they motored out the river channel, then tacked around the inner bay until almost dark, while Hawley tuned the rigging and gave him some pointers about sailing single-handed. Even with her heavy lead keel and masthead rig, the boat is really quite simple, a little crank (he likes that word, a condition he aspires to, though in sailing language it means initially tippy, not crotchety as in "old man") but big and powerful, with a much greater range than the other boats he's sailed. It used to be all he could do in the nineteen-footer just to beat up the lake a couple of miles and back in an afternoon, the wind seeming to blow perversely in his face which-ever way he wanted to go. Here, once you get into open water, the wind usually blows in one direction, just hoist the sails and keep on going, a couple of tacks at most, a quick turn around and a run home, the wind at your back.

"You can go anywhere in this baby," Hawley told him while they were pounding around the bay. "Mount Desert, downeast, even across the ocean. These early fiberglass jobs were built to last. You'd have to put a hole the size of a subway tunnel in her or open all the seacocks *and* the hatches before she'd sink on you. Even then you'd have to wait a while." Of indeterminate age, short and stocky, with ruddy cheeks and white moustache, trimmed peppery beard, black roll-neck sweater and Greek fisherman's cap, Hawley is the picture of an old salt. Phil thinks of him as his spiritual advisor in matters of sailing; his wise man. He's even sailed by himself to Lindiscove Island, Phil's favorite stopping point on the big cruise with Gus last summer—that transcendent vision of the deserted lifesaving station like a ruined monastery against the sky—and back in a day: "Nothing to it, just head out past the monument to Day Island Ledge, pop the chute, broad reach out around Barrett Island and you're there. Coming back you keep Barrett Light to starboard, Long Ledge to port and shoot in past Wertimer Rock. Head for Bergen's Head Light until you hear the horn. After that you can pick up the channel markers. Nothing to it. You can even do it in the dark. Just follow the flashing lights."

Hawley makes everything sound so effortless, so easy. That's what Phil likes, the easy confidence that makes all things seem possible. Phil wishes Sara could hear him. It might make her less anxious. Hawley offered to come with him today, but Phil said no thanks, such a short sail, he could handle it himself. Besides, he wants to be alone with his boat.

The tide is pushing the brown river water back up the channel now, and the mudflats are covered. The channel is marked with buoys and pilings, black cans and red nuns. " 'Black to port, back to port,' " Phil chants to himself as he starts the old clunker of an engine hanging down like a piece of petrified dog shit from the rear well, leaves it churning noisily in neutral, and casts off the mooring lines. He wonders what will happen when the Coast Guard finishes painting all the port cans international green. Oh, well, there's always "Red right return."

He's sorry to leave without saying goodbye and thanks, but the tide is full now, about to turn, and he wants to go out with it. As he motors out of the channel trailing the dinghy, feeling the cooler ocean breeze groping over the side of his neck, he hopes he won't have too much trouble getting back past Pondatear Island into the Indian River; the tide-rip can be quite strong, especially at dead

S u s a n   K e n n e y

low with an onshore wind, as he and Sara witnessed that day they bought the boat. Well, if it is, he can just take a few tacks around the bay until the tide turns again. After all, it's only nine in the morning, he can sail all day if he wants to. He told Sara not to wait up, and not to worry. He doesn't want to have to rush.

What could be better, he thinks as he raises the working jib and leaves it flailing wildly around the forestay, hopping over the sheets that writhe back and forth across the deck like berserk jump ropes, held only by the two stainless steel blocks on either side of the deck, as he hoists the main and lets it flap freely, crawls under the whipping sails, the noise deafening now, almost like thunder—rattle rattle boom snap boom—the wild flailing and flapping, snapping and fluttering that makes Sara nervous but he loves, not so much the noise itself but that moment, as he hustles back to grab the tiller, shuts down the engine, pulls in the mainsheet and holds it, trims the jib and lays off, when everything suddenly goes still: the sails fill with wind, the boat heels over, shoots forward with a whoosh . . . and he's off.

He wakes up choking, unable to breathe, some obstruction blocking his windpipe, burning in his chest. Oh God, he thinks in panic, struggling to sit up, catch his breath, I'm dying, after getting through all this crap, I'm fucking dying after all. He can't swallow, something presses on his chest, sucks in; he coughs, and feels his lungs expand full with air. What the hell is this? His mouth is stretched open around a huge piece of hose; he can feel it against his lips, down his throat and gullet, a sucking, hissing noise coming from it, or is it from somewhere else? He can't tell whether his eyes are open or shut; everything around him is a blurred confusion of dark and light. Oh God, help me! he wants to shout, but he can only think the words, not say them, his mouth distended in an involuntary yawn, air wheezing in and out in a regular rhythm beyond his control.

All around him he hears a weird cacophony of sound: thumping, humming, squeaking, beeping noises, like some broken-down barrel organ. A peach-colored balloon floats over him, bobbing perkily. Oh shit, he thinks, I'm at the circus.

Sailing

A flat, icy object presses firmly down on his bare shoulder, pushes him back onto the hard surface he's resting on. "Lie back, Mr. Boyd; try to relax," the balloon's voice echoes strangely. "We'll have that respirator out as soon as the doctor gets here. Don't fight it right now; just let it breathe for you."

A cold wave splashes over him and he shivers uncontrollably, feeling a million minnows with sharp scales slithering over his arms, his neck, his legs; they are all over him, his body . . . *Help me*! he tries to scream, but he's paralyzed by the pain that hits him like an ax and a horse rears up and stomps his head and the blurred colors whirl around and around the tiny pinpoint of light and down the drain and everything goes black.

When he comes to, there are two more blurred balloons nodding by his bed. He opens his eyes wide, trying to bring the bobbing ovals into focus, but he can't. He squeezes his eyes shut in despair. What have they done to him? His throat is killing him, and he's incredibly thirsty. He swallows convulsively, then takes a deep, shuddering breath he pays for with a sharp searing pain, as though someone has slit his gut open with a razor. He's so cold, and some idiot has filled his hand with little icicles. He twitches his fingers angrily, trying to get rid of them, but he can't; they stick. Well, maybe they'd be good to suck on, then, and tries to raise them to his lips. But he's so weak, his arm must weigh a hundred pounds . . .

"Phil." It's Sara's voice. Sara, here? He stares in the direction the voice is coming from, sees only an indistinct round shape, the features smudged.

"Sara," he croaks. "I can't see you. Everything's all blurry. Something's wrong . . ." He clutches at her fingers, his dry tongue cleaving to the roof of his mouth as he tries to make her understand that someone has blundered, too much anesthesia, irreversible brain damage, another fuckup . . .

"Of course everything's all blurry," she says calmly. "You're not wearing your glasses." To his relief, her features come briefly into focus as she bends down to kiss him, why he can't imagine, he's such a mess, tubes coming out of his nose and everywhere else, as far as he can tell, the bandage across his chest and belly as stiff and heavy as concrete. And it's not just his glasses he isn't wearing; he can tell by the feel of the chill air moving over his skin that except for the thousand pounds of bandage he's stark naked, bare everywhere. What will the nurses think? He really doesn't give a shit, to tell the truth, except that he's cold, cold, cold. He shivers uncontrollably. There are tears glistening in Sara's eyes. He hopes she isn't going to make a fuss.

She smiles. "Everything's fine," she says. "It went well."

That's her version. She raises his hand, wires and tubes and all, to her cheek, rubs her face against his knuckles. Everything is fine, whatever that means. He takes another deep breath—whoever thought one mere breath could be such a fine and painful luxury?— and drifts off to sleep.

The wind is light but from the south; he can sail right out into the bay. He cleats first the jib and then the main, sets a course for Indian Cove Point and leans back against the cockpit coaming, the tiller resting lightly in his palm. From where he sits he can see directly into the cabin, the narrow V-berth forward, the tiny marine head, the tiers of drawers, lockers under the settee berths filled with life jackets, flares and other safety equipment Sara insisted they put on board. Leave it to Sara to be ready for any possible emergency, even though with her heavy keel this boat can't capsize and turn turtle the way the nineteen-footer once did, dumping him and all the gear into the lake for Sara to rescue, which she did, in a motorboat commandeered from a cottage nearby.

But nothing's going to happen, not now, not anymore. He's paid his dues; they all have. He puts his head back, lets the sun beat down on his face. It feels so warm that with his free hand he hauls his canvas shirt out of his pants, unbuttons it and pulls it open. No more chalkface for him. "Why Mr. Boyd! What rosy cheeks you have!" the nurse at the Boston Clinic exclaimed when she saw him for his checkup at the end of May; he'd spent the last several weekends out in the sun getting the *Loon* ready, cleaning and waxing the topsides, painting the hull, varnishing all the mahogany brightwork; the wide coaming that surrounds the cockpit, the winch mounts, the tiller, the grab rails, the fancy, louvered drop-boards that fit in the companionway.

He was surprised that Sara wanted to buy this boat in the first place. He thought she was really stuck on Lightnings, the boat of her youth—Lightnings, Comets, Bantams, Stars, white flags rampant on a field of blue, stories of her father crewing in Lightning Number One—but then there was the little cabin almost like a dollhouse, a place where the kids could curl up and read if they got scared or bored. And of course she thought at the time they were going to have it hauled back home and sail it on the lake nearby. And so they bought the boat, the family boat.

As it's turned out, ever since the fiasco last summer, both David and Linnie have flatly refused to go sailing. That left Sara and him. Now Sara, who was supposed to be the big sailor, who got him into this in the first place, has begun to look at him funny and mutter about all the things she has to do besides go sailing with him every minute. Can't he take a day off now and then? It's true he doesn't need to be so compulsive; it's not as if he didn't have the whole rest of the summer to sail in, the May checkup already behind him, the next one not coming up until winter. But he regrets the loss of even one day pursuing this totally absorbing interest of his, an hour or two of perfecting his skill as a sailor, mastering the relation between wind and sail, cause and effect, the balance of conflicting forces. Wasn't that the idea in the first place, that sailing was good for him? After all, she's the one who insisted on buying the boat. Well, here he is, with a lot of catching up to do, perfecting his technique. And that he can do—would rather do—alone.

Passing abreast of the Indian Cove channel marker, Phil looks up and sees a mother-of-pearl cloud streaking the horizon far to the south and west, imagines more layers piling up in dark ledges behind the steep hills to the west. It will probably rain tomorrow. Too bad; he was thinking about staying over, going again tomorrow while the going's good, but it can't be helped. He puts the tiller over, and the boat comes about in that stately way he loves, the long heavy keel holding her steady as the sails dip toward the water, then begin to flutter wildly as the wind crosses the bow. He ducks the boom as it flies over the cockpit. The sails shudder briefly as he trims them for the other tack, then blow taut with a snap. The boat heels over, the emerald water curls back against the hull, foams and hisses, and the boat leaps forward, gaining speed, the wind at his back as he sits up on the deck, his feet in the cockpit, the ridge of the coaming under his knees, holding the tiller against the pressure of the boat heeling as the rudder slices through the water. A beam reach, the fastest point of sail. The boat lifts up and seems almost to plane. He can't remember the last time he felt this happy.

The wind is fairly steady in velocity, but switching around a bit, typical of sailing this close in to shore, so many land configurations deflecting the wind this way and that, so many things to watch for, rocks and shoals, races and tide-rips, so that gradually the beam reach eases into a gentler broad one, almost a run, and after a while he ties the tiller off, hops on deck, goes forward with the whisker pole to rig the jib for wing and wing, cleats the jib sheet as he comes back into the cockpit, lets out the main and cleats it, then leans his back against the coaming and puts his feet up on the other seat. Relaxed, even a little sleepy, he admires the mahogany brightwork as it glows warmly in the sun, the gleaming deck and topsides, the crisp white sails, the long graceful tiller tapping lightly against his palm, the running rigging as white and shiny as flax, all clean and bright, everything as good as new, here and now: his boat, himself, his life.

They've moved him out of ICU into a regular room, the whole surgical team, Hunker, Dalton, Mandelbaum and Greef, amazed at how quickly he's recovered. They can hardly contain themselves, stand around like a rowdy barbershop quartet, slapping each other on the back and telling operation stories; how the anesthesiologist dumped enough stuff into him to sedate a grizzly bear, and he still crawled onto the operating table himself, mumbling unintelligible jokes and chuckling the whole time, so they decided they'd better strap him down so "you wouldn't get up and walk away." People were watching from the gallery, doctors, nurses, students, and when Ristine started tying the blood vessels off the tumor would pulsate like a live thing, and everyone was yelling "Kill it! Get it! Kill! Kill!" When they lifted the main part out without having to resect the kidney, everyone clapped and cheered.

He listens to these stories with great fascination; it's as though it all happened to someone else. Even the incision doesn't bother him that much. "What a hack job," Hunker teases Mandelbaum as he removes the stitches. "They were going to sew up your belly button, but I told them your wife wouldn't like that, so they put it back."

Mandelbaum is just illustrating how he made the incision so that it would match the other one when Sara comes in. She's been home for a few days with the kids and his parents; now she's come to take him back. She looks exhausted, worn, and she doesn't get the belly button joke, or else she doesn't think it's funny. The team leaves, jostling each other out the door like Keystone Kops in lab coats, high as kites. Sara sits down on his bed.

"I have something to tell you," she says. Her face is serious but composed, even sadder-looking in repose, Phil thinks, than it used to be. Coming upon her unexpectedly, people often catch their breath and ask, "What's happened? What's wrong?" She just shrugs and says, "Nothing. This is my regular face." He feels a stab of regret that he is one of the things that's happened, added to so much pain already. But surely all that is over now; what else could there be?

"I didn't want to tell you before because I knew you'd be upset . . ." She hesitates, and he feels the icy clutch of fear; it's not over, he was a fool even to think it, something dreadful has happened, the children, his parents . . . "The dog died," she says. "The day they moved you out of ICU."

He stares at her, his head a jumble of relief and pain as the silly jingle "the dog it was that died" runs through his head. It's all right, it's just the dog, poor old Collie Cibber, the dog it was, as he reaches his hand out to comfort her, remembering all those months she spent caring for him after that awful moment when she'd run him over in the driveway, walking behind him as he staggered through the snow, holding him up by the tail so he could pee, bringing him back nearly to his old self again, the poor old friend, and the rescue, the heroic effort of recovery inevitably come to this, and he feels so bad for her because she tried so hard that suddenly he finds himself choking, inarticulate, racked with tears. It is the first time he's cried since that day almost two months ago Sam told them Phil was dying, that there was nothing they could do.

That's the trouble with a run, Phil reflects as he watches the land slip by with deceptive slowness, the wind at his back billowing the sails, rocking him and the boat up and down, the rhythmic sluicing sound of the bow plowing through yet another wave, the water washing back against the hull, apparent wind less than the true wind, so that though the boat's progress seems slow, in fact they're actually barreling right along at hull speed. A run is too easy, he thinks, not enough to keep you from remembering what you'd just as soon forget.

Even so, it's not so much the conscious recollections as the dreams that get him. The pain can't be recalled, only the knowledge that there was pain, and other details in time become abstractions, events in a narrative he sometimes feels compelled to go over and over, trying to understand why it all happened, what he did wrong, trying to get it all straight. But this at least is voluntary. Awake, he can choose not to remember, refuse to tell himself the story, think of something else, read a book, distract himself with this activity or that. That's what he likes about sailing; there is something so completely absorbing about the need to balance all these conflicting forces. But in his dreams he lies helpless, unable to stop the dream, reliving the distress, the panic, or some new version of it. He knows that he had dreams during the operation, but he can't remember any of them, and wonders now if in his sleep he is dreaming versions of those dreams over and over, just as awake he sometimes feels compelled to go back over everything, is dreaming toward something, understanding perhaps, and will keep dreaming until he gets it right. Still, he reflects, maybe it's not such a bad thing after all; whatever happened in these dreams has made

him no longer afraid of death. He doesn't want to die, but he is
not afraid.

Phil shivers; a cloud has passed over the sun and the air is
cooling. He buttons up his shirt, holding the tiller steady with the
pressure of one knee. It is a short sail to Indian Cove from the
mouth of the river, black cans to starboard, red nuns to port (black
to port, back to port), out past Eddy Island, around Sidders Point
bell, then back in past Big John Island and Eugene Ledge mark,
up the channel to Pondatear. Too short really on such a gorgeous
day, Phil thinks. He nudges the tiller a little to starboard, comes
about again, trims the sails for a broad reach, and heads toward
open water.

"You're crazy," Sara says. She is smiling but she means it. It's
right after Christmas, barely a month and a half after his operation,
and he's just told her he wants to leave the boat at the coast and
sail it on the ocean next summer instead of hauling it inland. "What
are you going to do, commute? It's a three-hour drive one way.
At least." Her hands are busy in clay, working on some sort of
figure, a woman's head. At least he thinks it's a woman. Right
now it's just a lump.

"We can sleep on the boat. All we need is a couple of sleeping
bags."

"What about the kids?"

"They can come too. There's room. It will be a real adventure.
That's the beauty of it. Something we can all do together," he says
hopefully.

She stops modeling. Her hands, resting on the tabletop, look
stiff and formal, as though she were wearing gray suede gloves.
"Well, maybe," she says after a moment.

He understands her reservation. She has grown up sailing on a
nice lake you could see the other side of, where if worst came to
worst you could always swim to shore. He knows she is permanently leery of sailing on the ocean, sees it as cold and inimical,
pitiless and unpredictable. Having the children along would make
it even worse; she could save herself if the boat went over, but

not both kids *and* him. Not such a bad way to go, Phil reflects, but Sara obviously doesn't see it that way.

"What's wrong with one of the big lakes closer to home? Champlain or Winnepesaukee? You can sail around to your heart's content. I thought that's what we were going to do."

He regards her for a moment; she really doesn't get it. He considers telling her that she's the one who's crazy. He can just picture them rattling over the mountains with a huge trailer looming behind, Sara frantic in the backseat, afraid either the boat will fall off (visions of the huge white hull bouncing down the cliffs, pitchpoling over and over, gear flying) or the hitch breaking loose, the whole shebang crashing into the station wagon (pointy bow smashing into the rear window, glass flying, everyone crushed). Trying not to sound too exasperated, he says, "Listen, it would take two hours to get to where we'd have to moor it on Champlain, another twenty minutes to row all the way out to the boat. Same for Winnepesaukee. And when you finally get going, you're still surrounded by land. When I go sailing, I just want to get in the boat and *go*. That's the whole idea of sailing. That's the idea of *boats*."

Finally she agrees; they will try the boat on the coast for a season. But by the time they get everything all thrashed out, there's no more winter storage available at Indian Cove, so they settle on a small marina on the river about five miles down the coast by road. On the first nice spring weekend they get up at the crack of dawn, load the kids in the car and drive over to the coast.

The boat may be a classic, but after a winter in the marina it needs a lot of cleaning and fixing up. The children are delighted with it, especially Linnie, who loves all the nooks and crannies, the little drawers and tiny closets, the miniature marine toilet, the bunks and V-berth. She treats it as a playhouse, which, sitting on its cradle in the yard, it might as well be. She is content to spend her time cleaning and keeping house, talking to imaginary companions while she douses the inside with Mr. Clean and Windex, polishing and scouring as she would never do at home.

Phil ponders her fascination, and concludes that it is not so much the idea of boats as it is the appeal of dwellings—the illusion one has that by changing your house you can change your life, not being trapped inside your house the way you are inside your body. But it is the same with boats, even more so, because they move over the water and take you to places you can't get to any other way. More than anything, he wants to do this, take Sara places she's never been. He's already been enough places without her.

David, who doesn't care much for the inside (not that Linnie will let him in anyway; she's like a mother bird in a birdhouse), helps Phil clean and polish the hull, overhaul the old engine. On weekends later in the spring when it's warmer Phil and the children drive over while Sara stays home to work on a new sculpture she has started in the studio at the college. They have a wonderful time, the three of them, staying late, dinner at a fast-food place, the children falling asleep in the car, the quiet drive home in the dark. This is just what they have been looking for, Phil thinks, something that they all like to do together at last.

Finally it's time; the boat is launched and moored back at Indian Cove, it's time for the great adventure. As soon as they get there the kids run off across the beach—of course it's low tide, a little detail he forgot to think of—picking up sea glass and mussel shells, while he and Sara hank the sails on, rev up the stinky little engine, and putt back to the dock to pick them up.

The weather is beautiful, the sailing perfect, Phil thinks, glancing hopefully at the faces of his family, ranged along one side of the cockpit. "Isn't this great?" he says as they tack out past Upstart Island into the bay. It is as before, when he came last fall with Sara, only nicer, not at all cold; wonderful. He grasps the tiller and looks to windward, settling down to enjoy the long day's sail in a brisk off-shore wind, mild swell, just a little chop.

"Daddy, I feel sick." It's Linnie, looking pale. Sara has one arm around her, the other around David. Her legs are stiff, her body rigid, braced tensely against the coaming. The boat is heeling barely twenty degrees, yet she looks terrified already. Phil's heart sinks. He eases off.

"This is boring," David says. "I want to go back."

The whole thing is an unmitigated disaster. Back at the mooring in the late afternoon, as the wind dies down, the mosquitoes are

as thick as a mourning veil. The persistent ground swell makes
Linnie even sicker, so Sara has to take her into shore in the boatyard
tender. Phil has put up the dropboards in preparation for their
night of camping out, leaves David inside setting up the two kids'
sleeping bags. He is stretched out on the deck in the sun slapping
mosquitoes when he hears scrambling noises inside, and David
suddenly appears, trying to claw his way out through the forward
hatch. "Let me out! I can't breathe!" He is pale and sweating,
wide-eyed with terror, clearly claustrophobic. It's hopeless. Phil
rows him into the dock. "Let's just go home," Sara says grimly
as she loads both children in the car. "I knew this was a bad idea."

So it comes down to just the two of them, day-sailing because
Sara won't leave the kids alone overnight, and not much of that
because she's always anxious to get back, always thinking of the
long drive home. It's as though she's determined to thwart him.
She won't let him sail alone, but she also doesn't seem interested
in sailing the boat herself anymore when she's along. She does the
occasional deckwork, but mostly sits and watches. It's as though
she's become his caretaker, his warden, his guard. He wonders if
she'll ever let him off the leash.

The air is clear, the horizon like a ruler, the wind steady. Clearing
the mark at Gunboat Ledge, Phil looks at his watch, then at the
chart folded in quarters in his lap. It's barely ten o'clock, the wind
is blowing just enough offshore so he can reach right across Middle
Bay. As he careens out into the main bay, he sees Stoners and Sink
Island Ledges dead ahead, not as far away as he thought, Midway
Rock clearly visible in the distance. Oh, what the hell, he thinks,
why not? The wind is perfect, almost due south out here; he can
reach out, reach back. He eases off into a beam reach, tears between
the marks going at what must be hull speed, heading for where
he wants most to go: Lindiscove, only thirty miles due east. It's a
little risky, the longest trip he will have undertaken by himself,
but what the hell. It's a nice day, the air is warm, and he's got
lots of time. Sara need never know.

She knows everything, or thinks she does, and always has. That's what gets him. The sky is getting dark, but since he doesn't have a watch he doesn't know whether this is because it's getting late and that's why Sara's so anxious, or because a storm is coming up. The sky certainly looks dirty enough, clouds with sooty undersides to the west, closing in on the wedge of clear blue to the east. He can hear her already—how can he be so self-indulgent, keeping the two of them out here forever while he pursues his compulsive activity, oblivious of the needs of other people; they won't get home till long past dinnertime, the kids rambunctious, everything thrown off schedule—well, they're heading in now, so she can't complain.

From the way the trees are tossing around inland, it looks as though they may be in for a bit of a squall, maybe even some rain. He thinks about starting the cranky old engine and motoring in the rest of the way, but sailing is faster, so he decides to take the risk. Sara goes forward with the boat hook, crouches down ready to pick up the mooring, while he hauls in the mainsheet and tacks across the wind, picking up speed so they can come about into the wind and coast past the mooring while Sara snags it. He cleats the mainsheet and drops the long coil onto the cockpit sole, reaches over to loosen the starboard genoa sheet. The *Loon* slices through the water at a slight angle of heel, main tight, genoa billowing.

He is just about to swing the tiller over when out of the corner of his eye just off the port bow he sees the surface of the water ruffling, darkening as though the shadow of a cloud were passing, gaining speed and rushing toward him, then the pucker of white foam. As he lunges in sudden realization for the cleated mainsheet, the wind slams into the already taut mainsail with a tremendous bang. The boat heels over sharply, and he is thrown across the seat, back and shoulders against the leeward coaming as the mast with its cross-shaped spreaders drops like a poleax toward the surface of the water.

Trying to regain his balance, he pushes himself up off the lee rail as the boat slews along on her side, dragging both sails through the water, the huge white genoa scooping under the surface of the water as though it were still filled with wind, then rumpling up like so much wet toilet paper, the tea-colored water turning its whiteness to yellow-brown. He hauls himself upright on the grab rails and peers over the edge of the cabin toward the bow, hoping Sara hasn't been thrown overboard. No, there she is, sprawled upright on the perpendicular deck, one elbow hooked around a stanchion, feet braced against the mast, hanging on for dear life and screaming at him to do something, what exactly he can't hear. Not only that, she's still got the boat hook.

Meanwhile the boat has rounded up into the wind and begun to right herself. And suddenly Sara is there next to him, slamming the tiller hard against his crotch, uncleating the mainsheet and letting the sail out as far as it will go. He's never seen anyone move so fast. "Jesus fucking Christ," she yells over the din of banging sails and whipping lines. "Are you all right?" She is as white as the sails used to be.

He watches the water sluice off the sodden edges of the genoa in a fringe. The *Loon* is now headed into the wind, the deck level, both sails flapping like thunder, spraying water all over them like huge hairy dogs. He is shaken. "Sure I'm all right," he says. "Are *you*?"

She nods, adjusts the tiller, and the sails slowly fill with wind as they head back out toward open water. She doesn't say he was incredibly careless, but he can tell she's thinking it. Holding the tiller steady between her knees, she opens the engine compartment and says in that cool, officious tone that drives him nuts: "I guess we should have come in under power."

Jesus Christ, as if he didn't already know that. "How come all of a sudden you're so damned quick with what to do?" he says accusingly, as though she's been hiding something from him. "You won't even take the goddamned tiller anymore."

She shrugs as she cranks the heavy engine. He should be doing that. God, does she think he's completely helpless? He takes the cord handle from her; she steps back.

"You didn't have to come tearing back here. The boat was already righting itself," he says as he yanks on the balky starter. Maybe she'd like to add *that* to her famous litany of unlost causes—

"whatever is broken can be mended, et cetera," as demonstated in her obsessive rehabilitation of the injured Collie Cibber, late noble dog, not to mention Phil himself: whatever is knocked down will right itself, if you leave it the fuck alone. The engine roars to life with a cloud of oily smoke; he bangs the choke in and shoves the motor into gear.

"You never know," she says.

Jesus fucking Christ is right, always the last word. Speechless with anger, he takes the tiller from her. She goes back up on deck.

The squall is over but a hard rain has started to fall, soaking everything that wasn't already wet. Now that the engine is running and they are headed back in, the helm requires little care and after a moment he finds his attention focusing on Sara's haunches as she kneels at the bow with the boathook, getting ready to pick up the mooring. Her shorts cling wetly, nearly transparent, and he realizes she is not wearing panties. He reflects on the roundness of her buttocks, the keyhole configuration of ass and crotch. Though she has put on weight over the years since he first saw that skinny arm upraised in the back of the room, thickened slightly in the waist and belly from the children, the thighs still stretch long and slender from the pale crescents of her behind. The shorts are wrinkled between her legs, suggesting clearly the hidden folds of flesh, wisps of dark pubic hair visible on either side. Feeling himself harden in his own soggy clothes he forgives her everything, thinking only how much he would like to run forward and grab her hand to haunch, take her from behind, thrust his core of hot flesh right in, doggy-fashion . . .

He looks down at his fly, bulging damply. He shakes his head and looks away, up the mast, down the shrouds, around the rail, anywhere but at her, hoping the hard-on will subside before they get to shore. No doubt she would be shocked, minding her own business, intent on getting the boat safely to shore, no thoughts of sex, even particularly of him, the culprit, the overturner of safe boats, of expectations. He feels a quick revulsion, a return of anger at her persistent belief in the continued necessity for rescue.

Once they are safely on the mooring, he goes around, still fuming, to check for damage while Sara unhanks the soaking wet sails.

It could have been worse. Nothing is lost or even broken. The standing rigging is undamaged, the sheets and other running rigging, even the anchor line are all intact, if slightly tangled up and damp. His running gear is still wedged in the corner of the bunk where he left it. He changes into his running shorts, picks up his shoes, goes back up on deck and sits down on the rail with his feet in the water.

"What are you doing?" Sara asks.

"What does it look like?" he says as lowers himself overboard. "Pick me up on your way home."

It's just past low tide; the boat has swung in toward shore and the water is barely over his head. Holding his running shoes out of the water, he sidestrokes in until he can stand, then wades ashore, puts on his shoes and starts off, leaving Sara in the boat, staring after him. If she knows so goddamned much, he thinks as he squishes down the road, she can put the fucking boat away by herself. Right now he wants to be alone. He who years ago would have given anything to have her full attention now feels oppressed by her constant vigilance, the overprotectiveness that is like a giant thumb bearing him down. Even though she no longer has to take his blood pressure three times a day, she is still assessing symptoms on a daily basis—how are you feeling, did you sleep well, are you all right?—and he resents the implication that his physical well-being is still negotiable. He used to be the strong one; now she is the take-charge person, always ready—as she has just demonstrated—to leap into the breach.

Later that night, in the darkness of their bedroom as she sleeps with her back to him, he reaches for her, grabs her by the haunches, as she gives a little start of wakefulness and squirms sleepily, tilts her bottom back toward him, then pressing down against her crotch with one hand, enters her from behind, thrusting hard as he rolls over on top, pushing her down into the mattress, and harder and harder, farther and farther at the odd angle, so deep he seems to be hitting bone, slipping more easily now in her wetness, moans half-smothered by her face pushed into the pillow, until he feels himself pulled up and forward toward the pinpoint of light and with one long shudder, comes. He barely hears her murmuring to him as he sinks into sleep.

"I don't get it," he says the next morning, standing at the kitchen counter with his coffee. There's no place to sit. It's raining outside, and the still-damp sails are draped all over the living room furniture, lines and sheets hanging from the stair railing, over doors, on coat hooks, over the back of kitchen chairs. "You buy the boat practically over my dead body . . ."

". . . Greatly exaggerated how dead," she interjects, dampening a hunk of clay at the kitchen sink.

He ignores her remark. ". . . You've grown up on the water, know everything you need to know about sailing a boat, it's all wonderful, something we can all do together. So now we have this boat of our own and you don't seem to want to have anything to do with it. Why don't you want to sail anymore?" He wants her to admit it; maybe then she'll let him go alone.

"I do want to sail. I just don't want to do it all the time."

"—Not only that, when you do agree to go out, I offer you the helm and you act like it's a red-hot poker. What's going on? What's changed?"

She sighs deeply, not looking at him. "The reason I get so nervous about taking the helm," she says, scuffing a bare foot over the kitchen floor (which could use a good hosing), ". . . is because whenever I used to skipper—which wasn't very often, because girls usually didn't—I'd get all panicky because I could never remember which way was which, and I'd say ready-about, and it would turn out to be a jibe, and everybody would be ducking and cursing, and the boat would go over and we'd lose the race. So they always put me on the bow. I was great at wing-and-wing."

He stares at her: the truth is out. "So what was all that stuff when you went and bought the boat last fall about sailing it yourself?"

"I lied," she says with a shrug. "I'm chicken. I bought the boat for you. I thought it would give you something to live for."

It is as he suspected. She did it all for him; it had been sheer bravado after all. Suddenly the burden of her altruism is too much for him to bear. He turns away. "Don't do me any more favors," he says evenly, trying to keep the annoyance out of his voice, because he knows she's tried, done what she thinks is best for him. But he wants to be out from under this laser beam of her anxious scrutiny, this perpetual taking care. He's recovered; now he wants to be free. "Let's get one thing straight," he says, turning back to face her. "I'm not some crippled old dog whose tail you have to hold up while I pee."

Her face instantly drains of color, then just as quickly flushes red. She stares at him, her complete lack of expression indicating how deeply his remark has hurt her. Turning away, she puts the clay down on the kitchen counter, covers it with a wet dishcloth.

He curses himself for being too harsh. "I just need to be alone, to get back to myself again," he says gently, reaching out to stroke her face.

"I'm sorry," she says, backing up slightly, stony-faced. "I was just trying to help." Her tone is formal, distant. "Just tell me what you want me to do."

He nods, feeling the space grow between them. He takes a deep breath. "I need to be by myself more. I don't want you always watching over me. And please stop asking me how I feel all the time. I feel fine. I am fine. Okay?"

"Fine," she says. "Okay."

"I'm sorry . . ." he begins.

"Never mind," she says. "It's all right. I'm glad we got that straight. Anyway I've got my own stuff to do." Crumbs of clay drop from her hands onto the kitchen floor. She turns and walks away.

He follows her into the living room, hears her running quickly up the stairs. The still-damp sails shroud the furniture, hump by hump. He feels oddly detached, as though he's standing on the set of a closed-up country house from a movie that he's never seen.

He screams by Tucker Rock at noon, already halfway there, the sails close-hauled now as he points higher into the wind. Of course everything takes much longer than he thought, the gaining of distance toward a given destination nearly always at the expense of speed, and even though this is where in the world he most wants to go right now, by mid-afternoon he's wondering if he hasn't been a little reckless, even foolhardy. Though he's still in sight of land, it's a couple of miles away, and the seas are building, rhythmic sloshings against the hull, bottle-green shards rolling off the bow. The boat does not feel quite as substantial as he thought.

He thinks of turning back, making a run for the mainland and safe harbor, but then he catches sight of Lindiscove off the port bow, long and low at either end, rising in the middle, faint but unmistakable, the old Coast Guard station with its ecclesiastical tower looming starkly on the promontory. He can put in there, he thinks, call ship-to-shore to let Sara know he won't be home until tomorrow. There's still food and water left on board from sleeping over; he'll be fine. After all, he's been here before.

He crunches down the long tree-lined driveway in his running shoes. The silver-dollar-sized poplar leaves flutter in the light breeze; farther down the jagged maple and oak leaves form a canopy over the rutted turnaround next to the house, the deserted sandbox, the partially collapsed woodpile. The tallest maple tree is already tinged with scarlet, even though it's hardly past the middle of August. The lawn needs mowing again, the rambling old house needs painting. He really ought to see to some of these things, he thinks as he walks by, throw what's left of the kids' sandpile into the ruts, do some scraping and painting, restack the wood and split some more. As it is they'll hardly have enough to get through the winter, let alone any to season for next year. The demands are endless, but he's let most of them go, hating to waste the fine summer days on chores when he could be sailing, this first season with his own boat. At least he can breathe freely now; he feels like his own man again. But the cost of this freedom has been Sara's almost complete withdrawal from him, mentally and physically. She has been remote and inaccessible since their quarrel a couple of weeks ago; the one time he tried to broach the subject she told him with a weariness that nearly stopped his heart: "I just feel all used up, as though there's nothing left."

He regrets this estrangement, but since it's all his fault for getting sick in the first place, for telling her to leave him alone, he'll just have to live with the consequences. But at least she's working again; that's something. He's seen the sculpture she has been working on all summer. It's modeled in clay at the moment, but she wants to have it cast in bronze. It is a figure of a woman from the waist up, life-sized, mildly attentuated, slightly abstract, but realistically rendered. Seen from the front the woman's body appears relaxed, arms close to her sides, hands clasped in front, one shoulder slightly raised in what seems to be a shrug. The face is apparently serene, without expression, eyes closed. But if you walk around the back, you see that the top of the woman's head is breaking open like an eggshell, and visible within is another head straining to emerge as from a cocoon or birth sac, its features blurred, the expression one of agony, folds of flesh dimpled against the jagged edges of the skull. When she showed it to him he was on the verge of asking her whether the figure represented her mother or herself, but when she told him she was calling the piece *Cracking Up* he decided he really didn't want to know. All around the house there are drawings on backs of envelopes, pieces of typing paper, figures of all kinds, family groups, mothers, fathers, children, husbands and wives embracing. He sees these drawings, but doesn't ask what she's going to do with them; it's part of their arrangement.

They have also come to an arrangement about sailing; she still goes with him, but he doesn't badger her about going all the time, or expect her to take the helm. It's part of their tacit agreement to go their separate ways, at least for now. Anyway, she no longer feels so uncertain of his competence; several days after the knockdown, when they were speaking again, she told him that she was relieved it had happened; now he was bound to be more cautious, and anyway, now he knows what to do. But she is still reluctant to let him go alone, has become adept at dragooning friends to crew when she can't go herself.

As he comes past the last maple he sees a strange car pulled up to the garage. It's packed to the gunwales with luggage, more tied on top, and New York plates; he didn't know they were expecting visitors. But as he's on his way to the stairs through the dining room, thinking he'll sneak past everyone and go take a shower, he hears a familiar voice, one he hasn't heard in several years, since before he got sick.

"Gus!" he shouts, bursting into the living room with his hand out. And there he is, Gus Worth, his old teacher, colleague, friend, sitting next to Sara on the couch.

"Philip!" Gus says, and bounces upright, looking as much like an amiable toad as ever, the flat broad head and wide smile, barrel chest and narrow banty legs in a faded green polo shirt and plaid Bermuda shorts. He thrusts a hand out. "Glad to see you."

Phil turns to greet the others, all old acquaintances from his undergraduate years: Eric von Sklar, a classmate, beaming his huge, dimpled Viking grin, as tall and even balder than ever; wiry compact Jack Short, his old lacrosse coach; white-haired and distinguished Lou Garrett, the English professor who inspired him all the way to graduate school; Lou's teenage son Ben retiring shyly by the fireplace. Phil can't believe his eyes as he shakes all their hands in turn. "What are you guys doing here?" he asks, still standing in his sweaty running gear.

"I know it's awfully short notice," Gus says apologetically. "But do you think you could be prevailed upon—and our dear Sara could be prevailed upon to let you—come along on the annual cruise of the good ship *Endeavour*?"

He sights the abandoned lifesaving station at four, standing stark and monastic on the headland in the golden afternoon light, the small empty window squares momentarily aligned so he can see right out the other side. But when he gets close to the mouth of the harbor, the southerly wind is blowing dead across the shoals and the breakers are ranged across the mouth of the harbor like giant foamy barricades. Mildly apprehensive, he heaves to and stands off out by the gong, listening to it clang as it pitches and rolls in the swell. Shit, Phil thinks, I've really blown it. I can't anchor in this stuff by myself.

Sweating a little now in the chilly ocean breeze, he rides up and down in the swell outside the bar, trying to think what is the best thing to do. The wind is still from the south and east; if it holds he can reach all the way back.

He doesn't feel the least bit tired; what's another four hours? He decides to cut and run for it, comes about well beyond the breaking ledges, trims the main and jib for a broad reach and turns back. It's getting on for five o'clock now; how many hours until nightfall? Though the days are long this time of year, he won't make it back before then. "Even in the dark," he murmurs to himself, trying to remember word for word the course Hawley gave him so casually this morning. Even in the dark. You idiot, he thinks as the bow crashes down hard through a wave and he watches the whisker pole he forgot to stow below bounce off the deck and fly overboard, vanishing in an instant. Oh, Christ, he thinks, you'll never make it, you fucking fool. Sara will never forgive you. Yet strangely enough, he isn't scared.

"They want me to stay on a while longer," he tells Sara, trying to sound casual, girding his tone against possible disappointment. "They think the wind is going to move around to the north so we won't have to beat, and Gus wants to try sailing all the way down the bay to Monhegan. It wouldn't be that much longer. Just a few more days." He holds his breath, fully expecting her to disapprove of his further indulgence in this luxury. He'll come home if she wants him to; after all she's had the kids on her neck for five days now.

To his surprise, she agrees, her voice a thin thread over the line. "No, really, it's fine with me. I'm just glad you're having a good time. As a matter of fact, I was thinking of taking the kids to to see my mother this week."

"I could take a pass on that."

"I know. You always can. That's why I thought I'd go while you're sailing. Good excuse for your nonappearance."

"All right then, that's settled. See you in a week." He hesitates, wondering if he should say he loves her. He wonders what she would say back. Feeling far away, remote, instead he simply says "Sara, thanks."

"Have a good time," he hears her answer faintly. "See you later. Bye." The phone clicks down at her end, but he waits for a moment before breaking the connection entirely, feels the thought of her tugging at him, an invisible cord binding him to her across the miles. Yet she has let him go, at least this far. He wishes he had said he loved her, but it's too late now. He just hangs up.

And after all, it's not so bad. As he sails past Barrett Light to starboard the wind begins to fall, along with the sea. It's barely dusk, but the beacons are visible all along the coast in the clear air, sprinkled over the ocean like Christmas lights, blinking at different intervals from different heights. He keeps the beacon at Tucker Rock to starboard, steers between the two lights flashing alternately at Midway Rock and Little Stark Island monument, and sets his sights on the Gunboat Ledge Light at the entrance to Middle Bay. He tacks along from point to point accompanied by the sound of gongs and whistles, bells and horns, until the sea goes flat and the wind dies out completely.

The moon is nearly full, and he is surprised by how much light it casts across the water, the brightness like a path of smooth shiny stones flung across the water, radiating outward. He is close enough in now to make out the marks huddled like watchful hooded monks along the islands and ledges, red nuns on the right, black cans to port.

He has to motor the rest of the way in from Gunboat Ledge. Though it's barely ten, he feels as though he's violating the night, the privacy of the air by starting his engine. But he gets used to it, putt-putting the last few miles into the harbor along with the tide.

"It sounds like quite a cruise," Sara comments as she puts down the last few pages of the log Phil has been typing up for the rest of the crew. "Now I understand why you're still in such a daze, even after a week. It's like you haven't come back yet."

"Hmm," Phil murmurs, not really listening. He is reliving the feeling he had that bright day as he stood alone in the tower of the abandoned Coast Guard station gazing out the open window over the wild meadow to the ocean and beyond, his sense of limitless possibilities, of questioning and searching, yet also of peace, all of which he associates with the meditative life, the religious calling. Maybe I should have been a monk, he thinks as he rolls the last page out. Do monks go sailing? Of course, think of St. Brendan the Navigator, crossing the ocean in a leather boat he sewed himself (or so the story goes). Maybe it's not too late.

Standing behind his chair, Sara says quietly, "I missed you." He feels the warmth of her body radiating against his neck, her hand resting lightly on his shoulder. "I still miss you. When are you going to come back? I mean, really back."

The children are at a friend's house, she tells him as she leads him upstairs, and won't be home for several hours. The sun is streaming in the bedroom windows. She goes to close the drapes, but he stops her. "No, I want to see you," he says as he unbuttons her shirt, then his. They fall into the bed, kicking the rumpled sheets out of the way. He kisses her neck, her breasts, feels a momentary surprise as she presses his head downward, past her belly, between her legs; he hadn't thought she'd ever really liked his kissing her there but now she writhes herself upward to meet his lips, the slippery tang of salty flesh as he probes inward, first with tongue, moving over the soft ridges salty-fishy wet so sweet like fresh scallops in the shell, then fingers too, gently, then harder, harder, and he licks his middle finger and thrusts it up her ass as she twists around, moaning, and her twitching becomes rhythmic, he hears her soft "unh-unh" as her hips rise and rotate, until finally she puts her hands on either side of his head and pulls him up, his throbbing prick heavy as a red-hot poker sliding carefully inside because he doesn't want to hurt her or come too soon, but finally he can't hold it, he comes and comes and comes, one wave after another smashing on the rocks and bursting . . .

No, he thinks as he lies washed up like some exhausted sea creature on the beach, limp and panting, no, I could never be a monk.

The boat is put away on its mooring in Indian Cove, everything shipshape. Even though he's exhausted, he's too restless and exhilarated to sleep; he misses Sara now, and the kids, so he decides to drive back home that night. He's on the road by eleven, still wide-eyed and giddy with fatigue, relief, and happiness, driving through the mountains at one in the morning, the hills rising up one after another like rollers, huge green-black waves in the moonlight. Where the road is being regraded, he nods off slightly, dreams for an instant he's back in the boat, and the roadside markers are red nuns and black cans, until he veers into one and to his surprise, sees it fly up into the air. It lands upright on its weighted bottom further down the embankment, bobbing back and forth exactly like a mark. Phil leaves it there, and laughing like a child bumps the rest of the row one after another, watching them fly up in the air and land swaying drunkenly along the road behind. Oh yes, he thinks. This is it. This is perfect.

And at last he's home. As he comes inside the house at two in the morning, sweaty and reeling with exhaustion, worrying that Sara will be angry, still grinning at the memory of the cans flying every which way, she comes running down the stairs in her nightgown, her face bleached white in the moonlight.

"I'm filthy," he says, holding up his grimy, dirt-smeared hands to warn her. "I stink."

She throws her pale arms around him and pulls him close, burying her face against his chest.

"Ah, you're still alive," she says. "You're here."

"You're right," he says, wrapping his arms around her. "I'm back."

PART

2

4

In Case You Don't Come Back

"Did you remember to flush the toilets?" Phil asks not long after they've left for Boston.

Sara slowly turns her head and stares at him. They haven't driven far, but too far to go back if the answer is no. She shrugs. "What can I say?" she says.

Phil gives her a quick exasperated look, then turns his attention back to his driving, both hands clenched tight around the steering wheel, the knuckles white as molars. "I just wish we hadn't left the house in such a mess," he says.

Sara, on the other hand, has just been congratulating herself on the way they left the house. It has taken her years to arrive at the point where she can walk out and shut the door on anything. Still, she understands how Phil feels. "Of course I flushed the toilets," she says not unsympathetically. "The babysitter can take care of the rest."

"Oh my god, what babysitter?" Phil groans, slumping against his seatbelt. "What's she going to think? If she shows up, that is," he adds ominously. They've driven off as soon as the kids got on the schoolbus, leaving the house not only in a mess but unattended, so they'll have plenty of time to make Phil's noon appointment at the hospital. At thirteen and a half and almost eleven, David and Linnie are old enough to stay by themselves except overnight; the babysitter is just in case.

"It's Wendy. Don't worry, she'll be there." Sara answers absently. She's trying to remember if she really did flush the toilets. For all her determined casualness she is still haunted by childhood recollections of those whirlwind cleanups "in case we don't come back," the whole family spurred on by her mother's cheerfully grim heckling: "You wouldn't want people to know we lived like pigs, now would you?" Not that she can blame her mother; Sara's father is one of the ones who did not come back, hoisting his new overnight bag one summer day, blowing them all kisses and departing forever at the age of forty, leaving behind a widow and three young children, very little money, and as is often the case with lawyers, no will.

Even now, though they both have wills—and matching powers of attorney thanks to a lawyer who, no stranger to life's ironies, insisted Sara was in more danger driving back and forth to Boston three years ago than Phil was having major surgery—Sara detects a certain thrill of doom, a sense of having goosed the gods by leaving the place in such a mess. If they were to be killed right now, whoever came in after them would get the shock of their lives; whiskers and dried toothpaste spit in the bathroom sink, crumbs on the table and down the cracks, beds hastily made up with last week's sheets, fly carcasses moldering in the overhead lights, dust lying like gray plush along the windowsills and tops of doorways, layers of unexaminable trash rising inexorably in the bottom of every closet, bureau drawer and cupboard, ready to spill out like so many guilty consciences. A veritable Pompeii of a mess, their sudden deaths falling over it like ash, transfixing it forever in people's minds. "Oh, yes, the Boyds, they lived like pigs." Oh come on now, Sara chides herself. Who cares? Besides, we'll never know the difference. "Anyway, she knows how we live," she says to Phil. "She won't be surprised."

Phil nods, says nothing more. The car drones on in the silence, seeming to acquire a momentum and direction of its own. As well it should, Sara thinks; it's certainly made this trip enough times, almost three years' worth, every three months that first year, then every six. After this checkup, they'll be down to one trip a year. Two more after that, and it will be over, Phil declared cured, no more checkups, no more trips to the Clinic. It is a consummation devoutly to be wished.

Meanwhile the conversation languishes, but Sara doesn't really mind. They never talk much on these trips any more, but it doesn't really matter, since talking no longer seems to have the power it once did to change things. Besides, Sara thinks, things aren't so bad. The fact is, this is not even a trip worth getting cleaned up for; these down and back routine checkups don't count. They're used to it. This time they won't even be gone overnight, or so she hopes.

As she stares straight ahead a spider swings down abruptly as a yo-yo, dangles for a moment, then busily begins to ravel up an eight-footed cat's cradle right in front of her face. She bats it to the floor, watches it scurry away under a crumpled milkshake container, then reaches up and swabs away its flimsy barricade. Never mind the house, she thinks; if they were to be killed right now the truth would be out in no time; the car is a traveling dump. There would be smelly sneaker soles, dirty socks and candy wrappers, trampled bubblegum and melted crayon ends strewn from here to the state border. But they're not going to have an accident; even if life is at best a gamble, they've certainly used up their share of disasters for a while. Nevertheless, she makes a silent promise to clean everything up as soon as they get home, puts her head back, shuts her eyes, and tries to sleep.

It's Phil's last day in the hospital; Ristine has promised to discharge him tomorrow, a mere ten days after the operation. The surgical team has been in twice, once to take out the stitches and once just to admire their handiwork, Dalton, Hunker, Mandelbaum and Greef all standing in a row at the foot of Phil's bed as graduated and inseparable as the fingers of one hand, joking and elbowing each other, still chortling over their great success. Mandelbaum the senior resident, as sleek as a penguin with his dark hair, white coat and glasses, has proudly pointed out to Sara that he has not only replaced Phil's belly button good as new, but also made the second scar, although much longer, go off across his ribs at precisely the same arc as the first, so that Phil's abdomen has all the symmetry of an uninflated basketball.

Now Ristine is sitting on the bed, as pale and lank as wheat. With his wire-rimmed glasses, pointed nose and mild manner he reminds Sara of a Mr. Peepers somehow stretched tall and competent. He has warmed up considerably over the days of Phil's recovery, which Sara thinks is a good sign. Phil told her earlier that for all Ristine's knowledge and appreciation of the body as machine, he suspects him of being secret philosopher; that's how he keeps his cool detachment. Sara has her suspicions about the detachment; she still remembers Ristine sitting there the night before the operation, his long pale hands clasped around one knee, describing to them in his flat Georgia accent all the awful things that could happen that he and the team were ready for. She had remarked finally on how calm and unruffled he seemed, and how reassuring it was to see he was not the least bit worried. He had swiveled his head around, blinked up at her as solemn as a cat and drawled, "Who me? Hell no, I'm scared to death."

But that is all behind them now, and they are discussing follow-up. "Well," says Ristine, pushing his glasses back up his narrow nose. It's an habitual gesture; watching him now, Sara wonders how he manages in the operating room. If he does it every three minutes, in eight hours that would be one hundred sixty pushes back up his nose. Not such a great number. There are one hundred eighty-four stitches across Phil's belly, all tied by hand. And that's just the outside. The rest of him they've stapled together, ribs and cartilage, muscle and bone. It will look funny on the X-rays, they have told him, like birdshot, but he'll never feel the difference inside.

"About the follow-up," Ristine goes on, "I'll want to see you in six weeks. I don't know what the others have planned." He pauses, looks interrogatively at the two of them, but they don't know either. It's all so complicated, two hospitals, three medical schools, and doctors who come in sets like Chinese boxes, attending, fellow, resident, intern, not to mention the occasional rotating curious medical student, all delighted with their part in unraveling the burden of Phil's mystery. "Somebody we can cure!" Sara remembers overhearing someone whisper excitedly outside Phil's room the night he was admitted to the Institute. Sara was sure they were talking about somebody else, but after all the tests were done—"Now I know what they mean by a battery of tests," Phil said, lying limp and exhausted after the last arteriogram— when Owen Hughes said: "We're going for a cure," she started to believe it. So far so good. Owen isn't here right now, having said his goodbyes earlier and flown off to accompany a dying patient back home to India, but they'll be seeing him again; he said he'd keep in touch.

"Right," Ristine says. "We'll fix up the appointment then. Don't do any lifting or twisting until those muscles heal. Expect to feel a little tired when you get home. It doesn't mean a relapse. Just take it easy."

"What else?" Sara asks. She is writing it all down in a notebook they've been keeping ever since Phil was discharged from the hospital back home almost two months ago, thinking he was a dead man.

"Well," Ristine drawls, adjusting his glasses, "that's up to the folks across the street. Technically, you belong to them. But my guess is the usual, CAT scan, X-rays, blood, urine every three months, then every six months for a while, then . . ."

"Hold it a minute," Phil says, pulling himself upright. "I thought you guys said you were going for a cure." He stares accusingly at Ristine. "I thought it was benign."

Ristine doesn't even blink. "Right. Nothing's changed. We're very hopeful."

Phil shuts his eyes and sinks back into the pillow. Sara looks at him, afraid for a moment he's going to cry. Since the operation he has had a tendency to break down easily. Dalton says it's the letdown; Hunker thinks he's still a touch anemic. Ristine says it's normal.

Phil is trembling now, but he doesn't cry. "So whose idea of a cure is this?"

"It's standard procedure," Ristine says mildly. "Just routine. We can't tell in the lab whether what you had was benign or not, only by hindsight. That first tumor you had two years ago seems to have been benign; chances are this one will be too. It's all academic anyway, because we got it all."

"Then why can't you just leave me alone?"

Ristine leans forward. Sara watches his glasses glide slowly down his nose. "The first couple of checkups are the worst. After you've had a few it'll get better. Two or three years from now you'll hardly notice. A necessary inconvenience. It won't bother you a bit."

Phil has shut his eyes again. As Sara watches him, she sees the months stretch ahead, the checkups—necessary inconveniences—like a series of barricades, and they are in a race, three, six, twelve, leap up and over, safe on the other side, then back up for the next. The longer you get to run before you have to jump, the closer you are to safety. But as she stares down the road the hurdles just fade off in the distance, infinite, a tunnel full of mirrors.

Ristine unfolds himself from the bed, shakes down his white coat, pushes his glasses back up his nose. "But don't worry, it won't be so bad. You'll get used to it." He pauses in the doorway, looks thoughtful for a second, then smiles. "Perfect is the enemy of good," he says, turns and walks away. Ristine says this a lot; it's one of the reasons Phil thinks he's a philosopher.

Of course she could have stayed home, Sara thinks, and spent her time bulldozing a path through the house instead of riding shotgun when she really isn't needed. They talked about Phil coming by himself this time, and even though she didn't really like the idea Sara had pretty much agreed, but as the time got closer Phil seemed to assume she was coming after all. To tell the truth, Sara is relieved. She hates the drive, but not as much as she hates sitting by the phone not knowing. She misses him when he's not around and besides, he might get lost. It's so confusing down here; even with all the driving back and forth she did, she never seemed to end up on the same road twice.

"There's the sign for Memorial Drive," she says too urgently, and Phil almost veers into a car merging from the left.

"This is crazy," he says through gritted teeth, falling in behind the next car, which speeds away aggressively, the driver waving a rude finger at them and honking contemptuously. There is concrete everywhere—bridges, over- and underpasses, roads going up, down and all around, signs the size of restaurant menus posted where you least expect them. Sara remembers the first time they drove down here, in the dark, at rush hour, car headlights shooting off like fireworks every which way. They were both terrified.

"There," she directs with a finger across his line of sight, not trusting herself to distinguish right or left. "That way."

"I see it," Phil says crossly. "I'm all right."

They shoot off the ramp into daylight; overhead the sky looks like the inside of a shucked oyster, and the river gleams mother-of-pearl just beyond the concrete gangways filled with noontime joggers.

"We're almost there," she says. "Keep left," as they whizz onto Beacon Street and head for Brookline. From here there's nothing to it; it's always easier to get there because of all the one-way streets. Sara remembers the first time, after she had left him at the Institute late at night, trying to follow the signs to Lexington, where she was staying with their old friends Jane and Mack for the duration. Suddenly lights seemed to flare at her from all directions, bouncing and weaving and streaming around in arcs as though she had driven into a crowd of runners holding flashlights; so that before she knew it she'd gone right through a red light. The cop who pulled her over shook his head and let her go with just a warning. Still, it's not the thought of getting lost or pulled over that worries her; she wonders what Phil would do, driving back alone, if there happened to be bad news.

But there's really nothing to worry about now, Sara thinks as she sees the buildings of the Medical Complex loom up, the Institute a great slab of coffee jello rising up among the brick and stone. Good news is good news, and bad news is negotiable. "Who knows what normal looks like in somebody like you?" Owen said cheerfully over lunch after Phil's checkup last spring. They won't be seeing him again, at least not here. He finally left the Institute last July after two tough years—"You were the good news," he told Phil—and lit out for private practice in the territories. So Phil will have another doctor for this checkup, someone he's never met. That's probably why they're a few months late with this checkup; they just couldn't seem to get up for it. Too bad; they both really liked Owen.

Phil pulls in past the entrance to the clinic and drives up the narrow corkscrew ramp. The machine spits a ticket at him; he passes it to Sara. They finally find a place on the top level. There is a nice view from the top looking north; you can see all of downtown Boston as far up as the docks. To the south the view is cut off by what look like giant concrete egg crates on end, the new ten-story patient tower of the hospital where Phil had his operation. It has been in use only for six months, and neither of them has been inside, but it's where they're going now, if they can figure out how to get there.

Sara waits by the car while Phil takes out a crumpled piece of paper on which he has scribbled directions from his friend Bonny in Radiology. "L2, A111, turn right, then left," he reads, then peers skeptically at the paper. "It sounds like the combination to a safe."

They walk across an enclosed footbridge leading from the garage into the next building. Sara takes out the small red plastic visitor's ID card they gave her three years ago, just in case. There is a wide yellow line down the middle of all the corridors that marks the path, left, right, straight, through the odor of stale egg yolk, for-maldehyde and mouse, past crumbling plaster walls stained with damp, down a flight of stairs to where three buildings come to-gether like jagged puzzle pieces, then straight on through increas-ingly dilapidated corridors past electronic checkpoints whirling and clicking and searching, jostled by people in white lab coats both coming and going. Sara holds the red plastic card up in front of her just in case, but no one challenges them.

The line stops at a door marked NO ADMITTANCE in partially rubbed-out letters. Phil yanks the door open and walks through,

Sara right behind him. He stops so abruptly she runs right into his back.

"Goodbye yellow brick road," he murmurs in a voice of wonder. "Where the hell are we?"

The old building is in the process of being renovated. Everything is dismantled, wiring and pipes exposed, partitions pulled down into piles of lath and plaster, new lumber and great sheets of drywall stacked everywhere. All along both sides of the corridor are large garbage bags full of unidentifiable debris; there's an intermittent ragged whine of drills and saws. A whiff of burning plaster dust and ozone mingles with the smell of iodine and lunch. Some mess, Sara thinks. Fascinated by the demolition, wondering if there are any unconsidered trifles she might snap up to use in her work, she is still peering curiously down the hallway when she feels Phil nudge her in the direction of the elevators to the new building.

Inside the elevator, Phil pushes a button marked with symbols matching the ones on his piece of paper and down they go. They walk down a windowless corridor that is hardly less beat-up looking than one they've been in; at the far end moving figures can be seen shrouded in polyethylene. There is a crackling sound, and sparks hit the plastic like fireflies in a dirty jar. All along the wall red fire-alarm lights blink and beep faintly, but no one seems to notice.

The CAT scan office is midway down the hall, marked with a small hand-lettered sign. It's smaller than the old one, painted cream, three-quarters full of metal shelves with manila folders spilling every which way. The rest of the small space is waiting room with rows of seats bolted to the floor along the wall. Phil stands in front of the counter; a slight, white-haired woman presses her knees sideways against her seat to give him room.

"Yes?" a pretty young woman behind the counter inquires politely. Phil gives his name, then stands there erect and nonchalant with his arms folded over his chest, looking big and broad-shouldered and healthy. His physical presence, Sara notices, is not lost on the young woman, who gazes up at him for a moment before she starts bustling through the folders on the counter. She probably can't believe he's ever been sick. Eat your heart out, Sara thinks; he's mine.

"Have you been here before? Ah, yes, I see you have," the young woman says as she pulls out Phil's thick file. She puts it to one side, then fills a paper cup from a large bottle of clear liquid. "Drink three of these." She bats her eyelashes at him. "You're so tall."

"Cheers," Phil says, taking a big gulp. He shudders, makes a face. "Gyuck," he says.

"I don't see why they can't put an olive in it," the white-haired woman says unexpectedly. "One little olive wouldn't show, would it?"

"We just ran out of cranberry juice," the young woman says from behind the counter. "Busy day. Sorry."

Phil nods gravely, and fills his cup again. The liquid gives off an odor of stewed Band-Aids; Sara wrinkles up her nose. Actually it's radioactive iodine and sterile water. Even with cranberry juice Phil says it's awful.

"Where's Bonny?" Phil asks after a moment. Bonny is Phil's special friend in the CAT scan office, another pretty young woman with long blonde hair and a perky figure. Phil is often surrounded by sweet young things; his office at the college is usually filled with students, mostly female, seeking advice of one kind or another. However, Phil seems generally oblivious to all this female attention.

"Lunch," the young woman answers, looking mildly disappointed. "But she'll be back any minute." She turns to Sara. "Yes? May I help you?" she inquires.

Sara smiles and answers, "I'm with him."

Phil strolls out into the hall, sipping from his paper cup. Not just because he's so tall but also because his insides have been so thoroughly rearranged, he not only has to drink three, they discovered after one of his scans looked bad two years ago, but do it while walking around, so that the contrast material trickles down into every nook and cranny. Sara glances around the new office. The other one was decorated with cat posters and old magazine covers; this one is all business, framed CAT scan sections on the wall, heads on one side, torsos on the other.

Sara steps up to one wall and looks at the photographs. Even in black and white the skull series resembles something from the deli, olive loaf with macaroni lined up slice by slice. She moves over to the torso series. These pictures are larger, about the size of a tea tray, and much more complex, mottled shapes in black and white and gray, each organ clearly labeled with little colored-paper spears stabbing into the appropriate area. The whole thing reminds her of a catalogue page of holiday gift packs, assorted delicacies you send by mail to sundry relatives in lieu of presents. She studies the ghostly slices, trying to make out what's what. These small round pears your kidneys, this bunch of grapes your small intestine, this large smoked pheasant your liver. The deluxe assortment. Phil's comes, she imagines, with only the one pear, the rest peppered with birdshot and a little jumbled up in transit. She shuts her eyes, reflecting that no one should know as much about another person's insides as she does.

She turns away, opens her eyes and walks into the hall, looking for Phil. He is standing at the far end with Bonny. Bonny is talking animatedly, her ponytail bobbing; Phil is smiling. As Sara is about to walk towards them, she hears a loud metallic rending noise behind her, turns to see two large flat doors sliding open like an elevator. Inside the machine looms like a giant Bendix. Phil has described having a scan as going through a car wash lying down, without the car, except you don't get wet. To Sara it looks like a giant oven.

The CAT scan attendant steps out, slides the door half-shut behind him. "Mrs. Crane?" The white-haired woman stands up, walks stiffly out into the hall toward Sara, her eyes wide with terror.

"Don't worry. It doesn't hurt," Sara says without thinking. The woman glances at her, smiles weakly, and disappears between the sliding doors. Why did I say that? Sara asks herself. What do I know?

Phil and Bonny have come back down the hall, Bonny hanging

on Phil's arm. "Doesn't he look great?" Bonny says to her as they go by. Sara follows them into the waiting room. Okay folks, she thinks, enough is enough.

"Isn't this something?" Bonny says, waving a hand around the tiny waiting room. "A brand-new ten-story building on top of us, and we wind up with this." She dumps a glass of clear liquid into the pot of a wilted azalea, tries to fluff up the leaves while the water gurgles out into the dish.

"I hope that's not what you're giving me," Phil says. "The damn thing'll glow in the dark." He holds out his cup. "If it lives."

Bonny grimaces, then says perkily, "Now there's a thought. I'll take it home and use it for a night-light." She fills his cup. "That's it. You're next," she says, still smiling. Sara wonders where the other young woman has gone. Probably to lunch. It's almost noon, after all. She doesn't feel hungry herself at the moment; anyway, she'll wait and eat with Phil when this is over.

Silence falls. They can hear the hum of the machine next door. It whirrs louder and louder, gaining speed, and when Sara shuts her eyes she sees the bright stainless steel rim spinning faster and faster, flashing like magician's hoops. The machine hums and hums. She stands next to Phil just inside the waiting room door. Out in the hall doors slide back. Someone calls Phil's name. Phil turns his head attentively toward the voice, then looks down at Sara. His face is pale, strained, and mildly apologetic.

"Are you going to have lunch now?"

Sara shakes her head. "I thought I'd wait for you."

Phil shrugs. "That's up to you. If you want we can get something to eat in the cafeteria next door after I'm done; the food's better. I'm starving. But I may be a while."

"You're always starving," Sara says severely. But she's glad he's hungry, remembering what he looked like after the first operation, like a ragged coat hung on a stick. He certainly doesn't look like that now, as his instant fan club will no doubt attest.

He winks at her as she stands there stiffly, staring at him. "See you later."

"See you later," she repeats, steps up to him and gives him a peck on the cheek. "Good luck," she says, as he walks off down the hall, his footsteps sounding in time with the red fire-alarm lights as they beep their unregarded warning to the air. Sara watches him disappear, then goes back inside to wait.

There has been considerable discussion whether Sara should wait out Phil's operation at Jane and Mack's house in Lexington, or at the hospital. Both Ristine and Phil have insisted it's unnecessary, even foolish of her to hang out at the hospital for what may turn out to be an all-day event, because there's nothing she can do, and it only increases her chances of getting mugged. "I don't want to have to worry about that," Phil said to her last night. "I've got enough to worry about."

"You worry too much," she answers. "Anyway you'll be asleep." But she is in fact thinking of not coming until Owen, stepping outside with her as she's about to leave, says "If I were you, I'd be here."

So she has been waiting here all this long day, part of the time with Jane, but alone now, standing in the long narrow corridor outside the door that leads to the operating room and to Intensive Care upstairs. Her head aches slightly, probably because she forgot to eat lunch, but she can do that later. She has been here so long that she feels invisible; no one seems to notice her standing against the wall of the main corridor as they go by and in and out, the doors whooshing and thumping constantly; she could be in another country, even on another plane of existence. Still, the worst is over; Phil hasn't died, and she has not been mugged.

The door next to her bangs back and Owen Hughes comes out, his white coat undone, his stethoscope dangling precariously from the top pocket. His face is rosy, cheerful, glistening with perspiration. He catches sight of her and comes over to her, smiling. "He's doing fine," he says, folding his arms. "Still out cold, though."

She knows that he is doing fine; she saw Ristine in the hall earlier so she knows from him it's gone well, the best that they could hope for. They did not have to take out the kidney after all, only a small part was damaged, and Ristine's sure they got all the tumor. Still, it is nice to hear it from Owen. She heaves a great sigh that leaves her head throbbing, and both she and Owen stand there mopping their brows for a while longer, while Owen tells her all about it, how brilliant Ristine was, how people clapped and cheered like onlookers at a major-league game.

"It's such a miracle," Sara blurts out, then, feeling like an idiot, realizing how naive, even ungrateful that sounds, adds quickly: "It seems like such a miracle to us anyway. But you guys must be used to it; around here it must happen all the time."

"As a matter of fact it doesn't," Owen says. "But that's what keeps us poor bastards going, the chance of the odd miracle."

As she stares at him, incredulous, he smiles and throws an arm around her numb shoulders, hugs her briefly. "I've got to go now. But I'll be back later. See you." And off he goes down the hall, his white coat flapping. Ah, the miracle, she thinks, testing the unfamiliar, even religious word, the odd pale miracle, as stern and still and fugitive as grace.

Later, after Ristine has found her still standing in the hall and taken her upstairs, even though he has told her Phil won't be awake, not for hours yet, and even though he has told her he's still hooked up to everything, Sara is so relieved and excited that she insists, and so she follows Ristine upstairs to see for herself that it is really over, that Phil is fine, and everything went well. There is some compensation in having been through all this before, she reflects as she passes the nurses' station in the center of the unit; she won't be horrified by all the tubes and wires and machines and other paraphernalia, the respirator hose rammed down his throat like a big vacuum cleaner hose.

But even though she has seen it all before, she gags a little and her ears start to ring. Ristine stands at the foot of the bed in his street clothes—he's not worried or he'd still be in his greens—looking pleased, his head bobbing up and down like one of those goggle-eyed long-beaked trick birds perched on a glass of water.

Sara walks forward and slips her fingers into Phil's partly curled-up hand. There is no response, but the hand is warm and rosy, not at all the way it was before. In fact, all of Phil is pink and rosy, at least what she can see of him under the huge bandage covering him from crotch to collarbone. To give herself something to do, she walks around, trying not to trip over things, and studies the machines and dials and meters. The respirator chuffs and sighs, the IV drips, the heart monitor bleeps a reasonable pulse of ninety-eight. Blood pressure ticks out 130/80, very good. She remembers the other time, the heart monitor line as furred as tinsel, the frenzied bleep almost continuous, the blood pressure so low they couldn't get a vein to run the transfusions. She looks around to see how many bags of blood he's getting, sees none, only an IV full of clear liquid. The nurse stands back, following her with her eyes. Sara walks back around the bed, carefully avoiding Phil's bare legs hanging over the end. She knows it's still early, a lot could happen, but, she thinks, so far so good.

She spends the next few days in and out of the waiting room, talking to families of other patients, the Greek brothers whose eighty-two-year-old mother has had a triple bypass and is not doing well, the sixteen-year-old black girl in grave condition, shot in the belly by her boyfriend during a party brawl. Phil on the other hand is doing fine; all tubes have come out except for one IV, and he is walking around the unit pushing it on a trolley, complaining about being hungry. Sara counts off days in her mind, haunted by the aftermath of the earlier operation; so many days and the danger of pneumonia is past, so many more and blood clots are less likely, and so on, each day bringing them closer to safety.

Then there is the business of the dog. Thinking she'll have to drive home to be there when he's put to sleep, Sara calls to get a report on Phil and finds out they've moved him out of ICU into a regular room on the floor where he was before the operation. Then she learns the dog has died during the night, and she doesn't have to go home after all, so she gets Phil's new room number from the front desk. Wondering how to break the news to him, she walks past the nurses' station, nodding briefly at a few familiar faces, down the hall and through the door of Phil's room . . . and stops dead. The IVs, the respirator, the heart monitor are all back, and Phil's body is once again enmeshed in a spiderweb of tubes and wires. Oh, no, she thinks, staring in horror at the still form. It's happening all over again, he's dying right here, right now, it's too soon, oh, shit, why did I ever mention miracles? "What's happened? What's wrong?" she practically screams, then claps a hand over her mouth and stares, confused by the sense that she has been here before.

A nurse comes running. "Oh, Mrs. Boyd! Your husband's in Room two twenty-three. He's doing fine."

Sara shuts her eyes and in the whirling rush of silence, knowing he is still safe after all, she laughs.

Phil gives his name to the receptionist behind the desk in the waiting room of the Clinic. Meanwhile Sara sits down in one of the nearby rows of chairs, picks up a magazine and begins to leaf through it. A nurse calls Phil's name, and he walks over to the nurse's station. After a moment, Sara gets up and walks around to where Phil is sitting with a thermometer in his mouth while the nurse pumps up the blood pressure cuff. Phil looks up at her, watching her face while Sara watches the mercury bouncing in the blood pressure tube on the wall. She learned how to use the cuff that fall three years ago after they discovered the second tumor had driven Phil's blood pressure upwards of 250/160, high enough to kill him if he sneezed. She still occasionally keeps tabs on it at home, just in case, leaving the kit lying around casually so the kids are used to it by now. "It's fine," Sara says.

The nurse nods, glancing at her curiously. "One-twenty over seventy," she tells them. "Nothing wrong with that."

Phil stands up, hands her the thermometer, and steps onto the scale. The arrow lurches around to two hundred and three pounds. Phil shrugs. "I had a big lunch," he tells the nurse.

"That's what they all say," she says dryly. "You can go sit down now."

Sara smiles, feeling proud of Phil as if he were her baby, gaining and thriving. They are about to sit down again when someone calls his name, a tall, thin, sandy-haired doctor with a scraggly beard and horn-rimmed glasses. The doctor looks very young, almost apologetic, certainly shy. Holding Phil's chart in one hand, he extends the other. "Hello. I'm Dr. Nevins."

They shake hands briefly, then the doctor starts down the hall. "See you later," Phil says over his shoulder to Sara as he follows Nevins down the hall.

"Oh, your wife is welcome to come along," Nevins says, and waits for Sara to catch up. They all file together into an empty examining room, sit down, and cross their legs simultaneously to get comfortable. Nevins flips open Phil's chart, stares at it briefly then closes it, laces his fingers across his knee and looks up.

"Well now. Tell me what's been going on since you were here last."

"Nothing really," Phil begins. He goes on to recite the medications, his diet, the precautions he's been taking, emphasizing that he feels just fine. It all sounds so normal, and Sara remembers the two hot meatball sandwiches he wolfed down at lunch. As he leans back in his chair, his jacket falls away, and the two long scars stand out momentarily as ridges under his jersey. Watching him, Sara thinks about the CAT scan. They told them they'd be reading it some time after three; it's now two-thirty. Sara feels the news pressing closer with the flat inevitability of a letter mailed but not yet delivered; it's all down in black and white now, fixed and irrevocable, good news or bad.

Nevins opens up the chart again, leafs through the various reports, blood tests, X-rays, urine tests, back at least an inch. When he begins to talk it's nothing new, nothing they haven't heard before, but coming from him it sounds different, even alarming. He knows something awful, Sara thinks, and then thinks, no, he can't. It's simply that he has no gift, not like Owen; she can tell already that for him there are no odd miracles, only triumphs of technology. He even makes *her* feel like a patient, as she listens to him talking about genetic predisposition, increased likelihood, unsettled pathology. Then he shuts the folder, clasps his hands over it with a gesture of finality, and clears his throat. "So I think it would be advisable to continue these six-month checkups for at least another year."

Slowly Phil turns his head toward her, stares at her stone-faced, as if to say, "What did I tell you?" Then he turns back to Nevins. "Dr. Hughes said after this checkup we could go to once a year."

"Six months is better," Nevins persists. "Just to be on the safe side. There's a great deal we don't know about your tumor; they're extremely rare, as I'm sure Dr. Hughes told you. This way we can catch anything that might come up early, while there's still something we can do."

Staring at Nevins, Sara sees the horizon of security recede a little further. Nevins shifts in his seat, then smiles.

"Though I must say, seeing you looking so well is most encouraging. If you get through a few more of these, you should be an excellent candidate for long-term survival." He stands up briskly, and their eyes follow him in tandem. "Now if you'd like to get undressed, we can do the physical exam. Then I'll call about your CAT scan." He nods to Sara, nods to Phil, goes out and shuts the door behind him.

Phil stands up, begins to pace around the room. Several narrow shiny instruments Sara hopes are designed merely to look up ears or noses rattle and clank on the steel cart as he brushes by; nearby a glass jar full of cotton swabs rocks precariously. He whirls around and glares at her. "Do you believe this? Did you hear that bullshit about long-term survival?" he says. "Formerly known as life, in case you hadn't guessed." He rolls his eyes toward the ceiling. "God, I wish Owen were still here."

"Doctors are different," she says as calmly as she can, studying her hands. "He's just being cautious."

"Right," Phil snorts. He stomps around a few more steps, then grabs his jacket by the lapels and jerks it off, throws it over the chair. He looks down at her. "See you later," he says pointedly.

"Don't you want me to stay?"

"Of course not. What for?" Phil says as he undoes his belt, drags his shirt out of his pants.

"I want to stay with you. I want to be here," she insists, aware of a vague compulsion; if it's going to be bad news it's better shared.

Phil bends down to untie his shoes. "Thanks anyway, but I'll be all right," he says. "You wait outside, okay?"

She opens the door just as Nevins is about to knock. After a brief feint and parry Sara steps out into the hall, and Nevins steps in. As she looks back over her shoulder, she sees Nevins peering through the crack. "So nice to have met you," he says, and shuts the door.

She wanders away from the doorway, down the corridor toward the waiting area in the lobby. With its soft, indirect lighting, its comfy overstuffed Design Research lounges and Marimekko drapes, its all-purpose carpet strewn with toys and books and coats and spilled crayons, coloring books and candy wrappers, a rapidly browning apple core set in an otherwise unused ashtray, it looks like someone's living room, everything left casually waiting for the owners to come back and pick up where they left off.

But Sara doesn't feel like sitting down, much less picking up, so she walks over to the big bulletin board in the middle of the hall between the adult and children's sections. It's a big, cheerful, busy-looking bulletin board, full of miscellaneous announcements and things to read, like bulletin boards everywhere. Its casual disorder—stuff tacked up every which way, plastered over in layers—reminds her of her own house, and for a moment she feels right at home. She starts at the top and reads across. "What to do in Boston": a list of places to go and see; "Have you been to the Top of the Rock? Ask for our hotel brochures, special discounts for patients and their families. Find out today!"; a mint-green mimeographed sheet announces the most recent interest rate for the clinic credit union. "Open your IRA today. Invest in the future! Time accounts available, up to 2 years. Patients welcome."

Sara stares at the words for a moment. Her eyes wander to a schedule of lectures for the week. "The Use of Immuno-factor D in recurrence of Renal-cell carcinoma after a remission of 18 years." She skips down the rest of the list, to a brightly colored travel brochure—sparkling water, sandy beaches, striped awnings and palm trees. A mostly naked, very tan man and woman, blond hair streaming, scoot down a bleached path in a candy-colored golf cart, laughing hysterically. "Beat the Boston winter blahs! Barbados in Spring! Think of it! Special group rates for patients and their families!"

As Sara stands there obediently thinking of it, a small figure comes barreling out of the children's area and bangs right into her leg. He looks up, startled, his face screwed up into a blotchy mask of outraged indignation. Then he takes off again, paper diapers swishing, tottering down the hall as fast as his little legs will carry him. Even from here, Sara can see the few sparse hairs on his round bald head, the yellowed waxen complexion. Then a harassed-looking woman pushes past, excusing herself, and races after the bald baby, calling "Larry! Larry!" The child doesn't get far before he's stopped by a blue-coated security guard. He arches his back, lets out a howl and pushes away, but the guard holds him until his mother hauls him up and hoists him over her shoulder. "Now, Larry," she murmurs as they come back down the hall. "Be a big boy. It's not so bad. It'll all be over before you know it." The little boy struggles feebly, kicking small hard shoes against his mother's hip until she reaches down and holds his feet. He drops his head on her shoulder, pops his thumb into his mouth, whimpering as they nudge past Sara in the direction of the Infusion Room.

Sara stares after them, remembering what Phil said the first time they came back here. "You know, it's not the place so much or even that I have to be here that really bugs me. It's all the little bald babies running around. What did they do to deserve this?" And as she stands there the whole place seems to turn dark, as though light can no longer penetrate the layers of smoked glass, and what there is seeps into the roughened concrete walls like paint, leaving long barred shadows all along the walls, and she wants to take a hammer and run through the place, battering and flailing it all down, the flashy Mexican wall hangings, the sky-high murals of kites and gulls, clouds and sails and other things that fly, the burbling fish tanks, the chipper carpets and dutiful chairs, the flushed or unflushed toilets, apple cores, anything and everything, smash it all down and trip off lightly through the debris, and not come back.

But it's all hopeless, she thinks as she sinks down on one of the butcher block sofas. She'd know this clutter anywhere, these flimsy fragments shored against the ruins, and she of all people should know what it's for. Behind the wall hangings and murals are concrete walls as blank and pitiless as stone; under the carpet littered with coats and toys and games and babies' pacifiers the surface is thin, dark, and translucent, and beneath it is the cold chalk face of death.

She sits there on the butcher block sofa, trying to pull herself together, and suddenly she is visited with the sharp physical longing to go back, go back before any of this, before even the possibility of this, to when her own children were small enough to hold all at once, their little starfish hands clutching at her, back to the time when life seemed so simple and so safe. *Go back, go back*, the voice says, and for a moment she doesn't know who she's supposed to be, wife, mother, daughter, so oddly does the past lie not just on the present and the future, but on the more distant past as well, so that in this moment she seems to be staring forever beyond the rims of many mirrors reflecting one another back and forth, transfixed by these long corridors full of time, and she sees her father, new suitcase in hand, slinging his jacket over his shoulder, kissing her goodbye, and disappearing down the tunnel full of mirrors. *Come back*, she calls after him, but it is too late, and he is gone.

She looks up. Someone is coming toward her down the hall, holding his jacket. *Why, he's here*, she thinks, momentarily confused. He's back. She stands up and starts forward to meet him, but as he comes closer she sees Phil's face, grim, preoccupied. Oh, no, she thinks. It's bad. Then he catches sight of her and smiles. Ah, she thinks, it's good. But as he walks up to her he shakes his head.

"They haven't read it yet. Nevins called twice. We're supposed to call him back after six. And not only that," he says, fluttering a piece of paper under her nose, "I've got to have a chest X-ray. 'Well now,' " he mimics Nevins' soft, nasal voice, " 'there is that spot on your rib we'd like to keep track of.' What did I tell you? I'm a goddamned research project." He tosses her his jacket. "I'll be right back," he says over his shoulder as he disappears down the spiral concrete stairs to X-ray.

How can he do this? Sara wonders as she leans wearily against the balcony of the stairwell. How can anybody? Just then she hears behind her the rapid thump of feet, the high-pitched gurgling sound. Oh no, she thinks, not again. She turns and sees the small bald child running toward her. His short legs churn, his hands reach forward, grasping at the air as if it would support him if he fell. Sara takes a step forward to catch him but he goes right by her, still gurgling, and abruptly Sara realizes he is laughing. His face is merry, his mouth stretched into a wide gummy grin in which two short rows of small, hard teeth glisten whitely. He rushes past her and throws his arms around the security guard's knees, tilts his head back and hugs her.

"Bye, Larry," the guard says cheerfully. "You're a good boy. See you next week."

Larry nods. "Week," he repeats, then looks around for his mother.

She has come up behind him, and now she quickly bundles him into his coat, shrugs hers on, and takes his hand. "Thanks," she says to the guard with a weary smile. "See you next week."

Sara watches them as they spin around through the revolving doors and out onto the sidewalk. A light snow is beginning to sift down, dusting the street like cornmeal. Then she turns back and leans once more against the concrete stairwell, elbows resting on Phil's coat. It has been a long day. It's getting late; most of the patients and their families have picked up their belongings and gone. But she's still here and Phil is just downstairs; he'll be back any minute, a chest X-ray is nothing, a minor inconvenience. It is so quiet now she can hear the hum of the air circulators, the faint clank of the elevators moving up and down. She feels the day collapse around her like an enormous multicolored parachute, settling gently over her in silken muffling folds, and lulled by the calm banality of bulletin boards, of time accounts and group rates and Barbados in the spring, of comic books and textbooks and all the assorted random trash of daily life, almost imperceptibly she feels her fear subside, soften once again into a familiar well-worn garment, pockets full of wadded string and paper clips, grit and rubber bands, loose change and sticky messages scrawled by the children, crumpled Kleenex and loose pen tops. It's almost over. We can do this, she thinks as she catches sight of Phil at the bottom of the stairs. It's not so bad. Perfect is the enemy of good, she thinks as she watches him come stomping up the stairs from X-ray. See you next week, next year, up and over, almost done.

It's not so bad, she thinks, handing him his coat, as long as you keep on moving.

"Come on, let's get out of here," Phil says as he grabs her arm and heads toward the elevator. "We can call from home."

Sara watches from the kitchen doorway while Phil punches out the number of the Clinic. "Dr. Nevins, please." The pause stretches thin and taut along the wire.

"Hello, Dr. Nevins, Phil. Right." He listens, face expressionless, nods, then shakes his head while the phone chirps like a cricket in his ear. He frowns, looks mildly perplexed. She shuts her eyes, doesn't open them again until she hears the sound of the phone being hung up.

Phil stands up, throws his arms out, begins to stretch. She watches the two long scars pull taut under his shirt.

" 'The chest X-ray was fine, and your CAT scan looks just great,' " he repeats verbatim, his voice squeezed oddly thin and breathless by his stretch. " 'See you in six months if nothing else comes up.' " Then he relaxes forward, regards her impassively, and shrugs. "That's it. It's over."

Sara walks across the room, puts her arms around him, rests her head against his chest, hears the gentle rocking of his heart, the slow smooth sift of breathing, feels the warm resilience of his skin beneath his clothes. But as she stands there with her arms around him, her face pressed hard against his chest, she feels the scars as thick as ropes between them, and as clearly as if it were this moment remembers the night five years ago this coming spring, just before the first operation, after his doctor had let him out on patient's furlough so he could spend the whole day with her and the kids, a day in April, a sunny day, a windy day, a day for flying kites, coming back late to his hospital room as though it were a hotel, just the two of them, remembers standing in the doorway watching him unbutton his shirt and slowly pull it off, hold it out at arm's length, then turn to face her, saying, "Take a good look at me now, because I'm never going to be the same."

She remembers moving toward him, slipping her arms around

him, hears her own voice saying calmly, spinning the bright disc of her innocence against the fear: "So who is? Just get through tomorrow and it will all be over," sees his face as he looks down at her, eyes fixed and intent as a runner's, and says: "Or just beginning," knows now, years later, even in this other place, that it will never be over, safety is an illusion, and it will always be too soon.

5

The Yellow Brick Road

She hears the sound of heavy bombers in the distance, a steady roar, faint at first, the horizon black with them, rising in a wave, a ceiling dense with sound, coming closer, no end to them, the noise rising to a crescendo until they are directly overhead, the noise intolerable, and she tenses herself, waiting for the ceiling to split and the bombs to drop through . . .

But no, they are passing over, the roar diminishing to a growl, then a whisper: ah, we're safe, she thinks. But then she hears another huge tidal wave of sound rising, rushing heavily toward her. *I must get away*! she thinks in panic, and she tries to run, but she can't move. There is no safety.

Sara wakes with a start of terror. It takes her a moment to realize that the roar she hears outside is not the sound of heavy bombers passing overhead; it's wind. Not that it makes much difference; she hates the sound of wind, especially this kind, wild, unruly, unpredictable, tossing the tops of trees, blowing the leaves straight out like flags, increasing in velocity with each succeeding gust. She puts the pillow over her head and tries to go back to sleep.

But it's no use. She sighs, sensing the space next to her empty. Time to get up. She can't put it off any longer. She'll never get back to sleep anyway; the wind noise is driving her crazy. She throws the covers back and gets out of bed. She peers out the window at her enemy the wind, lashing the tops of the big maples that line the long driveway, tossing the leaves inside out so their pale undersides are exposed and the foliage looks frothy white. There are several branches on the ground. Even the grass is blown flat. Sara turns away from the window.

Phil has tuned the radio to the weather station. The forecaster's noncommittal voice drones a litany of bad news, at least for her: "Wind from the south, ten to twenty knots gusting to thirty by mid-afternoon, seas one to three feet and building . . ." Fear gathers below her rib cage and sinks like lead into her gut. She twists the dial to another station. "Eee-yah-yah, ah-hahahaHa!" Elton John wails. "When are you gonna come down? When are you going to land? I should have stayed on the farm . . ." Sara flicks the radio off. Why did I say I'd go? she asks herself. A feeling of foreboding settles behind her eyes.

"Hi, you're up," Phil says as he comes in from the garage, his cheeks ruddy, his hair blown back from his forehead. "Isn't this great?"

It's the beginning of another sailing season, their fourth since they bought the *Loon*, and she has promised to help him move the boat from the marina to its mooring at Indian Cove. It's also the earliest they've ever put the boat in, Memorial Day weekend, a goal Phil has been working toward assiduously in an attempt to extend the season as much as possible. Because Phil wants to stay over and sail tomorrow and she wants to get back for the kids, they are driving to the coast in separate vehicles, Phil in the old red pickup, Sara in the station wagon. This is yet another variation on what Sara privately calls the Dance of the Cars, the Automotive Gavotte. Much of their life is now spent driving in opposite directions transporting either themselves or the children to work, high school, lessons, doctor or dentist, a friend's house, the grocery store, the library, the inevitable result of living in a house in the country. Often they will pass on the road coming or going and wave to each other, sometimes even stop to change cars or children, or simply to say hello.

Today at least they are going in the same direction. Following behind Phil on the way to the coast, Sara gets that odd feeling she has had before on trips they have taken together but in separate cars for one reason or another—too much luggage, different schedules, both cars a necessity where they were going—the sensation that they are connected by an invisible cord that lengthens and shortens with the distance between them, linked by the knowledge that even though they aren't traveling together their destination is the same.

So now she speeds up and slows down, keeping him in sight, trying to keep the distance even, the line taut. She does not like to let him out of her sight on these trips, afraid there will be an accident, she will come around a bend and find the truck belly-up, rolled over and smoking in the ditch, Phil bashed and bloody, dead, and nothing she can do. This is her responsibility, she still feels obscurely, to keep him safe by her worry and her watchfulness, her force of will. There is always this sense of connection, this cord between them, like an umbilical, the same feeling she gets when he's away, only then she sees the connection as the telephone line linking them over the distance: his call and her expectation of it, the voice coming over the wire, like the familiar car pulling into the driveway, both indications that whatever else has happened, that person—Phil or anyone else loved and worried about and waited for—is safe. Her mother must have felt something like this too; she remembers the look on her face when the call came and it was not his voice but the impersonal, unfamiliar caller in the night: "Mrs. Gilead, I'm afraid I have bad news . . ." She remembers too her mother telling Cousin Ralph, who had gone to bring her father's car back from Canada, to park it in a neighbor's driveway down the street so her little brother and sister wouldn't run out, thinking that it was all a mistake, that Daddy had come home after all.

She speeds up until she's close behind. Through his rear windshield she can just make out the margin of shoulders above the seat back, his neck and head upright and unmoving, fixed on the road ahead. She doesn't wonder what he's thinking about; she already knows. Sailing.

She glances aside at the passing landscape for signs the wind may be abating. Flags on flagpoles blow straight out as though starched and ironed, flat as cardboard. Trees toss and churn, and so does her stomach. There must be a God, she thinks grimly, because he's punishing me. She glares out the window and wills the wind to die before they get there. Then they can either motor up to Indian Cove, or just check to see the boat's all right, not flooded from some problem with the seacocks the way Phil found it one day, water practically up to the bunks, the inlet to the marine head left open by mistake, so he still has fits about the boat sinking when he's not there. He's even made her promise she'll drive over when he goes away on the fourth annual bluewater cruise with Gus next month. She doesn't really mind; she likes to drive, and at least when he's away she knows she won't have to force herself to go sailing.

A gust blows across the road so hard it makes the car swerve. She fixes her eyes on the road ahead, and tries to think of something else. But it's no use; the sense of foreboding increases the closer they get to their destination. She has the feeling something bad is going to happen. But then, she always does when they go sailing. It has become the focus for her free-floating anxiety. Phil doesn't see why she gets so upset, and neither does she, for that matter; they've been knocked down just that once three years ago, the first summer they had the boat, and that was only twenty yards from the mooring. But the fact is, she has never made the transition from sailing on a lake where you could tip over or fall in and still swim to shore, to being on the ocean, where survival time after immersion is twenty minutes or less and land always seems so far away.

But a promise is a promise and here they are again, driving down the winding rutted road to the marina this blustery day at the end of May, the earliest launch yet. Maybe Phil wants to get a head start on the season, but Sara would just as soon wait. It's about midtide, and the river looks calm at least. Maybe it won't be so bad. The wind no longer sounds like many invisible runaway freight trains lumbering overhead on unseen tracks across the sky, and here the trees do not lurch and toss. It could be worse. Twelve hours from now, maybe even sooner, she will be back home safe in her own bed.

"Well, that was really something," he says after they've driven home in silence, neither one wanting to say anything more about the knockdown. The sails, sopping wet from being dragged through the water, are spread out all over the living room. "I guess I wasn't too far off when I introduced you to Jane and Mack as Galahad. Sara to the rescue once again."

She might take this as a compliment, but she can tell from the edge of bitterness in his voice that flattery is not what's on his mind. Trying to sound casual, avoid a fight, she says, "Don't worry about it, these things happen. Just don't ask me to go sailing again for a while."

"That's it, isn't it?" he snaps. "You just don't want to do anything with me anymore. My getting sick has changed everything. It's not just the scars, or me. I was right when I said nothing would ever be the same. It isn't and it never will be. I know that. But give me a break, will you? Just stop trying to rescue me all the time."

She stares at him, speechless, too exhausted at the moment to try to argue him out of it, convince him that he's misunderstood. How can she tell him about the dreams, the nightmares of tossing waves, wind and sea out of control, the boat a roller coaster dipsy-doodle rocking her in and out of consciousness. She puts the lump of clay she's been working on aside, goes upstairs to bed. Even though he follows her later, and they make love in the dark it doesn't help, as he rolls her over abruptly, crushing her face into the pillow and coming in from behind so hard that she wakes up feeling bruised and sore.

The next morning they have a terrible argument. They hardly speak for days. It seems as though everything is falling apart, irreparable. She feels so exhausted and depressed that next time Phil approaches her to go sailing all she can say is, "I don't even want to talk about it. I just can't make myself do it anymore. I feel all used up, as though there's nothing left. I'm sorry." She tries to find friends who will go sailing with him; it's all she can do to bring herself to go even once in a while. She can tell he's trying not to be so insistent, but this makes her feel worse. She knows she's depriving him of something he really needs.

Then in August his old friend Gus turns up unexpectedly with a bunch of sailing buddies and invites Phil on a big bluewater cruise. Though he was the one who complained about feeling smothered, confined, pressed down, in his absence she feels a sudden sense of release, as though *she's* been let out of jail. She is on vacation. With this welcome respite comes the less-welcome realization that she is being constantly ground down by the conflict between Phil's needs, the children's, and her own. While he's away she finds she is no longer bothered by the wind noise; she knows that, whatever else, she won't have to make herself go sailing.

Putting the finishing touches on a piece called *Mirror Image*—the torso of a girl on a mirrored pedestal, framed on either side with mirrors so that if someone stands directly in front of the statue it looks as though she has arms and legs, but from a different angle she doesn't, an idea she got from a memory of going to the sideshow with her father—she wonders how long she can keep this up, trying to be all things to all of them. My strength is as the strength of three and a half, down from ten, she thinks as she shapes a big lump of clay into the rough semblance of a person's head and torso. Though she often dreams of running away—thumbing a ride from the end of the driveway, off with the raggle-taggle gypsies—she knows she never will.

But somehow, whether it's simply Gus's expert tutelage, or something more ineffable about sailing on blue water, Phil comes back from the week-long cruise transformed, no longer so dependent on her, more confident, almost his old self. She can tell as soon as he walks in the door with a dazed, almost beatified expression on his face. That night, she takes the first step toward reconciliation, knows from Phil's surprised intake of breath, his swift turning toward her, that he has been waiting for her all these weeks, and that everything is going to be all right again between them after all.

Sailing

There is still the problem of sailing, the bone of contention, his obsession versus her fear. Finally she convinces him it is fear of sailing, not of intimacy that holds her back—not lack of feeling for him or uneasiness about his competence, but the stress of the constant pressure to go, her own anxiety about being out on the ocean coupled with conflicts about everything else she has to do, so little time, the kids still too young to stay at home alone for extended periods, the housework, her own work constantly having to be put aside.

So they agree she will go sometimes, when the weather is nice and the sea calm, which turns out to be practically never. Phil promises not to be so compulsive about sailing whenever he can for as long as he can in all conditions. "I won't make you go if you don't want to, or if you're afraid," he says, and it is a promise he keeps, turning back even when she can see he is yearning to go on, to test his strength and prowess against the continually transmuting, demanding conditions of the sea. But she feels guilty, as though she is getting in his way, stealing something from him that he needs, that sailing is somehow connected with his sense of overcoming his illness, the loss of control regained by pitting his wit and strength across the wind, the sea, the balance of conflicting forces. So she often goes with him when she would rather not and is still afraid. But they seem to be emerging from under the shadow of his illness, life once more sustainable on a daily basis.

Sara dips her hand in the icy water. The noisy outboard is churning away as they head down the river toward the entrance to the bay, the channel marked by rough pilings sticking up like fingers crossed for luck. Further on the red nuns bob on one side, black cans on the other; she wonders why the nuns aren't black; whoever heard of a nun dressed in red? They look more like Little Red Riding Hoods ranged in a row, nodding to one another. She pulls out a piece of paper, begins to sketch the pilings, the image of the half-rotted timbers poking out of the eddying water, the cormorants perched on top, stretching their wings to dry. Absently she draws in a loon, even though she knows they come to the coast only in the fall and winter. The pilings remind her of telephone poles, and

S u s a n   K e n n e y

she finds herself thinking again about phone calls, about how odd
it is that a voice stretched thin over the wires across the miles—
just the sound of a different voice, of words, invisible—can carry
a message that changes everything. Even now when the phone
rings at odd hours she feels a shock, an involuntary clench of
readiness, girding for disaster.

She thinks of the portrait bust of her father she has been trying
to do for some time, and still can't seem to get right. It seems to
be mostly a problem with the hands, small fine hands she remembers quite distinctly from watching him while he did his wood-
working projects in his basement workshop in Ohio—the little
chair and table he made for her marionettes out of a couple of
cigar boxes for instance—hands she remembers also loosely folded
on his chest, pale and oddly puckered like withered rosebuds the
last time she saw him, in the funeral parlor when she was twelve,
so many years ago. Though his likeness continues to elude her,
she refuses to give up. She will keep coming back to it over and
over, until she gets it right. Meanwhile the figure sits shrouded in
the workshop Phil made for her out of a corner of the garage,
along with the other figures she is working on.

They are almost out of the river channel now, chugging between
two islands. She wishes they could just chug right close to shore
and onto the mooring at Indian Cove and get it over with, but
she knows the water is too shallow, and anyway, Phil has come
to sail. She glances over her shoulder at the water; there's not
much chop to speak of, and the sky is still crystal clear. It will be
all right, she tells herself. Everything is under control. Still, she
cannot get over this feeling that something terrible is going to
happen.

They come out of the channel into the inner bay, and Sara sees
to her relief that the wind is still light, the sea barely rumpled,
slopping gently against the hull. So much for predictions. Phil looks
disappointed, muttering under his breath as he stows the various
bits of gear in the cockpit lockers.

"We could motor up," she says hopefully, but Phil shakes his
head.

"There's always more wind farther out in the bay," he says.

"Anyway, we've got all day, right?" He shoves the tiller at her while he goes forward to raise the sails, a huge main and jib in a masthead rig, towering over them against a sky at the moment cloudless and intensely blue. Instead of the working jib he runs up the big genoa, which Sara really doesn't like, the way it blocks the view all the way down to the deck and lays the boat right over even in light air; she still remembers the sickening feeling that first summer, that time the boat heeled so sharply, then kept right on going over until the sails hit the water. But Phil claims it makes the boat point better. Oh well, if the wind starts to come up, they can always take it down. After all, she's done that before, and not in the best of conditions.

First one sail rustles up, then the next, as Phil grunts and grinds the winch handle, the muscles of his arms and chest bulging in his short-sleeved shirt. Before his operations he used to go bare-chested whenever possible, acquiring an impressive tan each summer, but not anymore, ostensibly because the sun will make his scars even more fibrous, but actually, Sara believes, because he's self-conscious. The scars invite horrified stares and painful explanations, so he stays covered up, and at the end of the summer wears a pale union suit etched on his naked torso, a shadow in reverse, in contrast to the deep tan of his neck and lower arms and legs.

"Lay off!" he shouts from the bow, and she pulls the tiller back toward her knee, hoping this is the right direction, watches the sails billow and fill momentarily, then fall slack. As she brings it a little closer to her, the sails stretch taut with a thump and the boat starts to move, gathering momentum, begins to glide in its stately fashion through the puckered sea. She rubs her eyes with her free hand (the other is white-knuckling the tiller) and continues to watch him as he pads along the deck coiling up loose tackle, making everything shipshape.

He looks so strong and healthy now. Of course he always has, comparatively speaking, that's the amazing thing, so that sometimes she thinks there is some perverse god who, seeing him look well in spite of everything, takes it as hubris and decides to hit him with something else. Anyway, it's a good thing, because there are practically no amenities on this old crock of a boat to make the going easier, a couple of winches for the jib sheets, block and tackle for the main and that's it, no traveler, no boom vang to keep the main from jibing unexpectedly, even the bilge pump takes two hands, not to mention starting the engine. Sometimes it's all even Phil can do to hold a course when they're laid right over, the pressure on the steering is so great. She understands now why it was always the young men who raised the sails and held the tiller steady against the sharply angled heel back home on the lake where she grew up, leaving the deck work and jib tending to the likes of her; it is not so much a matter of skill as of brute strength.

One of the things that worries her is that she doesn't think she's strong enough to sail this boat herself. She's already getting nervous with the tiller nudging her hand like an impatient puppy anxious to be let off the leash. She wishes Phil would hurry up and take it from her. She's sure the wind is coming up; having chased them all the way from home, over the hills and far away, it's just about to catch up now and blow their hair off.

Phil hops back along the deck, stopping to grind the winch that holds the jib sheet, and plops down beside her, grinning. She pushes the tiller into his hand and picks up the end of the jib sheet. "Sure you don't want to take the helm?" he asks. She shakes her head and hauls the jib sheet tight across the cockpit, hanging on for dear life. "You don't have to hold it, you know," Phil says. "Just tie it off. There's nothing going on out here."

That's your version, she thinks. Something always happens.

He glances at her, then reaches over and pats her leg with his warm, rough hand. "Don't worry, you're safe with me."

Sure enough, as they coast farther out into the bay the wind starts to blow, but gently, so though they are moving, they hardly heel at all. They are on a beam reach now, which, Phil has informed her, is the fastest point of sail. Or is it a broad reach? Phil knows more about sailing now than she ever did, could ever hope to. The more he learns about terms and technique, the relation between boat and wind and sail, the more she seems to get mixed up, not just between coming about and its opposite, jibing, but broad and beam reach, laying off and heading up, tack and beat. He gets impatient with her vagueness, no doubt interpreting it as lack of interest, even resistance, but she can't help it. As far as she's concerned they are only words. On these day-long sails, her mind wanders; she can't seem to pay attention the way Phil does, so intent on the business of sailing. Not only that, she's haunted by the fear the wind will blow up and knock them down, the rigging will break, there will be a thunderstorm and they will be struck by lightning, a rogue wave will swamp the boat, they will be run down by one of the huge tankers that come steaming through on their way up the bay.

She knows this is silly, that Phil is perfectly capable of sailing the boat in any emergency, that nothing is going to happen, but still she feels uneasy, vulnerable out here in this little boat surrounded by water too cold to survive in. It's not unlike the fear she feels in airplanes, which the psychologist she started seeing when Phil was so sick attributed at first to claustrophobia. "Maybe you don't like being trapped in an small enclosed space surrounded by people," she had suggested. "Maybe I don't like being trapped in a small enclosed space surrounded by air," Sara had replied.

She and the psychologist had finally come to the conclusion that her chronic anxiety was a form of shell shock, the result of so many traumatic experiences in her formative years, so many ups and downs continuing into adulthood. Right, Sara remembers thinking, I have been upped and downed by experts. That's how you get to be a manic-depressive: practice. She doesn't actually believe that, understanding now after all these years of dealing with her mother's illness that it is in fact caused not by sheer perversity but a chemical imbalance, some defect in the basic physical workings of the mind triggered by a series of extraordinarily distressing events, blow after blow falling on the already flawed mechanism.

In the years since her own children were born, the six years of Phil's illness, she has come to sympathize with her mother's predicament, her father's sudden, early death, hardly any money and what there was tied up by the lack of a will, unreliable relatives who first refused to help, and then proceeded to die themselves one after another within three years, shock following shock, until her mother was left alone with three children in the big but shabby run-down family house on the elegant street of the small upstate New York village where she'd been born. No wonder she tried to run away, both physically and mentally, over and over again. And she too never quite came back, at least not the way she was before Sara's father died.

Now the children are gone, all grown, and she is alone in the house with her knitting and her books, and there is peace (relatively speaking) at last. They've all survived; Fran's about to graduate from medical school, Vic's happily married with a couple of kids and a house in the suburbs. Sara doesn't really worry any more about taking after her mother, feeling that if she were going to go crazy, she would have done it by now, and with good reason. But no; she sees in their lives only this likeness, that they are both the somebody else to whom the bad things always happen. And of course there is this one difference; unlike her father, Phil did not die after all. He came back.

Sara looks at him now, thinking how glad she is he's here. The sun on his face, the wind in his hair, smiling happily, intent and absorbed in what he's doing. The sailing has been good for him, no doubt about it, and that is worth everything, including this small cold lump lying just below her ribs that will not melt even in the warm sun and mild air, the apparent reliability, at least for the moment, of the wind.

She wedges herself in the corner of the cockpit next to the companionway with her back against the cabin, and stretches her legs out along the seat. This is her favorite place to sit, out of the wind, facing the stern, so she can see where they've been, not where they're going or what's coming up; she'd rather not know. They haven't come far, really; the shore is no more than a stone's throw away, and there are islands dotting the inner bay on every side. The seagulls wheel and screech overhead, diving toward the water and then skimming back toward land.

Phil was right; today it all seems perfectly safe. As the boat slides easily through the water with a reassuringly steady hiss, the mast barely leaning, she looks at him. The sun is directly behind him now; everything is bathed in golden light and the waves are tipped with molten bronze. She sees him silhouetted, surrounded by a faint aureole, and is reminded of the first time she saw him naked, or almost. He'd come to her apartment to take a shower because the water was off in the rooming house where he lived. Not realizing he was finished, she had wandered into the bedroom for something and there he was, standing in the doorway with the fluorescent light behind him, steam pouring out all around. He had filled the whole opening, it seemed, and she could see the whole long shape of his body as he stood there gazing at her, casually drying himself with a towel held up in front, the muscles of his arms made even heavier by a summer of construction work, the wide arc of one shoulder curving out, the broad chest tapering to his waist, the line of his deep tan clearly visibly across the narrow hip and flat belly.

Her mouth had gone dry, her tongue cleaving to the roof, she had stood there speechless, gulping, riveted, staring at him, while he simply looked at her, unembarrassed, smiling faintly. Finally she'd babbled "Oh, excuse me," and fled back into the kitchen, but it was too late; after that it was just a matter of time. Though she resisted the idea, not wanting to get involved, afraid of committing herself, she couldn't get the sight of him out of her mind, and then the arm flung casually around her shoulders, drawing her to his side in the library, as they came out of the graduate student lounge together, walking next to him, pulled close, so that she could feel that whole long, hard length of his body, chest and hip and thigh . . .

. . . she can't get the sight or the feel of him out of her mind. She follows him everywhere, sits next to him in classes, at the study tables in the library, at lunch. Whenever he looks up she's there, just minding her own business, of course. They are friends; they talk to one another on study breaks, take long walks through the linked quads of the campus, kicking through the leaves like children. When winter comes, to avoid their intrusively curious friends who think all this is so romantic, they take to meeting in seldom-frequented stacks, standing together between the narrow aisles of dusty books. Though she is not ready for this, her mother's most recent breakdown still occupying her attention, her own nameless fears nagging at her, she can't seem to help herself, knows it is just a matter of time.

He has a gift for mordant observation, the quick and witty remark, an ironic, almost cynical view of life that fascinates her. Nothing that smacks of absurdity or affectation gets by him. He teases her unmercifully, but she tries to give as good as she gets. She has brought her bike to school, even though the University is steeply uphill from where she lives, and the thing is practically useless. "That's the silliest thing I ever heard of," he tells her. "You walk that thing around like a pet dog," he says.

"Yeah, but it's great going home, downhill all the way," she replies. "Anyway, look who's talking. You look like a polar bear stuck in a kayak in that little sports car of yours."

Gazing at her, he replies absolutely deadpan, "My father picked it out. Personally, I wanted an old Chevy. Sports cars are insincere."

She stares at him in disbelief. "That's *my* line!"

He grabs her, pulls her to him, holds her, and they laugh and laugh. He makes her feel funny and smart and cute, and he laughs at all her jokes. For the first time in many years she can imagine living happily ever after. But her mother's statement, made time and time again, continues to haunt her. "There are no truly happy marriages; one of you always dies and leaves the other one."

After the first kiss in the stacks, sudden, unexpected, yet welcome, she accepts what she has known from her first sight of him yet resisted for reasons more or less obscure to her, that he is everything she ever wanted, forget the others, always with this one quality or that but always too short, too skinny, too blonde, too overbearing, too timid, too dull. There he was that day, grinning his odd spade-shaped smile at her from across the seminar table, that ironic, knowing look in the big brown eyes under the heavy Byzantine eyebrows, tall, dark, handsome, funny, smart; he is the one, and though she doesn't want to get married for a long time, wants to get on with her life, her career, be on her own for a while after all these difficult years of dealing with her father's death, her mother's illness, he is big and strong and sturdy, with such an aura of steadiness, of integrity, that she knows she will be safe with him.

But first she has to put her life in order, get her mother squared away (the doctors at Seneca are talking about discharging her, but she will have to live with someone responsible for a probationary period), her sister and brother taken care of; her brother Vic hates boarding school and wants to come home, but there is no home to come to, her sister Fran loves her school and never wants to leave, even for vacations, and why would she, considering her past experience. The burden of sorting everything out falls, as always, on Sara. But he is patient, he can wait.

After her mother is released from the mental hospital, Sara moves her back into the family house with Vic and a housekeeper, and commutes back and forth from school on weekends to make sure everything is all right. It is. Her mother is fine, a little subdued, but she gets along with the housekeeper, and things seem to be working out just fine. Sara can't believe it. All of a sudden she can't seem to get her own head straight. Now that she is more or less free of family responsibilities, she can't make up her mind what to do with her own life. Having lived with uncertainty so long, trying to protect herself against all contingencies, constantly temporizing, when it comes to making a real decision, she finds herself panicking, unable to act. It's all been too much, and now that things finally look better, she feels herself going under, paddling as hard as she can just to keep her head above water. She's more confused than ever.

Phil senses what is going on, though he misunderstands the reasons, taking her desperate emotional water-treading for equivocation, and suddenly stops seeing her, even speaking to her. School is almost over; not really understanding what has happened, finally she seeks him out, chases him down in the library just before she has to leave. She traps him next to the circulation desk. "I just wanted to part friends . . ." she begins.

"I love you," he interrupts with a look of hopeless vulnerability that nearly breaks her heart, "I can't go on with this any longer." They talk for a while, but resolve nothing.

She goes back home—he even drives her—feeling sad and hopeless. He doesn't believe she loves him, will never believe it. Wanting just a little more time, not knowing how much, she has tried his patience too long and lost him. Sara, she says to herself, he was perfect, and you blew it.

She misses him terribly. After a week or so in the house with her mother and brother and Bertha the housekeeper—Fran has refused to come home from boarding school—she goes to stay at their big old run-down summer house on the lake at Carpenter's Point, to try to sort things out. She thinks that with her family history—either you drop dead or go crazy—it's just as well she's not going to get married and have children. She resigns herself to spending the rest of her life alone. She settles down and tries to draw and paint, reads biographies and diaries of famous artists. It seems that sooner or later most of them also drop dead or go nuts, and she wonders if she is doing the right thing.

Then one bright afternoon she hears the crunch and scrape on gravel of a low-slung sports car bottoming out at the curve, looks up and there he is. "I couldn't do it," he says from the seat of his tiny sports car, the dust still swirling around him, his hair blown back, the ratty leather bomber jacket unzipped. "I couldn't stay away."

She takes one look at him, his smiling face turned toward her, shirt open at the collar, big strong hands gripping the steering wheel, and that's that. They walk through the house, slowly, room by room, as she points out this or that item of interest, knowing the moment is inevitable, until suddenly, in the last room, upstairs in the back, her room, here he is in the golden light, and she turns to him, and the rest is a blur of arms and legs and slippery skin, the gleam of the sun striking off brass bed knobs, everything happening so fast, a roller coaster so steep all she can do is hold on for dear life while her body arches and throbs with a will of its own, zooms up and plummets down over and over, until she just can't stand it any longer and lets go.

Afterward, in the late afternoon, the two of them go out on the lake in the beat-up aluminum canoe, floating around the edge of the point where the inlet stream feeds in, fishing. There is nothing in the house for dinner, neither of them has much money, and they don't want to go anywhere anyway, not now, so they've decided to try their luck with the fishing poles the kids left behind last summer.

The air is still, the surface of the lake so flat and the water so clear it is as though they are suspended in air above the pebbly bottom several feet below, the fish darting beneath them unaware, the glassy surface disturbed only by the occasional trout rise, the eddy from Phil's paddle fanning out in tiny whirlpools as he slowly propels the boat closer to where the fish are feeding. They drop their lines in, baited with worms they've just dug up, and one after another the silvery spotted brook trout bite, are caught. They couldn't find a bucket or a net, so they scoop the slippery flailing bodies out of the water with a kitchen colander and drop them into a dishpan in the bottom of the canoe. "I don't believe this," Phil exclaims with a quick amazed look in her direction as he winds his reel. "Is it legal?"

Probably not; neither of them has a license, and for all she knows it may not even be fishing season yet. "Poached fish always taste better," she says. He laughs. They catch six and cook them for dinner on the old wood stove in the kitchen. Then they go back to bed.

Six months later, they are married in the little stone Gothic church by the lake.

When she looks around, the sea, no longer roughened by the wind, looks for the moment as slick and shiny as a pool of oil. She has an odd sense of déjà vu; the first time they sailed the *Loon*, over four years ago, it was like this.

Phil sits back, fingers just barely touching the tiller, looking mildly aggrieved. "Not much wind. Hmm. We could start the motor, but . . ." he ruminates, "let's not, at least not yet. Let's just see how she ghosts."

. . . *see how she ghosts*, Sara murmurs to herself, settling back, closing her eyes and letting the sun warm her face. See how she ghosts, she mumbles sleepily, not sure whether she is talking to Phil or someone else in the lonely space between dream and recollection. Another vision of flat water, of sails seen not up close and towering over, but from far away, mere pennants against water improbably blue, the boats so small, herself small, watching, long before she learned to sail herself, long before her father's death, before even the possibility of death.

They are back at her grandmother's for the annual summer visit. She and her mother are standing on the golf course overlooking the lake, watching the Sunday regatta at the country club. Whenever they come back to visit her grandmother, her father crews in a race with Jack Myers, and old friend and builder of the first Lightning. Lightning Number One has been sold, but Jack still has his Rebel class sloop, a savage pirate of a boat with a sharp black hull and brightly colored rebel flag for ensign emblazoned across the main. Her father walks by, rattling the silver martini shaker with the tiny screw-on top linked by a chain, flourishing two narrow, thin-stemmed glasses between the fingers of his other hand, a cigarette dangling from his lips, as handsome as a movie star. He cocks an eyebrow at them and winks. "This is a no-class race," he says jauntily to Sara's mother, standing there in her white dress and shoes, with her black hair and angular, sharply shadowed face, holding Sara's hand, "but that doesn't mean we can't go first class."

"Oh, Jimmie, be careful," her mother says. "Don't lose it," which Sara takes to mean the race. How silly, she thinks, Daddy will never lose.

And off they go, the men in their white golf shirts and knickers, while the families sit in white wooden chairs like picket fences on the green lawn above the water, the ladies in white embroidered tennis or golf dresses, the children in swimsuits, sand grating in the creases of knees and crotches, the sting of water drying on sunburn, the heat of the sun, the clink of ice in glasses. And far away, the white sails gather like teepees in the sun.

There is enough wind to get the boats—all kinds of boats, all sizes, designs, a one-of-a-kind race, Lightnings, Comets, Bantams,

Stars—around the first two buoys, tantalizing, taunting, giving the nod first to this one, then that, a fickle wind, a flirting wind. Then just as they all round the last buoy to run for home, the wind dies, the blue water turns so dark green it looks almost black, and the boats coast to a halt, motionless in a pool of tar.

"Dead in the water," someone says behind them. Sara looks anxiously out over the water at her father, so small, sitting on the deck of the Rebel. Dead in the water? But they are still laughing and talking, and as she shields her eyes from the bright sun, she sees her father wave to her. Something flashes, gleams for a moment like a mirror. Even so far away, so small, he can still see it's me, she thinks. The boat is still moving, leaving a V-shaped rumple in the water behind.

"The Rebel will win," her mother says. "It ghosts well." And Sara stares, bemused, watching for ghosts to rise up out of the water, push the boat with Jack and her father in it, send them home.

The Rebel indeed ghosts well, although Sara never discerns any. It comes in first, passing over the invisible finish line, its prow as slick as a razor, Jack and her father standing in the stern, urging the boat forward with their bodies. The gun cracks, an instant later the puff of smoke floats up from the committee boat. Her father waves his hands excitedly, jumping all over the cockpit. The boat rocks wildly, and as Sara watches, her father loses his balance, sits down abruptly on the deck, then leaps up again with a wild war whoop of victory. She is glad he is so happy. Not until he limps gingerly up the ramp onto the lawn, red-faced and grimacing, a towel wrapped around his waist, do they realize that in his excitement over the imminent victory (he had never won a race before) he had absentmindedly stuck the two empty martini glasses in his baggy hip pockets, and when he sat down suddenly, smashed them to smithereens. The rebel yell had been a howl of pain; her mother spent the rest of the vacation picking glass splinters out of his rear end. Yet almost instantly the incident became a funny story, and even now, as she remembers him, tries to picture his face, there are no lines of pain or worry and he is gay and laughing, always laughing, frozen in time, forever a young man. If only she could reconcile that image with her last sight of him, lying in the funeral parlor with folded withered hands, so solemn and so still.

Watching Phil now, sitting at the far end of the cockpit in almost the same attitude as that day in the canoe, head turned slightly, torso upright, one leg bent, the other straight, tiller in his hand instead of a paddle, she is overcome with the sudden sharp sense of how much she loves him, remembers the sight of him framed in the bathroom door, the feel of his long muscular body relaxing into hers after their lovemaking, remembers how after the punishment of both operations, weak and skinny, wasted by months of illness, he worked to rebuild himself, so that in spite of the scars, the body is as straight and strong as ever. She has always wanted to model his torso, even if she has to do it from memory; she knows he is too shy, too private, too proud to pose for her, especially now. She would make it without the scars, she thinks, the way he was that day, like a Greek statue, standing in the doorway with the towel.

Phil shifts position as though uncomfortable, looks over at her. "I'm not feeling so great," he says matter-of-factly. "Must have been that second sandwich I had for lunch. How old was that tuna?"

Just then the boat heels sharply, swooping over with the big genoa bellying so that she has to brace her feet against the seat opposite. Just as abruptly it lurches back upright. Oh no, Sara thinks. "Where are we?" she asks, suddenly apprehensive.

"Just off Tucker Rock," Phil says. "I thought we'd make a run for Lindiscove." She can't see his face clearly, but she hears him chuckle as she feels the blood drain from her face. "Just kidding," he says. "But the wind's perfect," he adds hopefully. "We could reach all the way."

She shields her eyes and studies the horizon at his back. The sun is midway down the sky, its light sparkling off the waves in a fanlike pattern as though someone had splashed a bucket of gold paint across them. They are still heading east, but on a closer reach now; the wind seems to be coming more from the north than it was earlier, and Phil has had to harden up several times. Although it is hard to judge distances out here, they seem quite far from land, several miles at least from the low-lying sandy tidal shore that lies like outstretched fingers all along the northern part of the bay. Even the seagulls don't seem to come out this far. She wonders how far away they are from where Phil wants to go, this Lindiscove he keeps talking about as though it were some sort of holy place.

They have been reaching across a southerly wind, so they should make good time going back, she is thinking to herself, when from directly behind her she hears a rustling noise, and suddenly her hair blows forward around her face like a sun-bonnet. The sails snap in then out with a sharp crack, and she sees Phil stiffen at the tiller. She looks toward the far-off shore and sees between the boat and land a line of whitecaps moving toward them, the water dark and riled-looking behind. "Phil," she warns. "Look there."

"Okay, okay, I see," he says calmly. "Wind's coming up. I knew it, as soon as it started swinging around to the northeast. We'll start back, but you'd better hold on to your socks. Here, take the helm while I break the gennie down."

As she moves back toward him, heart in her mouth, she sees the muscles of his forearm bunch as his hand tightens into a fist. Another gust of wind hits like a slap, thundering in her ears, and the boat heels sharply, throwing them both off-balance. Just as abruptly it rounds back up. "Don't worry," Phil says, but where his face was ruddy before, it is now pale under his tan, and there are beads of sweat along his temple. She takes the tiller from him and watches him make his way forward toward the mast, staggering against the cabin bulkhead as he climbs up to the mast.

"Keep it headed into the wind!" he shouts at her. As she struggles to bring the bow around into the wind, the boat begins to pitch and heave, slamming straight across the waves, and the sails lose their tension, flapping madly, the noise so loud that although she can hear him yelling something behind the thrashing mainsail, she can't make out what he's saying. She uncleats the mainsheet, holding onto it as she grips the tiller with her other hand, then stands up in the cockpit, dodges her head around the flailing boom, trying to see him. She hears the reassuring zing of the genoa coming down the forestay; at least that's done, and even though she feels as

135

though she's gone deaf from all the noise, now she can see him just behind the mast, kneeling on the foredeck unhanking the sail and stuffing it down the forward hatch. Maybe he wants her to get the working jib? But who will mind the tiller? Frankly, she'd much rather do the deckwork than be responsible for the helm, especially in this wind. "Phil!" she yells as loudly as she can. "Phil!" She sees his head go up; he's heard her. He stands up quickly, a fold of sail draped over one shoulder, and turns toward her with a quizzical look, a look so familiar her heart nearly stops, an ashen look she has seen before . . .

. . . and her father throws his coat over his shoulder, goes out the door, down the steps, turns to wave goodbye once more. But his face is ashen, and his skin is slicked with sweat; it is the face of a dead man . . .

She stares in horror, reaching toward him as he sways, then staggers, his face like chalk, drops to one knee in front of the mast, reaching for the handrail, and falls forward on his face.

Sara lets go of everything and rushes forward. Phil is sprawled limply across the top of the cabin. He's dead, she thinks, just like that, it's happened, Oh, God, I should have known, I could have stopped him, it's too soon, too soon . . .

She sees his hand contract around the handrail, his shoulders tense slightly as he tries to raise his head. A miracle. He's still alive, even conscious, trying to get up. She crouches next to him as the boom flies over, then back, the boat pitches and wallows, washing around broadside to the waves. But she doesn't care, he's still alive after all. She puts her hands on his shoulders, trying to turn him over, manages to get his head up just enough so that he can turn and look at her. His mouth is slack, and his eyes, looking roughly in her direction, are jittering back and forth as though he were watching a tennis match in fast-forward. His eyeballs dance across, then back, unfocused. He takes a deep breath, then blinks.

"Phew, I'm dizzy," he says in an almost normal voice. "Who's sailing the boat?" His lifts his head, starts to get up, his eyeballs jitter and he slumps back down.

She feels for his pulse; his heartbeat is fast but strong and regular. Not a heart attack then, anyway, not as far as she can tell. "Dizzy," he mumbles again, then stretches his head over the side of the cabin and starts to retch. Yellow liquid dribbles down onto the deck. His eyes roll back into his head, and he passes out cold, his body limp as seaweed.

Meanwhile the boat has swung around and is now lurching downwind through the waves. She's got to get him off the deck and into the cockpit, where at least he won't go overboard. Bracing her knees on either side of him, she straightens his body out and grabs his arms between the armpits and elbows as though she were going to give him artificial respiration, then hauls with all her might, crawling backward on her knees until she can feel the edge of the companionway.

"Shit!" she yells as she barks first one shin, then the other on the hatch opening. The pain makes her angry, and pulling on Phil's flaccid shoulders (but he's still breathing, she can see his chest rise and fall) she continues to curse, softly at first, then louder, "Son of a bitch . . . " pull, ". . . Goddam wind," yank, ". . . out here in the middle of the fucking ocean . . ."

Losing her grip, she falls backward right on her fanny into the cockpit, and bangs her head against the tiller, flailing back and forth across the stern. Phil's limp body gathers momentum and starts to slide down off the cabin under its own weight. She leaps up, scrambles forward in time to catch his head and shoulders and partly lifts, partly guides him as he does a slow-motion somersault off the cabin roof. She manages to lower his head and shoulders into her cozy corner, then unfolds him backwards like a blanket until he is stretched full-length on the seat, head toward the cabin, feet toward the stern. His head lolls back and forth with the motion of the boat. Grabbing a life cushion, she wedges it against his face and neck.

Now what? Should she lash him in? Not now; there isn't time. She has to get back to shore as soon as possible. Maybe it's not a heart attack or stroke, she thinks, remembering his comment about the sandwich. Maybe he just has food poisoning, needs his stomach pumped and he'll be fine. She doesn't remember that food poisoning makes your eyeballs go funny, but that's beside the point. There are things to do.

Her mouth is dry, and she's out of breath now, but she can't spare a moment. All right. Fire up the engine, and then you can steer into the wind, take down the sail, and head for shore, run the boat right onto the beach if you have to, but get to safety and get help.

The tiller is jerking a restless arc across the width of the cockpit, just like Phil's eyeballs; she straddles it as she lifts up the hatch of the engine lazarette and gazes down at the old ten-horse Evinrude, its casing rusty and battered as an old mortar shell. Push this in, pull that out, squeeze this and yank the starter cord. Nothing to it. At least she knows a little bit about outboards, thanks to her teenage years spent bumming around the country club. She braces herself and pulls.

Yank, yank, splutter, gasp, time after time, the engine shudders briefly and then dies. Finally it won't even turn over. As she stares down through the well at the ocean below, the translucent water seems to fall away. Momentarily distracted, she watches this curious phenomenon, thinking Hmm, that's interesting . . . until the other side of the huge wave that has just rolled under the hull pushes up through the hole in the boat and drenches her with oily-smelling water from head to waist. "Fuck!" she yells, and slams down the cover.

She sits down at Phil's feet, nudging him to see if she can wake him up. His lips move, but through the slits of his eyelids she sees white gleaming. Not a good sign. Sighing, she rubs her hand across her face, twiddles Phil's foot with the other, trying to think. The boat bobs aimlessly up and down, scudding over the waves, mainsail flapping like a wounded seagull, her enemy the wind picking up the spray and flinging nastily it in her face, howling around the mast.

"All right, now what?" she howls back, her mouth wide. The wind rushes past her cheek and makes a hollow booming noise across her open mouth, mocking her. The mainsail sways and billows over head, all the rigging gyrating like a dozen jump ropes in the hands of frenetic schoolchildren. "Now what!" she screams up at the sky. The wind and spray roar over her like a giant waterfall. She sees land in the distance, faded, remote, a dream of land, the waves ranged between like so many barricades between her and safety, and they are in a race, up and over . . .

She grabs the tiller and pulls it back toward her, thinking she'll lay off a little and try to get underway, pulls the mainsheet in with her other hand so she can just let it go in case they start to go over. Suddenly with a whoosh the wind billows the sail inside out, then throws it right past her with a huge bang, and out the other side. Oh, shit, she's done it ass-backwards, the boat has accidentally jibed. Pulling the tiller straight, she freezes rigid, watches in despair as the bow goes sideways into one wave, emerges shedding water in a cascade only to crash into the next. All right then, we'll go with it and come about. She mutters the old litany to herself: Ready-about, Hard-to-lee. Push the tiller toward the side the sail is on. Flap, flap, bang! and the sail swings noisily over to the other tack. Oh, well, it beats an accidental jibe. The words come back to her from long ago: Straighten the stick and pull the sail in till it luffs.

Holding the tiller steady with her knee, she grabs the mainsheet with both hands and hauls with all her strength until the main is trimmed. As the sail flattens out the boat leaps forward—in the opposite direction from where she wants to go. They are heading out to sea. The bow rides up into the air, then skids down over the first wave, pushed ahead by the following sea, then up the next, a furious roller coaster ride. Water sloshes up through the outboard well and into the cockpit. Frantically she once more jams the tiller toward the sail—that much she can remember—and they come about again, swooping around and heeling violently as the wind catches the sail and lays the boat right over. Sara sobs in terror.

Petrified with fear, she watches helplessly as Phil rolls off the seat and flops like a raggedy doll face-up in the bottom of the cockpit, one hand ricocheting off the cockpit sole. His eyes flutter open momentarily, and he fixes her with a puzzled look.

"Where are we?"

Sara can't help herself. "Where the fuck do you think we are?" she screams at him. "Out in the middle of the cocksucking ocean with no engine and it's blowing like stink and I can't sail this goddamned boat by myself. You know that! Why the fuck did I ever let you get me into this mess? You promised me I'd be safe!"

Phil blinks up at her, puzzled. "I'm sorry," he says faintly, shutting his eyes. "I guess you should never have married me."

Oh, Christ, he thinks she means their whole life together! "Don't be stupid!" she screams. "I just meant in the boat! Out here!" but the words die on her lips as he raises his head, struggles up onto one elbow, goes deathly pale and falls back down, banging his head on the companionway.

"Wait! Don't pass out on me again! Tell me what to do!" she yells. His eyes fly open wide, focus on something, staring past her into space. His lips move. Intently she watches, trying to make out what he's saying. If these are his last words, she hopes they'll be directions.

"Follow the yellow brick road," he says. "Follow the yellow brick road." With that, he smiles beatifically at her, folds his hands on his chest, leans his head back against the cabin, closes his eyes and snores.

" 'Follow the yellow brick road'?" she screams, stamping her feet on the cockpit sole. The wind slams by like an express train. " 'Follow the yellow brick road'! What the fuck is that supposed to mean?"

Meanwhile they are boiling along at a terrifying angle of heel, smashing crookedly into the white-combed waves one after another, the bow breaking the wedges of water into smithereens that fly back over the windward side as though someone has thrown a bucketful of crushed ice into her face. Sobbing for breath, her vision blurred, she turns away to wipe her eyes. As she looks around wildly, the silly refrain babbling in her head, sung by hundreds of midgets in their high-speed voices, "Follow the yellow brick road, follow the yellow brick road!" she sees over her left shoulder the sun, shining low in the western sky, reflecting across the water toward her a path of golden light, reaching all the way back to the distant shore. The waves are tipped with molten gold. It looks just like a yellow brick road.

Oh hell, why not? What has she got to lose? Pulling the tiller toward her body, she holds the sheet and eases the sail as the boat starts to bear away from the wind, the angle of heel decreasing until they are nearly upright, no longer slamming hard against the waves. She continues to let out sail as the bow swings around and the boat heads on an even keel straight into the glimmering path of light, toward the west, the wind now almost at her back, the sea no longer a barrier crashing and foaming between her and safety, instead now washing gently behind, pushing her obliquely toward shore.

And that's it. They are on a broad reach, the easiest point of sail. If he had told her that in so many words, she wouldn't have had the faintest idea what he meant.

Sooner than she would have thought possible, they are passing just inside Midway Rock, and looking northwest she can make out the mark at the mouth of Indian Cove. She studies the chart she's snaked off a shelf just inside the cabin; with all its mysterious marks and whorls and blobs it reminds her of a CAT scan, and is probably about as useful. But she can see that if she keeps the boat headed straight on the path of light much longer she'll run across something resembling several half-chewed anchovies laid side by side, called the Sea Island Ledges. Ledge is not good to run across; she knows that much. She could try to thread her way around them and get back up the river, but that is several miles away, and practically all mud flats at low tide.

The seas are much calmer behind the barrier islands that line the inner bay, and the wind seems to be dying down at last. Phil is curled up comfortably in the fetal position in the front corner of the cockpit. Unable to reach the jacket, she has covered him as best she can with his foul-weather gear pants. She chucks the chart down the companionway and decides to risk it. Keeping her eye on the markers—black to port, back to port, red right return, those dumb red nuns again—she shifts the tiller, hardens up—if that's the word, no wonder men associate sex with sailing and call boats "she"—and threads her way close-hauled up toward the river mouth, nuns to the right, cans to the left, letting the sail out whenever they start to heel too much, but keeping up as much speed as she can to buck the tide.

And soon she is passing inside Pondatear, the tide coming in now and pulling her along with it, so that the boat seems to glide effortlessly through the calmer water, land on either side, keeping to midchannel, a little bit closer to the wind, until at last she sights the dock and float.

Fortunately for her not many boats are in yet, the big orange mooring balls bobbing empty all around her, that many fewer obstacles to crash into. Feeling like a loose ball in a pinball machine, she maneuvers through the harbor, letting out more and more sail to slow the boat down as she comes closer to the dock. Not wanting to risk coming about in these close quarters, she swings around just short of the eye of the wind, then lets the sail flutter loose and waits while the wind pushes her gently sideways and the boat fetches up neatly at the dock.

She leaps out with the rear docking line, wraps it around a huge cleat bolted to the weathered boards and stops the boat. Suddenly wobbly-legged, rubber-kneed, she staggers to the bow, retrieves the other docking line and ties the boat up firmly to the float: Safe.

She quickly drops the main, letting it fall any which way into the cockpit; there is no time to furl it now. She has to get Phil to a hospital before it's too late. Ducking under the boom to check on him before she runs for help, she's surprised to find him sitting up, one leg of the bright yellow foul-weather pants draped over each shoulder like a huge banana peel, arms folded around his knees. He's staring straight ahead with a somewhat dazed expression, but more or less upright and awake. Not moving his head, he gazes at her owlishly from under his eyebrows. "Are we where I think we are?" he asks.

"You can sure as hell bet we're not in Kansas anymore."

"No need to be sarcastic," he says with dignity. As Sara stands there with her mouth open, he stands up, walks slowly, somewhat unsteadily but with great deliberation to the car they've left here for the trip back, gets in the passenger side.

He sits there staring straight ahead as though nothing has happened, while Sara puts the boat away, wondering furiously if he's tricked her. It's now past six o'clock. Sara gets in the car. "Are you really all right?" she asks, squinting at him closely. He looks much better. Even though she already knows the answer, she asks anyway. "Do you want me to take you to the hospital?"

"Are you kidding?" he says, waving a hand dismissively. "Of course not. I'm fine, just a little woozy. But I think you'd better drive, okay? We'll just have to come back tomorrow or the next day for the truck."

They hardly talk on the way home; Phil falls asleep almost immediately, his head lolling from side to side, finally coming to rest against the window. Sara decides to take the turnpike; even though it takes longer it's smoother than the winding, hilly "short-cut" Phil is so fond of. She drives carefully, as though he were an egg balanced on a spoon, her precious cargo, trying to keep him from rolling around too much. It's dark when they get home.

"I'm calling the doctor," she says.

"Can't it wait until morning?" he says wearily. "Right now I just want to sleep." He falls into bed, is instantly asleep. Sara gets in beside him, but lies awake for a long time, listening to him breathe. Finally he starts to snore. She nudges him.

He opens one eye; the other is buried in his pillow. The wind still roars a hollow curve across the sky. "The big cruise is coming up in three weeks, you know," he mumbles. "I'm going no matter what."

She starts to say something, but drowsy now, instead begins to dream. Phil will go on the cruise and she will let him, because then she will be on vacation. Every morning for a week she can wake up thumbing her nose at the wind, knowing she won't have to go sailing. In her sleep she still hears the wind noise, but now she is no longer dreaming of heavy bombers flying over while she stands riveted to the spot, of treading water, drenched and terrified, under a thunderous waterfall, of boats rocking and careening out of control, dizziness, disaster, death, and yellow brick roads. When the distant roar begins to rise again, she just hops over the side, tripping lightly from one gleaming puddle of light to the next, and doesn't even get her ruby slippers wet. She doesn't look back or even where she's going; she just runs away.

6

To the Dump

It's Saturday morning, Phil's been gone five days now, and Sara hasn't heard from him since he called Tuesday night to tell her he'd arrived safely, that they were getting started first thing in the morning. She keeps expecting the phone to ring any minute, Phil's voice on the line, bringing her up to date. She can't call him—that's not part of the deal—but she has always been able to count on him to call her at least once while he's away, let her know what's going on and how he's doing. She likes this sense of connection, the telephone lines stretching over the distance like a cord between them, so that even when they're not talking, they're still somehow in touch. Right now the line is stretched pretty thin, the connection tenuous. She's tried watching the morning and evening news so she can see where he is on the satellite map and what the weather's like out there, but that doesn't help much. Never mind, she tells herself; no news is simply that, no news.

To help pass the time while he's away, Sara and the kids have been going through the house cleaning out closets and bureau drawers, digging into one glory hole after another, kitchen, attic, basement and garage, clearing the decks so they can surprise Dad when he gets back. Sara has made several trips to the dump with the resulting true trash, leaving the negotiable trash for some future yard sale. Now the kids are rearranging their rooms while Sara is in the process of resurrecting her old marionette theater, one of the last things her father made for her before he died suddenly one Friday while he was away from home on business. Sara couldn't believe her eyes a few weeks ago when she caught sight of the faded blue proscenium stuffed back under the eaves of her mother's house in upstate New York; she thought it was long gone along with most of the other stuff from her childhood, hauled off to the dump by someone who didn't recognize these odd pieces of hinged plywood, wooden brackets and nailed-together floorboards as something worth saving.

So she's lugged it back home with her and here it is, more than thirty years after her father made it, set up in her workshop, having survived fairly intact—well, salvageable anyway—the intervening decades of multiple house moves, assorted breakdowns, fits of demolition, simple neglect. Her mother designed it, and her father had constructed the entire theater to fold up and fit in the trunk of their 1950 Buick so Sara could take her marionette shows on the road, which she did, her mother driving her around to birthday parties, school assemblies, even a stint on local television. Since Phil wasn't there to object, it was no problem to cram it into the back of the station wagon, even with the kids and all their stuff. David and Linnie were really excited, talked most of the way home about fixing it up, putting on a play, even charging admission. Their interest waned quickly, Sara suspects partly because she insists on making everything exactly the way it was. So they have concentrated on their rooms, leaving the theater to Sara, which is fine with her. But meanwhile, she's still got some serious cleaning up to do. Before she knows it, Phil will be calling to say he's on his way home.

The catch-all basket that has rested on the kitchen counter for many months now contains, among other things, three pieces of sea glass from the beach at Indian Cove, one plastic ice-cube with a fly inside, a small round white rubber band for Linnie's braces that Sara momentarily mistakes for a maggot, assorted nuts and bolts, three pen tops, eight pennies, one dried-up mascara brush, two slightly-used birthday candles, a flattened tube of Neosporin, a needle with knotted white thread, a cut-off rose stem with thorns, six paper clips (four colored, two plain), several fly carcasses without benefit of ice cube, random dust-balls, lint, gum wrappers and other debris. Where does it all come from? Sara asks herself as she sorts the items worth saving into several piles, hers, David's, Linnie's, medicine cabinet, workshop. There is no pile for Phil; he always throws his junk out on the spot. She pockets the pennies and dumps the rest into the large kitchen garbage can painted with bright Pennsylvania Dutch leaves and tulips Phil gave her for her birthday, moves on to the next glory hole.

Sara is beginning to feel a certain lack of progress. It's been almost two whole days since she watched Phil drive off down the long driveway, looking as always incongruously large and fit, his head and shoulders dwarfing the cab of the rusty little red pickup. Even though she's made a couple of trips to the dump already, most of the time she seems just to be moving messes from one place to another. Still, sorting junk seems to hold her interest as well as anything; she doesn't feel like working on any of her sculptures. There's always the marionette theater, but she's saving that, doing it bit by bit. Anyway, she's beginning to think it's the process and not the end result that matters.

She's already rearranged the attic to hold more boxes, and gone through her own drawers and closets. The kids are working in the playroom, having caught some of her fever, so she decides to take a look at the basement. A musty, dank odor floats up the stairs at her as she gropes for the light switch; the floor is partially dirty and water runs through the granite and rubble foundation most months of the year, so they have never put much down there, but she goes down anyway, thinking she can always sweep away the cobwebs and check which cans of paint have dried up, whether any more rats have drowned in the cistern.

As she turns on the stair light, she hears a rustling noise and then a soft flop, flop, flop. Cautiously she peers down the stairs, and sees, frantically leaping off in all directions to get out of the circle of light, several pale green frogs of varying sizes. One stops in mid-flop and settles back down onto the floor, squats on its haunches at the bottom of the stairs regarding her solemnly with eyes as large, round, and glistening as two fried eggs. He is huge, the size of a desk telephone, the biggest frog Sara has ever seen in real life, with iridescent, slimy-looking skin draped around him like a green satin cloak. His eyes fix her with an inscrutable look; his throat pulsates with significance. "Knee-deep," he comments in a tone as deep and resonant as a bass viol. "Redd-up."

Wow, Sara thinks as she retreats up the steps, this certainly gives new meaning to the tale of the Frog Prince. She slams the door. A faintly guttural "—the-DUMP" vibrates up through the floor. "Okay, okay! I'm trying!" Sara shouts back. Oh fine, she thinks, Phil's only been gone since yesterday, and already I'm taking orders from frogs. She shoots the bolt on the door.

This is just the beginning. She is soaping herself in the shower Thursday morning when an earwig drops from the ceiling onto her shoulder. She looks up and sees more crawling out from a hole in the corner to parade around the ceiling moulding. Suddenly they are everywhere she looks. They infest the damp cracks by the kitchen sink, crawl out from under unused flower pots in the garage. She lifts up several loops of garden hose to wash off the ones crawling up the side of the house, and hundreds drop off the coils like oblong, wet black beads, their ice-pick pincers at the ready, scrambling for safety. It's the earwig capital of the world. She hoses them into the ground.

Fleas pop up off the floors like soda fizz, landing on ankles, lurking in the bedding and upholstered furniture. Prowling the house with her can of insecticide, she descries glistening beetle bodies huddling inside cracks in the walls, spiders swinging from all the corners, moths caroming inside lampshades in broad daylight, tiny worms waving their heads at her like minuscule beckoning fingers from the bag of flour. There are ants in the sugar bowl. She finds a platoon of gnats in her toothbrush. "What is this?" she shouts to no one in particular as she blasts them off under the hot water tap, "the Bug-of-the-Month Club?"

Bugs everywhere. She knows they aren't all bugs, technically speaking; some have four pairs of legs, and many have wings, even the ones that come through the screens, crash against the wall and land on their backs with their legs flailing helplessly. But as far as she's concerned, any insect is a bug, and even though she knows it's the hot, humid summer weather, and this happens every summer, she feels invaded. Thinking if you can't beat them, at least you can identify them, she goes to the town library on Thursday afternoon and gets out a book on bugs.

As if this weren't enough, she finds evidence of mice in the kitchen, a trail of rice-sized turds like a tiny wagon train winding from under the stove, behind the refrigerator, along the underside of the dishwasher and into the broom closet. The cats are waiting for her to feed them, sitting on the kitchen counter smug as owls, watching a mouse saunter past with a crumb of doggy kibble in its mouth. They look at her, then back at each other, start to bat and hiss, fighting as usual over their food. She picks one up under each arm, struggling and swiping at each other, tosses them both down into the basement, muttering, "Catch mice. Chase frogs. Eat bugs."

The collie puppy they have recently acquired, even actually paid for, unlike the legendary but gratis Collie Cibber, it turns out *does* eat bugs. At night, tossing in her disturbed sleep, she hears the whine of a mosquito, then a snap of teeth, smacking of lips, and the mosquito whines no more. She watches the puppy snare house-flies and moths in mid-flight or as they flutter against the screens, his nose quivering like an anteater's. In the garage she finds him crunching on a June bug, which he shortly spits out with a dis-appointed expression indicating it tastes nasty. But he continues to relish mosquitoes, flies, and moths, bumping his long nose along the screens and windowsills to snap them up.

But even with the puppy's help, by Friday Sara is beginning to feel as though she's losing control of the whole house. First the washer starts lurching across the floor like a demented troll, then the dryer makes a noise like a helicopter coming in for landing. The dishwasher sends a river of sudsy water that pools in the middle of the sagging kitchen floor, and the refrigerator begins defrosting on the outside. None of the doors will shut, and the ones that are shut won't open. She imagines the whole house collapsing into its foundation. At least that will take care of the frogs.

The children are increasingly irritable, wanting to know what they are going to do for fun. Ignoring Sara's admonitions to get busy with the cleanup, they start to fight each other too. Sara puts them in their rooms, threatening to keep them there until Dad gets home. They want to know when that is. Since Sara still hasn't heard from Phil, she can't really tell them. "Next week!" she yells. They don't believe her. But it keeps them quiet for the time being, all that time with just one parent to exasperate, too risky; usually they take turns. Before she knows it, they have announced their intention to seriously clean up their rooms.

In her workshop, Sara looks at the torso she's started, modeling it on Phil's from memory, but without the scars. Right now it is not going well. She fiddles with the marionette stage for a while, then comes back inside, and goes upstairs to tell the kids they can come out.

Overhead she hears a fluttering sound. She looks up, sees a dark shadow fluttering inside the frosted globe chandelier hanging over the stairs. It's much too big to be a moth. She lets out a scream. It's a bat. The children hear her all the way upstairs. They come running.

She catches the bat—a small one, clearly a baby, but still dangerous, since bats carry rabies—by throwing a towel over it in midflight while the children dance around in a frenzy of fear and excitement. They want to see it up close, but Sara refuses. She knows she mustn't touch it and she certainly can't just let it go—rabid animals are purported to behave strangely, and she considers the act of fluttering around in someone's hall light in the middle of the afternoon pretty strange even for a bat—so she carries it outside still wrapped in the towel, places the bundle in the driveway and runs over it several times with the car, while the children watch from the kitchen window. Then she throws the whole thing in the garbage and slams down the lid. She will take it to the dump with her on the final run tomorrow, right before—she hopes—Phil gets back.

The puppy is nearly housebroken, but has to be monitored frequently, so Sara takes him out for a noon run. While he trots up and down the long driveway going about his business, Sara turns and stares back at the old house. Tall, stately, just what they always wanted, now it seems to be in a state of perpetual disrepair, the roof leaking, the paint peeling, a shutter hanging by one hinge, attached to what's left of the other with a trash bag twist-em tie, all the doors cockeyed, the wind whistling through chinks in the foundation.

Standing in the driveway, looking around at the house, the trees, the yard, she contemplates the day-to-day chores she and Phil usually share, feeling them drag on her like a heavy winter garment these hot summer days: the cooking, shopping and washing, the vacuuming, folding of laundry, paying bills, making the dump run.

Then there are the seasonal chores, divided into his and hers. So it has always been Sara's job to cover the drafty old granite and rubble foundation with sheets of plastic to keep out the winter wind, bury the rose bushes, pull down the recalcitrantly sticky self-storing storm windows, set out the garden in the spring and tend it in the summer, rake the leaves around the house in fall, while Phil mows the huge lawn, grinds the leaves up on the big lawn, cuts and splits and stacks the woodpile for the stove, shovels the snow that piles up on the roofs and at the head of the driveway, rototills the garden. These chores signal the rotating seasons, the passage of time, week after week, year following year.

There is a rhythm in the seasons going round, in their cooperative effort to keep things going on as even a keel as possible. Now, in Phil's absence, staring at the rambling, ramshackle house, the lawn in need of mowing again, the sickly trees with bony leafless limbs in need of trimming, she wonders how she could ever do everything all by herself. Could she learn to run a chain saw? Split wood without throwing her back out? Just for a moment she tries to imagine what life would be like if Phil did not come back.

Not that it would be all bad. For one thing, she wouldn't ever have to go sailing. With Phil away, she would be free to leave the various messes she's created in the process of "cleaning up" around for as long as she liked. All this week she hasn't felt compelled to wash the dishes and tidy up the kitchen every night. She has stayed up late reading; she and the kids have had pick-up dinners and junk food. If I were by myself, she thinks, I would buy a microwave oven and three hundred sixty-five frozen entreés, and not cook dinner for a year. I would buy paper plates and plastic spoons and live like a gypsy.

But she knows she wouldn't, not really. She loves their life, this house. She would go on just as they are, even without him; maybe she would even keep the boat, learn not to be afraid to sail it herself.

She calls the dog and goes back inside. Phil is due back any time—a week at the most, they said—and even though he hasn't called to say when he's getting in, he hasn't called to say he isn't, either. No news is no news. But time is running out. The cleanup has to be finished before he gets home. Back in the kitchen she feels her wedding ring tight on her finger, swollen in the July heat and humidity, takes it off and puts it on the kitchen counter next to the latest basket now collecting junk.

When the children were smaller and she was too busy even to think of doing serious sculpture, Sara used to make hand puppets and put on plays in a refrigerator box with her friend Joyce for the local schools. Going through the attic right after she and the kids have returned from her mother's, she comes across some of the props she collected over the years, including the little wooden chair her father made, and several of her old marionettes, dusty, beat-up, bald, and unstrung from years in the attic being chewed on by squirrels and who knows what other vermin, but still workable. Once she's completely refurbished the theater—replaced the missing parts, repainted it, made new hangings and a backdrop, added draw curtains and the lights—she'll restring the marionettes so she and David and Linnie can put on a show. It will be just like old times.

She will then, as Phil has observed more than once, have recreated yet another element of her childhood; the rambling old run-down house in a picturesque village near a nice lake, full of cats and dogs and children and accumulated junk (only one dog really, the puppy they have recently acquired after four years of being without, but she includes dog ghosts as well, and yes, she must confess, lots of junk; it runs in the family), even an aluminum canoe identical to the one they used to paddle around at Carpenter's. And the sailboat, too, though that, since they have decided to keep it at the coast, is not quite the same. Sometimes, though, she wonders if these correspondences are an illusion, if the way she remembers things is the way they really were. More than once lately her mother has revised the story of her life to parallel Sara's in what Sara takes to be some obscure attempt at establishing the fact, if not the words of sympathy, so that sometimes her mother's past seems oddly to be repeating Sara's present.

For instance. Whenever Fran comes across an article in her various medical journals about Phil's kind of tumor, pheochromocytoma—they can both spell and pronounce it now, after years of practice—she Xeroxes it and sends it along; "In medicine what you don't know *can* hurt you," she maintains, and certainly their experience, particularly the too-hasty and nearly fatal first operation six years ago, has borne this out. "You never know when these might come in handy," Fran says. Sara hopes they never will, but she and Phil read them anyway.

The latest one describes a new diagnostic test developed by doctors at the University of Michigan Hospital, so that even very small tumors can be located and identified with much greater accuracy than heretofore was available through CAT scans, obviating the need for exploratory surgery of the kind, Sara thinks to herself as she reads, that nearly killed Phil that first time. Even though they are used to a certain amount of medical jargon the text is pretty hard going; Phil declares it to be decadent bureaucratic gobbledegook and gives up after one paragraph. Sara gets far enough to learn that what the tumors do is take up the radioactive isotope, and light up on the screen. They look at the illustrations, fuzzy reproductions of X-rayed torsos, ghostly skeletons with spines like strings of popcorn, rib cages like upside-down Christmas trees glimpsed through thick fog. Some look as though they're decorated with clusters of tiny lights, four, five, even ten. The clusters of light—like gangs of fireflies—are tumors.

"Phew! How do they make heads or tails out of these?" Phil wonders. "Why don't you tell your sister to stop sending us this stuff?" He gestures at the Xeroxes draped precariously on the edge of her desk, looking as though they will slither off and scatter all over the floor any second. "All it does is pile up and add to the mess." Sara adds the article to her stack, just in case. After all, there was that dizzy spell in the boat last month; though Phil has seemed fine since then, you never know.

When she tells her mother over the phone about the new test, her mother says, "Isn't that funny? A hospital in Michigan again, after all these years."

"Why?" Sara asks, wondering if her mother means funny ha-ha or funny peculiar. What could be so funny about a hospital in Michigan?

"That's where your father died, didn't you know that? The land he was negotiating for was in Canada, and so was the motel he was staying in, but when he got sick, they took him across the border to a hospital in Michigan. That's where he died."

Sara goes upstairs to see how the kids are doing. Throughout the morning she's heard various thumps and scraping noises, the sound of large objects being dragged across the floor. All has been quiet for some time now, and this usually means trouble. But she finds David in his room peacefully wrapping his comic books in plastic food-storage bags. He looks up momentarily. "Those can go to the attic," he says, waving a hand in the direction of several boxes stacked by the door.

"Not to the dump, huh?" Sara says, picking her way across the room from clear space to space as though on stepping stones until she can see inside the closet. David gives her a withering glance and continues wrapping comic books. That way, he has assured her, they will be real collector's items.

All the rooms in the house have large walk-in closets, she supposes because people had very large clothes in the nineteenth century, when the house was built. Sara has been particularly fascinated over the years by the changes in the children's use of their closet space. So David's, known as Headquarters during his commando phase, stuffed full of army clothing, weapons, helmets, books on war, toy soldiers and World War I posters, has more recently become the Dojo, a martial arts studio, complete with an old pair of Phil's pajamas, a navy blue sash from an outgrown bathrobe, several crude wooden swords, half-a-dozen pieces of cut-up broom handle connected with swing set chain into what Sara has since learned are called numchucks, or something like that.

Right now it is filled almost flush to the doorway with assorted toy cartons David has insisted on saving since he was a toddler (they're worth more in the original boxes, he explains, ignoring the fact that the toys themselves are largely destroyed), ragged stacks of magazines, empty shoe boxes, books mainly coverless, half-a-dozen old cameras, several undistinguished rocks, a chunk of ersatz Kryptonite, and more items that formerly reposed all over his room, mainly under the bed. Carefully arranged across the few inches of floor space left are several brown paper lunch bags. Sara opens one; it is filled with used plastic sandwich bags, slightly redolent of stale peanut butter. Another one contains the label wrappers and black hanger rods from several dozen pairs of tube socks. To one side is a stack of purple dittos and notebook papers; school work. She flips through to the papers on the bottom. They are printed in shaky block letters. Kindergarten. She turns to David. "What do you call this?" she inquires politely, pointing a thumb back over her shoulder at the mess.

"Land of the Lost," David replies, and rolls over on the floor, chuckling. He bobs upright, tears of laughter welling in his eyes.

"Are you kidding me? Sock wrappers? Used baggies? All your old school papers?"

"Only the A ones," he says nonchalantly. "I threw the rest away. I threw away a lot of junk. Don't worry, Mom, I'm going to clean the whole thing right out." Then he adds, apparently without irony: "I've been thinking it would make a really great place to hang clothes."

Shaking her head, Sara goes down the hall to investigate Linnie's room. Her closet, similarly piled to the rafters, has been variously transformed from a ten-bed stuffed-animal hospital to dollhouse apartments to miniature riding school, with various sizes of stalls for the twenty or so model horses, sawdust and bundles of tall grass clippings smuggled in for authenticity, discovered by Sara when the odor of rotting vegetation spread to the rest of the upstairs. It is now being transformed into Linnette's Fashion Boutique (Linnie's given name is in fact Linda, but she has informed Sara that "Linnette" sounds more "boutique-y") of which Sara is given an extended tour, considering the space is only about four feet by six, a good part of it taken up by a chair "where the customer sits for the showings." In the course of it, Linnie informs her she wants to be a model when she grows up.

The rest of Linnie's room is a disaster. "How can you tell what's clean and what's dirty?" Sara asks, pointing to the piles of clothes spread all over the floor, clearly every item of apparel Linnie owns, except for the ones chosen to be shown in the Boutique. "What are your bureau drawers for?"

Linnie shrugs. Sara opens a drawer at random; it contains old coloring books, rolled-up posters, bent record albums and numerous candy wrappers.

Sara sighs. "One of these days I'm going to sell this house and build a new one," she announces loudly, "and each room will be containerized like a giant dumpster. Then I'll have a room-sized bulldozer and one of those huge garbage trucks with an elevator on the back, and once a week I will bulldoze everything together, back the garbage truck up to each room, empty it, and haul everything to the dump."

Linnie grins at her. "No, you won't."

"Ha, ha," David shouts from his room. The kids are clearly on to her; they know she is as bad as they are.

By now it's clear that neither child is inclined to give anything up. "You can sell the house any time you want, Mom," they have assured her many times, "but we're keeping our rooms." The best she can do is a few boxes up to attic; taking any of it to the dump is out of the question. A yard sale is a possibility, but not with Phil expected back so soon.

The fact is, she's hardly one to talk. The attic is already full of her stuff, including college essays and notebooks (Sara: "You never know when they might come in handy . . ." Phil: "Like when? Don't you think the kids will want to take their own notes in college?"), *her* old school papers, report cards, and so on. Phil may come from a neat and tidy clan whose idea of redecorating has always been to put the entire contents of a room out on the curb for the trashman, but Sara is one of a long line of pack rats, or as she prefers to be called, keepers.

At this very moment, she can feel bearing down overhead, bulging the ceiling plaster downward, the many boxes of family artifacts, all with their stories to tell, useless but beautiful objects handed down through generations, divided and redivided, spewed out like grains of salt from the machine at the bottom of the sea, seemingly undepleted after numerous tag sales, years of breakage and attrition, not to mention her mother's famous house-trashing episode.

Sara's share now gathers dust in the attic, slender white lawn dresses with baggy fronts her big-bosomed grandmother wore as a girl, the ruby decanter with gilt stopper, the only thing of value her Scottish great-great-great-grandfather brought with him from Inverness when he emigrated after the First Jacobite Rebellion, sets of dinnerware for twelve, pewter porringers and saucers, odd cups, crystal goblets.

Not to mention the old letters and photographs, fading and yellowed in their albums, stiff-collared ancestors, flapper aunts and bespectacled grandmas, stern grandfathers and joking uncles, her father as handsome as a movie star in his white golf knickers, as his college yearbook (also there) described him, "with laughing hair and curly eyes," her mother walking down a windy New York street in a huge raccoon coat staring at the camera with huge raccoon eyes, her parents at their wedding, herself when she was a little girl in short skirts with her underpants hanging down.

Probably the primitive camera that recorded all this is up there too, if it's not in David's closet.

So too the various transmutations over the years of the children's closets, all their belongings treasured in turn, piling up in layers like an ancient city, marking the progress of their growing up, a more tangible record of their lives than photographs in an album, and as far as she's concerned, theirs to keep as long as they want. After that, maybe *she'll* keep them, just in case, the way her mother kept things for her she never dreamed she'd want again, like the marionette theater. Now her children are as fascinated by her childhood things as she is by theirs.

In a way she is glad they are getting older and can understand more; as her mother said on their last visit, "At least your children are older." But she also remembers the earlier times, when the children were small and all of them were so innocent about what life might bring, and she feels a stab of regret that soon their closets will be no more than a place to hang their clothes. Then those too will be gone.

On her way downstairs, thinking now that it's way past lunchtime Phil will probably call and she should be near the kitchen phone so they can talk without the children interrupting, she passes by the bookcase in the back hall between the kid's rooms, and her attention is arrested momentarily by the sight of an old snapshot propped among the books, probably a reject from Linnie's latest cleanup. She takes down the dime-store frame; it's a photograph of her mother as a little girl. As she stands there looking at it, she is struck by the image of her mother standing there in the picture proudly holding up a tattered, one-eyed teddy bear to the camera. Holding the photograph in her hands, she thinks *How strange*; to see her now as she was then, small, knobby-kneed, so eager, so hopeful, so unsuspecting, not an inkling in the world of what was to come.

And suddenly, gripping the little picture in its frame, she misses Phil so sharply she wants to cry. She wants him home and safe, as though he'd never left. She knows they can't go back, but she wishes that they could just stay as they are, with nothing changing, not go back *or* forward. If we could only stay right where we are, she thinks, held like the photograph, safe in this house, this place, this time.

"Your father had a heart defect, you know," her mother says casually, stretched out on her bed under the covers with her hands under her neck, elbows pointing toward the ceiling, so her still slender arms seem to form a huge bow behind her head. Her body has grown heavier with age but her arms haven't, and with the covers pulled up almost to her chin she looks just the way she always used to, just the way Sara remembers her, except for the white hair. It's late at night on the last day of Sara's visit, the kids are asleep, and they are talking. Sara has just finished telling her mother how hard it is to deal with the uncertainty of Phil's illness, one doctor saying this, another that, the possibility the disease could recur at any time.

"What?" she asks, not sure she heard her mother right.

"Uh-huh," her mother says. "It was a mitral valve defect from rheumatic fever when he was a boy. We knew he could go at any moment. There wasn't anything the doctors could do then, so we just had to live with it. Of course he could have been more careful, but he didn't want to live like an invalid. But it was like the sword— whoever's it is, some Greek name I can't remember, my mind is going—hanging over our heads. You know." Her mother sighs. "I used to lie there with my head on his chest, listening to it. His heart didn't go thump-thump, it went whoosh, whoosh."

"Damocles," Sara murmurs without even thinking, momentarily distracted by the unexpectedly intimate image of her mother all those years ago, lying in bed with her father, head on his chest, listening to his heart go whoosh. Then she realizes what her mother just said. This is the first she's heard of any valve defect, rheumatic fever. Her father's death came so suddenly, without warning, a shock from which none of them, particularly her mother, has ever quite recovered. The phone call from the hospital at dawn, a strange voice telling them he was dead of a heart attack, just like that. And now she's saying that they knew beforehand?

"Why didn't you *tell* us?" she practically shouts at her mother, then claps a hand over her mouth; she doesn't want to wake the children. She's outraged at the idea that she wasn't told, not even she, the oldest. She could have been warned. If she'd known, it would not have come as such a shock, there would have been time to get ready, even to do something before it happened . . .

Sara sits back in her chair. It's the same old futile fantasy of rescue; she should know better by now. But this is a change of tune in her mother's long recitative of grief, which though altering somewhat over the years has always included this bitter refrain of blame: "If he had only done what the doctors told him and lost weight and quit smoking, taken better care of himself we might have had more time together"; in other words, this terrible desertion was all his fault. Sara, on the other hand, has always felt obscurely that it was hers for not being there to save him, so he ended up dying all alone so far away from home. It occurs to her that her mother may have felt that way too.

"What good would it have done?" her mother says matter-of-factly. "It would only have frightened you children and made you worry. And there was nothing you could do. You kids were so young. You understand. It was better that way."

Better than what? Sara contemplates her mother's face, the light from the soundless television set next to her bed flickering over it like a silent movie. The fact is, Sara *does* understand. The same old bind, forewarned is forearmed, but the cost is great; always watching, cataloguing symptoms, the blood pressure cuff casually left around so the children will take it for granted as part of their lives, know in some subliminal way they're still not completely safe; the anxious waiting for the outcome of checkups, all part of the price they have to pay for Phil's continued survival. This is better: he did not die, and they are warned. But this is what they live with, the worry, the necessary inconvenience.

"Oh, well," her mother says. "At least your children are older."

Sara gets it now. It's all too much of a coincidence, this tale of her father's heart defect. Her mother is making it all up, in another of her oblique and slightly loony attempts at comfort. Though she is sure her mother means well, this is comfort Sara can do without. Besides, it doesn't really change things.

But when she repeats the story to her sister Fran, now a first-

year resident at a huge medical center in Massachusetts, she says
it's plausible. Their mother's new version is so medically detailed
that Fran thinks it might be in fact be true. A heart with a defective
valve does go whoosh-whoosh instead of lub-dub. If he blew a
valve, she speculates, that might explain why the doctors couldn't
save him. *Nobody* could have saved him. Sara reminds her the
cause of death was listed as coronary occlusion. "Meaningless,"
Fran the doctor replies. "A blanket term. All that says is that his
heart shut down." Fran shrugs. "Since there was no autopsy, we'll
never know. But where would she get enough terminology to make
it up, much less make sense?"

" 'General Hospital'?" Sara suggests, still skeptical. " 'St. Elsewhere'?" After all, why save it until now, more than thirty years
later?

Finally she chalks it up as one more song without words, the
burden of which is that her mother understands how Sara feels,
that their experience is similar. This is the last thing Sara wants
to hear, so she resists this and other parallels, not just because
they are probably apocryphal, but because she knows they are
irrelevant as well. She is her own self with her own choices, and
this is her own life, not some repeat performance. Yet sometimes
the temptation to see it as a chance to do everything over and do
it right is very strong. Otherwise why does she keep piling up these
tokens of the past?

Sara is in the kitchen, cleaning out the broom closet. She is down
to the papier-mâché model of Mount Vesuvius with the orange-
juice-can crater and three left-handed rubber gloves with the thumbs
cut off when she hears David thundering down the stairs, landing
with all his weight on the lowest step. Strange-looking silvery
insects shaped like tiny dolphins drop out of Vesuvius and loop
in panic toward the cracks and crevices of the closet walls, where
they make their escape.

"Mom! Mom!" He skids to a halt beside her in the kitchen.
"There's this really funny rustling noise in the wall. Linnie's scared
it's a ghost!"

On her way upstairs to investigate, Sara reminds David that one of these days he is going to hit the battered bottom step with both feet and go right through into the basement. But he has already leapt up the staircase and disappeared around the corner into Linnie's room.

The back chimney goes up behind the wallboard between the children's rooms, forming part of the wall on either side. It's a new chimney, recently rebuilt of cinder block with a smooth clay flue, unlike their other chimneys made of ragged, disintegrating brick several layers thick. Linnie is hiding in her bed, the covers pulled up over her head, quivering. She's overdramatizing of course; Sara doesn't think kids her age believe in ghosts unless it suits their purposes, like Santa Claus or the Tooth Fairy. Not that there isn't a noise; when she puts her ear to the wall she hears a fluttering sound, the hum of desperately beating wings, faint scratchings at the clay flue. The sound whirrs down past her feet, accompanied now by frantic chirping.

"It's just a bird," she says calmly.

"How did a bird fly all the way down there?" asks Linnie, leaping out of bed and pressing the whole side of her head against the wall. Then she turns to face it, lips nearly touching. "Hi, bird," she shouts. More frantic fluttering, like a child in the womb.

"It's probably a swift," Sara explains. "They like to nest in the tops of chimneys."

"Don't they burn up?" David wants to know.

"They usually nest when winter is over and we don't have fires any more," Sara says evasively, hoping she won't have to go into detail about nests built too early in the spring when fires are infrequent but still occasional, the parent birds surprised by smoke, the sudden squawk and beat of evacuating wings dislodging the nest down into the blazing fireplace, eggs still in them, or worse, baby birds, the times she has surreptitiously scraped up the ashes and dumped them over the bank behind the house where the children won't see the grisly remains, tiny bird beaks and skeletons, some with scorched feathers still attached. "This chimney is so smooth inside it probably couldn't get a foothold and just kept slipping further down."

Linnie's face is creased with anxiety. "How will it get out? Won't it die in there?" Tears well in her eyes.

"I'm sure it will fly back out somehow," Sara says, patting Linnie's shoulder. She looks around for David, but he has left the room, either squeamish or indifferent.

They find him in the kitchen, his ear pressed to the base of the chimney. "It's all the way down here!" he shouts. "I can hear it beating!"

"But it can't get out!" Linnie wails. "It's going to die in there!" She puts her hands over her face and runs away, sobbing.

Linnie is right. The top of the chimney is three stories up, more than thirty feet; the flue is seven inches square. A bird could flutter down; a bird could never fly back up. "Poor bird," David says. That's it. He shrugs and walks away, hardly a sentimentalist. There is nothing to be done.

A little later, Sara is sitting by herself in the kitchen reading the newspaper, not really waiting for the phone to ring, yet wanting to be near it in case it does. In the silence, she hears a faint scrabbling behind the cast iron clean-out door. She gets up and kneels down in front of the small black door, carefully eases it open and peers inside.

The bird is wedged in a corner of the flue, wings partially extended, chest heaving. It looks out at her with bright beady eyes, desperate with fear yet obviously too exhausted to move. Bird lime spatters the inside of the chimney, chalky against the soot. She stares at the bird, wondering what it is thinking, what it sees. Alone in blackness, fluttering helplessly further and further down the dark sooty hole, the bright square of sky diminishing to the size of a pocket mirror, safe air beyond impossible to reach . . . then suddenly when hope is gone, a noise, a clank, light opening up at the bottom, air rushing in, then, horrors! a huge face peering in . . .

Don't be silly, she tells herself, sitting back on her heels while the bird tries to press itself back out of sight, fluttering up a few inches, then flopping back down. This is just a birdbrain we are talking about here. What do birds know? Survival instinct, nothing more. "Here, birdie," she says reassuringly. "I won't hurt you. Come on out."

The bird stares at her, obviously in a bind as far as survival goes, can't fly back up, too scared to come out down here. On second thought, Sara isn't so sure she wants a scared-shitless, soot-encrusted bird flying around loose in her kitchen any more than she wants a dead bird decomposing in her chimney. But she can't just squat there and wait for the bird to croak so she can remove its carcass; it is not, after all, in her nature to do nothing.

She pushes the clean-out door almost shut so the bird can't get out, goes to get a towel and one of the kids' shrimp nets she remembers seeing in the broom closet, purchased by grandparents at the Jersey shore for fifty cents, cheap and flimsy, tutu netting on a stick, largely useless and heretofore unused. But not thrown out; you never know when something like that might come in handy.

In a matter of seconds she has snared the bird—she was right, it is a swift, the dark points of the forked tail feathers sticking out of the mesh like calipers—dropped the net and gently thrown the towel over the bird, just the way she captured the bat yesterday, the same way they used to capture bats all those summers ago at Carpenter's. She gathers the small mound up, motionless in her hands, takes it outdoors into the fading light, thinking that it is probably dead of fright by now, its little heart blasted to bits with frantic beating.

But no, when she lays the towel on the ground and flips it open, the bird hops upright, ruffles its feathers, then with a single shudder of movement flings itself into the air, wings humming as it swoops low to the ground straight into the shadows of the trees, obviously none the worse for wear. Sara smiles as she watches it go. One more bust in the chops for the powers of darkness. She walks back into the kitchen, thinking she'll stay by the phone a while in case Phil calls. But he doesn't call.

"To the dump, to the dump, to the dump-dump-dump!" the children sing gaily to the tune of the Lone Ranger; they think these are the real words. When they were smaller they always went with Phil on the weekly dump run; it was an occasion. They have lost interest now they're older ("The dump is so *bor*-ing," Linnie says disdainfully. "It's gross," says David.), but Phil still regards it as "one of the few pleasures left to a man of my age and condition." Now Sara goes along with him, for the ride since he won't let her get out of the truck, even to unload the garbage. He's always afraid she'll bring something back.

"Why are you doing this?" he asks suspiciously as they rattle down the dump road in the little red pickup loaded with the week's haul of garbage.

"Doing what?" she replies.

"Going with me to the dump."

"Why not? I want to go everywhere with you," she says. It's been almost two weeks since Phil fainted in the boat, and he's been just fine, but Sara still isn't taking any chances.

Phil snorts in disbelief. "Not sailing," he says.

"That's not fair," she says. "That's different." He knows she loves going to the dump, in fact comes from a long line of dump-pickers, has long since been wise to that speculative "you-never-know-when-it-might-come-in-handy" look on her face. But these days Sara is content simply to look around. While it's true that one person's garbage appears much like another's, when you get right down to it, you can tell a lot about people from what they unload at the dump, if you take the time. Maybe that's why Phil always ties their trash bags up tight and carefully deposits them on the fringes of the pile instead of flinging them over the top, where they might burst open. He doesn't want anyone to know what's inside.

After badgering the kids into finishing their part of the cleanup, Linnie vacuuming, David lugging out trash cans, Sara makes one last sweep and does the dump run, hoping Phil won't be too disappointed that he missed it. But tomorrow's Sunday, the dump is closed, and she's afraid if she waits too long, she or the kids will start putting things back; leaving all the full trash cans around is too much of a temptation. Not to mention the bat. So she loads the cans, plus a few cardboard boxes and grocery bags containing the overflow into the station wagon and takes off, grateful for the chance to go to the dump alone for a change.

Sailing

The truth is, she's not just an ordinary run-of-the-mill dump-picker, whatever Phil may think. Her attitude toward dumps is much more complex. Some of her fondest childhood memories are of going with her mother to the village dump, picking through the trash long before recycling became fashionable, motivated not so much by their reduced circumstances as by a desire not to let perfectly usable items go to waste, coming home with lamps and chairs, pots and pans, all in more or less salvageable condition, her mother's idea of a good time. Those were the days before the breakdowns started, before her mother trashed the house they were living in and two others the year Sara was seventeen, ran through the back lots until the police caught up with her and hauled her off to the state mental institution.

Even after her father died and they moved back to Skaneateles, into the big old run-down house with her grandmother and her aunt, there were still lots of good times. Going to the dump, for instance. Sara just assumed it was perfectly natural to bring things back as well as take them there, a sort of informal trading post for items no longer used but not necessarily useless. Her mother frequently went empty-handed just to look around, Sara now supposes more as a way to pass the time, an excuse to get out of the crowded, dreary house, just as she used to load Sara and the younger kids into the old Buick and drive around the lake, up and down backcountry roads, exploring, all the time telling them stories of her youth. Everything was an adventure, like rediscovering the mysterious place her mother called Frozen Ocean, no more than an old abandoned gravel pit, but still exciting to the four of them, because it did look like a frozen ocean with its peaks and valleys, waves of eroded clay. That was in fact how they happened across the house at Carpenter's, which her mother bought with what was left of the insurance money, so they would have a place of their own at least part of the year. It is one of Sara's continuing regrets that Carpenter's was something they could not keep.

And all those times her mother faithfully lugged Sara and her marionettes around to schools and birthday parties, even after they moved, until finally Sara lost interest, and put everything away. Sometimes Sara wonders why it took so long after her father's death—five years, in fact—for her mother to go completely nuts. But who can understand the inner compulsions of grief? Here at the local dump she once spotted an entire woman's wardrobe, dresses still on the hangers, shoes still in boxes, coats, pants, even a couple of wigs, unceremoniously tossed onto the pile like garbage. She hadn't understood at the time, but now she thinks it must have been a woman who died, probably of cancer—the wigs—and her husband, in his grief, had just grabbed everything out of her closets and drawers and taken it to the dump. She could never do that, she thought at the time. But who knows what she'd do?

She hauls the cans and boxes and bags out of the station wagon, and throws them on the heap, dead bat and all. Then, with a little time to herself—after all, the kids can answer the phone as well as she can—she watches the seagulls wheeling and screeching and pecking over the undulant heaps of garbage, the piles of gravel waiting to be bulldozed over when the garbage gets too ripe. It reminds her of her mother's Frozen Ocean, of the real ocean, of sailing, of Phil. With all the conflicts between them, his intolerance of her sloppiness, her fascination with the dump, with the found objects he refuses to let her bring home, her refusal now to sail with him, how much their lives have changed, somehow they have adjusted to the pressures and demands. So far. Even here at the dump she feels the invisible cord tugging between them, the distance lengthening and shortening, but still the connection holding, the lines stretching over the distance, his voice, her voice. This is how she sees their life together, the adjusting of distance, yet always the sense of this attachment, this connection she has with no one else.

She drives home, thinking he has probably called while she was gone. But there have been no calls.

It is a mess to end all messes. There is stuff everywhere, clothes, books, toys, pictures, blankets, pillows, shoes, coat hangers strewn all over in every room, through the halls and down the stairs, every bureau drawer, cupboard, closet in the whole house emptied onto the floor, the contents of every trash can, flour bin, cereal box, sugar bowl thrown on top, then several containers of paint, laundry detergent and motor oil poured over that. Sara picks her way through the debris alone; she's told her sister and brother to stay outside in case their mother is still somewhere in the house smashing things up. At seventeen she is the oldest and therefore responsible; she doesn't want them to get hurt.

She moves through the house, each room worse than the next, until she comes out the other side. Her mother is not there; she is in the house next door. Sara can hear the thud of furniture being overturned, the slamming of cupboard doors. She tells Vic and Francie, who are by now peering curiously in at the windows, to stay put, then picks up the phone and calls the family doctor, who says to call the police. By the time they get there, Sara's mother has moved up the street, through the third and last of the houses her family once lived in. Seeing them coming, she runs away across the fields in the twilight, but Sara guesses where she is heading, tells the police. When they finally catch her, she is hiding in an old carriage house nearly a mile away.

Standing in the kitchen after her mother has been taken away to the state hospital, Sara contemplates the cornflakes stuck to the gobs of wet paint on the walls, the sheets and blankets soaked with oil, the broken kitchen plates and jelly glasses, the cracked windows, and wonders how she's ever going to clean it up all by herself.

Not until she, her cousin's husband Pete, and Dick, an old family friend, have picked through, sorted out and cleaned up the whole mess as best they can does she realize that, crazy and violent and wild as her mother was that day, as much as she ruined, she has nevertheless gone through the entire house without destroying one single object of any value. The family artifacts remain intact.

After this episode, her mother is committed involuntarily to the state mental hospital for a year, which means she can't sign herself out when she feels like it. The court-appointed guardian (all their relatives are either dead or too far away or just plain unwilling) arranges to rent the house unfurnished, so Sara and Vic and Fran move in with a kind neighbor and everything in the house is packed up by a moving company and put into storage. Everything. When

Sara's mother is discharged and they all move back into the house, they find the movers have carefully packed away and stored for the whole year three garbage cans. With the garbage still in them.

It must have been this way with her mother and father, Sara thinks as she finishes up the supper dishes, the same sense of connection between the two of them she feels with Phil. Not long after the funeral, Sara's mother drove to Canada by herself, leaving Sara and her sister and brother with her grandmother. She stayed at the same motel, visited the friends he had had dinner with the night before, went to the hospital—in Michigan, she reminds herself, not Canada—and talked to the doctors and nurses. Sara didn't understand it at the time, although she had wanted to go with her, but now she does. The connection had been broken so abruptly, and her mother wanted to know about him, be able to see where he had been and what he did right up to the end, so she could be in touch with every second of her husband's life. The connection was broken, but she had followed the loose end as far as she could, to find out everything she could, to know how it was.

Oh well, she thinks as she walks out to the workshop after the kids have gone up to bed, he'll have to call to let me know what time he's getting in. If not tonight, then first thing tomorrow.

. . . *"I'm not feeling too hot," he says to the friends he's just had dinner with. "I think I'll go back to the motel and make an early night of it."*

"Sure you're okay, Jim? Maybe you should see a doctor."

"No, I'm okay; it's probably just a touch of flu. I'll be fine in the morning." He's too polite to tell them it feels like indigestion, that gassy feeling, tightness in the chest, the heartburn. When he gets back to the motel he tells the manager. "Don't wake me up too early, I just want to sleep."

It's getting late, but Sara decides to set up the marionette theater anyway. She unfolds the royal blue proscenium, a little tottery, split in places, but bright and clean-looking in its new coat of paint, attaches the wooden brackets that prop it up. The hardware is old, the brackets are slightly crooked, a little warped, and the separating hinges her father put on are rusty. But she sprays them with lubricating oil, and after a little pressure, they go together and the front stands by itself.

. . . the rattling of the stretcher, his face gray and sweating, "Save my room, I'll be back tomorrow," coming in gasps, because his chest is tight and he can't quite get his breath. "Sure, Jim, don't worry, we won't rent your room. You just take care. . . ."

She fits the new floor over the tops of the brackets, has to jiggle it a little because the old wood has shrunk unevenly, doesn't quite match the new. But at last the floor settles down level with a satisfying clunk. She opens the two small wooden step stools she bought at the local hardware store, surprised that they were still made, and places them several feet apart behind the floor. The old bridge her father made out of leftover oak floorboards from the house in Toledo fits right down over the tops of the step stools, just the way it used to. She steps up on the bridge, affixes the railing she has made to hold the backdrop, the back railing with hooks to hold the marionettes. The bridge feels as sturdy as ever under her feet.

. . . the heart monitor bleeps and jumps a jagged line, the IVs dangle from rods on either side. The respirator hisses oxygen into the tent, the nurse reaches inside, pumps up the blood pressure cuff, tucks the stethoscope head into the crook of his arm. "Doctor!" she calls. The white-coated man comes running . . .

She bolts on the extensions, threads the curtains on the rods, and puts them up, red velvet curtains she found at a garage sale just last week, the same red-wine color as the old ones. But not quite enough to cover the front; she has had to fill in with another kind and color of material. But it looks just fine.

. . . the oxygen hisses, then stops; the nurse has turned it off at the valve. The heart monitor hums a steady tune, the line is flat. That too is switched off, with one last blip, meaning nothing except the interruption of the current. They pull the sheet up over his head. "I'll call his wife," the doctor says. It's four-thirty in the morning, in a hospital in Michigan, far away from home.

She puts the draw curtains up on their brackets across the proscenium, swishes them open and closed a few times. They work smoothly, better than the old ones.

169

Was he lonely? Did he know? Did he really think he would be back tomorrow?

She takes out a string of Christmas lights. Though these are new they are just like the ones she had before, not really satisfactory then or now, but all right for the time being. She strings the lights across the inside of the stage, the way they used to be, plugs them in. She goes around front and stands back, looking at the stage with curtains, all lit up. It looks just the way it always did; magic. Sara smiles.

The phone rings.

She runs inside, picks up the receiver. And it's Phil.

"Where are you?"

"I'm still at the hospital. But I'm planning to catch the early flight out of Detroit tomorrow, so I'll be home by noon."

"Good. See you then." She tries to picture him, standing in a corridor of the hospital in Michigan, holding the phone at his end of the line. But she has never been there, and she can't. The open line hums. "So."

"So."

"What's up?"

"All the news is in."

"And?"

"There won't be another operation. It was Christmas in July out here. I lit up all over. It's in my bones."

Sara shuts her eyes. This is even worse than she expected. Who would have thought the chance of just one tumor and another operation would be the *good* news? The line stretches taut with grief.

Phil clears his throat. "But it's not the end, at least not yet," he says, his voice a little stronger. "I'll tell you more when I get home, okay? I love you." There is a rustling sound. Before she can get any words out, she hears the abrupt clunk of the phone being hung up.

Sara stands in the kitchen holding the phone, staring blankly at the receiver. Suddenly her chest feels tight; she can't seem to get her breath. Jamming the receiver down, she yanks open the back door and hurries outside. She stands in front of the garage under the light, breathing deeply in the still-warm summer air. A swarm of insects gathers around her head, swirls around her, into her eyes, her nose, whining in her ears. As she swats them away, she hears the hum of bat wings, looks up to see them flitting overhead in their peculiar zigzag flight.

Stepping out of the ring of light, she starts to run, slowly at first. She jogs by the decrepit side porch, past the weed-covered turnaround, and starts down the driveway, going faster now: past the half-split, tumbled-over woodpile, down the line of huge over-grown trees, past the ribbed grass-piles mouldering on the lawn; runs as far and as fast as she can, away from the big old run-down, vermin-infested house, the woodpile, the lawn, the leaves that seem already to be falling in her path. As she runs she feels the air stirring an unfamiliar bareness around her finger. Her wedding ring is not there. In a flash she sees it resting on the counter next to the basket full of junk, knows with the bitter certainty of an irony long-practiced that it has gone, by mistake but just as irrevocably, with everything else to the dump.

She stops, gasping for breath, at the head of the long driveway where it meets the road. She stands by the road and thinks of winter, the snow falling deep and covering the road, the plow throwing up the snow like surf, curling along the shoulder in waves that block the driveway, freezing in the bitter air. Shivering now, she turns back toward the big old house. Its lighted windows cast pale oblongs across the lawn, making the summer grass look bleached and stiff with frost. Behind the house the faded summer trees rise up as frail as wood-smoke, beyond the ragged trees the random stars, the dark.

PART
3

7

The Long Haul

Lying awake in his hospital room, Phil can see the flicker of colored lights from the Christmas tree at the far end of the long hall. On off, on off, no sound, just blink, blink, blink. The nurses turned them on when they came in for the 7 A.M. shift, and now they are flashing away, throwing reflections of red and green and blue along the dimly lit corridor walls. The colors are pretty washed out by the time they get all the way down to Phil's door, but the rhythm is soothing, and Phil can feel himself starting to nod off.

Though it's past eight in the morning, it's still pitch dark outside. Even after almost a week here this continues to amaze Phil, who's used to the sun rising much earlier, before everything else gets going, the way it does back home. That's his idea of the crack of dawn; whoever heard of watching the sun come up during your coffee break? Around here people spend hours bustling around in the dark, heading off to work in cars and buses with the lights on, streetlamps lit as though it were the middle of the night. He knows it has something to do with time zones, home all the way at one end where the sun rises at a reasonable hour, while here in Michigan, a thousand miles the other way, it's just getting light by midmorning. Still, he can't get used to seeing stars out the window while he's supposed to be eating breakfast.

Not that it really matters; he's been awake most of the night, as usual. He's been having trouble sleeping ever since he got here. Usually he's been drifting off in the early morning, just in time for them to come and get him for yet another test, CAT scan, more MIBG scans, assorted chest X-rays. Then there's urine to be collected, blood to be drawn, temperature, blood pressure, the works; they really keep you busy around here. The bone marrow tap was the worst; he can still feel the grinding pressure in the small of his back over his right hipbone. "I've never seen anyone tolerate one of these so well," Medina said while he was drilling away. Big deal. He'd just as soon not think about that, but the place where they punctured him still aches as though someone pounded on it with a hammer.

This morning there are no tests scheduled; presumably they've found out everything they need to know, so he could go back to sleep if he wanted to. But even though he's drowsy, he wants to stay awake, in case the doctor decides to cruise by early with the report. Phil hopes so. Even though he knows the news isn't good, he'd like to get it over with so he can pack up and go home, salvage what he can of Christmas.

When the call comes for him at the office, Phil knows right away there's something wrong. "Dr. Nevins is on the phone," the message from the departmental secretary reads. "Needs to talk to you as soon as possible." It's been a little over a week since he sent the urine specimen to Boston, time enough for them to run the tests, and Nevins is not one to call up just to chat. He excuses himself from the appointments committee meeting and takes the call in his office. Nevins's reedy voice comes over the line. "I'm sorry to have to tell you this, Mr. Boyd, but your tests are off." Nevins's voice seems to shrink inside the telephone, then expand; Phil imagines his long, somber face with its pallid complexion growing larger and smaller, larger and smaller. He feels a little dizzy, the first time this has happened since his episode in the boat over a month ago.

"The values show a significant increase in your catecholamine levels, which may indicate new tumor growth," Nevins is saying. "I think we'd better schedule some more tests. How soon can you get down here?"

When he's finished talking to Nevins, he comes back in and sits down. A few of his colleagues look up at him curiously, then go back to discussing dossiers for the as-yet-unhired sabbatical replacement. They should probably be replacing him. He tries to pay attention to the discussion, but as he looks out the window at the trees swaying slightly in the summer breeze, the leaves take on a peculiar sharpness of outline and color, the voices and the room seem to fade far away, and he feels himself, once again, afloat.

"Good morning, Mr. Boyd," his nurse Carol says brightly as she squeaks in on her rubber-soled shoes, stethoscope draped around her neck like one of those fancy fox-biting-its-tail fur scarves his grandmother used to wear. There is nothing warm or furry about the stethoscope. "I just want to get a pressure on you one more time."

She pulls the blood pressure cuff out from the wall and wraps it around his arm, sticks the stethoscope prongs in her ears and presses the cold disc against the inside of his elbow. Phil closes his eyes and tries to will his blood pressure to be lower; it's been sky-high ever since he got here, much higher than it is at home when Sara takes it. This has gotten Matsu, the Korean resident in charge of his case, all worked up so that he keeps increasing the medication trying to get it under control. Phil's tried to tell him this always happens when he's in the hospital, but the guy is obsessed with the problem and won't let it alone. Oh well, he probably regards it as something he can fix, unlike the rest of Phil's problems, or else he's scared to death that Phil will have a stroke and die on him, which will mess up the research program. Phil wonders what it's like for the residents who wind up here in the Clinical Research Unit, fresh out of medical school thinking they know everything— two whole corridors full of diseases no one's ever heard of, much less knows what to do about. But they try, he's got to give them that. They try.

The air sighs out of the bulb with a faint "phew." Phil opens his eyes and watches Carol as she loosens the cuff but leaves it on his arm. She's frowning slightly. Phil's heart sinks; it must still be high. "So what is it?" he asks, even though he knows she's been instructed not to tell him. Matsu thinks it gets him too upset.

"A little lower," Carol answers in a noncommittal voice. That leaves her a lot of leeway, since it's been running 200 over 120 and up. If it were really much lower, she'd tell him in a second, in spite of the orders. All the nurses on this unit are so nice, kind and thoughtful without being disgustingly cheerful; they know the patients have enough to worry about without a lot of hospital rigmarole to deal with. She looks at him and smiles. "One-sixty over one hundred. Not bad, huh? Must be because you're going home. Okay, you can stand up now."

It sounds pretty high to Phil. Obediently he swings his legs over, stands up carefully, waits quietly by the bed for a few moments. One of the symptoms of his disease is that the blood pressure is always higher lying down, and tends to drop precipitously when you stand up. You can even pass right out, the way he did that day on the boat. So they've been taking his blood pressure both ways ever since he got here. He and Sara only do it sitting down. Maybe that's why it has always been so much lower at home.

Or maybe it's really gaining on him now, the cancer out of control spreading all over his insides. He feels himself breaking out in a cold sweat inside his hospital pajamas. The ones he brought with him got blood on them from the bone marrow; he tried to wash the blood out himself so Sara wouldn't get too upset when she saw it, but they weren't dry last night, so the night nurse brought him clean ones. He hates hospital pajamas, though as things go these flannel ones aren't too bad, but Brooks Brothers they are not. He supposes he'll have to get some new pajamas now that he's going to be in and out of hospitals again. He hates to waste the money; he doesn't like to buy new clothes he'll never have a chance to wear out. This drives Sara nuts, so she goes out and buys things for him, new underwear, pajamas, shirts, sweaters. He makes her take most of the stuff back, but not the pajamas. Those he'll probably get to use up.

Carol removes the cuff and folds it back against the wall. "About the same. The blood pressure medication must be working," she says. "All done. You can go for your walk now if you want."

Phil sits back down on the bed and contemplates his running shoes, neatly lined up with his loafers underneath the nightstand. Because his blood pressure has been so high they won't allow him outside anymore, but one of the things he's been doing to keep himself in shape is taking long walks through the hospital corridors. This also helps the swelling in his legs, which has been bothering him on and off ever since the big cruise with Gus in June. All this time he'd been getting worse, only they hadn't realized it, because the false test results of his September urine sample made them all think everything was the same. Oh well, they had almost five months after his trip here in July when they found out that the tumor had metastasized, thinking nothing had changed since then, even if it was all an illusion.

It is a disappointment not to be able to get outside and run; when he was here six months ago, in July, he brought his gear and flabbergasted the intern who came to do the admitting exam by asking him to come back later because it was time for him to go running. Of course he had no real symptoms then other than the slight edema, not even any firm evidence of tumor growth from the CAT scans they did in Boston, just the lab reports showing his urine test results were now considerably above the range of normal. He can still hear Nevins's reedy, nasal voice on the phone. "Something has changed, Mr. Boyd, and we've got to find out why." Then he came here and found out the real story, and it's been downhill ever since. He has trouble running now, even though the swelling hasn't gotten any worse, can't even walk very far without getting bad cramps in his legs. He also gets short of breath. But he has kept on going, finished the first semester of teaching at any rate, and here he is.

He gets up, stretches his stiff leg muscles, and walks to the doorway. None of this bears much looking into. Instead he looks up and down the hall. At one end is the Christmas tree, blinking away, at the other end the nurses' station. There is a standing joke among the nurses and Phil about the layout of the unit. Phil's room is on the long hall; on the other side of the nurses' station is the short hall. When he came in July, they asked him if he preferred the long hall or the short hall, and Phil broke up. Now it's not so funny anymore. "Good for the long haul," was the word then. That too has changed.

Anyway, there's no time for a walk now; Dr. Bierstadt will be coming by with the latest, and, Phil hopes, his discharge papers. Right now all he wants to do is get home and help Sara do Christmas, such as it is. He crosses back over to his bed and lies back down.

He and Sara are sitting in one of the examining rooms at the Clinic in Boston. Sara is watching Nevins, and Phil is watching Sara. That was the hardest part, after the phone call, telling Sara. He put it off all afternoon, staying later than usual at the office. When he came home dinner was in the oven, the kids were off somewhere and she was in bed reading; she hadn't been feeling well, another one of the colds she seems to get every summer. "Hi," she said, glancing up at him curiously. "Where've you been?"

She looked so girlish, with her round rosy cheeks and curly hair, so innocent and unsuspecting that for a moment he couldn't even speak, just sat down on the edge of the bed and put a hand on the covers over her legs. And that was it, of course. She knew. She had gone very still, her face expressionless, laid the book face down, still watching him, and said: "What's wrong?"

He still doesn't know why he thought the news would finally do her in, maybe because she has always been so hopeful, the optimist, the stubborn one who had always insisted, even that time four years ago in September when Sam told them it was hopeless and there was nothing to be done, on exploring every avenue, refusing to give up. He wasn't about to give up either, but for him it was more a matter of hanging on, enduring what he had to right there where he was, not looking around for somewhere else to go. Maybe it was because she had tried so hard, not just with him, but all her life practically, that he feels he has really failed her; three times and out. How she had clung to that word "benign," looking forward to the five-year anniversary and his being declared cured. One more year and counting. So much for that illusion.

But she had hardly missed a beat, didn't cry or even blink; it was as though she'd been expecting it all along. She made arrangements the next day for the kids to stay with friends, asked their neighbor Punch to feed the animals so they could drive to Boston right away, and as she put it, "get this sorted out."

So here they are, several blood tests, one three-hour CAT scan, one chest X-ray, two bone scans and a lung and liver scan later, and nothing is sorted out. On the contrary, it's more of a puzzle than ever. Not only that, there has been one fuckup after another, and they've spent the whole day running from place to place, getting more and more exasperated. First the lung tomograph wouldn't work, and then the Clinic's scanner broke down right around Phil's belly button, and they had to start the whole thing over. Nevins sent them to the big hospital across the street for the lung tomos, but after they waited around for two hours and collected yet another little plastic patient ID card, the resident radiologist sent them back, officiously pronouncing that the cost-benefit ratio didn't justify doing this test at this time.

Nevins was embarrassed and apologetic, even a little flustered, regarding this as rude and unprofessional behavior. Not only that, all but one of the Clinic's nuclear medicine guys are off at a convention, and there's an incredible back-log on the readings. So Nevins went and read them himself.

All along Phil has been assuming—hoping even, weird as that seems—they'd find another big tumor right away, since that is what it was before. It would seem to to be the pattern, and means another a operation, but he can deal with that. After all, he got almost four years from the last one. But Nevins is sitting there shaking his head, tapping his fingernail on Phil's folder, looking more like an undertaker than ever. If there is another big tumor, they haven't found it. Nevins is now thinking in terms of several little ones, which has always been a possibility, even with a benign condition. They know from reading the articles Sara's sister Fran keeps sending them that Phil's kind of tumor, even when benign, can occur in multiples, in one recorded case as many as eleven. Sara is still holding out for the designation of benign, though at this point, Phil can't see that it makes much difference; it all sounds pretty academic to him. He doesn't think anybody's going to go chasing all over his insides after a whole bunch of little tumors; they might not even operate on one if it's in the wrong place. He also doesn't think Nevins is buying benign anymore, if he ever did. In the pessimist sweepstakes, Nevins leaves Phil standing in the gate.

"Of course there is that spot on your rib," Nevins remarks, and he and Sara begin discussing once more the issue of the spot discovered during the work-up before the second operation, the spot Owen Hughes badgered the radiologists so persistently about that finally he got them to declare once and for all it was a benign cyst, so Ristine could go ahead and operate and "get it all." That was Owen's little miracle. Now Nevins wants to biopsy it, and maybe one of those mysterious pea-sized nodules in his lungs (which have been there right along on the so-called normal CAT scans, but which nobody has seen fit to mention before), as well. I'm just full of surprises, Phil thinks, as he leans back in his chair, crosses his legs, and stares up at the ceiling. The voices murmur on, the ventilator fan drones in the background.

He's practically in a trance, trying to keep himself from thinking about another operation, when he hears the voices rise slightly. Sara is asking Nevins about the new test for locating this kind of tumor they've been developing at the hospital in Michigan, as described in one of those incomprehensible articles Fran has sent her. The tumors take up whatever special sauce they use, and light up on the screen like fluorescent popcorn.

Nevins is shaking his head again, trying to keep a straight face, his eyelids fluttering with skepticism, either about the procedure itself, or at the idea of a layperson poring over technical articles and then presuming to discuss them with an expert. But he doesn't know Sara; once she gets ahold of something she never quits and she doesn't get embarrassed about telling people their own business. "Just checking," she said to Owen when he told her to stop looking things up in the medical books at the Coop next door and just let him worry about Phil's case. "You can't be too careful. After all, somebody's got to keep you guys honest." Phil almost died of embarrassment, but Owen just laughed, while Sara hit him with another question without even stopping for breath. She used to drive Sam crazy with all her questions. But he's got to hand it to her; when there weren't enough good answers they took it on the road, and here he is, alive to tell the tale. For now.

Phil watches the two of them with interest; he can almost predict what's going to happen next. Nevins sits back and laces his hands over one knee, clears his throat, about to pronounce. "I think that whatever can be done can be done here," he says.

Phil can hardly believe his ears. He represses a guffaw as Sara's face flushes crimson, her lips tighten and her jaw sets, Sam's old familiar words like a red flag in front of a raging bull. He feels sorry for Nevins.

Sara reaches into one side of the huge pocketbook she uses as a portable filing cabinet and hauls out the article she's been talking about, places it carefully on her knees where Nevins can see the Magic Marker underlinings, the fuzzy stars and question marks and comments squiggled in the margins. "Dr. Nevins, how many cases of this kind of tumor have you treated?" she asks quietly.

Nevins rolls his eyes back, contemplates the air duct overhead. "I believe we have had—all told—um, eight cases here at the Center."

"How many have *you* treated?" Sara repeats.

Nevins looks at Phil, then at her. "One," he says finally, and inclines his head toward Phil. "He's it."

I'm it all right, Phil thinks, while Sara taps a finger on the Xeroxed article. "They've had over eighty at the University of Michigan, the largest group so far in the literature, even more than the NIH study. With their test they can find these tumors whether they're little or big, one or several. They can do it without an operation requiring general anesthesia . . ."

"So they say," Nevins interjects mildly, with a faintly pleading look at Phil.

Sara ignores him, barrels right on. ". . . so let's just stop pussy-footing around. We know Phil has to have another tumor some-where or his catecholamines wouldn't be elevated, but you can't find it with the tests *you* have available. Their test is specific for pheos and it's noninvasive, so what have we got to lose? Either they'll find just one tumor in a place that can be operated on, or else it'll be Christmas in July out there. Either way, we'll know what's going on and what to do next."

Nevins's face pales considerably, a condition Phil would not have thought possible, since his usual complexion is parchment gray. Phil is not sure whether this is because of Sara's challenge, or the seeming callousness of her remark about his lighting up like a Christmas tree. He feels a little pale about that himself, because if that's the case, he doesn't believe there's anything that *can* be done. It's the ball game.

Still, he's got to hand it to her, remembering all this stuff, keeping it in her head all this time. He feels sorry that he's left her holding the bag, carrying on the argument to do something while he just sits there. But he's so tired.

It doesn't really matter, because Nevins in effect rolls over and sticks all four feet up in the air. "I don't see any problem there, if that's what you want to do," he says, looking inquiringly at Phil. Phil nods, even though he's not really sure he wants to know. Yet there is still the hope of just one tumor, another operation, if not a cure, then at least a few more years. He'd rather have an operation and get it over with than do radiation, or worse, chemotherapy. That is the worst nightmare of all.

"That's it, then," Nevins says in a voice that sounds almost cheerful, in marked contrast to his usual measured, sepulchral tones. "I'll call them in the morning to make the arrangements and let you know as soon as possible." Probably glad to be getting rid of us, Phil thinks. Nevins stands up, smiles, shakes both their hands, and shuffles out of the room.

"Don't you think you were a little hard on the old Grim Reaper there?" Phil says to Sara on the drive home. He's still chuckling over the whole incident, probably an inappropriate reaction, given the circumstances, but who's to say?

"I'll write him a note," Sara says. "After all, even if he is a jerk, at least he tried."

Lying in his bed, Phil can feel a rush starting. The top of his head begins to prickle, his fingers and toes tingle and go cold, and his heart begins to pound. He tries to keep his breathing steady, but the pounding of his heart is so rapid and strong he can't get his breath; he feels as though his heart is going to leap right out of his chest. Oh, God, don't let me die right here, he thinks. He squeezes his eyes shut and tries to take slow if shallow breaths, feeling the beads of sweat roll down his forehead, the sides of his nose, along his temples where the pulse throbs painfully, finally trickle into his beard. This is a fairly recent symptom, just since earlier this summer, what they call a spike, the sudden sharp rise in blood pressure caused by the release of adrenalin from the tumor, resulting in an exaggerated fight-or-flight response. He understands this all, but it really doesn't help; when it happens it still scares the shit out of him. It's the most frightening symptom he has right now, and the most dangerous. Since they upped his medication he's had fewer of these, and Dr. Bierstadt says that as long as they can keep his regular blood pressure under control the spikes aren't really that dangerous. He wonders what will happen when they can no longer control his regular blood pressure.

He can feel his heart slowing now, the numbness in his extremities replaced by the tingling sensation of capillaries opening up. The hair lies back down on his head, and the throbbing stops; he can feel the color coming back into his face. The flight is over. He wipes his face with a corner of the sheet and shuts his eyes, wishing Bierstadt would come.

"Pleased to meet you, Professor Boyd," the doctor says in his cultivated, not-quite-British accent. "I'm Ephraim Bierstadt. Do come in." He is a big man, about Phil's age or a little older, with brown eyes, a Colonel Blimp mustache, and a belly over which his rumpled shirt—it's late July and too hot for the white lab coats—strains its buttons, failing to prevent a small triangle of pale flesh from being exposed just above his belt buckle. He looks so much like Popeye's old friend Wimpy that when Phil hears a rustling in the hall, he turns his head expecting it to be the button-eating chicken, but it's only the mail robot running by on its little track. It stops outside Bierstadt's office door, hums expectantly.

"Oh, bother," Bierstadt groans and waves a dismissive hand.

"Come back later, will you?" To Phil's amazement the robot scoots off. He has come to the right place; this is clearly a hotbed of technology. "Now, Dr. Boyd, let me explain what we are going to do."

There are a number of doctors on the team conducting research into the nature of his disease—endocrinologists, radiologists, on-cologists, neurologists. Bierstadt himself is a specialist in nuclear medicine and endocrinology, and an associate professor in the School of Medicine, Rhodesian by birth, an odd series of degrees after his name, only one of which is M.D. He insists on calling Phil "Dr. Boyd" in deference to his advanced degree and position as a full professor, much to the confusion of the nurses, who assumed for a while Phil was also a physician. He is one of the few doctors Phil has encountered who treats him like an equal instead of a mere patient, or worse, a nuisance. There are advan-tages in being a research project.

Now the tests are finished, the four-day series of X-rays com-pleted, and all the news is in. The mystery is solved.

"There are four areas of uptake on the scintigrams," Bierstadt tells Phil. They are in the viewing room, and Phil's X-rays are ranged along the lighted wall. They are not as large as he thought they would be, not much bigger than a sheet of construction paper, but there are a lot of them. They all look as though they've been taken underwater. The front view shows a faint transparent image grayish-white against the light, like a Halloween skeleton in a dark aquarium; in the side view, ribs and spine resemble a sea horse floating in murk. Bierstadt points to four small round clutches of pale luminescent pearls, here, here, there and here. As Phil stares past Bierstadt's finger, the skeleton begins to gyrate in an eerie dance; the sea horse undulates its version of a swim. Phil shuts his eyes for a moment. That only makes it worse.

"It is not immediately clear in what organs these tumors are located," Bierstadt is saying, "but by a system of measurement and comparison with your other studies, we have concluded"—here he puts up the bone scan series, more bits of skeletons, more sea horses, lumps and spurs of coral, a wrecked ship—"that these correspond to a disease process here in the right iliac crest," he points to a black spot on the little dancing skeleton's flared hip bone; "the eighth thoracic vertebra just here," a finger tracing a garland of coral to mid-spine, one segment a lump of coal among the rest; "the adjacent seventh rib . . ." a tusk of bleached white ivory with one end smudged.

No shit, Phil thinks with interest; so it's that old rib spot after all. So much for miracles. He sways a little on his feet, leans forward and puts his hands on the shelf in front of him. Four places. Four tumors in four places. Bone, bone, and bone.

"That means it's malignant, isn't it?"

"I'm afraid so, yes," says Bierstadt. "This indicates a metastatic condition."

Without warning Phil has a sudden vision of himself sailing, feels for a moment as if he were actually in the *Loon*, rocking over the waves. That's where he'd be right now if he weren't here, the only place he ever really wants to be. But all that is over now, no more summers with the boat. "I guess I'll have to sell the boat," he murmurs without thinking.

Bierstadt blinks. No wonder; it's a pretty strange thing to say. Phil doesn't even know why he said it. He feels a surge of guilt; what he really should be worrying about is how to break the news to Sara. He hasn't called all week, since they started the series, partly because they didn't find anything at first and he didn't want to raise false hopes. Good thing, too. Mentally he tries out the words. Malignant. Metastatic. Cancer. He wonders if he can bring himself to call now, hear her voice on the phone, hopeful, expectant, eager, hear his own voice telling her this, the worst news of all.

Bierstadt reaches over, turns on the overhead lights and helps Phil to a chair, lowers himself into one next to him. "I'm sorry to be the bearer of such bad tidings, Dr. Boyd," he says gently in his quiet, cultivated voice. He leans back and folds his hands over his straining buttons. "I know this is a disappointment, but things may not be quite so disastrous as they appear."

Oh, sure, now for the good news. Phil looks at the kindly, intellectual face, the brown eyes behind heavy horn-rimmed glasses, fleshy hands clasped over the big belly, one foot casually crossed over a knee. "That's only three," he says. "Where's the fourth? My wife will want to know."

As it turns out, they aren't too sure about the fourth, probably nothing to worry about, a small, soft tissue tumor, possibly a lymph node somewhere at the midline. After an hour or so, Bierstadt has convinced him it isn't the end of the world, Phil listening at first mostly so he will have something to tell Sara, some lifeline to toss her, even if he has none himself. "Mainly slow-growing, indolent tumors, these pheochromocytomas"—he'll have to learn to pronounce it now, roll it trippingly off the tongue—". . . can't tell how long these have been present, but we know the rib lesion has been there at least four years with no visible change, according to the Clinic scans back in Boston, which is encouraging." Compared to what? Phil wonders. The tumors are not large, and not at the moment life-threatening. As long as they can keep his blood pressure under control—"And you have a lot of leeway there, you're taking comparatively little medication at the moment"— he could go on for a long time. Why, they have been following one man, a short-order cook in a diner in Detroit, "bones like Swiss cheese, mets all over, still going strong," for lo these twenty years.

When Phil presses him about survival time, Bierstadt admits reluctantly that the average is four and one-half years from the time a patient is first seen here. There are a few who, for some as-yet-unexplained reason, go fast. Many live longer. He walks Phil back to his room, and as he is leaving, looks Phil up and down. "Of course this has no medical validity," he says, "but I have observed many cases, and my sense of things is that you are one who is good for the long haul." He smiles and shakes Phil's hand. "There will be more summers. Please don't sell the boat."

He hasn't sold the boat, at least not yet. But here he is, back again after just six months, not even one more summer, most of that time spent under the illusion that nothing was changed, while all the time the disease was filling up his insides as though he were one of those popcorn machines in the old movie theaters. He had faithfully sent a urine specimen via the local hospital to the lab in

Boston. They all breathed a sigh of relief when the report came back saying the levels were just about the same.

Exactly the same, they had discovered early in December, when his blood pressure skyrocketed and his symptoms—swelling, leg cramps, headache, shortness of breath—got even worse, because they *were* the same. The lab had either never received or had lost the September sample, and had sent copies of the June results. No one had noticed they were identical. The December test results were right off the fucking scale.

Oh well, at least he'd made it through the semester. But it wasn't easy; he knew all along there was something badly wrong with him. So much for Bierstadt's sense of things. He is obviously one of the few who go fast. The only long haul I'm good for, he thinks, is the one I'm on right now, the one with the Christmas tree blinking away at the end of it. "We're down to the short haul," he says to himself, trying out the sound of it.

Long hall, short hall; he thinks he likes the literal version better. Listening for footsteps, trying to distinguish nurses' soft-soled whispers from the brisker sound of doctors, he thinks of all the time he's spent in hospital rooms, waiting for doctors to show up with the latest report. Good news, bad news; it hardly seems to make much difference anymore. He's beginning to think that none of this is real.

He closes his eyes, and the faces appear, ranged in one long ethereal line like ghosts at the banquet in *Macbeth*, each with their own version of reality: Crane the surgeon, like a great goggling bird, standing at the foot of his bed in ICU after that first bloody operation seven years ago, when he was still practically hemorrhaging to death; "I'm willing to bet that it's benign"; Sam with his dire predictions, his over-sympathetic identification with Phil culminating in his quasi-suicidal "If I were you I would do nothing." Owen was always his favorite, with his cheerful cynicism, his skeptic's temperament, busily choreographing the new diagnosis. "Renal cell carcinoma? You must be kidding. Don't know where they got that idea, that's *really* out in left field!" Then the second operation, the miracle of a cure, or rather the illusion of a cure: Owen's assurance, "This rib spot is going to turn out to be nothing"; and cool Ristine, "We got it all. Everything went fine; it was just long."

They hadn't gotten it all, and now he wonders if that's just something surgeons say as a matter of course. He suspects that Owen, now out of the medical profession entirely and enrolled in law school in California, knew the odds all along. But it was a good ride. Until Owen left and he inherited Nevins, the Grim Reaper, who seemed to know all the time that it would somehow come to this.

Still, always the need for certainty, for belief, the assurance of the designation "cure" that someday it would be over, while all the time the terms of reality keep being revised. So when the blood pressure went back up, that was nothing too, a residual effect, as long as the urine tests stayed normal. Oh, sure, there was this and that on the odd CAT scan, but "who knows what normal looks like in you?" All those scans declared just fine, up and over, almost done, two years, three years, four, the benchmark five coming up; then the urine tests up above normal (but they were drifting up all the time, you see) and now they look back and see stuff everywhere. Then more doctors, new tests, okay it's metastatic, malignant, but not that bad, slow-growing, many years ahead. Up and down, like the waves, but with smaller and smaller increments of belief.

Now there is no more romance of illusion. Lying in his bed, eyes closed, listening for footsteps, waiting for the latest report, Phil suddenly feels all at sea, clinging like a shipwrecked sailor to the pathetic flotsam of hope, too flimsy now to bear his weight. He is tempted to let go and just go under.

Lying there, he wonders if any of it is real, or if it's all a dream. Suppose I never woke up from that first operation, he thinks. That's it; I've been in a coma ever since, dreaming this bad dream. None of this is real.

He tries this concept out for a minute or two, to see if it makes things any easier to deal with. It doesn't. Any way you look at it, awake or asleep, it's still a nightmare.

Male voices rumble, heels click down the long hall toward his door. He sits up as Bierstadt comes into the room with Medina in tow. If Bierstadt resembles Wimpy, white coat open and flapping, both his tie and his moustache askew, then Medina, with his upright, military bearing and clean-shaven face, tie carefully tucked in above the knife-pressed lapels of his buttoned-right-up white coat, is the Steadfast Tin Soldier. He is also the Unit's head chemotherapist, an expert in last-ditch, experimental protocols. He is a hard, no-nonsense man, brisk and unsentimental sometimes to the point of seeming cruel, but Phil respects him for this. At least with Medina you always know where you stand. Today, as always, he does not mince words.

"Well, I'm sorry, Mr. Boyd," he says in his flat, midwestern voice, as clipped and controlled and tucked in as the rest of him. "You've failed to qualify for the experimental radiation therapy; your tumors don't take up enough isotope to make it worthwhile."

Phil feels suddenly sick, tremulous; though not unexpected, this is a blow. Even when all hope seems to be gone, when he thinks he has disciplined himself to cling no more, another piece of the wreck pops up, only to slip from his grasp. While he stares at them, his mind gibbering *now what now what now what?* the doctors pull up chairs. The two of them sit down in unison as though rehearsed, one big and round and rumpled, one short, wiry, and dapper. For a moment they remind Phil of Laurel and Hardy. But they aren't telling jokes.

"I think we must consider the options," Bierstadt says in his careful, measured voice, so oddly soft and small for such a large man. Just the tone of it takes the edge off of Phil's agitation; he blinks several times to clear his vision. Of all the doctors he has known only Bierstadt seems to be able to hold the balance between sympathy and detachment. Owen was the best, but he burnt out early, left the profession. Phil wonders what he would think of all this. "We could do nothing," Bierstadt continues, "and conceivably you could go on for years, as long as your blood pressure remains under control, and a tumor doesn't come up in a vital spot. By the way, your worst symptoms now are caused by either tumor or clot in your vena cava, but that situation may begin to resolve somewhat as collateral circulation develops around it. The body has many ways of coping with disaster. You are still in remarkably strong condition, Dr. Boyd."

For a dying man, Phil adds silently. But there is still another country to be heard from. He looks at Medina, who's sitting there with his arms folded and one leg crossed over the other. The crease on his pants leg sticks out from under the hem of his white coat as sharp as a machete. He is clearly the bad-news bear.

Medina clears his throat, but his voice is still rusty when he speaks. "Frankly, the amount of tumor you have is terrifying," he says bluntly.

Phil looks at Bierstadt. Somehow bad news never sounds quite as bad when he tells it. This time it does. Bierstadt's eyelids flutter slightly as he looks down at his toes. "It seems your disease is rapidly extending."

Even though Phil has known this all along, it's another thing to hear it said flat-out by someone else. Two someones. His mouth goes dry, and he feels himself pulled upward and away, all the voices, the sounds, the blinking of the colored lights faint and distant. With an effort he draws himself back, trying to pay attention. His scalp starts to prickle. Oh, shit, he thinks, not again.

The upshot of it all, Phil gathers as he tries to listen and ride out his rush at the same time, is that they, particularly Medina, are not especially keen on doing nothing. They want to try something else. "There is no cure for your disease," Medina points out—so what else is new?—"but there are still things we can do."

"Ah, yes," says Bierstadt cheerfully. "We've lots more up our sleeve." He begins to talk about local radiation, mainly for reduction of bone pain. This has minimal side effects; it will not make him sick or bald. Such a treatment is palliative; it will make him more comfortable, enhance the quality of life perhaps, but not the quantity. He will in all probability not live any longer than he would otherwise.

"Over the long haul," Medina adds, "it probably won't make much difference."

Phil shuts his eyes. He does not have bone pain, at least not that he knows of. The voices buzz on around his head. There is another treatment they have been experimenting with, a new protocol that combines a number of different chemotherapeutic agents. They are trying it on one other person; if Phil will agree, they want to try it on him too. "With this treatment," Medina explains, "there is a chance we could prolong your life somewhat. You might get one good year, maybe more. We just don't know. But the side effects may slow you down considerably."

Phil, still feeling remote, detached, can hardly keep from laughing. He's heard this all before, in another context. "Distance at the expense of speed," he murmurs. "There you have it." He leans his head back against the pillow, trying to smother the deep, inappropriate welling up of mirth. A balance of conflicting forces. Sailing close-hauled means gaining distance to windward at the expense of speed. He opens his eyes.

Laurel and Hardy are staring at him with identical puzzled expressions on their dissimilar faces. Phil smiles. They continue to stare, less puzzled now, he sees, than expectant. It occurs to Phil that he is supposed to say something. "Well, that's it then," he remarks.

Both doctors smile, and continue to sit, waiting. Apparently just saying something isn't enough; they want more from him. Could it be they want him to decide? Right now? Speed or distance? Quality or quantity? It's all just too much, and his head is spinning, his heart still pounding. "I guess I'd like to think it over for a while," he says at last.

The two nod in unison, bobbing their heads wisely.

"Can I let you know in a week or so? After Christmas, maybe?" He doesn't know exactly what putting it off till after Christmas will gain, but it seems to be the right thing to do. After all, this will probably be his last Christmas; why not make it as nice as possible? Suddenly he feels the urge to get out of bed. He throws back the covers, swings his legs down into his slippers and stands up, feeling like an idiot in his baggy hospital pajamas. He wishes he had gotten dressed for this one.

Medina bounces out of his chair as though he were on springs, stretches out a hand and shakes Phil's briskly. "Fine," he says. "That's good. Just give me a call, and we'll set things up. We've already got the baseline bone marrow, so . . ." He hesitates, perhaps realizing that he's slightly jumped the gun. ". . . whatever you decide." Then one last—and for him uncharacteristically hedging—shot. "So far, the side effects don't seem to be too, *too* bad."

Baseline, Phil thinks, gulping down the laughter that still threatens to bubble up; why it's a whole new ball game. One, two, three strikes you're out . . .

Medina whirls toward the door, then turns back with a snap of his heels. "Oh, by the way, I signed your discharge papers, so you're all set. You can leave any time. Have a nice trip." Phil almost expects him to salute as he goes out the door; his own fingers twitch toward his eyebrow.

Bierstadt watches Medina march off, then turns to Phil. "Dr. Boyd, I think you are weathering this difficult and disappointing turn of events extremely well. If there's anything I can do, if you have any questions in the meantime, don't hesitate to call." He extends a soft, fleshy hand; there is a small card in it. "Here is my home phone number." The small kindness makes Phil want to cry.

After Bierstadt leaves, Phil sits down on the bed. Chemotherapy. He pictures himself, weak and bald and skinny, puking his brains out, looking like death even before the fact; his worst nightmare of all. I'm not going to do it, he thinks. I'd rather just die and get it over with. Then he puts on his clothes, packs his bags, and calls the airport limousine. When he stops at the desk to pick up his discharge papers, the nurse chirps, "Merry Christmas."

The ride east is rough and turbulent. The plane pitches up and down, sways back and forth, surrounded by air as opaque as cloth yet swirling constantly, as though they were suspended in a sling of smoke. The other passengers are blowing lunch into barf bags right and left, and he's not feeling too hot himself, but as always he resists the impulse to throw up. He considers the possibility that the plane will crash, perhaps a consummation devoutly to be wished, he thinks, if it weren't for the others. After all, there are worse ways of dying, and his is one of them. Like a plane with a bomb hidden inside, he is carrying his own death within him; it is his only real destination.

As the plane drones and lurches eastward, he wonders what Sara will say when he tells her that it's over. He'll have to say something about the experimental treatment, his decision not to do it, to go out, as Sam put it four years ago, "quick and dirty." No more of this long day's dying to augment our pain. Then of course she'll try to talk him into it; he can imagine what she's going to say. "Why, look how everything turns out for the best, if we'd known even a year ago, there would have been nothing we could do. Now there's this new therapy. Things are turning up all the time. Maybe in the meantime they'll even find a cure." Hoping, always hoping. Something will turn up. How can he make her understand that he has come, finally, to the end of all things?

Lulled by the motion of the plane, he shuts his eyes and tries to think of nothing, here at the end of all things.

It's a bright warm day in October, an Indian summer day, relatively calm, and a good thing too, because Sara has decided to come with him. It's the last sail of the season; they are taking the boat back up the river to the marina. There's just about enough wind to move the boat and no sea, just the way she likes it.

Sitting in the cockpit, the tiller just nudging his hand, he looks around at the islands, the low-lying shore fringing this part of the bay. The leaves have turned, the colors past their peak, and it occurs to him that it is four years almost to the day that he and Sara first sailed the *Loon* through this channel and out into the bay. Four years since the operation in Boston, since they "got it all." He is now going into his fifth year. Five years and you'll be home free. It is also five months since he passed out in the boat and this whole new phase started. If there had been no follow-up, no tests, there would have been no phone calls, no trips to Michigan, and by now he would have been considered cured. He wonders briefly if not knowing would somehow have altered the reality of what has happened, but he knows that isn't true. He would have gotten sick again just the same. It is his fate. Still, he wonders. "Do you think it would have made any difference?" he says aloud.

"What?"

"If we'd known earlier. If it would have changed things."

Sara shrugs, then looks off into the distance. "Probably not," she answers after a moment. "Knowing doesn't change things, except the way you feel about yourself. You're just the same outside; you look the same. Nobody knows how long you've had those bone mets, maybe for years. The rib spot was there four years ago and hasn't gotten any bigger. Bierstadt said you could go on for years. The test results haven't changed, not since June, anyway. It looks like the disease is at a standstill. Nothing has changed except the way you think about yourself. Who knows? If you ask me, it's all a head job."

He smiles, listening to her rattle on, lining up all the evidence on the bright side, as usual.

She shrugs again. "Anyway, even if we had known earlier, there wouldn't have been anything that we could do. That's all I ask," she adds. "Just to know that we've done everything we can."

The plane rocks so hard that Phil's head bumps the window, waking him out of his daze. He can hear her now. "We should do everything we can," he thinks. She'll argue, badger, cajole. What does she mean, "we"? It's all very well and good for her to talk about this in the abstract. Nobody's doing anything to *her*. He's the one who's doing all the suffering. "Right, and nobody does it better," he can imagine her saying, "but suffering clouds judgment. That's why I'm here, to provide an objective view." He wedges his coat between the window and his head, and shuts his eyes again.

She stares at the sunlight on the water, not at him; he knows she doesn't really want to talk about this. Lately they have talked less and less. She is probably thinking of a way to get the feeling of that glittering ephemeral light in one of her sculptures or paintings, not of him or his disease, or even sailing. She seems abstracted, as she is more and more these days, absent in spirit, if not in body. It reminds him of the way she was so long ago in graduate school, before they were married, before the kids came, before they had finally seemed happy together. Still, it is nice to have her here where he can look at her, believing that nothing has changed.

He, on the other hand, knows something has changed, even if the figures haven't. The swelling in his legs is not as bad as it was this summer, but there is now a heaviness about them, a constant aching, and he can trace blue veins knotting along the surface he doesn't remember seeing there before. Although he puts on his shorts and running shoes at the end of each day and hits the road, he does not run far; it's really all he can do to walk, much less chug up the hills at full speed the way he used to. He's short of breath a lot of time, and though he doesn't actually get dizzy and faint, he has been having these spells when his scalp prickles and his fingers tingle and his heart starts pounding, and his blood seems to be rushing through his body so furiously he can almost hear it. He simply doesn't feel the way he did. Autumn is closing in, it's the last sail of the season, and without warning his eyes fill with tears. He grips the tiller hard, until his knuckles pop, and concentrates on sailing.

The plane pitches up and down, almost as if it were breasting invisible breakers in the air. "Of course you could just simply walk away," he remembers Bierstadt telling him. "Many do. They leave here and we never see them again. It is their right, of course." Bierstadt sighed. "Still, I often wonder what's become of them, if there mightn't have been something more we could have done or learned."

So many variables, wind strength and direction, tide changes, rocks and shoals, so much to look out for, so much to learn. And then there are the matters of discretion, whether to sail closer to the wind to gain distance at the expense of speed, or lay off to gain the fastest point of sail. If he keeps his eyes shut, he can imagine he is sailing into the dark, breasting the waves one after another, either homeward, or away.

They sail all afternoon, out beyond the islands at the mouth of the inner bay, but never too far from their eventual destination. The wind is gentle, the sailing leisurely; he doesn't want to spoil this last time for Sara. Finally they chug up the river to the marina. As they are tying up at the dock, another boat pulls in, a big old wooden yawl with classic lines, the long stern counter, swept-up bow, teak brightwork gleaming, everything shipshape, a young man—well, their age maybe, but Phil still thinks of himself as young—at the helm. In khaki coveralls and wearing a captain's hat, clearly he's not the owner of the dream boat. Phil wonders who is. He hears voices from belowdecks, so he knows someone else is on board.

While he is stowing gear and breaking his boat down, unhanking the main, detaching the boom, Phil watches the other boat out of the corner of his eye, hoping to catch a glimpse of the owners. The hatch slides open and two of the oldest people he has ever seen come crawling up the companionway. They are both dressed in tattered wool pants, flannel shirts, down vests and windbreakers. One appears to be a woman, the other a man, but Phil is not sure how he knows this, certainly not from any difference in their clothes or hair, the configuration of their bodies. The old man is wearing what at first appears to be an ice bag on his head, which on closer inspection turns out to be a faded tam-o'-shanter. The woman puts on an equally ratty-looking scarf, ties it under her chin babushka-style.

Squabbling quietly between themselves, they stagger along the deck to the lifeline gate, and shakily disembark, the young man handing the old man a steel walker frame he opens like an umbrella, the old woman a cane. The bent-over old man snaps a crabby thank-you, and shuffles along the deck behind his walker. He looks up from under the brim of his tam and catches sight of Phil, flicks a two-fingered salute. "Not much doing out there today," Phil hears him mutter in disgust. The old woman mutters back, "That's your version. Shut up, you old coot." She takes his arm, and together they make their way up the gangplank toward shore.

As Phil watches them, suddenly he is seized with a sudden, sharp longing, and the tears fill his eyes again, blinding him for a moment. He sits down abruptly in the companionway, while his breath catches in the tightness of his throat, and the tears roll down his face.

"What's wrong? What is it?" Sara hops across the cockpit and tucks herself close to him, wiping the tears with her small fingers, the cuff of her flannel shirt. "Tell me."

He just shuts his eyes and shakes his head, the grief a hard inflexible lump inside his throat. Finally he's able to speak. "I just feel so bad," he says, not looking at her. Tears glisten on his lower eyelids like rows of cold glass beads. "It's been so short. I wanted more. I wanted to see the kids grow up. I wanted us to get old together."

"Shhhh," Sara says, stroking his face. "Don't say that. Why ruin this beautiful day? Beside, you'll see them grow up. We're going to get old together. I know it."

She knows it. Of course. And suddenly he's angry; this is just one more example of her evasion, her inability to accept reality, the cockeyed optimism that has no basis in the way things are, are going to be. What's she going to say next? You'll be here? Just because it worked before doesn't mean it will again. But she knew that; this too she knows, with her prim certainty. "How can you say that?" he says, looking her straight in the eye. "Sara, I have a terminal disease. There is no cure. It isn't going to go away. You can't go on living in this illusion forever."

"Okay," she says. "You and I and the disease are going to get old together."

The plane swings northward, coming into clearer, darker air, as far to the west the late sun rolls down over Michigan. He takes out the discharge summary—for what it's worth, these doctors in the Clinical Research Unit, unlike the others, have no secrets from him; he carries his own papers now, just like a passport from another country. He supposes Sara will want to read it; she always does. He skims the first page, wondering if there's anything about the experimental therapy. No surprises here, still it all sounds pretty awful, malignant metastatic, rapid extension, disturbing new symptoms, uncertain prognosis. Who are they kidding? There's nothing uncertain about his prognosis. So much for Bierstadt's lo these twenty years. No mention of the new therapy, but he supposes he'll have to tell her anyway, and his decision not to do it. It seems as though his whole life has been heading toward this outcome, hounded by some obscure karma, and there has never been anything he could do to avoid it. It's as though he's been blown willy-nilly by the wind, tacking back and forth, buoyed up by the illusion of control, only to come to port at last here in this place and in this time, as he always knew he would. It is his fate.

He pictures Sara's face, the round rosy cheeks, the fuzzy hair, remembers watching her as she sat there jabbering away about getting old together in the cockpit of the boat, remembers his surprise at seeing several white hairs among the blown-back curls, a web of minute lines around her eyes, and just a hint of sag along her chin. Her face had blurred, and for a moment he could see how she would look old. Not very different at all; the truth is, the faces you know well don't really change. People don't change. That was what she was saying, as in a soft murmuring voice she talked about the children, drawing pictures in the air, molding their faces, their bodies, predicting how they will look grown-up by the way they look now, not very different from the way they have always been, the consistency of their faces and their personalities, old familiar stories of how they felt and acted in the womb, so none of it, David's restlessness, Linnie's quiet determination, has been any surprise to her. People don't really change. What you know now is what they will always be, so you can imagine them grown up. Nothing really changes. You already know what we will be like. You can imagine us old.

And as the plane begins to circle now, coming in to land, all at once he recognizes in her words the oblique attempt to comfort him and realizes this: she has never believed for one moment that they would grow old together. All this time he has been sternly resisting the bright persistent fallacy of her hope, she has been fighting against her own bleak twilight vision of despair. She has seen this bitter outcome, been expecting it all along: you can imagine now the way we will be when you're gone. This is the only way he can be with them as they get older, the only way he can be with them years from now, or even next year. This is what she knows.

He remembers that gathering around his bed in the hospital, a couple of days after Sam had come in to tell them there was new tumor all over his belly, and that radiation and chemotherapy had been shown to have no effect on this kind of tumor, and that anything that could be done could be done here (even now he can recite everything word for word, each one burned into his memory), then paused and said: "If it were me, I would do nothing," and walked off. Sara had jumped up out of her chair; he thought she'd run away.

What she had actually done was start to raising hell, calling everybody she knew who had anything to do with medicine, her sister the medical student, her brother the chief financial officer at Penn Medical School, her former psychiatrist, her old college friend at Hershey Medical Center, the head lab technician at the hospital and his wife the nurse who live around the corner, finally working her way up to the director of the entire hospital. There they all were, standing around his bed—well, not her sister and brother and college friend and former psychiatrist, but everybody else, it seems, even the Episcopal priest, for God's sake . . .

"I'm not going to let you go down the tubes without a fight," Sara says, and he, weary and dizzy and drugged to the gills with stuff for his high blood pressure, his anxiety, his kidney failure, his sinus infection, lies there staring at her round, determined face, feeling like a lost mountaineer who wants nothing more than to go to sleep forever in the warm snow of the mountain pass, instead finds himself dug up, dragged out wet and shivering, caught in the soft but firm jaws of some huge, resolute St. Bernard. "We're going to take it on the road," Sara says.

"There's a lot that we don't know about your tumor," the chief doctor murmurs. "So we've all agreed that further evaluation is needed. I've talked to my old friend Dr. Spencer at the Cancer Center in Boston, and they'll take you as soon as they have a free bed." Phil looks around at the circle of faces. He feels at a disadvantage, the only one lying down, but if he gets up, he'll probably pass out.

"Have you changed your mind about doing nothing?" he says to Sam, who nods.

"I think we should go for broke," Sam says.

"Yeah, sure," Phil replies with a bitter laugh. "And I'm the one who's going to be broken." Then suddenly it all comes home to him, what they're talking about, and he struggles up on one elbow, the panic freezing his blood, the image of himself helpless, wasted, sick, in pain, tubes and needles and monitors everywhere. "I don't want to be kept alive on machines."

Sara sits down on the bed, her hand on his chest. "It won't come to that," she says calmly.

"How do you know?" he says, falling back exhausted, searching for a way to say it. He doesn't want to use the word "quit." "How will we know when it's time?"

"When the time comes, we'll know it," she answers. "Won't we, Sam?"

"I hope so, Sara," he says. "I sure hope so."

"Well, anyway, it isn't now," she says. "Not yet. It's still too soon."

. . . and remembering her sad, determined face that awful day, in this instant as the plane banks steeply around for its final approach he knows that he will do whatever it is he has to do, for a chance to see the kids get bigger; if not to grow old, then at least to stay with Sara a little longer. After all, what does he have to lose? His hair, a few pounds, some dignity? When it's time, he'll know it. And so, he hopes, will she.

He flips over to the second page, to see if Medina has written any additional orders or explanations. There is just one line, written in his usual precise script, "It is hoped the Pt. will return for further treatment," followed by his signature in ballpoint pen. Next to this, in the space labeled "Discharge Status": scrawled in pencil probably at the last minute by some poor desperate intern without a clue, is the single word: "Alive."

The plane begins its descent. The streets below glitter like ropes of tinsel, the runway lights blink on and off, blue and yellow, red and green; the frayed, elusive sparks of one more Christmas.

8

Nativity

"So what are we going to get Daddy for Christmas?" asks Linnie as she and Sara walk down the brightly lit street.

Sara doesn't answer. At the moment, she's feeling too irritable to risk saying anything, especially to Linnie. They've come straight downtown after dropping David off at his evening swimming practice, and they've got barely an hour and a half to shop before it will be time to pick him up and meet Phil's plane. Sweet, oblivious David; as they were driving into town tonight, after she'd yelled much too loud at both kids for what was really only minor squabbling, he looked over at her and said, "Jeez, Mom, how come you're so grouchy these days?"

"Well, you can't expect me to be Little Merry Sunshine all the time," she'd snapped, and he had come right back in his tone of sweet reason: "Well, you don't have to be Little Mary Raincloud, either."

So of course she had to laugh, then all three of them were laughing just as though nothing were wrong, as once again she wondered, hearing the giggles and splutters, how any of them, especially her, could laugh at all, considering. But of course the children don't know the whole story. Then again, neither does she, and won't until Phil gets back from Michigan tonight with the results of the latest tests.

Over her head, festoons of greenery sway in the biting cold wind. Illuminated plastic Santa Claus faces the size of stop signs grin at her out of wads of balsam stuck onto the streetlights all the way down the main street of the business district. People are milling in and out of stores, all of which are open late these last few remaining shopping days; jolly Christmas music recorded on what sounds to Sara like an organ played underwater gurgles out of loudspeakers and dribbles through the air. Christmas in New England; big deal. There's no snow, and if she had her way, there'd be no Christmas either. That was Phil's reaction when they found out the results of the preliminary CAT scan; let's cancel Christmas. But of course they both know that would be foolish, even self-indulgent; there are still the children to think of, the semblance of a normal life to be carried on as long as possible. But Sara has the distinct impression she is merely going through the motions. This is what we get for holding out, she thinks, for Phil's insistence on finishing the semester, a full-blown medical crisis, and Christmas ruined. We should have known better, should have waited until after, should never have found out, should have, should have . . . any number of possibilities. But "should-have me no should-haves," she chides herself, echoing the pact she and Phil have made. "If-only me no if-only's." There's no going back.

"Mom? Did you hear what I said?" In Linnie's voice Sara hears an echo of her own impatience, the way sometimes she still hears her mother's tone echoing in hers, and for a moment she feels buffeted by disembodied voices strangely like her own. "About what to get Dad? I think it should be something really special, don't you?"

"Mmmm," Sara replies noncommittally, looking at her daughter, whose face, at twelve-and-a-half, is almost level with Sara's. The child has been a little spooky lately. Both children know their father is sick, but they are used to this; he has been in and out of hospitals most of their lives. Right now neither of them knows how sick (and neither do you, she reminds herself sternly, not until the latest word from Michigan is in), but Linnie is more sensitive, or perhaps just more open, about what's in the air. The other night, after Sara had come back from taking Phil to the airport, she went up to make sure the kids were both tucked in. There was David, sound asleep, head thrown back, mouth open, snoring away in his squeaky adolescent tone, but Linnie was awake, waiting. She'd clutched at Sara's hand, pulled her down onto the bed.

"Is Dad all right?" she'd whispered. "Tell me really."

They've agreed they would never lie to the kids, or cover up what was going on, but that didn't mean you couldn't put the best face on things, soft-pedal it a little for the time being, so she'd begun by saying, "Not exactly . . ." and Linnie had burst into tears.

"I knew it! I did!" she sobbed. "Does he have another tumor? Will he have to have another operation?"

"Maybe," Sara had hedged, "but operations aren't necessarily a bad thing, if they can make people better." She doesn't believe there will be another operation herself, but that was Linnie's chief terror at the moment, and thus the one she had addressed. "Do you remember the other operations?"

"Yes, but I didn't understand then. Mommy, I'm so scared."

And Sara, crumbling, had replied with the easy, slick evasion, feeling like a cheat: "Don't be, sweetie. It will be all right. Let's think about Daddy coming home, and making this the best Christmas ever."

Much to her relief Linnie latched right onto that, and has been pursuing the concept intently ever since, specifically the question of what to get Dad for Christmas. Phil's attitude toward Christmas can only be described as Bah, humbug. It is only recently that Sara has realized the source of this, the old religious asceticism of his Catholic background resurfacing after all these years, perhaps in response to his illness, a monkish longing for the sanctified occasion of the purely religious holiday. Over the years it has taken the form first of impatience with and now contempt for the getting and spending, the growing bombardment of every minute from Columbus Day on by commercials on television, radio, daily four-color newspaper inserts blaring forth Christmas specials, limited supply now through Sunday no rainchecks, Christmas in July no joke anymore, his disturbance over what he calls the children's greed lists, and ultimately his general resistance to the whole idea of Christmas, period. For the more pagan and acquisitive members of the family this attitude is explained (somewhat solipsistically) by their suspicion that he has never gotten a Christmas present he really liked.

This is an exaggeration, but certainly there have been some spectacular failures, Sara thinks, and starts to chuckle to herself; take for instance the slimline leather attaché case with genuine brass fittings his parents thought would be a nice substitute for the ratty old canvas rucksack he carried his books and papers to school in. Not only did he guess—as usual—what it was before he even opened the box, he had refused to look at the inside with four different compartments, both legal and letter size, fat and skinny, button and strap. And blamed Sara for letting his mother think he'd want it in the first place.

Over the years Sara has taken to watching him on the rare occasions they are in stores together, looking for clues. So it was a reasonable assumption that he would like the woodsman's rip-stop canvas flak jacket with the hatchet loop, buck-knife sheath, shoulder vents and corduroy sweat collar (though Sara thought it was hideous), since he spent so much time admiring it in the work-clothes section of Farrin's basement. But when it turned up as his Christmas present he didn't want it after all, though he did submit to trying it on, to the great hilarity of the children, because the extra-large, his usual size, was this time ludicrously enormous even on his tall frame, the shoulder vents hulking out like condor wings, the hatchet strap hanging down to his knees. "What's this, my dick sling?" he'd asked, sending the children into hysterics. Nor had he liked the miniature twelve-volt stereo tape deck with cigarette-pack-sized speakers Sara bought for the boat, though she had to admit he had a point about its not being waterproof.

So Sara keeps a special return file for sales slips and over the seasons back have gone the wrong-colored Shetland sweaters, the all-in-one quick-dry nylon running shorts ("I hate sissy jocks"), the gold neck chain ("Are you kidding me?" he had remarked with a look of horror, dangling it from his index finger like a length of river slime, but at least he'd been surprised), the environmental noise tapes (*Ocean Surf*—"Sounds like a toilet flushing"; and *Wooden Boat*—"If I want to hear something creak in the wind, I can just sit in the living room and listen to my own house") and more neither of them can now remember, but it certainly gives her something to think about.

Not that there haven't been successes, too, the stereo speakers secretly installed in his truck during what he thought was a routine oil change, so that when he turned on the ignition he nearly got his eardrums blasted with one supersonic shriek from Elton John; the cord of cut and split firewood delivered Christmas morning in a red truck by a friend in a Santa Claus suit (though the cord, as Phil noticed while it was being stacked, was short, and Santa had to make good on it later).

Certainly his attitude has been a challenge to Sara's ingenuity. But now the problem is compounded. Phil has refused to buy any new clothes since they found out in July his disease was metastatic; he's convinced he won't live long enough to wear out his old ones, let alone new, so why spend the money? The same goes for sailboat gear, because in his weakened state he doubts he'll ever sail again. Ditto cross-country skiing. Even a year's subscription to *Cruising World*, his favorite sailing magazine, raises the issue ("Here's a six-month offer; now that's about right"), not to mention the irony of lifetime guarantees ("I'm a real bargain"), even the shelf-life expiration dates on cereals and vitamins. For Sara, the gallows humor is wearing thin, although she doesn't know what else he's supposed to do. Herself either. What do you get for what may be someone's last Christmas that isn't either a reminder or a reproach?

"Hold still," she yells at Phil, pointing the camera at him as he comes around the side of the shed with the leaf rake in his hand. She's been trying to surprise him so she can get a good shot of his face. But he's too quick for her. He puts his hand up and ducks his head as always. "Oh, come on, Phil," she says, lowering the camera in disappointment. The shot is ruined. "Why won't you let me take your picture?"

"Because I know why you're doing it," he says.

She watches him disappear into the shed. He is walking slowly, as though his legs were bothering him. His once-slim behind is still a little swollen, filling out the formerly crumpled seat of his ancient jeans. She turns and walks into her workshop, shuts the door. On the table where she keeps her drawings are stacks of photographs, sketches of Phil alone, with the children, the dog, doing things around the house, nothing special, just random photographs recording daily life.

Except that they are not, really. What he suspects is true; that she has been creating occasions, saving up memories, trying to preserve as much as she can of their life together, in an attempt to freeze the too-rapid progress of time. Once she looked forward to time passing, because she thought it was bringing them closer to safety; now it just brings closer the time when she will be without him.

Putting the camera down, she walks over to her work table and lifts the damp cover off what she is working on now. It is a man's torso, life-size, reclining, from shoulders to upper thigh. She would like it to be Phil, but somehow she can't seem to get it right. Though Phil jokingly calls it his surrogate, the figure is really not at all like his body. It is still blurred and lifeless, lumps of clay fashioned into a merely generic semblance of muscle and bone. She runs her fingers lightly over the contour of chest and hip, idly pressing here, molding a bit there. The clay is cold under her hands.

"So, Mom," Linnie says. "You got any ideas?"

As a matter of fact, Sara does have an idea. It came to her during a phone conversation with Phil's parents right after Thanksgiving, when everyone was already talking Christmas. "We got a new manger this year," Phil's mother said. "Would you want the old one?" Phil had responded eagerly, yes, it was something he'd always wanted, so while the kids were nudging her on the extension and asking what's a manger, she heard his mother say, "This is just the barn part now, not the figures, you realize. The figures got all chipped and broken over the years so I just heaved them. If you want, we'll bring it the next time we come to visit, maybe in the spring. There must be a store up by you where you can get more figures for it."

Phil had been quite excited, but that was before the CAT scan turned up more trouble, confirmed by the latest urine test levels going right off the scale, and Sara knows that he's forgotten all about it. She thinks getting the figures is a nice idea, and since it would never occur to him that she would buy him anything religious, agnostic that she is, it's also a pretty safe bet he'll never guess.

Crèche is what they always called it in her Presbyterian-Episcopalian family, why she has no idea, since none of them were French, perhaps because it sounded more refined. She doesn't like the term, it sounds so hoity-toity, but the inaccuracy of "manger," as Phil and his family call it, has always bothered her even more, since as far as she's concerned, that's just the feed-trough part, no crib for a bed, and she thinks the children might get mixed up. Of course *crèche* isn't much better, since it originally meant the same thing, only in French. The fact is, she doesn't really know *what* to call it. What do they say in shops around here? "Remember the crèche Grandma and Daddy were talking about?" she says to Linnie now, using the English pronunciation.

"Huh?" says Linnie, giving her a blank look.

"The Christmas scene, you know, the barn and figures . . ."

"Oh, you mean the Baby Jesus set," Linnie says, enlightened. "So what about it?"

"I thought we might look for one for Daddy. To go with the old stable that Grandma is going to send us."

"Oh, yeah!" Linnie replies, her upturned face brightening in several colors under a string of garish Christmas lights. "He told Grandma he always wanted one. Great idea, Mom!" Then her face falls. "But where are we going to find one around here?"

"Just follow me," she says to Linnie, and off they march, to a little shop around the corner Sara has noticed before that inexplicably stocks both a line of clothes for mature women in the half-size range and an assortment of various religious items, usually displayed side by side behind the tiny plate glass window. "Angels We Have Heard on High!" the loudspeakers announce, and sure enough, in this holiday season, the whole of the window space is devoted to a full cast of Christmas figures in the Baroque style, two-thirds life-size, with rumpled plaster angels suspended on wires dangling benevolently over the Holy Family, the parade of shepherds, the three kings, the gifts of gold and frankincense and myrrh, the camels, donkeys, sheep, embarrassed innkeeper and wife, and more characters whose role Sara cannot even begin to identify. "Hark! The Herald Angels Sing!" bawls the chorus, and Sara's heart lifts with relief. This is it.

"Oh, Mommy," Linnie gasps, clapping her hands. "You found some!" Sara pulls the door open, and they go inside.

The religious items, being seasonal, are all over the store, on counters, shelves and in bookcases, as well as a special display rack obviously set up for the occasion. Linnie peers around, sees a large statue of an apparently adolescent Jesus in vestments, holding a sacred heart, anatomically correct and dripping blood. "Wow," she whispers reverently, transfixed.

"Do you have just the figures?" Sara asks of the sweetly smiling woman who inquires whether she needs assistance. "We already have the stable part."

"Oh, yes, right here," the woman replies eagerly, pointing to a tall open case resting against the back wall. Her hand continues the gesture around to a high shelf, chockablock with figures. Sara realizes right away there's going to be a problem. The figures come in all styles, from cartoon cute to graceful Gothic, in a variety of materials, and—here's the real difficulty—a wide range of sizes.

"Lin," she says, remembering to address her daughter in the shortened and hence more mature diminutive of her given name Linnie now prefers to use in public, "do you remember how big Grandma's stable is?"

Linnie tears her gaze away from the bleeding-heart statue and looks perplexed. "Gee, no, I don't. Does it matter?"

Sara gestures at the rows of figures, Mary, Joseph, Baby Jesus looking extremely mature for a newborn, hands spread wide, fat toddler legs dangling over the manger, wearing what is probably meant to be swaddling clothes but looks more like a disposable diaper. The figures come three-inch, five-inch, seven-inch and so on, up to at least a foot.

"This big?" Linnie offers helpfully, holding her hands about a foot apart. It's clear she's just guessing. The woman stands patiently, hands folded in front of her skirt, a serene smile on her face.

"You do want them to fit," she says. "It should look right." She stands and waits, while Sara desperately tries to picture the old manger set in her mind. She studies the figures on the shelves, thinking the five-inch size looks about right. She picks up Mary, turns her upside down. The figure is hollow plaster—a real plaster saint, Sara thinks—made in Taiwan. The features are blurred, the expression more simpering than beatified. Sara replaces the Mary, and looks at the others. Baby Jesus beams smugly from his haybale, and Joseph looks constipated, praying for relief. All the other figures are of the same molded plaster, painted on the assembly line, characterless, identical, only bigger or smaller. No, she thinks, not these.

"I was thinking of something in wood . . ." she says tentatively.

The woman shakes her head. "Nothing in wood in the separate figures," she says. "Perhaps you'd consider one of these sets. They're simulated wood, really very nice." She moves over to the large center display rack. There, carefully positioned in the straw, are several small structures, complete with a multitude of figures. "This is one of our most popular ones," she says, pointing to a moss-covered, rustic-looking stable with several levels. The shepherds are down below, the Holy Family in the center, and the three kings on a small round platform almost like a theater box. She gives the tallest king a little tweak, and the platform begins to revolve to the tinkling tune of "We Three Kings of Orient Are." Sara watches the three kings go round and round, wondering what Phil would think. Of course she already knows the answer. "This one plays 'O Little Town of Bethlehem,' " the woman is explaining, as she starts up another, "and this one . . ."

"That's all right," Sara says quickly. The tinkling crèche music boxes sound a dizzying cacophony in her ears, louder and softer, louder and softer, and she feels a need to get out of here before she bursts into hysterical laughter. "I think I'd better go home and measure the stable," she says to the startled saleswoman as she heads for the door. Hauling it open, she babbles a guilty "I'm sure we'll be back another time . . . really very nice," over her shoulder and darts into the street.

"Hey, Mom, what was that all about?" Linnie says, catching up to Sara a little way down the sidewalk. "You sure left in a hurry. Didn't you like those crèche sets, mangers, whatever?"

"Did you?"

"Um, not really. They just don't seem—you know—right for Dad."

"What did you have in mind?" Sara asks, curious to know what Linnie thinks is right for Dad. She takes her daughter's hand, but as usual Linnie twists her cold fingers away with an exasperated "Oh, Mom," and marches on ahead. Sara realizes with a start that Linnie's fingers are as big if not bigger than her own. As her mother said once again on the phone last night, "At least your children are older." But still not old enough. Yes, the children are older; he had not died during that first operation when they were so little, nor when he was forty, like her father. David is fifteen, Linnie twelve and a half, both children older now than Sara was when her father died, another hurdle leaped. His had not been the sudden death after all; he has spared her that, given all of them that gift, but at great cost, each succeeding year scraped out with such effort and such pain.

Tears sting her eyes, and she wonders whether any of this pretense is worth going on with. So many Christmases she has felt this way, the effort of business-as-usual; the first Christmas after her father died, at her grandparents', people bursting into tears and hiding in the cloakroom, running upstairs sniffling into handkerchiefs, her grandfather the Presbyterian minister beating his breast and wailing at the heavens, "Oh, Lord, Lord, why couldn't you have taken these old bones, instead of my boy Jamie?" She remembers not thinking much of a Lord who couldn't figure that out for himself.

She still misses her father at Christmas; his presents, though last-minute, were always right, and her mother played the piano and he sang Christmas carols in his light baritone so round and rich, unlike his high light speaking voice with its funny, western Pennsylvania twang. And here she is again, forcing herself to endure another Christmas with a soul of lead. Is it worth it after all?

"Hey, Mom! Get a load of this!" Linnie is waiting for her a few yards up the street, in front of the New England Candy Factory. There, in a cloud of green cellophane grass, is a chocolate crèche set. "Wouldn't Dad just love it? Munch, munch, munch, bye-bye Baby Jesus." Doubling over, Linnie grabs onto Sara's arm, and holding their hands over their mouths they sneak away together out of the store's range, then burst out laughing, holding onto each other helplessly.

But it's the last laugh of the evening. An hour later, exhausted, discouraged, Linnie complains, "I'm starving." They've been to every store on the street, seen plaster crèche sets and chocolate crèche sets, plastic and pewter and papier-mâché, even a hand-crafted ceramic one. They paused over that one, but it wasn't quite right either. "Too bad you didn't think of this before, Mom. You could have made him one yourself," Linnie had commented. "Maybe you still could."

Sara, who has already thought of this, says simply, "There isn't time now, honey, and even if there were, Daddy would be in the house, so I couldn't work on it without him knowing." There isn't time, she thinks, there will never be time. Over the loudspeakers "Away in a Manger, No Crib for a Bed" gurgles wetly, as if to mock them. Time is running out. In another half hour the stores will be closing; it will be time to pick up David and head for the airport. "Come on," she says wearily to Linnie. "Let's go to the deli and get something to eat."

In the dark, she runs her hands over his back, feeling the hardness of the muscles over his shoulder blades, the long roped ridge on either side of his spine, the indented valley between, along the slight smooth curve of his waist over the small of his back to the beginning of his buttocks, as far as she can reach. This is the part of his body she loves most, the broad, heavy shoulders and long back tapering into his flanks, and it's still the same. She pats his ass gently with both hands, but he continues to breathe a gentle snore into her ear, out cold, draped over her sound asleep.

They've gone to bed late this Christmas Eve, tired and a little giggly from splitting a bottle of champagne while they wrapped the kids' presents and stuffed the stockings. But that didn't stop him, and now he's lying here snoring away, exhausted from their lovemaking. It's been barely a month since he was discharged from the hospital in Boston, but things are certainly back to normal. She never dreamed he'd be able to recover so fast, not after the sight of the long reddish scar, winding from under his arm around his ribs across his belly, down toward his crotch, except for its length, nearly a match for the other one, now paled to skin color, but thick and convoluted as old rope.

The night he got home, barely ten days after, as they slept on their sides like spoons she awoke to the feeling of his hard prick poking at her through her nightgown. She still isn't sure who was more surprised, not to mention relieved, that everything still worked.

He rolls over on his back, taking her part way with him, and she nestles into her favorite position on her side, shoulder tucked in under his, head in the crook of his neck, ear and cheek over his left breast, her body lined up along the whole straight warm length of his side, arm across his belly. She can hear the slow steady thump of his heart, her head rising and falling with the rhythm of his breathing. She can also feel, pressing against the inside of her arm, the two raised bands of scar. And suddenly she feels the tears well in her eyes, and she takes one ragged breath and starts to cry.

He's instantly awake, peering at her in the dark. "What is it? What's wrong?"

"I'm just so glad you're here," she whispers. "So glad it's over, and you're still here."

"Merry Christmas."

"Merry Christmas."

"Gee, Mom, there must be something else we can get him," Linnie persists over her hot ham-and-cheese turnover. "For the boat? Maybe new skis? I mean there's always next year for the manger."

Sara shakes her head, squints her eyes against the access of tears, grief at the absence of next year, and stares past Linnie out the window. Linnie looks at her suspiciously. "Mom? Are you okay?"

"Wait a minute." Sara says, her breath catching. Across the street in a jewelry store they've patronized for many years, on a shelf behind the front window, visible only from this angle, she has spotted what is clearly a class act in crèche figures. She hasn't even thought of looking in the jeweler's, but there they are, Mary, Joseph, and the Baby Jesus, gathered reverently all by themselves on a center shelf. Even from here she can tell they are beautiful. "Finish your sandwich quick," she says to Linnie. "We're going across the street."

The figures are porcelain, Royal Doulton, the jeweler tells them as he sets the six-inch Mary gingerly on the glass counter. She is exquisitely modeled, glazed and fired, the colors of her face at once transparent and glowing, her expression fond, beatific, a mother's face. "They're lovely," Sara says, hearing Linnie's intake of breath beside her. The figures are so happy-looking, rosy, and gleaming, that though porcelain was not what she had in mind, more something carved in wood, austere, attentuated El Greco figures, like Phil himself, she thinks that these will do. She hesitates, then pops the question. "How much?"

"Six hundred dollars."

Sara gasps. Even for a grand gesture, it's more than they can afford. "Oh, dear," she says, thinking she should have known. Now she's gotten Linnie's hopes up.

"Is that too much?" Linnie whispers tensely at her elbow. Sara nods, feeling Linnie's disappointment as she turns away.

"Oh, well, it was a nice idea. Maybe next year, if we save our pennies," she says, and smiles apologetically at the jeweler, who has furnished them with many charming though relatively inexpensive gifts for all and sundry through the years. He nods sympathetically, and Sara follows a drooping Linnie out the door. It was a mistake, she knows, to have made so much of this to Linnie, the special trip while Dad's away, the secret, perfect surprise present at last, something to comfort all of them, mere self-indulgence. She should have thought of it before, when there was time, and now she curses herself for not paying more attention to all those catalogues of special gifts that have inundated them since mid-summer; she is certain that somewhere in one of them, now reposing out of her reach at the bottom of the sanitary landfill, there is the perfect set of figures, just made to order, and she missed it. It's too late now. And no next year.

"Mom." Linnie, no longer adroop, is yanking on her sleeve with one hand. The other is pointing at the jeweler's window. Sara peers through the glass, past the confused reflections of Christmas lights. In the corner near the top, barely visible in the shadows, is what appears to be a small chalet or cuckoo clock. They move closer, and Sara sees what Linnie has seen, the small figures clustered round in the unmistakable configuration of a crèche.

Sara grabs Linnie's hand without a word and they turn around, go back inside.

"Oh, the little carved nativity? I'd forgotten about that one."

Of course that's what they're called, Nativity, the birth, Sara thinks as the jeweler climbs a step stool, takes down the little figures one by one, then the stable. The roughly shingled roof is dusty; he blows on it, then wipes it with his sleeve. "Sorry about that. We've had this one around for a long time." Carefully he positions the figures in their places, Mary, Joseph, and the infant, the ox and the ass, on the wooden platform of the little stable. In an alcove behind there is actually a stall with a gate, on one side a bent leafless tree and a fence; the weathered eaves hang down protectively over the huddled family, while a cherub looks down happily, perched on a shingle with his banner stretched wide, "Gloria in Excelsis Deo."

Linnie, her eyes glowing, clutches Sara's arm with both hands in a spasm of delight. "Oh, Mom," she says. "Oh, Mom. It's wood and everything. It's perfect, isn't it?"

Sara is studying the little Mary, not much bigger than her index finger, the folds of her shawl and gown so meticulously rendered, her features so delicate yet clear, the colors so soft, so subtle, that she wonders for a moment if these can actually be wood after all. The time, the care . . .

"Oh, yes, it's wood, all hand-carved by elves in the deep dark forests of the Alps," the jeweler says to Linnie, who gives him a withering glance.

"No, actually," he says to Sara, "everything in this line is hand-carved individually by master European craftsman from original designs . . ." He reaches under the counter and brings up a thick color catalogue, begins to flip through the pages. "ARTISTIC WOODCARVINGS" the catalogue reads, with texts in German, Italian and French, side by side. "There's yours," he says, pointing to a page. "Of course that's only one of the many nativities they offer, among other items. We thought it was the nicest, and quite reasonable." The jeweler is beaming happily, sharing their enthusiasm.

Sara stares down at the catalogue page. Not only is the nativity pictured, along with it are a whole array of other figures, adoring shepherds, supplicating kings, skeptical innkeepers, amazed sheep, snooty camels, dour elephants, bored retainers, even a barking dog.

"Wow! We can add on, buy Dad a new piece every year!" Linnie says, hopping up and down, beseeching. "Mom, can we get it, Mom? It's so perfect."

It is perfect. The thing itself, the nativity, the small family huddled together in the shelter of the rustic stall, perfect for this year. And more for Christmases to come, a new one each year, on and on; there must be twenty figures on the catalogue page. Neither a reminder nor a reproach.

"I can give you a real deal on it," the jeweler says, getting down to business. "But I have to tell you why." He picks up the Joseph and turns him upside down. "The Joseph was broken . . ." Linnie moans in disappointment. Sara's heart sinks; not perfect after all. ". . . but he's been mended." He points to a line across the base of the figure, nearly invisible, a shiny film of glue over it. Again he looks apologetic. "I can order you a new Joseph, but it will cost more. But if you still want it . . ."

"Yes, we'll take it just the way it is," says Sara quickly. Linnie claps her hands. "Would you mind wrapping each piece separately? It's for my husband, and we . . . we want it to be a surprise."

"Be glad to. It will take a little while, so if you have other errands—"

Outside, Sara and Linnie can contain themselves no longer, they squeal and hug each other, then dance off down the street toward nowhere in particular. When they come back the packages are waiting, all wrapped in different paper, in different-sized boxes, six small ones and one big. They head back toward the car and hide them under the driver's seat, where Phil won't see them. She wonders briefly which one has the Joseph, which the Baby Jesus. But then, it really doesn't matter which is which.

The wind has died down, and it's begun to snow, small flakes sifting down, dusting the ice along the pavement like lace. Sara turns on the heat, the defroster, the radio, while they wait for the car to warm up. Linnie is silent now, and Sara looks at her profile, outlined against the steamed-up window of the car, and is surprised to see a single tear roll out and down the still slightly baby-rounded cheek.

"Linnie, what's wrong?" She reaches over, but Linnie shakes her head.

"I'm afraid he won't like it. After I saw it everything was so wonderful, you said it was perfect and I felt so good, but then there was the part about the Joseph being broken and I got all worried that he wouldn't like it after all, and I . . . I just wanted it to be the best Christmas ever and now it seems all spoiled . . . oh, Mom, I'm just so scared. What will it be like?" And Linnie plummets toward her, head on her shoulder, and begins to sob. Sara cuddles her for a moment, then wipes along the soft, wet hollows under Linnie's eyes gently with her bare fingers, first one cheek, then the other.

"Oh, Linnie, honey, don't be scared. I'll tell you what it will be like. We'll all get up on Christmas morning, just like always. All this time Daddy will have been looking at all the boxes, and wondering what's in them and shaking them and poking them the way he always does, but he won't be able to guess and he'll want to open them right away, but we'll tell him he has to save them all till last, because—but we won't tell him this—as soon as he opens the first one, he'll know, right?" A nod and a sniff from Linnie.

"And after we've all opened all the other presents, then we'll put the packages on Daddy's lap, and he'll start to open them . . ."

"Which one first?"

"I don't know, because I don't know which is which, but I think that probably it will be the Joseph, and then Daddy will know what the whole present is, and he may even cry a little because he's so happy, and we'll all gather around him and he'll put his arms around us and say this is just what I always wanted, and it's the best present ever, and the best Christmas ever . . ." Sara stops and takes a breath. "And that's what it will be like."

"Are you sure?" Linnie hiccups. But her eyes are dry and she is smiling.

"Darn right I'm sure." Sara starts the engine of the car. All down the street lights are going out, the stores closing. Even the strings of colored lights blink off, and everything looks dull. But as she pulls out, the radio begins to play the stately Baroque strains of "How Brightly Shines the Morning Star," one of Phil's favorite Christmas hymns. Overhead the traffic lights turn red, yellow, green. The snow has melted into droplets on the windshield, and now the wipers flick back and forth, flashing all the colors across their faces, and suddenly the car seems filled with Christmas.

9

A Balance of Conflicting Forces

In an hour or so the infusion room will be filled up, but right now Phil is the only one here. He always arrives early on the days he gets chemo because they have to drop Linnie at school first. On Thursday and Friday mornings every four weeks for over a year now, Phil has gotten up a little later than everyone else, taken his shower and dressed while the rest of the family is eating breakfast. All he has to eat before they leave for town are the pills that are supposed to keep him from getting sick to his stomach. He's not sure they really work since he still gets sick, but they are what the doctors in Michigan ordered, so he takes them. Maybe he'd feel even worse if he didn't.

Then he and Sara and Linnie get in the car and drive Linnie to the junior high—David has his own ride to the high school, which starts even earlier—and from there to the hospital on the other side of town. He drives in but Sara has to drive back, because after the chemo he's too doped up to stay awake, let alone drive a car. He tries not to think about where he's going because it always makes him feel as though he's driving over a cliff, and not only that, doing it on purpose. This is the way it has been since they started this a year ago in January, two days of getting sick on chemo plus another week of feeling lousy every month. Lately it's been even longer. As soon as he walks in the door and smells the stuff they use to clean the floors he starts to get nauseated.

But it could be worse, as Sara keeps reminding him. After all, he's still on his feet. He hasn't lost much weight to speak of, and though his hair and beard are slightly thinner, he hasn't gotten bald, either. Sara says it's because they went out and bought the wig in expectation that he would lose his hair, which guaranteed he wouldn't; if they hadn't, it would have, because that's the way things work. Phil thinks it might be the ice cap they put on him the first six months. The nurses just shrug. He's still teaching full time, except for the days he misses because of the treatments. So outwardly at least, he looks and acts pretty much the same, but it's an effort. Inside he's very tired.

After he's seen the doctor for the usual quick checkup—what's the blood pressure, how're you feeling, any problems since the last time, over and out—he sits in one of those simulated-leather lounge chairs with the footrest that pops up when you lean back and Elsie the nurse sticks the needle in and hooks up the IV, starts running the pre-meds, and pretty soon he's cruising. Well, not quite. They give him a drug to make him drowsy, a drug to kill the pain, a drug to control the vomiting, and a drug to make him forget what it all feels like so he'll come back next time. Usually he sleeps, but he still throws up, still feels the pain, and he doesn't really forget. Sara says he doesn't remember some things, like whether he's had lunch or dinner, or what she's said to him on the way home. So he does forget, but not enough. And he still keeps coming back for more.

He sits down in the middle lounge chair, the one he always uses. They are all in a row, five of them, and they look just like the chairs his grandfather or his uncles used to have in their dens (when they had dens), except that attached to each one is a tall metal pole with a loop at the top for hanging IVs, and on the ceiling above is a track with a curtain hanging down that can be pulled around for privacy, just like in a hospital room. Otherwise, they try very hard to make the place as pleasant and homey as possible. So there is real wooden furniture in rustic colonial maple—end tables, chairs, even a credenza with a record player inside—that reminds him of his parents' old living-room set, a television inexplicably and permanently tuned to "Sesame Street," a bookcase with popular novels and magazines as well as inspirational literature and information about cancer. The walls are papered with some sort of forest scene, and there are coordinating curtains on the windows. Today there is also a styrofoam wig stand sitting on the credenza, with a man's dark-haired wig tilted at a rakish angle so that it resembles a beret, probably waiting for someone to come in and pick it up.

At first glance, the place looks just like someone's apartment; you could imagine that they just called up the local condo unit company and had it dropped right in. The maple cabinets full of drugs and supplies are discreetly closed, as is the door to the examining room, and the nurses' station, secretaries, phones, and medical records are behind the wall in what would be the kitchen. The pass-through is where you check in. All it lacks is wall-to-wall carpeting, but of course that would be too risky. You never know when someone is going to blow lunch all over, or worst yet, spill one of the drugs they give him. The stuff is so caustic it would burn a hole right through to the linoleum. Sometimes he feels as though that's what it's doing to his veins.

Elsie pops her head out of the nurses' room. "Hello, Mr. Boyd," she says cheerfully in her squeaky little girl's voice. "You're here bright and early." This is what she always says. She is always cheerful but never inappropriately so—let's face it, she seems to be saying, this is no picnic but we might as well get on with it—and she tries to be as sympathetic, as accommodating, as matter-of-fact as possible, even when things go wrong and the drugs aren't up from the pharmacy and he has to wait for the doctor to get here and give the go-ahead and he's getting sicker and sicker just at the thought of the needle and the first fat bag of fluid trailing its tentacles like a pale, transparent, stinging jellyfish.

But that's not true today; it's Friday and he saw the doctor yesterday so Elsie sits right down and starts to fish for a vein that hasn't collapsed yet; the stab and pain like an aching tooth, then the burning and stinging as the chemicals start flowing drip-drip into the big vein in the back of his hand, and then he starts to float away, up and down over the surface of the water, up and down, rocked so peacefully asleep—until the first wave of nausea hits and he pitches forward suddenly awake, doubled up, retching into the little kidney-shaped pan Elsie has tucked into the crook of his elbow while he was sleeping, and he retches and heaves, finally dribbling a thin stream of greenish puke, all there is for now, and then lies back exhausted, sick and dizzy, the back of his hand throbbing, his arm swollen to the elbow from the IV, and sleeps again.

Sara watches him walk down the hall into the oncology unit— "down the rabbit hole" as they jokingly refer to it these days when Phil more or less disappears off the face of the earth for a while. Most of the time now she just drops him off and goes about her business, unless his blood counts are borderline and there's some doubt about whether he's going to get the treatment on schedule. Then she goes in and waits until he sees the doctor, sometimes idly flipping through his two-inch-thick medical record to see if they've missed anything. If there's something she doesn't understand, she'll go look it up in the medical dictionary her sister Fran gave her, or in one of the reference books in the college library. After all, you can't be too careful, especially after the experiences they've had.

Phil is scheduled to go to Michigan for a follow-up evaluation in a couple of weeks, and before she does anything else she has to drop off his latest bucket of pee at the hospital lab so they can send it out there for analysis ahead of time to get an idea of how well the chemotherapy is working. She put the liter container in a brown paper bag before they left the house, but it's full right to the screwtop and as she walks down the hall toward the reception area she realizes it's been leaking. She pulls the amber plastic jug out of the soggy bag and stands it on the counter next to the receptionist's computer terminal. "Listen carefully," she says to the young woman, who looks up startled, a chipper "How may I help you?" frozen on her lips. "This is a 24-hour urine specimen, and it has to be sent to Michigan for analysis as part of an experimental program. It is very important that it not get lost, or be processed here by mistake."

She's in the middle of giving the address to the receptionist, who is really very cooperative if somewhat baffled by the whole arrangement, when she sees Sam come out of the lab. She hasn't seen him over a year, not since the screwup with the lab reports. She turns sideways trying to be invisible but it's no use, he's seen her, and with a smile of greeting walks over and stands next to her while she repeats the address for the young woman. He's nodding like a loose-hinged ceramic Buddha, his expression sympathetic, all-knowing, familiar. "Another specimen on its way to Boston, I see," he says.

"Referring physician?" the receptionist inquires.

Sara can see it coming, the cat out of the bag along with the jug of pee. She tries to fake it. "Uh, Dr. Richard Medina."

The receptionist looks puzzled. "Is he on the staff here?"

"No," Sara says. Sam is standing next to her, their shoulders nearly touching.

"Then I need the name of your local physician. Just for our records," the receptionist beams helpfully. Sam is still smiling expectantly, waiting for her to finish so he can chat about how things are going.

Sara clears her throat and gives the name of another doctor in town. Out of the corner of her eye she sees the smile jerked off Sam's face, leaving his mouth as abruptly pursed up as a drawstring bag.

"Wait a minute until I get these entered and I'll read them back to you." The receptionist turns to her machine, types out the instructions in a series of clearly audible beeps.

Sam clears his throat. "So that's why I haven't heard anything lately," he says after a moment, his pouchy face expressionless.

"He's just a liaison," she says wearily. "Everything is being done in Michigan now—"

"—I feel left out," Sam says.

Sara looks him straight in the eye, tired of the whole business.

"—And they wanted a doctor here who was qualified . . ." She stops to take a breath. ". . . to deal with cancer."

Sam stares at her for a split second, then turns on his heel and walks away.

"All set," the receptionist chirps, handing her a copy of the lab slip. "Have a nice day."

"This protocol we're starting you on is highly experimental," Medina says in his flat, no-nonsense voice. They are sitting in Phil's room at the hospital in Michigan, or rather Sara and Medina are sitting; Phil is lying in bed. This early in the morning, unmussed as yet by rounds, Medina is so neat and buttoned up and shiny he looks as though he's been shellacked. "There have, however, been some encouraging results," he goes on. "In two cases, there has been normalization of the C-T scan, and considerable reduction in the level of catecholamines, with consequent reduction in blood pressure. In the third case, rapidly progressing disease was stabilized, with reduction of symptoms." Medina crosses his legs, barely denting the knife-edge pants; his white coat crackles. "It's not a cure, but at the very least we can hope to achieve a balance, the treatment inhibiting the disease enough to make the cost-benefit ratio worthwhile. It's possible we may be able to arrest the progress of your disease entirely for the time being." Then Medina leans forward as though speaking confidentially, says in English, "Let's face it. It would be a big plus even if we could just keep you where you are."

Medina is looking at Phil while he explains this; Sara is looking at Medina and nodding her head; she's read the article he's quoting the statistics from, which Bierstadt sent them after they decided to go ahead and do the initial treatment here in Michigan, then continue it back home on an outpatient basis if the side effects weren't too bad. That's what he means by cost-benefit ratio. Phil is about to become the fourth case in this experimental program, the first at Michigan, and they're hoping the results of the treatment will be worth how sick it's going to make him. Will there be life after chemo? That's what they're here to find out. Medina has promised him they will do everything in their power to alleviate the immediate side effects, particularly the incessant vomiting, "even if we have to put you to sleep for two days."

That is the main reason Sara insisted on coming with him, or so she said, even though it was right after Christmas, hardly time to catch their breath. "If you're going to be out of it you need to have someone with you. It's just common sense, Phil," she'd argued. And of course he could see her point, though this is something he'd rather do alone. He also knows she's curious, wanted—no, needed—to see what the place looked like, see where he's been, meet the doctors and make sure they know what they're doing, ask questions, her mission as always to keep everybody honest, make sure that everybody's doing whatever can be done, and pronto.

Now, looking at the apparatus they're lugging in, IV trolleys and drip counters, and blood pressure monitors, wires and tubes and bags, Phil shuts his eyes, and envisions an old-fashioned balancing scale like the one held by blindfolded Justice in her nightie, his tumors on one side, beakers of chemicals on the other, with tubes connecting them. The chemicals shoot through the tubes and drench the tumors, which start to shrivel up and die, and the scale on that side goes up. Then the cancer cells begin to get fat again and multiply, and the scale goes down. Justice weighed in the balance: crime and punishment, sin and retribution.

But he's not supposed to think that way, at least according to the shrink they have taken to seeing on occasion when things really get rough. Contemplate the randomness of fate, the plight of Job. Her point is that there is no justice, at least not in this case; it doesn't apply here as a concept, so think of something else. He's not so sure; nevertheless he obediently visualizes two children on a seesaw. Up, down, up, down, sometimes balancing, sometimes not, depending on what each kid does in turn.

"It may not work forever," Medina says, his voice less formal, verging on sympathetic. "But at least it's worth a try."

Phil pops his eyes open. "What happens when it stops working?" he asks without really thinking. Dumb question. What happens when one kid hops off the seesaw? The other one falls down and busts his ass.

What he really meant was "how will we know?" but Medina is already off and running. "Let's cross that bridge when we come to it," he replies, standing up so briskly that whatever dust has had time to settle on him flies off and whirls around him, motes glistening in the beam of light from overhead. "Meanwhile why don't we just get started?" He rubs his hands together with a dry whisper like leaves rustling, nods to them, nods to the nurse with the needle, about-faces and marches from the room. The words "Back later . . ." float crisply down the hall.

Sara is now standing at the foot of the bed watching, so Phil tries not to wince as the nurse sticks the needle into his vein, but it hurts too much, and he sees her grimace and go pale at his sharp intake of breath. She turns away, for which he is grateful; he wishes she would leave. Then, as the drip-drip starts and he begins to feel sleepy, he decides he doesn't care.

Some time later, half-asleep, without even a moment's warning he suddenly starts to retch, and groping in his daze for a receptacle, reaches over the side of the bed and vomits into his shoe.

"He has some Nemesis," he hears the nurse tell Sara. Some, ha, that's putting it mildly, he thinks, not bothering to open his eyes; he's much too drowsy; it's a good thing he's in bed. Nemesis is right; an agent or act of retribution, an opponent or rival a person cannot best. The best we can hope for is a balance of conflicting forces, distance at the expense of speed, a fair wind and moderate seas.

Nestling his head into the sailbag, he rolls on his side and goes back to sleep.

Sara stares blankly at the nurse, who is standing next to Phil's bed adjusting the drip machine. "What did you say?"

The nurse frowns at the apparatus, twiddles a dial. "He had some emesis," she repeats, then explains, "He upchucked in his shoe." She turns and smiles brightly at Sara. "Missed the kidney basin entirely. But it's all cleaned up now, and he's doing great."

It will be a couple of hours before the treatment is over, so after she leaves the hospital Sara stops by the college to check the mail.

Then she goes to Phil's office and waits for Elsie to call and tell her Phil's ready to go home. She's been teaching an introductory drawing course for several years now, and this last year took on the upperclass course in sculpture, but she doesn't go to her own office in the art building on these days because though her office hours and classes are in the afternoon, there are always a few students around wanting to talk, even at this hour of the morning. On Fridays she's out of here by ten o'clock, without having to say anything to anyone except the secretary and the odd colleague or two. This is the other part of her life, the private part. If she didn't have to be someplace where the hospital can get in touch with her, she wouldn't come in at all; she'd stay home and scratch away at one of her sculptures, or clean the house, do something by herself so she wouldn't have to see or talk to anybody.

The fact is, she feels so distracted on the days that Phil gets chemo, cross and resentful, worried and angry at the world, that it is all she can do to be civil, much carry on a normal conversation. It takes all the strength she can muster to keep herself from telling perfectly innocent people like bank tellers and grocery clerks to fuck off. But today she won't be here that long; she has to go downtown to pick up Phil's airline ticket and go to the bank. While she's there she might as well get a few things at the grocery store. By then he ought to be ready to come home.

She's just letting herself into Phil's office when she hears a step behind her. It's one of Phil's colleagues. He sidles up to her in mock surprise, asks archly, "Why, fancy meeting you here! To what do we owe this unexpected pleasure so bright and early this fair morning?"

Clenching her teeth, she takes a deep breath. "Hospital run," she says. "It's Phil's week for chemo."

Face blanching, the man stutters, "Oh. Oh yes, oh dear." His mouth wobbles up and down a few times, then with an stricken look he turns around and heads the other way.

Really, you'd think the penny would have dropped by now, she thinks in annoyance, shutting the door behind her, not turning on the lights. After all, she's been here this early on a Thursday and Friday morning every four weeks for fifteen months now, just like clockwork, and it's always for the same reason. Lately it has also coincided with her period, which makes her even more irritable and snappish. She supposes the students who catch her on these days think she is cold and distant, not to say mean and nasty, but there's not much she can do about it. On these days she not only doesn't feel like talking, she feels like biting the mail open and chewing on the telephone, banging the desk and kicking the walls, throwing books around, snarling and making ugly faces and generally behaving badly. But she can't. The public facade must be maintained at all costs. It was Phil's decision not to take full medical leave until he had to, to keep up the semblance of a normal life for as long as he can. This is possible partly because he still looks so well, his hair a little thinner perhaps, his appearance slightly more ascetic. In fact, he looks more like a monk than ever, pared down to his essence, if anything enobled by his illness. This is horseshit, of course, but here they are, carrying on the pretense of business as usual.

It isn't easy. The gulp followed by the swift about-face and the cut-and-run is infinitely more tolerable, Sara has come to believe, than the sight of someone she barely knows, indifference suddenly transformed into a solemn, knowing look, the head bowed close to hers in confidence, the question, "How *is* he doing?" so lugubriously inflected that she is tempted to reply, "Dead, thanks."

But of course the required answer is a bright "Oh, just fine, thank you!" if she wants to avoid the morbidly curious inquisition, sympathy disguising the compulsion to know each gory detail like gawkers at a burning house, to what end Sara has yet to figure out. "So what's the story here?" they prod. Do they imagine there is something to be learned, or that making her talk it out will help? What she really needs is a great big button that reads: DON'T ASK.

Then there are the babblers, accosting both of them with the latest popular theories of diet or meditation that worked for friends of friends of theirs, or worse yet, mindless retellings of death and dying anecdotes meant in some misguided way to be comforting, she supposes, the only other possible explanation sheer sadism: "So and so had that, and suffered terribly, but in the end it was so beautiful . . ." Another button: DON'T TELL CANCER STORIES.

The ones who really get her, though, are those smug mind-over-matter types she privately calls the cheerleaders who "just know that Phil can beat this," implying if he doesn't it's because he has a bad attitude. But of course that's how he got cancer in the first place, that and not eating right. Button number three: DON'T MORALIZE.

In idle moments she tries to think of some conversation stoppers, since the real story is too complicated to explain, and she gets so tired of retelling it to one person after another. To the ubiquitous "How is he doing?" she's tempted to answer simply, "Rotten, and I don't want to talk about it." But she's too well-behaved to do this; she still feels bound to tell the truth. Better, yes, for a while, but since then, for months now, everything the same, all their energies engaged in a holding operation, trying to stay on an even keel, maintaining the precarious balance between side effects and symptoms, treatment and disease known in the supermarket magazines as "Living with Cancer." Or worse yet, "Making Every Moment Count." The best she has come up with is a ploy she learned from her cousin, developed after several years of dealing with a chronically ill child: a noncommittal "Enh . . ." accompanied by an exaggerated shrug and a wry look.

What the articles don't prepare you for are people like the dental hygienist who after getting wind of the diagnosis, shows up to clean Phil's teeth with a surgical gown, rubber gloves and a face mask, "just in case"; or the close, dear friends who take it all in, express sincere sorrow with a hug and a tear, say "I'll call you," and are never heard from again, no doubt believing it is kinder not to notice, to pretend nothing is happening, spare her the agony of embarrassment, the reminder of pain. Surely it is easier to avoid her on the street. In her heart she knows she would not—does not—know what to do herself. Don't pretend it isn't happening, but don't pry either. Don't give advice or tell grim stories. Don't moralize. Wait for the clues. Pay attention. Care. It could happen to you.

Some people get it and some just don't, Sara thinks as she deposits most of the mail in the wastebasket. She doesn't really blame anyone anymore for not knowing what to do or how to act. People are damned if they do, damned if they don't. This good news-bad news seesaw of Phil's illness has been going on so long now that most of the people who know them well are tired of hearing about it, and those who don't, think Phil is either cured or dead. But how can one carry on business as usual without seeming callously to ignore? Surely not by pretending nothing is wrong, asking Phil why he doesn't serve on more committees, write more articles, run three times a week the way he used to—"Boyd, what's with you, you're just going to pot!"—when it's all he can do to get himself out of bed and dressed. But it's Phil himself who insists on making things look good.

Crumpling envelopes, Sara sighs. If we really wanted sympathy and understanding, she supposes, we should be more open about what's going on. Over the years she has learned to respect Phil's need to be private, even secretive; in the long run it's easier than always having to respond, explain or justify, even tell people what they can do to help. Most of the time it's like having an eager cleaning woman you have to pick up for ahead of time, who follows you around asking what she can scrub next the whole time she's there. One of these days, when someone asks "Is there anything I can do?" she'll say "Sure. How about cleaning my oven?"

These encounters make her all the more grateful for those who somehow, either through experience or some mysterious access of sympathy, seem instinctively to know what to do or how to act in any given dire circumstance. This is, Sara has come to believe, a rare gift indeed, a combination of tact, persistence and creativity that allows these few to transcend their fear of seeming helpless and inadequate, their own egotism. Ultimately, she has decided, it all comes down to an utter lack of self-consciousness, at least in these matters of the heart. They don't care if their behavior might be construed by others or in the great scheme of things as foolish or intrusive or tactless, in the long run or the last analysis demonstrative of nobility or weakness of character. They just show up out of nowhere, in the daytime or the middle of the night, in the kitchen or the hospital waiting room, bringing the gift of their full attention, without even being asked.

And for some of them, it goes back years. More than five years now since Jane, harried wife of corporate-executive-on-the-way-to-the-top Mack, mother of two active teenagers, a boy and a girl, both needing transportation to some activity or other at any given moment, refusing to take no for an answer, sat with her in the Boston hospital during those long hours of Phil's second operation—one entire day, from 9 A.M. until 5 P.M.—wiggling her toes and knitting, talking nonstop about absolutely nothing; or Dave, the Episcopalian priest who, even though he knew she was a skeptic, possibly even an atheist, read her mind and refused to let her go alone that first time more than seven years ago into the Intensive Care Unit where Phil was hemorrhaging, near death, stayed with her in the waiting room into the small hours reading not from the Bible but the *Norton Anthology* she had inexplicably grabbed up from the bedside table in Phil's room when the nurse told her he'd been taken to ICU, and had forgotten to put down.

But in a way the emergencies are easier to get up for, because they don't go on and on. What to do to help in the face of what they now deal with on a daily basis? Sara knows she is not always a nice person to be with, to listen to, obsessed as she is with symptoms, with survival, her mood at best depressed, at worst so dissociated from her immediate surroundings she hardly knows what's going on around her.

She jumps as the phone rings, grabs it up, even though it's probably for Phil. It's not.

"Good morning," says the familiar voice. It's her friend Patience, who has for months now called her three times a week at 7:59 A.M. with what she jokingly calls her "morning wake-up call, just checking to see if you're still alive," a joke that is no joke, at once acknowledging the seriousness of the situation and treating it in such a way that Sara feels the opportunity but not the necessity to talk. So what if it's a little early, sometimes waking Sara out of an uneasy sleep; the call's long-distance, and that's when the rates are low. She could take the phone off the hook if she wanted to sleep but the fact is she's grateful for the company, even though most of the time they just pass the time of day discussing such mundane matters as child rearing, the latest in college gossip, or absolutely nothing.

"How did you know I was here?" Sara asks, smiling as she tucks the phone into the crook of her neck and puts her feet up on the desk.

"I didn't. I called your house and then your office and you weren't there, so I tried the next place I thought you'd be. Pretty good, huh?"

They talk for a while, until finally it's time for Sara to go and run her errands. Patience heaves a huge sigh. "How do you go on?" she asks. "How do you do it?"

"You know what Schopenhauer says," Sara says nonchalantly, repeating an old joke from graduate school, "you can't fall off the floor. Sometimes you can even get your chin up on the piano caster." She smiles and holds the phone away from her ear as Patience breaks into hoots of delighted laughter. That's what I need, Sara thinks, someone to laugh at my jokes.

Finally, out of breath, Patience says skeptically, "Did Schopenhauer really say that?"

"No," Sara replies. "It was the Mad Hatter. And I made up the part about the piano caster."

Finally they hang up. Sara is now pressed for time, but the conversation, maybe just the contact, has put her in a better mood. On the way to her car she thinks of the couple who never fail to call on the days Phil has his treatment to ask "How's he doing?" even when they know the answer is the same; lousy, and follow it with the question nearly everyone forgets to ask, "How are *you* doing?" Sara wonders if they mark it on their calendar, counting week by week, or just remember when the time comes around again. Either way, Sara finds the mere fact of their taking notice profoundly comforting, the bleak routine that much less lonely shared.

Perhaps the most creative is Jean, a colleague of Phil's, busy with her own work and family, who has on several occasions supplied various charms and totems, among them (on loan) the baby rattle her son clutched before and after successful open-heart surgery to correct a serious birth defect, three "lucky" Bicentennial quarters taped to a card containing an elaborate history and instructions for their use, as well as delivering (also long-distance, from her house some fifteen miles away) huge dishes of lasagne, one of the few meals everyone in the Boyd family enjoys, which last the whole time Phil is away in Michigan for his evaluation, with some left over for when he gets back. How she knows when these ministrations are appropriate Sara has no idea, since Jean has never asked her in advance, the totems just showing up the day before Phil is due to go for this or that checkup or procedure: the rattle for his series of painful bone marrow taps to see if the drugs were being taken up in sufficient quantities; the quarters before a trip to Michigan for yet another evaluation, one for the flight out, one for the flight back, and one for "while you're in that other country"; the lasagne appearing on her doorstep while Sara was sweating it out at home, too upset to cook. Or the friend, bless him, a sailor from his youth who, sensing desperation when Phil was too sick from the chemo last summer to go sailing at the coast, brought his own small day-sailer rattling on its trailer out to the nearby lake and insisted on taking them all for a transcendent moonlit sail. Little things, done without being asked, showing that someone is paying attention, awful as it is, to what is going on . . .

Sara thinks of these and others, a narrow fringe of upturned faces ringing the net under this fragile balancing act they call their life, and as she heads over toward the hospital to check on Phil, thanks them; thanks too (just in case) a God she still can't quite believe in—but how else to explain the relentless, seemingly vindictive quality of it all?—for giving them such friends.

Up and down, up and down, rocked in a sea as black as ink, the waves invisible in the dark air except for frills of phosphorescence breaking at their tips, the hiss of froth, the momentary glow and then the huge wave billows underneath, lifting the boat up only to drop precipitously down the other side, chasing the frill of foam. Phil, stretched out in the cockpit with eyes wide open, back against the coaming, feels the rhythm, hears the slosh, but hard as he stares, can't make out the delineation between night sea and sky. He takes a deep breath, resisting the urge, gropes for the tiller, thinking if he turns the boat into the wind slightly the pitching may ease a bit and he won't feel so sick, as he fumbles for it in the darkness feels it inexplicably wedged between his elbow and his ribs, transformed into a shallow plastic dish shaped like a comma, and as the nightbird pecks sharply at the back of his other hand, he thrusts the flimsy useless object from him, leans over the side and heaves.

He lies back, breathless, shivering, and lets the boat sail on.

In the medical section of the Coop next door to the Boston Institute for Cancer Research where Phil has finally been admitted for re-evaluation, Sara looks up one word after another, following definitions like a trail of bread crumbs: "*diastolic*, from the Greek *diastole*, to expand; q.v. *systolic*, to contract. *Pressure*; the force exerted by a body, usually a fluid or vapor, against the entity constraining it, as in the circulation of the blood." Thus blood pressure, she concludes, is a result of the balance between the force of the blood as it is pushed through the blood vessels by the action of the heart muscle, and the tension exerted against this flow by the vessels themselves, and high blood pressure is a morbid imbalance of these two conflicting forces. "Its causes are varied, often undiscovered; a small but significant percentage of cases are caused by tumors of adrenal and extra-adrenal tissue in the paraganglion or sympathetic nervous system. See also *pheochromocytoma*." Obediently she flips over the requisite number of pages and reads on. "From the Greek: *Pheo* or *phaeo*—meaning dun-colored, from *phaeophyta*, a division of brown algae mostly marine, diverse in form, often of gigantic size, anchored by holdfasts to the ocean bottom . . ." That's enough. The rest she can look up as they go along.

"So it looks like we may be dealing with something entirely different from that earlier diagnosis of renal cell carcinoma, possibly even something we can cure, an extremely rare kind of tumor called pheochromocytoma," says Nancy, the admitting resident at the Boston Institute. She flips his record shut, waves her hand dismissively and says in an unbearably chipper voice, "Oh, but I'm sorry, this is so technical, it must all be Greek to you."

Phil looks at her. "That's because it *is* all Greek," he says solemnly.

Nancy blinks, stares at him and then at Sara in momentary confusion. "You're right," she says, and starts to laugh.

He stares at the lighted X-rays, past Bierstadt's pointing finger, beyond the knobs of coral, through the ribs of sunken ships, into the sea of darkness, where the shadows lie. They loom before him, diverse forms often of gigantic size, anchored to the bottom by holdfasts. Ah, he thinks, looking at the dark shapes lurking under the surface, here, here, and here, it is the Other. But no, he thinks as he stares at diverse shapes enclosed within the chalk white smudge of bone, shadows enclosed in other shadows, trying to feel the presence of this alien other deep inside, stretching and extending as the light shines bright behind. He feels nothing, only himself. Ah, not the Other, he thinks. Flesh of my flesh. The Shadow. Me.

"How's he doing?" Sara asks, sticking her head in the door of the infusion room. Phil is stretched out on the recliner, head back, snoring gently, a thin hospital blanket covering him from neck to knees, tucked in all around. His face is pale, waxen-looking, his lips chapped and dry.

"Sleeping like a baby," Elsie croons softly as she hangs another bag. She looks apologetically at Sara. "He's not quite done yet; can you come back in a little while?" she says in a small, squeaky voice, obviously puzzled that Sara has not waited for her call. On the telephone she sounds just like a little girl calling with a message from her mother: "Hello, this is Elsie at the hospital. Mr. Boyd is ready to go home now."

"That's okay, Elsie. I have some other things to do. I just stopped in on my way downtown. Half an hour?"

Elsie glances at the bag. "Give it forty-five."

In his sleep, Phil grimaces, and his body lurches forward slightly. She hears an odd noise, an intake of air sharply cut off. She moves forward in alarm as the strange sound is repeated, a strangled chuckle deep inside his chest, because it sounds like he's going to heave, and his plastic dish has fallen on the floor.

"That's just hiccups," Elsie says. "He already tossed his cookies a little while ago. But he's doing just fine now." She moves to the next chair, sits down next to a frail, thin woman in a turban, eyebrows scrawled across her marble forehead as though with charcoal, and picks up her limp hand.

Sara smiles what she hopes is encouragingly at the woman over Elsie's shoulder. "See you later," she says, turns and walks out of the room.

In the hall she runs into an acquaintance from the college, a woman who knows her and Phil slightly, impeccably groomed from the top of her dutchboy haircut, her magenta boiled-wool jacket and paisley skirt to the tips of her discreetly fashionable low-heeled pumps, sweeping through the main entrance on her way, no doubt, to do good works. "Oh, come on now!" the woman says heartily, barely breaking stride as she reaches out a tsk-tsk finger to tap Sara on the shoulder as she breezes by. "Smile! It can't be that bad!"

Sara stops in her tracks, turns her head slowly and just looks at her, then continues out the door without a word.

Sitting on a bench just outside the entrance to the hospital, waiting for Sara to pick him up, Phil inhales deeply of the cold, damp air. It's getting on for spring, but the ground is still frozen, remnants of tired-looking snow still on the ground. He shivers. He wonders what month it is. February? March? In June it will be eighteen months since he started chemo. One more summer, the eighth since his first operation, sixth since he got sick again. He wonders if he'll make it that far.

Suddenly without warning, he feels his stomach contract, churning upward. God, what could be left? He moves his knees apart, bends forward, and vomits discreetly into the dirty snow.

As Sara wheels the car into the turnaround, leans over and opens the door, he stands up, walks as steadily as possible on feet as huge and numb as paving stones over to the car and gets in, hoping he can make it home without getting sick. As he fastens his seat belt, Sara hands him a towel and the big white plastic basin they always bring from home. He cradles it in his lap and looks at her, turned toward him from the driver's seat, an anxious expression on her face.

"You okay?" she asks.

She means does he need to blow lunch. He doesn't at the moment, not that that means anything. With this kind of vomiting—projectile, chemical-induced, so Sara tells him—there's usually no sense of the stomach in an uproar, no early warning wave of nausea. One minute you're sitting there minding your own business, the next minute up it comes and you've got your face in the bowl. If you're lucky. He nods his head and smiles. "Sure."

Sara moves her foot from the brake to the accelerator, starts to let up on the clutch. His eyelids rotate downward, irresistible, heavy as soup-spoons. Reduction of pressure on the inhibiting mechanism accompanied by increase in application of propelling force results in motion. Thus when you can no longer hold your eyes open, they fall shut. When a moving object is inadvertently stopped by a stationary force or one moving in an opposite direction, an accident results. For every action there is an equal and opposite reaction. When an irresistible object meets an immovable force—or is it the other way around?—stasis, usually temporary, results. He wonders which is the force and which the object, the treatment or the disease. He wonders which is worse. Not that it really matters; whichever way you look at it, he is the accident. He wonders how long temporary stasis lasts. Evidently not long enough.

"Wait," he mumbles indistinctly, his tongue still thick from the last drug they shot him up with, which makes his face swell up and his jaw not work right for a while. He might as well be drunk.

She shoves the clutch back down and hits the brake, probably thinking he has to pitch, but that's not it. He reaches across her, and pulls the seat belt buckle out. "Fashion your sheet—seat belt," he says as distinctly as possible. "Case of an accident. Can't be too careful. Right?"

"Right," she says, clicking the buckle into the slot.

Even though she knows it doesn't help, she still tries to drive home carefully, as though he were a crate of eggs or a plate-glass window, not going around curves too fast, or flying too precipitously over frost heaves in the road. This runs counter to her instinct to drive too fast, get home as soon as possible, before he starts to throw up in the car. She still remembers the first time she picked him up after they started the treatment here, a year ago January. He'd walked right to the car on his own, a little groggy but still upright. He hadn't gotten sick, he told her proudly, didn't even feel nauseous. The drugs they gave him to keep him from puking his brains out—correction, that's "inhibit the emetic reflex"—must be working; maybe this wasn't going to be so bad after all.

Elated, eager to get away from the hospital, she had driven off lickety-split down the street, up and over the little bridge, around the curve and down the hill, whoops-a-daisy. Suddenly she was aware of a noise like a balky pump next to her, Phil cupping his hands over his mouth, saying in a choked voice as though he were gargling, "Quick, give me the bowl, I'm going to be sick." Looking wildly around the car she had realized there was nothing remotely resembling a receptacle, not even a paper cup, so she'd pulled the car over to the curb. Phil had flung open the door, seen where they were and reared back, horrified. They had stopped right alongside the house of their friends Ralph and Alice.

"Oh, Christ," he groaned, "not here—" Then retching noisily, he'd leaned over and heaved repeatedly into a snowbank not ten feet from their friends' living room windows, while Sara had stroked his arm, saying "just let it go, don't fight it," all the time expecting the shades to fly up, the windows to rattle open, cries of alarm, a dismayed Ralph and Alice running out the door with wet towels and glasses of water, wanting to know what they could do to help.

The shades had stayed pulled, the windows shut, and Ralph and Alice, not at home that day, never knew that Phil had whoopsed all over their snow. Phil had wiped his beard and moustache with grocery cash-register slips and a crumpled wad of Kleenex that Sara had found under the seat. "Jesus, it looks like piss," Phil said, and kicked fresh snow over the patch. Then they had snuck down the block and continued on their way. Since then, for the half-hour ride home on these days, they are their own traveling sick bay, portable sink, towels and wet washcloth. When he starts to retch Sara just rolls the window down, and once out of town with no cars in sight, they stop to empty out the pan.

She's heading for the city limits when she sees the blue lights twirling in her rearview mirror. Damn, she thinks. Carefully she steers the car over to the curb, trying not to disturb Phil, who is sitting upright with his head lolling precariously against the seatback, eyes shut, mouth hanging open, face flushed, snoring gently. As soon as the car stops, he opens his eyes and looks around, beaming happily, completely out of it.

The officer leans in her window. "Hey, lady, do you know you were doing forty in a twenty-five mile an hour zone?"

"I'm sorry, Officer," Sara says. "I'm just trying to get my husband home from the hospital."

"*From* the hospital?" the cop asks skeptically, already reaching around into his back pocket for his ticket book. "That's a new one. Isn't the story usually '*to* the hospital'?"

"No, Officer," Sara says politely, trying to calculate the fine; five bucks for each mile over twenty-five; damn. "He's been there already. I'm trying to get him back home before he gets sick."

The cop looks at her as though she's crazy. "Let me get this straight, lady. You were speeding because you're coming *from* the hospital so you can get back home *before* your husband gets sick," he says with elaborate patience. "Is that correct?"

Hearing him repeat it, Sara realizes what she's left out. "He's a cancer patient on chemotherapy," she explains. "He just had a treatment—"

The cop peers over at Phil. "He doesn't look that sick to me," he says. He turns to her with an accusing look, says in a flinty voice, "Your license and registration, please."

Sara is rummaging through her pocketbook for her driver's license when she hears the familiar sound, as though someone just punched Phil in the gut. "Unh." Then again, louder: "Unh!" She watches the policeman's face as his eyes flick in Phil's direction. A belch, more gasps, then the sound of a huge yawn, of liquid splashing into the plastic bowl, the smell of rotting seashore. The color drains from the officer's face. Sara smiles sweetly and offers him her driver's license.

The officer quickly steps back from the car, flipping his ticket book shut. "Uh, that's okay, lady. Never mind," he shouts as he skips backward toward the patrol car. "Just watch it next time, will you?" Sara watches in her rearview mirror as he hops in, turns off the blinkers, pulls quickly out and around their car.

"What's going on?" Phil mutters indistinctly. "Is there an accident? Are you okay?"

"Everything's just fine," she says, handing him a towel. He wipes his face, then opens the car door and dumps the contents of the basin in the street. She starts to chuckle, then to laugh. Phil looks at her, puzzled. He won't remember this, but perhaps she will tell him later. "Perfect," she says. "You were great."

Phil lies as straight as possible in bed, on his back, not turning his head one way or the other until the worst of the dizziness passes, thinking about the conversation he heard yesterday. While the doctor was examining him, the phone rang. "Oh, hello," his doctor said. "Thanks for admitting that patient of mine." A pause, then with a dismissive wave of his hand, oblivious of Phil sitting there right in front of him. "Oh, yeah, he's just dying. Uh-hmm. Cancer, of course." A sympathetic chuckle. "I know. You must have felt like you'd just liberated Auschwitz."

It is not the first callous remark Phil has heard this doctor make, but right now he hardly cares. He feels just awful, still sick to his stomach, the muscles sore from retching, his throat burned by the bile, a rotten taste in his mouth. What else? His bones ache inside his skin, sick bones so sore he can feel each and every one, floating like slivers of hot glass in flesh that feels like jelly. He feels as though he's been run over by a truck. His teeth hurt, and tomorrow the hinges of his jaw will start to ache. The tips of his fingers and his toes are numb and tinglingly painful at the same time. Though the other effects will lessen in a week or so, his toes and fingers will stay this way, worsening with each treatment. For a while he was afraid he eventually wouldn't be able to hold a pen to grade his papers, or run anymore. That, like his hair falling out, hasn't happened, not quite, and he's only lost eight pounds. He can still write, and run, even though he can't quite feel the pavement or the pen. He doesn't know if this nerve damage is reversible with the cessation of treatment; he certainly hopes so. He doesn't look like the victim of a concentration camp, at least not yet. But he has been thinking about all this, and has made up his mind.

Head whirling, thoughts disconnected and nightmarish, he opens his eyes. Sara is standing next to the bed. He wants to say something to her, but his tongue is thick inside his mouth, the buzz and rush of blood so loud inside his brain he can't think of the right words. He probably has brain damage, too.

"Here's your bucket," he hears her say as though from far away. "I'm taking the dog out for a walk. The phone is off the hook so you can get some sleep."

"Thanks," he whispers as his eyes roll shut. The last thing he wants to do is sleep and dream, but he can't help it; he's dragged down by the heels into the vortex, twirled around and around and down until the black water closes over his head.

Sara watches Phil's heavy-lidded eyes roll back, then slowly close. Smiling over some secret, he rolls onto his side, disturbing the covers like a great fish, then brings his knees up, presses his hands together flat as though in prayer and tucks them between the pillow and one cheek with a sigh. He looks like an angelic child in a false beard. Relieved that he is more comfortable now, the worst of the vomiting over, she straightens the covers, pulls them up around his neck and tucks him in. It will be a couple of hours before the kids get home from school, so he has some time to sleep it off.

Outside, watching the dog yank his leg up next to the woodpile, insert his long nose like a hummingbird into the rumpled snowbank at the end of the driveway, she ponders once again the mystery. Here is a man who respects his parents, is loving and faithful to his wife, kind to dogs and children, doesn't smoke, drinks little and not often, has always followed a nutritious diet high in bulk and fiber with plenty of fresh fruit, has an aversion to red meat, drinks plenty of liquids, gets his rest, takes his vitamins every day, flosses his teeth each morning and night, always wears his seat belt, observes the speed limit, pays his bills promptly, and wouldn't be caught dead walking on the grass. What else is there, what fault to be construed? He has been a loving son, spouse, and father, a responsible citizen, teacher, and friend. What has he done, she demands of the air at random, to deserve this suffering, this pain?

Close to tears, a thought occurs to her. Maybe it's me you're mad at? she queries, staring at the sky. The sky does not stare back. The bare tree branches overhead rattle like castanets. If I say Okay, okay, I give; you're up there, will you let him off the hook? How about if I give up orgasms? Let's make a deal.

Of course there is no answer. Clouds cover the sky like the inside of an oyster shell, soft clouds like mother-of-pearl, nacre over pain.

The dog starts to bark, bounces stiff-legged down the lawn and disappears behind a petrified snow bank, his ears bobbing up like furry butterflies. This dog is sweet-natured, eager to please, but dumb, no match for the legendary Collie Cibber. Not that they wanted one, knowing the other dog could never be replaced, in fact set out deliberately to find one different in almost every way, given that they wanted the same breed. So they purposely got and even paid for a full-blooded collie of a different color, long nose, and large, sturdy parentage, no joke names this time, St. Brendan the Navigator for the Kennel Club, Brennie for short. There is just this one strange thing. Bred to be much larger, he has grown, black like a shadow, to exactly the same size, as if to fill the empty dog-shaped space in all their hearts.

"See, whatever's gone can be replaced," Phil said the other day, watching her and the children, all of whom had mourned the old dog bitterly for years, frolicking on the lawn with the new one.

"Rolled-newspaper remark!" she yelled, and started to whack him with her glove. She tripped him, wrestled him to the ground, and she, the children, and the dog all fell upon him, pretending to beat him up. Rolled-newspaper remarks—pessimistic observations assuming his own imminent death and subsequent replacement—are comments, on the advice of their shrink, that she no longer tolerates. No more gloom and doom, dire predictions about life going on without him. They'll jump off that place when they come to it, and it isn't yet.

Lying in bed, Phil hears Sara talking to the dog in her Minnie Mouse voice, the one she reserves for pets and small children. He listens as she comes inside and shuts the door, hears the jingle of the dog's tags as he shakes crumbs snow from his coat, the ritual thump of the two dog biscuits she tosses on the floor. The dog flops down with a groan and starts to crunch his biscuits.

The stairs creak as she starts up them, trying to be quiet in case he's asleep. He props himself up into a sitting position and slowly swings his legs over the side of the bed. He hopes he isn't going to be sick anymore, because there's something he wants to tell her right now, before the kids get home.

She stands in the doorway, watching him retch into the plastic bowl. The immediate effects seem to be getting worse each time, and it's taking him longer and longer to get over the long-term ones. How much more of this can even he, the strong, the indomitable one, endure? She moves toward him to take the basin, but he waves her aside, stands up on wobbly pins, staggers past her out the door. She hears him dump the contents in the toilet, flush it, then rinse the basin in the bathtub. He clears his throat, comes back down the hallway into the bedroom carrying it in front of him, flops back down in bed, panting, his eyelids at half-mast. She pats his hot thigh, strokes his arm, feeling as though she might burst into tears at any moment, scream and cry. But she won't let herself; it would just upset him, and crying is no relief to her, either. It has been a long day.

He shuts his eyes and takes a deep, ragged breath, then opens them. His lips tremble. He looks at her, eyes round with effort. "This is it, Sara," he says. "I quit."

A chill spreads over her. "What do you mean?"

"I mean this is it, the end. I'm not doing this anymore. It's not worth it. *I'm* not worth it. Or what's left of me."

Before she can even open her mouth to say "rolled-newspaper remark," he clutches her hand, face pleading for silence. "It's over, Sara. I wanted to be a hero, but I'm just a patient."

"You are a hero," she says.

He shakes his head. "No, I'm not. I wanted to do good in the world, and all I did was get sick. Heroes don't spend their lives puking their brains out."

"Heroes puke their brains out and then clean up after themselves."

His smile is fleeting, the distraction momentary. "It's not doing any good, Sara. I can tell. Let's face it, this has just been one long holding operation. And now it isn't even that any more. I'm getting worse—again."

Sara feels as though she's been turned to stone, the resistance hardening to anger, the old impulse to argue, to cajole, if necessary browbeat, welling up instead of tears. "How can you say that? You can't tell that, at least not until you go out there next month."

"I'm not going. It would be a waste of time. I know just what they'll tell me. 'You've had some benefit, but the treatments appear to have only arrested the disease temporarily, and now it's starting to progress again . . .' " He pauses. "Listen, my blood pressure yesterday morning was one-ninety over one-twenty. I'm short of breath, I wake up with a headache almost every morning, and I'm starting to get dizzy spells. Not to mention that I feel like hell from the chemo all the time."

"It could be just the treatments, tumor breaking down maybe, not necessarily a bad thing . . ." Sara babbles, talking as fast as she can, more afraid than angry now. "You should wait to find out, you should go to Michigan, let them sort it out, before you make any long-term decisions. Maybe they'll come up with something else." She drops her eyes, unable to face the stern, pitying resolution in his glance. "Anyway, I already bought your ticket," she says desperately. "You have to go."

"Take it back. Save the money."

"Phil, please. Who cares about the money? Can't we just go on as we are, the way we planned? I don't care what it's like, as long as I can see your face, talk to you, hear your voice . . ."

"Come on, Sara, face it. I can't go on forever. There's going to come a time when you'll just have to let me go."

"But don't you want to live? Don't you want to go on as long as you can?" she pleads.

He shakes his head. "Not like this."

"What do you want?"

"I want to quit while I still have something left. I want to be left alone. I want one more good summer." He closes his eyes, swallows painfully. "I just want to sail."

Sara stares at him for a moment. She wants to say something, but her throat is tight, all the space for words enclosed by sobs. Feeling the tears start, she jumps up, runs blindly out of the room and down the stairs, barely noticing the startled faces of David and Linnie and she brushes by them at the door. "Hey, Mom, what's wrong, where are you going?" she hears them call behind her.

"Away!" she shouts back at them as she runs down the long driveway as fast as she can, out onto the street and down the road.

She does not go far. After a few hundred yards, out of breath, she slows down and just walks along the shoulder, trying to straighten out her thoughts, listening to the sounds of the cars whizzing by, waiting, hoping that she will hear the familiar sound of their car engine behind her, slowing down, Phil coming after her, finding her and comforting her. But she knows this is impossible; even if he could drive in his condition, the stern unyielding distance he has begun to put between them forbids it. This, she realizes, is the beginning of their inevitable separation: "There will come a time when you'll just have to let me go." The Shadow knows. She looks up. Too soon, too soon, she protests, but again the sky, dark now, vouchsafes no comfort. She is alone.

As she starts up the hill and rounds the corner back toward their house, she sees in the distance a figure standing at the head of the driveway. Oh, Phil! she thinks, and starts to run. But as she comes closer, the figure separates into two, and in the dusk she see the faces of her children turned toward her anxiously, David grinning foolishly, Linnie dissolved in tears. "Mom, where have you been?" Linnie demands. "We were worried! You acted like you were running away."

"I just went for a walk," she answers, and puts her arms around both of them, murmurs soothingly routine questions about their day as they walk back down the long driveway toward the old house. The dog frisks out of the tumbledown garage, wagging his tail in greeting. This is what I will be left with, Sara thinks. We are the ones who will grow old together. This is how it will be.

After she puts the dinner on, she goes upstairs to see him. He's sitting up in bed, looking exhausted, but not quite so pale and heavy-lidded. "I'm sorry, Sara," he says. "You don't have to take the ticket back. I'll go, even if it's going to be nothing but bad news."

Sara smiles and nods, relieved that after all he's going. Then she will know that they have exhausted every effort, done everything they could.

What she doesn't tell him, at least not yet, is that she would have had to take two tickets back, because this morning when she picked his up she bought herself one too. Bad news is always better shared.

IO

Last Things

"I wish you'd tell them," Sara says. It's Saturday morning, a nice day for a change this rainy June, and they're standing around in the kitchen wondering which overdue chore to do next. Or rather Sara is; Phil is thinking about going to the boat. "Just talk to them about it," she says. "Give them a chance to get ready." The kids are upstairs, happily watching television. The last thing Phil wants to do is tell them anything. What he really wants to do is go sailing.

"Okay, okay," he answers. "I'll get around to it. I just don't know when." He's been meaning to say something to the kids for several weeks now, ever since he and Sara got the final word, but there never seems to be a right moment.

"Well, it'd better be pretty soon. You're running out of time," she says, yanking open the back door. She's wearing her old jeans and a flannel shirt, and there is a pair of ratty work gloves—his work gloves as a matter of fact—hanging out of her back pocket far enough to make it look as though they're trying to grab her ass. He smiles. He'd like to grab her ass himself. But before he can get into position she stalks out the door into the garage, clearly not in the mood.

She's probably going out to her workshop, to take another look at the collection of sculptures she's been working on for about a year now, figures done in plaster and clay he hasn't seen because she keeps them under wraps, covered up with old sheets and blankets as though they were real people she had to keep warm. One of them is of her father, and he suspects another one has something to do with him, as far as he can guess from the shape under the covers. He used to peek once in a while, or she would show him something, watch his reaction, ask his advice, but lately she has kept her work pretty much to herself. He has a feeling it's not going well, but that's her business. The fact is, he is no longer even curious about what she's doing, and if it's about him, he really doesn't want to know. He can't help her anymore; she's gone ahead without him, which is just as well. He's sure she'll work it out, particularly after he's gone and she isn't so distracted all the time. Anyway, he's still got some tidying up to do in the kitchen. Then maybe he'll go upstairs and tell the kids.

Sara picks her way through the pile of sailboat gear that Phil has yet to put on the boat, at the moment spread all over one side of the garage, so they have to park the old rusty pickup in the turn-around. It looks tacky, but so what? The whole place is falling down anyway. She just can't keep up with it. One evening last week she heard a loud rending noise right outside their bedroom window, followed by a rhythmic plop-plop-plop. She rushed to the window thinking the chimney had finally gone over, but it was just a shutter inexplicably split apart, attached by a single hinge and swinging out at a drunken angle as one by one the slats separated from the loosened frame and dropped onto the ground below. She had opened the window, lifted what was left of the frame up off its hinge and tossed it down.

It's sitting in the workshop now, a pile of intact slats arranged like pick-up sticks, the frame in several pieces, old green paint as thick and checkered and mud-stained as a crocodile hide. They have more shutters stacked up over the eaves of the garage, but none of them is the same size, so she'll have to put it back together. It's just one more thing on her list, along with the half-cut woodpile fallen in a heap and rotting alongside the driveway, the peeling paint, the broken storm windows, the tottering chimney, the leaky basement, the overgrown lawn. The list goes on and on. No wonder she doesn't have any time to work on her sculpture anymore; she's too busy shoring up the ruins. But maybe she'll get back to it one of these days.

She's looking for the wood glue and duct tape when she hears a crunch of gravel in the driveway. She pokes her head out the garage door opening to see an unfamiliar, neat-looking car roll up and park in the wrong place, as though whoever is driving doesn't know which entrance to try first. As she stands there in her torn jeans and work gloves an unfamiliar, neat-looking woman gets out. She's elderly, short, rather frail, wearing a lightweight beige flannel suit, and there is a fat book in her hand, which probably means she is not canvassing for a favorite charity. She smiles in a restrained but hopeful way as she totters somewhat uncertainly toward Sara, flicking a look out of the corners of both eyes as though expecting to be attacked by something. Sara wishes the dog would start barking, but the only time he ever does that is when someone in the family comes home.

Not only has Sara had experience with itinerant encyclopedia and book salespersons, not to mention the odd vacuum-cleaner peddler and religious maniac, she regards them as a real intrusion. Whatever this woman is selling, she doesn't want any, and is about to say in a polite but firm voice, "I'm not interested," when the woman stops about six feet away, folds her hands over the book, fixes her eyes on a point just over Sara's left shoulder, takes a deep breath and says in a reverent falsetto: "Hello. I'm here to talk to you about the future—"

"Well, I don't want to. Go away," Sara snaps, turns on her heel and walks back into the garage.

Phil climbs the stairs and stands in the doorway of what used to be the playroom, now the home of the television set. The kids are too old to play as such anymore—no more coloring books and crayons and Lego and toy cars all over the floor—but they still watch television. David is sprawled in his sweatpants across the sleeper couch and Linnie is sitting on the floor in one of Phil's old tee-shirts, strands of brightly-colored embroidery floss tied to her toes, weaving a bracelet that resembles multicolored rickrack. They are watching a program featuring real people. Could it be they have finally outgrown cartoons?

"Hi, Dad," David growls as he lifts the remote control and waves it in the direction of the television. The human faces are replaced by smooth, bright images straight out of a comic book with sound effects to match. Both kids grin and start to chuckle, eyes glued on the flickering screen. Suddenly they look very young. No, not a good time, Phil thinks. He watches them watching for a few moments, then turns to go back downstairs. Maybe tomorrow, or next week, when he can talk to each of them alone. Better to tell them separately, so they have a chance to take it in.

Sara is gazing speculatively at the slats, wondering if they are all different sizes—graduated maybe, crazy as that sounds, otherwise why can't she get this thing back together?—when she hears the phone ring. Someone inside answers it. Press this, squeeze that, insert tab A into slot B, on to the next. She's already reinforced the frame with angle irons; this is the tricky part, getting the slats to go.

At one time or another she has tried her hand at most of the heavy chores Phil usually takes care of—splitting wood, raking snow off the roof, digging up the septic tank, even running the chain saw—but her real mission in life is fixing things. The Fix-it Queen: she is legendary in the family, at least to her children, for being able to find, fix or replace anything, her motto "At least it's worth a try." She grabs the shutter by the top of the frame and tilts it on its side. It's so heavy she has to rest it on her thigh. Several supposedly replaced slats fall out. She puts it back down on the workbench, wondering who's on the phone.

Phil sticks his head out the back door. "You ready for this?"

Sara nods, wiping her sticky hands on the back of her pants. But Phil's attention is momentarily distracted by the sight of the shutter. "What are you doing with that?"

"Trying to put it back together," she says.

"Don't be stupid," Phil says. "It's not worth it. It will just fall apart again. You can always get a new—"

"Who is it?" she interrupts, coming toward him. They can sort out the shutter controversy later. Phil doesn't want her to put it back together, but she knows a new one won't match, besides being outrageously expensive. She can't buy a new shutter every time one falls off the house. They'd be broke in no time.

"That was Mack," Phil says. "He wants to stop and see us. Not only that, he wants us to meet his new woman, Buffy or Muffy or whatever her name is."

Sara groans in exasperation. She doesn't want to see anybody in the first place, and if she did, Mack would be the last person. You'd think he could take the hint, his letters and cards unanswered ever since he left Jane for another woman after twenty years of marriage and two kids. They had all been good friends for a long time—Mack was even an usher at their wedding—but after the separation Sara had decided that Jane needed friends more. After all, Mack had Biffy or Cissy or whatever her name was. Phil has been more neutral, but he didn't exactly keep up the correspondence either. She dusts her hands off. "Well, I don't want to see them. Tell him we won't be home. He can come sometime when I'm not here."

"I can't. He called from the phone booth at the bottom of the hill. They'll be here in thirty seconds."

Sara can hardly believe her ears. "You're kidding!"

Phil shakes his head.

"But I can't be here! I promised Jane I'd be *her* friend!" She whirls around, suddenly agitated, looking for an exit. She is about to race toward the turnaround, jump in the pickup truck and drive away when she sees a station wagon loaded with camping equipment turn in at the top of the driveway. "I think I'm going to be sick," she says. Phil holds the door open for her as she goes inside.

"The worst thing is he's taken away my memories," Jane sobs over the phone. She's just called Phil and Sara to break the news of the separation. "All this time, for twenty years, I thought everything was wonderful. Now he's saying none of it was true."

Sara can't believe it; she feels like banging the phone against the wall, or better yet, ripping it right out.

At the other end of the line Jane heaves a huge, shuddering sigh. "I hate to say this, especially to you, but it would have been better if he'd died. Then at least I'd still have my memories. But he's ruined them all."

Hearing Jane's choked voice over the telephone line, Sara remembers the last time the four of them were together, in the art museum cafeteria that time two years ago when they were in Boston to see Nevins, sitting there in the atrium, laughing and talking, eating cheese and bread and drinking wine, good old friends, just the way it used to be back when they were in graduate school. And all the while keeping their secrets: Jane and Mack had been separated for over a month; she and Phil had just found out the disease was back. Business as usual, just like old times, but it had all been a pretense, an illusion.

"That day in the museum, when you called, said let's get together, oh, I don't know," Jane says now. "You'd both been through so much—and there was still a chance then, so we . . . we decided to act as if nothing were wrong. I guess we fooled you, huh?" Fresh barrage of sobs. It's all Sara can do to keep from joining in. Jane and Mack, good friends all the way back to graduate school, insisting Sara stay with them in Lexington while Phil was in the hospital for his second operation, faithful Jane, who jabbered and twiddled her bare toes and did needlepoint for eight hours straight, sitting next to Sara in the hospital waiting room; handsome Mack, who said little but suffered much, and always had a stiff drink waiting when she came back to their house at night after a long day standing vigil outside the intensive care unit; Jane and Mack the high school sweethearts, the romantic June wedding, reception in the garden of her parents' house on the Hudson, so much in love, the perfect marriage, perfect children, the perfect life together as Mack mounted the corporate ladder toward his vice-presidency, Jane the perfect executive wife, the homemaker, enthusiastic party-giver, always at his side; Jane and Mack are getting a divorce.

Sara simply can't believe it. Surely there's some mistake? A chance they'll make it up? No, the papers are all signed, the decree is final in a month. What about the kids, a boy and girl not much older than David and Linnie? Joint custody. Everything is done, finished. It's not until Sara hangs up the phone that she realizes she doesn't even know the reason why.

Phil can't believe it either, but he gets the rest of the story when Mack calls *him* at the office the next day. "Their paths have diverged," Phil repeats to Sara. "He says their interests are no longer the same and they've drifted apart. He says it goes back at least ten years. He's been pretending all this time, trying to make it work."

Twenty years of perfection, ten of it illusion. So much for the memories. "So what's the grounds?" Sara asks.

"Irreconcilable differences. He hopes we can all still be friends."

"Ha," says Sara. "Sounds like bullshit to me. I'll bet it's another woman."

Phil and Buffy are sitting in the living room when Sara comes back downstairs; Mack has headed straight for the john. Supposedly she was changing her clothes, as good an excuse as any for being upstairs gathering her wits when they first arrived. She was up there for an inordinately long time, Phil thinks, considering that she has only changed into a slightly more respectable pair of pants, but Mack and Buffy don't know that. Phil supposes he should be glad she came downstairs at all. He smiles encouragingly at her as she walks over to the couch and sits down next to Buffy. Her face is stiff, her expression not overtly hostile, but not exactly friendly either. He sees she has put on eye makeup. He winks at her, hoping she'll loosen up.

Mack reappears, starts talking away as fast as he can, nervous, Phil can tell, about bringing this Buffy person to meet them; Phil feels sorry for him, especially with Sara sitting there silent, her face immobile, her expression all but a glare. He had no idea she'd taken the breakup so personally.

They've been camping out in the mountains, Mack tell them, are now on their way back to Boston, can't stay, but wanted to stop in and say hello to old friends. Buffy is younger, slight, soft-

S a i l i n g

spoken, reserved, dark, and quite pretty in a sharp-nosed patrician way, about as different from big, hearty, buxom Jane as you can get, which is something of a relief to Phil. His observation has been that their divorced friends seem to pick the same sort of person all over again, which makes the split seem that much more arbitrary and inexplicable, not to mention the problem of mixing up the names.

Phil asks if they want coffee or tea or a drink. After all it's nearly lunchtime, though lunch is clearly out of the question, Sara with her bats on, sitting there as though she's been shot up with Novocaine; he briefly imagines her mixing a laxative into the chicken salad or some other dark revenge. Mack and Buffy both leap at the chance. He starts to get up, but Sara stops him back with a look. "No, I'll do it, you just sit."

Over the sound of much banging of crockery in the kitchen, they converse a while longer about mundane matters. Nothing is said about the divorce, but eventually Mack pops the other loaded question, "How are *you*?" just as Sara is coming back into the room with a tray of iced tea and coffee. Phil is glad she has something to do with her hands and her face and her mouth, asking about cream and sugar and so forth, because it's clear she still hasn't reconciled herself to this visitation. Although he doesn't like to have to go over everything again—it always gives him nightmares when he talks about his illness now—he sees it as a way of easing the silence, and so spends some time giving a slightly laundered but extensive account of what has been going on since they last saw—he almost says "you and Jane," but stops himself in time.

Mack listens and nods sympathetically, rocking back and forth in the creaky old upstate New York rocking chair they've had since graduate school, fingertips together in a thoughtful, Gothic peak, his handsome face impassive; after all, he's used to this, has been in on it almost from the beginning. After a minute or two Buffy excuses herself, also to go to the bathroom. Sara listens intently as usual, her eyes on Phil's face. You'd think she'd get sick of listening to the same old story—he knows it gives her nightmares

255

too—but she says it comes out differently each time he tells some-body else. Since the two of them hardly discuss the subject any-more, he supposes it's her way of finding out what he thinks.

He's just started telling Mack about what he's going to do next—the public version, that is—when he notices Sara clearing her throat, wiggling her eyebrows, nodding her head significantly in the direction of the door. Mack glances over, then hops up with a huge grin. "Hi, guys!" he says in his best camp-counselor voice, extending his hand to David and Linnie, who, Phil is glad to see, have finally decided to get dressed and come down. Mack is pound-ing David's bicep and rubbing Linnie's hair in his old Uncle Mack fashion when Buffy comes back into the room. The kids turn to her expectantly, and go goggle-eyed. They stare speechless, their mouths hanging open, from Mack to Buffy to Phil and Sara and then at each other while the introductions are made. What the hell's eating them, Phil wonders crossly, why are they acting so strange? What is it with everybody in this house? Can't people even be polite?

Sara, picking up on it, hands David the tray and tells him to go to the kitchen and start lunch; she reminds him he's got to help with the lawn later. Both kids nearly knock each other down getting out of the room, and from the kitchen there's an outburst of excited comment, quickly smothered.

It is not until after he and Sara have waved goodbye to Mack and Buffy, seen them roll safely down the driveway out onto the road and he's about to go inside and bawl David and Linnie out for being so rude that he realizes what has happened. The kids come tumbling out of the house, pointing and gesticulating at the disappearing car with expressions of total astonishment on their faces. "Mom! Dad!" they shout in unison. "What happened to Jane? Where are the kids? What was Mack doing here with another woman?"

He and Sara exchange a look. No one has thought to tell the children about Jane and Mack, and their lack of information has left them vulnerable to this rude shock. This time the result was vaguely comic; another time it might not be. Plans or no plans, the fact is that with the disease barely under control now, he could pop off at any moment, just the way Sara's father did. Bad as the situation is, according to Sara that would be worse. Whatever happens, he owes them the chance to get ready, so they won't be taken by surprise the way Sara and her family were. It can never be too soon.

"Okay, I get it," he says to Sara. "I'll tell them both this afternoon."

Sara lifts the cover off the smaller of the two shrouded figures in her workshop, peers at the recumbent head and shoulders, hands folded over the middle of the chest so it resembles the top half of a tombstone effigy. The face is good enough, eyes closed as though in sleep, skin smoothed, lips faintly smiling, but the hands continue to elude her. Small hands, but not a woman's hands. These are dead hands, pinched and lifeless; after all this time she still can't get them right. She thinks of the last time she saw her father alive, hoisting his new suitcase, blowing kisses, waving goodbye that day in June, a sunny day not unlike today, thirty-four years ago this week in fact. "See you when I get back." She wishes she had never seen him dead.

She uncovers the larger figure, clay over an armature of wire and lath, a life-sized nude male from head to thighs, reclining on its side. Classic in form, it resembles Phil, or rather Phil the way he was before (the patient is a well-nourished and well-developed white male, with no distinguishing scars or marks) the first operation. This too she can't seem to get right. She thought she might be able to do it from memory, working from feel alone, but the sense is lost. She's not even sure why she's doing it.

Ranged along the walls of the darkened workshop are the other figures in the series, *Cracking Up*, the one based on her mother that won the big award, the *Mirror Image* abstract, the slightly corny *Little Girl Lost* that ended up being bought in a limited edition for a fancy mail-order catalogue and is now in living rooms all over the country as decorator art—she's still embarrassed about that, but it was more money than she imagined possible and they needed it for the boat—and her current favorite, a shaggy dog done in the plaster-impregnated fabric doctors use for casts, wound and draped over an old wooden sawhorse, molded and fringed with garden shears before it hardened, tongue hanging out, limpid agate marbles for eyes, fuzzy pipe cleaners for the cocky caterpillar eyebrows. The dog is the only one who is smiling.

Piled in a corner looking like a stack of used lumber is the marionette theater she worked so hard to salvage summer before last. No one ever uses it; she's too busy and the kids aren't interested anymore. Maybe she should just get out Phil's chain saw—if she can get it to work, the thing's so tricky and she's a little bit afraid of it—and saw it up for kindling, add it to the bonfire of things she'd like to get rid of, broken shutters, old doors, piles of boxes and newspapers, scraps of wood, all the unidentifiable and indescribable junk they've accumulated in these years of living in this old house.

But she didn't come out here to take inventory. Rummaging under the workbench, she pulls out the mahogany box containing the Plath sextant and a copy of Bowditch's *Practical Navigator* she bought for the kids to give Phil on Father's Day. She can wrap them both while he's explaining everything to David and Linnie. At least she hopes that's what he's doing. Then maybe they'll have an idea of what the presents are for.

As she's coming back through the garage to get some wrapping paper, Phil sticks his head out the kitchen door. "I'm going to talk to the kids now. Is there anything special do you think I should say?"

"I don't care what you tell them," she says, trying to keep the impatience out of her voice. "I just want them to be ready for whatever comes." She and Phil disagree on this point, Phil leaning toward the "the less they know the better" school, but Sara knows what it's like to be caught unawares, and her attitude has prevailed. At least she thinks it has. Anyway, he promised. Now if he would just get on with it . . .

"I'm going to talk to them separately. Which one do you think I should tell first?"

Sara rolls her eyes up, drops her head onto her chest, sags her arms and shoulders like a dispirited scarecrow in a pantomime of "I give up."

"Okay, okay," Phil says. He shuts the kitchen door. She hears him shout "Linnie!"

"Yeah, Dad?" comes Linnie's high, clear, unsuspecting voice.

"I'm sorry to have to tell you this. I know it is a disappointment," Bierstadt says in his mellow, reflective voice. "We had hoped for a more long-lasting result. Still . . ." He pauses.

Still what? Phil wonders. Sitting on his hospital bed, fully clothed because they've got a plane to catch, Phil watches Bierstadt's face. Medina has left already, his own visibly bitter disappointment striking Phil almost as a reproach, along with his parting shot, "We've done everything medical science has to offer you at this point in time."

Bierstadt has stayed on, clearly for damage control, trying in his kindly philosophical way to help them salvage something from the ruins. After all, the doctors wanted this to work as much as he did. But here we are at last, Phil thinks, once more at the end of all things. The final reckoning. Still, it was worth a try. And he has gained another year and a half, not so much for himself—let's face it, this has been no picnic—but for Sara and the children. He waits for Bierstadt to go on.

But Bierstadt does not continue. It is strange to see him at a loss for words. "So what next?" Phil asks after a moment. Sara looks up, her face impassive. Phil has to hand it to her. He hadn't wanted her to come, believing it would be easier for him to deal with this alone, but she promised she wouldn't badger the doctors with questions, bug them about this and that, and she has kept her promise. She's been sitting in the lounge chair, ostensibly looking through a magazine the whole time, hardly moving a muscle. No crying, no screaming and tearing of hair. He admires her equanimity almost as much as he is puzzled by it. It's as though she expected this all the time. He on the other hand is a wreck, soaked with sweat, limp and tremulous, short of breath. That's what comes of getting his hopes up; the funny thing is he didn't even know he had any. He thought that he was ready for this.

"Oh. Well." Bierstadt considers his answer. "I expect you'll just go on as you are, at least for a time. As long as the blood pressure can be controlled, and the tumors don't pop up in a vital place, you should be able to function. Actually, you will probably feel better than you have for a while, as the side effects of the chemotherapeutic agents wear off. After that . . ." Bierstadt represses a shrug. "It's a largely a matter of keeping on top of the blood pressure. It will go up at a greater or lesser rate, depending on tumor growth. So it must be kept track of and regulated. But you do that at home, don't you?" he says, nodding at Sara. "As you know, it's the cardiovascular effects that are usually fatal, not the tumor *per se.*"

"How long?"

Bierstadt's eyelids flicker and he looks away. Phil is instantly sorry that he asked; he should have learned by now. Oh well, might as well hear the worst. Medina would tell him quick enough. Bierstadt clears his throat, then shrugs, an uncharacteristic gesture. "I don't think anyone really knows," he says. "It's possible you could go on for years."

It's nice of him to say that, but Phil doesn't think he really believes it. Possible, but not probable. Months yes, years no. And what will those years be like? It doesn't bear much looking into. Still, Phil would like to pin him down, because he needs to know. "Will I get through the summer?"

It seems little enough to ask. Eyes on the ceiling, Bierstadt purses his lips, considering. "Oh, I should think so," he says after a moment. "Oh, the summer certainly, yes, I'd say so. Quite probably," he says in his careful, cultivated, not-quite-British tone. He looks directly at Phil. His eyes are sad.

Well, that's it then. One more good summer, and after that, a long day's dying, to augment our pain. But Phil already knows what he's going to do; he's got it all figured out, no extended disability, no long drawn-out process. He wonders if Sara suspects what he has in mind. He thinks of Sara, of the children, his parents going on without him, the people he has disappointed, the life he won't get to live, and has to squeeze his lips tight between his teeth to stop their trembling, his eyelids hard against the sudden sharp access of tears.

Bierstadt takes a deep breath and stands up. "Please keep in touch," he says. "Let us know how things are going." He extends his fleshy hand to Phil. "I'm terribly sorry about this, but please remember that we haven't abandoned you. One never knows when something may turn up."

It's such a ludicrous remark in context, yet so in character coming from chubby, red-cheeked Bierstadt, that Phil can't help smiling. "Thank you for everything," he says, standing up and shaking Bierstadt's hand. This is, of course, goodbye. The lights seem to dim, and for a moment he feels light-headed, his body floating as though cast loose, adrift. He turns away, ostensibly to zip up his suitcase, while Bierstadt says goodbye to Sara.

"Well," he says to Sara when Bierstadt has gone, the "well," repeated so often now Sara says it is his version of a sigh. "That's it, as they say in the old country. We're on our own."

Sara's not even paying attention. "Look at this," she says, waving the magazine in his face, her expression disgusted, almost outraged. He peers at the headline; it's an article about the latest treatments for cancer. Phil feels his knees go weak. God, doesn't she ever give up? How can he convince her that it's over? That he'd like the rest of the time off, while he's still got it in him to do what he has to do, the one last good summer. "Sara, not now—"

"Not the whole article, dummy," she says. "Just read this line." She thrusts the article under his nose, jabbing her finger into the flimsy page so hard it pokes a small crater in the slick surface.

The line runs under a photograph, clearly posed, of a grinning white-coated doctor next to a hospital bed containing a smiling patient, flanked by a hopeful-looking family member, presumably his spouse. The rest of the room is taken up with machines, charts, tubes, IV bags and poles. The line reads: "It's hard to describe what it's like to take care of people who have failed all other treatment."

Phil looks at Sara curiously. "So what about it?"

She jabs again, making further dents along the page. " 'People who have failed all other treatment'?" she quotes with emphasis. "Isn't that a little backwards? I mean, who the fuck failed whom?"

Sara threads her way back through the collection of sailboat equipment. It really doesn't look like much, considering: ship-to-shore radio, knot log, depth finder, a couple of fire extinguishers, safety harness, first-aid box, distress kit, wind indicator, sea anchor, assorted boxes of tools, extra hardware and rigging, a sail-mending kit—the bare minimum for someone sailing single-handed, which is what Phil does most of the time now anyway. The kids aren't interested, and she can't even bring herself to go day-sailing any more; the mere idea makes her sick. There is something so threatening, inimical about the ocean, the coldness of the water, the mindless rhythmic surging of the waves, the unpredictability of wind, the slick, nearly impenetrable surface always moving, never still, the sense of some dark hostile presence lurking underneath, with purpose to appall. To her it is the enemy.

David comes out, grumbling, to start the lawn. "How come I have to do it all?" he says to Sara, who is looking at the section in Bowditch on celestial navigation using a micrometer drum sextant before she wraps the book up. "Dad usually does half."

"He's talking to Linnie about something important," Sara answers. "Besides, you're big enough to do the whole lawn. Get used to it." Ignoring his dirty look, she shuts the book, wraps the paper around it and tapes it up. This whole process of finding out where you want to go by shooting angles of sun, moon and stars is completely unintelligible to her; it might as well be written in code. Maybe it is; it makes Phil's chain saw look about as complicated as a nail file. But Phil took a piloting and navigation course this spring, has been listening to tapes on his long drives to the coast, so he ought to be able to decipher it. She pictures him out there on the ocean, tossing up and down, taking sights and measuring speed and distance, walking the little dividers across the chart, adjusting the parallel rules.

She supposes the traditional method, without the intrusion of electronic gadgetry, cords and wires, beeps and blips and lines and graphs, has its appeal. When she had tried to talk him into getting more equipment, if not for comfort, then at least for the appearance of safety (and just in case, though she would never say this to him now, he happened to change his mind), Loran or Sat-Nav instead of just the sextant, only another few hundred bucks, or radar even, he'd just shaken his head. "Why waste the money?" he'd said, adding quickly before she could accuse him of another rolled-newspaper remark, "I want to do it the old-fashioned way. You know, '. . . All I need is a tall, tall ship, and the stars to steer her by.' " Then he'd looked at her absolutely straight-faced. "Besides, I can always fall back on dead reckoning."

"Do you remember the time we sailed down here all those summers ago in that first sailboat, the one we borrowed?" Phil asks David. They have walked down the dirt path that winds through the District Watershed Reserve to the small beach at the head of the lake. The path is marked here and there with NO TRESPASSING: VIOLATORS WILL BE PROSECUTED signs, the beach supposedly only accessible by boat, but the signs are faded, barely legible, and the local inhabitants generally ignore them. David was a little concerned about this point when they set out, but suspecting a possible avoidance impulse, Phil had assured him everything would be fine; the signs were not enforced.

Out of the corner of his eye Phil sees David frown, as if trying to remember. After a moment he grunts tentatively, "I guess." It is not clear whether he does or not, which is the whole idea, as far as Phil can tell.

David's character has been and remains a mystery to him, although Phil is haunted by the suspicion that in many ways the boy's temperament is oddly like his own. Never a particularly forthcoming child, David has lately become even more remote and inaccessible, especially, Phil feels, toward him. He supposes this is no wonder; after all, Phil has been sick now over half David's life. It's probably the most persistent memory he has, and Linnie, three years younger, remembers nothing else. Yet the children are so different in the ways they have reacted to this strange presence in their lives.

The difference is summed up for Phil in two incidents—or rather an incident and a pair of objects. He remembers just before he and Sara were about to leave for Boston that fall almost six years ago, not knowing whether he would have the operation, or if he did, whether he would survive, waiting on the porch to say good-bye to the children. Linnie came running out of the house and flung herself at Phil, grabbing onto his pant legs, clutching him, bawling her heart out, until Phil's mother came and peeled her off, took her back inside. Phil can still see the small shoulders bunched in hiccuping shrugs, the tragic face blubbered with tears watching him through the window, the small hand raised in a last despairing slow-motion wave. Upset as they were, he and Sara had to laugh at the extravagance of it all: Linnie the tragedy queen. No one will ever need to wonder what's on her mind.

David, on the other hand, was nowhere to be found; he had simply disappeared, hiding out in the tree house Phil's dad was building until they were gone. These opposite ways of reacting have persisted all these years, oddly symbolized not long ago when Sara let the children choose mugs with mottoes on them for toothbrush holders. Linnie had picked one that read THE BIG CHEESE. David's read GRIN AND IGNORE IT.

"Do you remember?" Phil repeats. "In the first little boat we borrowed, all four of us crammed in, and the picnic basket?"

"Yeah," David says, his eyes on the path. "Sort of."

"I guess you never really got into sailing, huh?"

David shakes his head. "Not really."

This is no news. What Phil once hoped would they could all do together he now must do alone. But enough preamble; no sense putting it off any longer. He takes a deep breath, wondering exactly what to say, how much to tell. He's already spoken to Linnie, but that really doesn't help much; the children are so different. She had a fit of course, insisted she was coming with him to make sure he got back safe, so he had to talk her out of it and ended up telling her more than he intended, probably more than she should know. But David is older. "David?" he says.

The boy is standing on the rocky beach, lobbing flat stones across the calm surface of the water, so they skim and skip in a series of overlapping and ever-diminishing circles. He remembers watching Sara on the beach at Carpenter's, surrounded by an endless supply of small flat rocks as thin as wafers, Sara a past master at this, sometimes making a stone do as many as twenty-four hops. David slings a rock with an impressive sidearm pitch. But his baseball days are over, Phil thinks with a twinge of sadness; he is too old for Little League now and doesn't want to go on to Legion ball. He still has a good arm, bats left, throws right, but has no interest; baseball, he says, is boring. He has never hit that one thrilling, gut-wrenching home run. The rock bounces over the surface at least ten times, then finally sinks, the circles eddying out like desultory raindrops from overhead.

Phil sits down and drapes his hands over his knees, starts to talk to David's back. "I wanted to tell you that I'm going on a long sail this summer. Across the ocean, in fact."

David pauses almost imperceptibly, then whips another stone. Half-a-dozen skips. "By yourself?" David's voice floats back.

"That's right. I'm going alone."

David bends, rummages through the rocks between his feet. "Isn't that kind of dangerous?" he says in a muffled voice. Phil can't see his face, but at least he's talking, asking questions.

"Yes, it is, and it's possible something might happen to me, that I might not come back. We can talk about that if you want, but first I want to tell you something else." He takes another deep breath; this is the hard part. "You know this chemotherapy that I've been doing is experimental, and they didn't know whether it would work."

David picks up a rock and heaves it. Three skips. "I thought it was working."

"Well, they thought it might, and it did for a while, but then it didn't. That's why I stopped doing the treatments."

"But you've gotten better since then, haven't you?"

Phil nods, even though he knows David isn't looking at him. It's true, he is better than when he was on chemo, but not for long. Phil looks away too; suddenly he finds the sight of his son's back—shoulders just beginning to square and broaden, the body lengthening, slimmer but still wearing that slight pad of baby fat around the waist, the boyish vulnerability of neck and ears—too much to bear. He has grown this last year, but is not as tall as Phil, perhaps never will be. Phil will never know.

He tries to keep his voice from breaking. "Yes, I am feeling better now, and will for a while. But the treatment isn't a cure, and now the disease is coming back, and it looks as though there isn't anything more that they can do to stop it."

No crunch of rocks, no slight repeated splash of water. Though he can't look, the quality of stillness tells him that for once he has David's complete attention.

"What does that mean?" he hears him murmur. "I mean, are they sure?" Then plip, plip, plip, another rock hurled across the water.

Oh, God, Phil thinks, this is ridiculous. David the literalist wants everything spelled out, chapter and verse, just like Sara, questions, always questions. Annoyed at the drawing-out of this process, David's dogged, even perverse resistance to information the meaning of which is perfectly self-evident, his refusal to accept the obvious—just like Sara, for Christ's sake he's got two of them to contend with—Phil raises his voice, enunciates with the clarity of barely concealed exasperation, "Yes, they're sure. What it means is I'm not going to get any better. It means that I thought I'd better take this chance, while I'm still feeling good, to do something I've always wanted to do. And I want you to understand, in case I don't come back . . ."

. . . and as he pauses for breath, meaning to tell his son that he is dying, force him to understand, because he is almost a man and must grow up soon, meaning to tell him that that he is about to undertake a lone and dangerous voyage from which he has no intention of returning, this lone voyage on the sea infinitely preferable to the other voyage that as much as he might wish it he cannot make alone, the slow corruption of the flesh, the wasting away to hollow cheeks and strengthless skeletal limbs, the helplessness, loss of control; meaning to tell him this is his worst nightmare, this inevitable hungry process of decay, being kept alive on machines until there's nothing left, this vision of them being forced to witness the terrible business of his dying that he can't bear, must spare them—Sara, David, Linnie, his parents, his sisters—all the ones he loves and hurts so with his body's revolt, its mindless persistence in continuing to exist in spite of the disease that's slowly killing him; meaning to tell him this is a nightmare he cannot and will not share, he takes a breath, looks up . . .

. . . and sees David's face turned toward him, white and stricken, eyes wide, staring at him, his hands clutched around as many rocks as he can hold.

David starts to speak, rapidly, and in a higher tone than he generally attempts to maintain since his voice started changing. "You know, that time we sailed here we had a picnic, and I ran through the woods and got caught on some barbed wire. And I was frightened, and so were you because we were so far from help. But you and Mommy looked at the wire and the place where it was sticking in, and figured out the barbed wire was only pinching me, and Mommy held on to me while you squeezed on the barb and it came free and the skin wasn't even broken, just pinched and I didn't even bleed. And then I fainted because I had been so scared, but when I woke up you were all there. And then we all got in the boat and sailed home and everything was really okay, I was just fine, and it all turned out to be not as bad as we thought. We all got back just fine." He gives Phil a quick, sidelong glance, then looks away, all around at the trees, the sky, the path ahead, anywhere but at Phil himself.

Phil stares at David for a moment, surprised at his detailed recollection of that incident so long ago. And watching his son's face as they walk along shoulder to shoulder, the boy almost as tall as he is but not quite, Phil realizes that in fact David does understand. So much like Sara, he still clings to the forlorn hope that things will somehow "turn out not to be as bad as we thought." David has missed nothing, and hope is all he has.

"Right," Phil says, slinging an arm around David's shoulders for one fugitive quick hug, all the boy will tolerate these days. "Sometimes things turn out not to be so bad."

Sara stands in the doorway of Linnie's room. Linnie is sitting cross-legged on the floor, humming quietly to herself as she rearranges the contents of a small plastic box that looks like a miniature milk crate. It contains various kinds of makeup—eyeshadow, lipstick, liner, mascara, nail polish—which they have agreed to let her experiment with at home, as long as she doesn't wear it anywhere else. Small cones of breasts are barely visible under the tee-shirt she is wearing; her feet are as big as Sara's. Soon she will be grown. But not soon enough.

"How can he do it?" Linnie asks, without looking up.

"Do what?"

"Just go away and leave all the people he loves."

So. He's told her, but she doesn't really understand, can't accept Phil's decision. Sara starts to explain. "You know Daddy's been sick, honey—"

"Not Dad," Linnie interrupts with a little wave of impatience. "Mack. How could he do that, just leave Jane and his family and go off with someone else?"

"Uh, well," says Sara, somewhat taken aback. "Sometimes it happens that people stop loving each other, they grow apart, and don't want to stay together anymore." Sara pauses. "Is that what you think is happening with Daddy and us? That's why he's going away?"

Linnie shakes her head, and starts to hum again.

"Did Daddy talk to you?" Sara asks, shoving her hands in her pockets and leaning against the doorjamb, trying to look casual.

Linnie nods, but doesn't look up. Then Sara realizes she isn't humming, she's murmuring to herself, as though talking to an unseen companion. Oh, oh, Sara thinks. Marigold is back.

For years Linnie had had an imaginary friend named Marigold, who lived between the wallpaper and the wall and sometimes slept on the shelf of Linnie's closet. She could get bigger or smaller, had friends but no family, and was "me when I grow up." She usually showed up when Linnie was either upset or bored, for instance on long car trips. Sara still remembers the time she rumbled Marigold by mistake on one of the trips to her mother's. Linnie was sitting in the far back of the station wagon, carrying on a conversation with her imaginary friend, but all in her own voice. Listening, Sara had said without thinking, "Isn't it funny that Marigold talks with your voice?" There was a stunned silence, and then Linnie had burst into tears, saying, "You ruined it! You killed her! Now Marigold is gone, and she's never coming back. You ruined everything!" Sara, contrite, had spent the rest of the trip undoing the damage, convincing Linnie that Marigold was just fine, still living between the wallpaper and the wall, and could talk in any voice she wanted.

But she'd thought Marigold was long gone, Linnie too old for this sort of retreat into fantasy. "What exactly did Daddy tell you?"

Linnie still does not look up. "That he hasn't been feeling well but now he's feeling better, so he's going on a long trip in his sailboat." She fumbles with the articles in the box, arranging and rearranging them at random.

Sara kneels in front of Linnie, trying to get her full attention. She has to know what Phil has told her, if it's enough. "Is that all?"

Linnie shrugs. "That it would be dangerous, and he won't let me go with him." She pauses, glancing up at Sara from under her eyebrows. Then she adds, "But that's okay, because I know he'll be just fine." She drops her eyes, and the low murmuring continues.

Oh, God, Phil, is that what you told her? Suddenly angry, wanting her daughter to face facts, not carry on imaginary conversations with invisible companions instead of her, not retreat into a dreamworld where people don't get sick and die and fathers always return from the trips they go on, Sara reaches out, yanks the little milk crate away, and says, "Don't you think you're a little old to believe in Marigold now?" She just barely stops herself from adding, "And happy endings."

Linnie looks up quickly, her eyes wide, and Sara sees her face is stained with tears. "Marigold's not real," she says. "She never was. I always knew that. I only pretended I didn't after that time in the car, because I thought you wanted me to. It seemed so important to you. I thought you were the one who wanted to believe in Marigold." Linnie shuts her eyes, takes a huge breath and bursts into sobs.

Oh, God, she does know, Sara thinks as she leans forward and draws Linnie to her, cuddling her still slightly baby-round cheek against her shoulder. She knows everything; she knows he's not coming back. She was trying to protect me. All these years, preserving the illusion. And she rocks the sobbing body, almost as big as hers yet still with the flat simplicity of childhood, murmuring over and over the meaningless soft words of comfort, "Yes, baby, yes, I know, it's okay. Everything will be just fine."

After supper, sitting in the kitchen chair next to the wood stove, he watches as she comes toward him, the look on her face intent, purposeful. He unbuttons his shirt, slowly pulls one arm out of the sleeve. She moves closer until she is standing over him, his thigh between her legs. She grasps his wrist and tucks his hand between her arm and side next to her breast. He feels the warmth emanating from her body. Stay calm, he tells himself. Cool it. Wait. He takes a deep breath, exhales, trying to stay relaxed as she moves into position.

She sticks the prongs of the stethoscope in her ears, letting the diaphragm dangle while she wraps the cuff around his upper arm. She moves her left hand underneath his elbow, supporting it, and with her thumb presses the cold disc of the stethoscope into the crease. With his free hand he holds up the blood pressure gauge so she can read it. "Relax your arm," she says, jiggling it. He makes a conscious effort to go limp everywhere.

Whoosh, whoosh, whoosh, as she pumps air into the cuff. It stiffens, rises, presses on his skin, his muscle, harder, and harder, until he feels first his fingers, then his whole arm start to go cold and numb. Then the hiss and rush of air as she releases the valve, relief of warm blood rushing back into vessels momentarily squeezed shut. He watches her face, head bent, eyes down, sternly concentrating on the arcane noises of his pulse. At last he has her full attention. This, he thinks, is our most intimate moment.

She is frowning now as she watches the arrow float downward. Out of the corner of his eye he can see the little arrow bounce energetically for a moment, float gently down toward zero. He watches her face, stern in its concentration, detached, as she lets the rest of the air out with a wheeze. She drags the stethoscope from her ears, and unwraps the cuff, pulling it apart with the familiar ripping sound. "Well?" he says, nudging her inner thigh gently with his leg.

"About the same," she answers, not smiling. "Maybe a little higher." He knows she is trying to break it to him gently, but it only confirms what he already knows. She sighs. "I guess it's time to up your pills again."

She looks oddly disappointed, considering it's not the first time. He wonders if it's possible that she still hasn't accepted the inevitable. Time to change the subject. "That visit was pretty awkward," he remarks as she's putting away the blood pressure kit. "Mack must really have wanted to see us and have us meet his girlfriend."

"Either that, or they really had to go to the bathroom."

It's getting dark. David is still droning the lawn mower around the front lawn; it takes him three times as long to mow the grass as Phil. But then, his legs are shorter. Sara is kneeling next to the shutter to see if the glue is dry yet when Phil comes out into the garage. He stands next to her, surveying the pile of sailboat equipment.

"It's too bad, isn't it?" he says. "I thought sailing was one of the things we could do together."

"We did do it together," she says.

"Not for long. And now it's over."

"What's over?"

"Doing things together."

"We're doing this together."

"What's 'this'?"

She waves a hand around at the equipment, the rest of the garage, the back of the house, vaguely in the direction of the kids' rooms. "This. Getting ready."

"And this somehow has to include the shutter?"

Sara glances up at him. "The kids still think it's going to be all right. At least Linnie does."

He shrugs. "I did the best I could. Maybe they just need to go on believing in the romance of illusion."

"The saving illusion," she says, removing the pieces of duct tape she's used to keep everything together until the glue dried.

"Big deal."

"Yeah, well, it got us this far." She wedges her foot against the bottom of the shutter and swings it upright. The frame creaks, but the slats do not fall out.

"Not far enough," Phil says, watching her.

"*This far,*" she says through gritted teeth, and taps the shutter gently several times. Thump, thump, thump. She picks it up with both hands and bangs it lightly on the concrete. Knock, knock, knock. Everything holds.

"Fucking amazing," he says. "I'll put it up for you. It's heavy. You might hurt yourself."

He wraps one hand around the frame, lifts the shutter effortlessly. He is still so strong. Sara stares at the back of Phil's hand clenched around the frame. She has always loved his hands, big, long-fingered, strong, the nails well-cared for, the skin fine and unmarked: beautiful hands. As she looks now, she sees the veins knotted like tangled string under the skin, mottled and puckered from the IVs, a blue bruise still slightly visible from his last treatment three months ago. Her lip starts to tremble, and she puts a hand out to touch his, just as he swings the shutter around and leans it against the wall. He turns toward her.

"I still think this is a bad idea," he says. "One good bang against the house and it'll be kindling. Face it, Sara. Going around fixing broken shutters is about the last thing you need to do." He pauses, looking at her seriously. "But you'll do whatever you want when I'm gone anyway," he says after a moment. "After all, you can fix everything. Except me. I'm something glue and duct tape and baling wire won't mend." He smiles wryly, almost apologetically at her, the old joke between them, as she stands there trying to hold back the tears. "Anyway, this isn't exactly how I imagined us spending our last days together. Speaking of which, I read over the insurance policies the other day. I'm worth more to you dead than I am alive. And the boat is worth more sunk."

She stares at him, unable to speak.

"You think I'm a coward, don't you?"

She shakes her head, but he isn't watching. He brushes his hands together, showering flakes of old green paint. "Oh, well, what difference does it make? We both know I'm a dead man. I'll put the shutter up in the morning. Right now I'm too tired. I'm going up to bed." He turns abruptly and goes inside.

Sara stares after him for a moment, feeling her eyelids sting as the tears well up behind them. What difference does it make? What *difference* does it make? "Damn you, Phil Boyd," she mutters. "Damn you!" She picks up the shutter, thinking the hell with it, she'll just hurl it down, let it crash apart right here, right now.

Behind the garage she hears David, mowing the back lawn by himself. "You're goddamned right," she shouts, knowing no one can hear her over the noise of the mower. "What difference *does* it make? Fuck you, Phil Boyd! I *will* do whatever I want when you're gone! I'll have a garage sale and sell all your clothes! I'll buy a microwave and three hundred sixty-five different frozen dinners, and not cook for a whole fucking year! I won't mow the lawn on time! I'll let the leaves pile up, the chimney fall down, the septic tank overflow, the sills rot, the whole goddamned house collapse! I'll stay up as late as I want reading and not worry about keeping you awake! I won't have to do your goddamned blood pressure three times a day! I won't have to watch you get sick and bald and skinny! I won't have to worry about you anymore. I'll be free, goddammit. Free!"

Sobbing now, holding the shutter over her head, she kicks open the door of the workshop, sees the shrouded figures silhouetted in the light. "If these are our last days together," she screams at the covered torso, "they really suck! 'What difference does it make?' I'll tell you! None! You're so busy acting like a dead man you might as well go be one!"

She advances toward the torso, thinking she'll push the shutter onto it like a hardboiled-egg slicer, squeeze the clay up through the slats, cut it up into slices just like all Phil's CAT scans, salvage the clay, and start all over. But as she reaches with one hand to pull off the blanket, the other one, numb from the strain of trying to hold up the heavy frame, slips off, and the shutter drops from her grasp as she jumps back, clatters to the floor. She shuts her eyes, wondering if it's broken. All that work for nothing.

It isn't. It lies there intact, too heavy, thick with paint. I couldn't hold it with one hand, she thinks. How am I ever going to climb

a ladder and put it back? There are some things I'm just not strong
enough to do without him.

Tears streaming down her face, she pulls the blanket back, shuts
her eyes and runs her hand from the hollow of the neck up over
the angle of shoulder, then down along the line of waist, hip, and
flank. The clay is cold, hard and unyielding as stone. It takes hours
of stroking and pushing and molding to make the clay soft enough
to work, time that might have been better spent with him. Why
is she even doing it? Something to remember him by, the way he
was? How stupid. It isn't Phil, only a version of him, and not even
a good one at that. Now it never will be. There are some things
she just can't do without him.

Everywhere she looks she is reminded of what is to come, all
the last things, Linnie's softball glove hanging on a hook, left there
after her final game, a heap of crumpled book covers and school
papers carelessly tossed down on the last day of school, the rake
and chain saw where Phil left them the last time he raked leaves
and cut wood. Last things. These last days with Phil.

She turns away and yanks the blanket up. Leaving the shutter
where it fell, she walks out of the workshop and through the
garage, shutting off lights as she moves through the kitchen, the
living room, up the stairs. In the darkened bedroom, she hears
the faint sound of his breathing as she undresses, thinks of the
silence after. She creeps into bed, trying not to wake him.

But as she feels the warmth emanating from his body as he lies
there on his side, turned away from her but so close, still so substantial, she misses him so much him already that she can't help
herself, she nestles closer until she is in the old familiar position,
like spoons, face pressed between his shoulder blades, breasts
against his back, belly against buttocks, thighs folded under his
thighs, knees behind his knees. Sound asleep, his body acknow-
ledges her presence, his elbow lifting slightly so she can slip her arm
around him.

. . . and as she rests her head against his back, hears the gentle
rocking of his heart, the slow smooth sift of breathing, feels the
warm resilience of his skin, she feels the scars as thick as ropes
winding across and down, and clutching him to her, she holds him

in her arms, feels his flesh dissolve like smoke, leaving only air.

This is how it will be, she thinks. This is how it will be after he's gone. Where this substantial presence, this solid warm bulk is now there will be nothing but cold empty space.

A catch of breath, interruption of snore. Muscles relaxed in sleep tensing almost imperceptibly as his head lifts slightly off the pillow, attentive, listening. Then he starts to roll over, lifting his elbow slightly so that her arm slides up and over his side as he turns to face her. Breath warm on her face, he throws an arm still heavy with sleep over her shoulder and hugs her to him.

"Ah, you're here," she whispers.

"Yes," he answers. "I'm still here."

I I

As Long As You Keep on Moving

"Hi, Phil. How're you feeling?"

"Fine," Phil says with his eyes closed. It's a lie of course; he has a headache, his nose is stuffed up, and his stomach is bothering him. But one of the rules of hospital behavior is that you don't complain.

"Good," the voice says.

Phil hears the rustle of pages, whoever it is shuffling through his record again. The narrow hospital bed gives a sudden lurch as though someone has just bumped into it, then continues to rock gently up and down, and Phil starts to feel even sicker. In fact, he may heave. Pressing his lips together, he opens his eyes, peers all around the hospital room to see who's there.

Except that he's not in a hospital room. He's not even in a bed. He's lying in his narrow bunk in the slanted cabin of the *Loon*, hundreds of miles from land, and of course there's no one there.

Although it's not the first time he's heard voices, or what seem to be voices, a vague chorus murmuring just out of earshot, mumbling in the wake that churns behind, whispering in the hiss of water cleaving off the bow, this is the first time he's actually understood the words.

And the distinct sound of someone turning pages? He squints around the still-dim cabin. The sun is just coming up, slanting off the surface of the ocean, casting pale fluttering ribbons of bluish light that ripple up and down the white cabin walls, so that for a moment he has the panicky feeling that he's underwater, the boat filled up and sinking, himself about to drown. His ears buzz with fright and his head throbs even harder; drowning is not really the way he wants to go. Almost against his will he takes a deep breath, feels with some relief the effortless sift of air into his lungs, the steady rocking of the boat as it moves across the surface of the water. They are still sailing.

Maybe it would help if he put on his glasses. Trying to stay flat on his back so he isn't turning sideways against the up-and-down motion of the boat—it's usually the combination of pitch and roll that makes him puke—he carefully reaches his right hand over and gropes in the little cubbyhole next to his left shoulder, loops the elastic strap over his ears and sets the glasses on his nose. He peers through the watery light at the other bunk, where the rustling noise seems to be coming from. Aha. The big blue copy of Bowditch that Sara and the kids gave him has fallen off the shelf onto the other berth, and is now lying open on its spine, pages quietly riffling back and forth as the boat pitches gently through the waves. As he watches, the book collapses shut with a wheeze. Water percolates along the hull in a low-pitched babble almost as discrete as syllables.

Phil smiles. So much for hearing things. He glances at the watch on his wrist: not even sun-up yet. He could doze a little longer. He puts his glasses back in the cubbyhole, shuts his eyes, and tries to go back to sleep.

Rocked on a sea as black as ink, waves invisible except for the frills of phosphorescence ruffling their tips, Sara listens to the wind prowling the rigging, zooming in the shrouds, and, frightened, reaches an arm toward Phil and tries to clutch him to her as the boat heels sharply. To her horror she feels his solid bulk of flesh and bone dissolve into huge slimy strands of seaweed that tug and pull away no matter how she tries to gather them, until at last her arms are empty, and she slides overboard, goes under, the icy graphite surface closing over her head.

With a jerk her eyes pop open and she lies there gasping, momentarily unable to move. In the dark it takes her several moments to realize she is not on a boat, not in the water. She is shivering, uncovered, at home in her own bed. But she is not on her own side. In her sleep she has moved over to snuggle against Phil's back, has flung an arm out to embrace him. But Phil is not there. She is lying at the edge of the indentation his body has left in the mattress, about to tip over into it, and her groping arm has encountered only air. In her nightmare she has frantically wound the topsheet and blanket into a tangled mess, then let it slip over the side of the bed onto the floor.

She reaches over and retrieves the wadded covers, spreads them out over herself, then rolls onto her back so she can see the windows. Steeples of gray light are just visible where the curtains split. It's barely dawn, not anywhere near time to get up yet. Turning onto her side, she inches her way into the hollow Phil has left, takes her pillow and wedges it in the empty space next to her stomach the way she used to do after the kids were born. Resting her head on the pillow that still smells faintly of Phil even after seven nights, she pulls the sheet up over her shoulder, and tries to go back to sleep.

There is no wind, not even a hope of wind. The sails hang ghostlike, billowing randomly with the corkscrew motion of the boat as she gyrates aimlessly up and down across the waves. Then he hears in the distance, still far behind him but clearly audible, the hollow roar of an express train speeding through the subway tunnel, pushing the air ahead until it bursts out, whirling up everything in its path. His heart starts to pound faster and faster, his breath shortens as he turns his head and looks to windward, sees behind him a great wall of water pushing forward, foaming, hissing, the wind whistling toward him through the air with the tense finality of huge bombs falling. This is it, he thinks, panting in rhythm with the rapid ticking of his heart. It's almost over. At last the time is now. Hand gripping the tiller, he tenses himself for impact . . .

Phil wakes with a start, the sunlight bursting in his eyes. He swings his legs over the side of the bunk and sits up, head throbbing at the temples, around the eyes, a wide band tightening around his forehead, worse each morning since he threw his pills overboard three days ago.

Sunlight is now streaming through the portholes, glinting through the slits between the dropboards in the companionway. The *Loon* is still pitching diagonally through the waves in the same steady rhythm she has for days, the wind unchanged, from the south at ten knots, the same wind that has been blowing him offshore on an easy beam reach ever since he left six, no seven days ago.

He shakes his head with a trace of impatience; he really hoped it would be over by now—Pow! a blinding flash behind the eyes or a slam in the chest and dot dot dot—especially when his heart started galloping in his chest, cramming a breathless pain behind his ribs and down his arms. Trembling, soaked with sweat, he feels the arteries pulsing in his neck, his groin, behind his knees, his scalp tingling, the hair on his head standing up, the flesh along his spine creeping as the tumors send their signals unblocked by the medications he's been taking for so long: Danger! Run! Flee! Fight! The arteries squeeze down, the heart pumps faster, and the surges keep getting worse the higher his blood pressure goes.

But obviously not yet high enough, or he'd be dead by now. As soon as he stands upright the pressure will begin to subside, and after he's been up for a while his head won't hurt at all. Not only that, his heart has slowed down somewhat since the first day, apparently adjusting to the lack of medication, at least for now. Things aren't going quite the way he planned. In fact, he feels pretty good, for a dying man. The boat seems to nod in agreement as she heaves forward over a bigger swell.

A wave of nausea reminds him that if he doesn't get up on deck pretty fast, he's going to heave himself. The Dramamine he took last night—before he tied off the tiller and went sound asleep, hoping a nice strong gale would blow up in the night and do the job for him, overwhelming the *Loon* and him with her—has obviously worn off.

Hell, he thinks dizzily, numb fingers fumbling with the dropboards, head pounding, stomach churning, ears buzzing; this really sucks. It's hopeless. I might as well still be on chemo.

He sticks his head up through the companionway, shades his eyes and looks out over the ocean, the same textured, slightly luminous surface, billowing slightly as though it were a huge lady in a giant satin ballgown with someone blowing air under her skirt. He glances at his watch; 7 A.M. As good a time as any. Carefully unscrewing and lifting the sextant out of its mahogany box—God, what a beautiful instrument it is, the delicate wedge-shaped lattice of the brass frame catching the early morning light like a spider web touched with dew—he tucks the *Nautical Almanac* under his other arm and climbs up into the cockpit to check the taffrail log. It squats there on the afterdeck with its line streaming out behind, grinning like a boy who's hooked a fish.

The knotmeter reads 420, the total miles he's come thus far, twenty-four miles since last night, not bad, but he doesn't know in what direction or at what speed. The gulls are off and running, converging on him from the west, the landward side, wheeling around the boat looking for a handout, their squeals as sharp and grating as chalk scraped across a blackboard.

"You're out of luck!" he shouts. They ought to know by now he's stopped eating. He glares up at them, flung across the sky like so many bits of torn-up paper. He wishes they would leave. Their presence this far from shore means there probably isn't much wind coming from that direction for the foreseeable future, in other words, for the next few hours. Gulls fly out this far only if they know they can get back without having to buck a headwind.

Already he senses the wind dropping slightly. He looks up to where the mast revolves in lazy half-circles high in the air, around and back, around and back, unable to shake the feeling that all this has happened before. He leans against the coaming, head back, watching the cross-shaped silhouette against the sky. The sky goes on forever, uniform, clear, vast. There is not a cloud in it. There is no hope of wind. It's all so damned picturesque he feels pasted on a calendar, with the permanent fixity of a painted ship upon a painted ocean.

Looking around, he wonders briefly what made the boat lurch so abruptly just as he woke up, almost as though someone had stepped off. There are no squalls or cat's-paws in sight, no rogue waves tossing a white peak as far as he can see. Probably a curious dolphin, or even a small whale, coming upon a lone hull all the way out here and deciding to give it a little nudge. He sticks his head over the rail, but sees no shadows passing under the surface, only his own fractured reflection, undulating strangely in a sea of broken glass. The blood rushes to his head; he can hear it roaring in his ears like those same voices whose words are as yet too low and indistinct for him to understand. Maybe this is what he's been hearing all along.

He moves to the port side, facing the sun, opens the logbook and starts his entry. He won't be doing this much longer, but he might as well make it look good right up to the very end. After all, isn't that what he's been doing all along? If by some chance the boat is found, then everyone will know he did it by the book, fixed a course and kept on sailing, as far as he could for as long as he was able.

Day 7, 0700 hours, he writes. He looks at his watch again, and notes the date. Ha, he thinks, calculating briefly. Seven o'clock in the morning on the seventh day of his voyage, the seventh day of the seventh month. It has a nice ring to it. He counts the years on his fingers since that fall they bought the boat. No, not seven yet, but never mind; perfect is the enemy of good. Today's as good a day as any.

After a moment he continues his notation. Conditions fair, sea swells 1–3 out of the SW, wind force 5–10 and diminishing. The rest he leaves blank; the latitude and longitude will have to wait until he takes a couple of sun sights to get a running fix. Then he'll know exactly where he is, whether he's finally gotten past the shipping lanes and fishing zones marked on his chart, far enough to be out of sight of passing boats so there will be no chance of rescue when he does what he has to do.

He shivers slightly in the expedition-weight long underwear he's been sleeping in, a present from his sisters. Even though the sun is shining brightly, the air is still a little chilly; surprising how cool it gets out here on the ocean at night, even in July. He feels better already, the nausea passing as soon as he stuck his head out into the air and could see the horizon. He thinks he'll wait until noon to get a sight and plot his position. After all, there's no hurry; he's got all day. Meanwhile as long as the wind doesn't die altogether, he can just keep right on sailing.

Putting aside the logbook and the sextant for the time being, he unfastens the tiller jock and takes the tiller in his hand, feeling the smooth wood rubbing against his palm. Ever so slightly he corrects the course until the telltales lie flat against the foresail. "Ah, that's good," he murmurs as the hull cuts smoothly through the rippling sea. "That's perfect. I could do this forever." Nothing has changed.

In this relatively calm weather the gentle sea swells seem almost stationary, like a series of rolling hills, rising one after another, even taking on the same mossy green, flatly opaque color, so that sometimes he imagines he's riding in a car up and down over the hilly road on his way to the coast, or else back home. It has been this way for seven days now, the sky and sea conspiring to provide wind and weather so consistently beautiful, the sky overhead going on forever, uniform, clear, vast, a deep blue that translates itself to streaks of violet and emerald reflecting on the darker basalt surface of the ocean, like shadows of cloud passing over land, so that he feels almost against his will a pool of calm spreading within him like a warm clear light, and he has to keep reminding himself what he's come out here to do.

But really, there was no point in going on any longer, better the quick clean exit than the slow painful decline. He's not afraid of the pain really; it's just that he did not want Sara and the kids to have to watch him waste away and suffer, kept alive on machines (though Sara promised she wouldn't let that happen), IVs and tubes and bags, first his strength, then his dignity, then his mind and finally his body—the stupid flesh always last—helplessly draining away.

He glances through the companionway at the expensive video

depth sounder his parents gave him as a bon voyage present, an "added safety feature, so you won't run aground or anything." What do they think he's going to run aground on in the middle of the Atlantic Ocean, the Lost Continent of Atlantis? Moby Dick? His parents, even now, wanting desperately to keep him safe. But there is no safety. Safety is an illusion; he certainly knows that by now.

The depth sounder now sits blank and silent; he turned it off along with the ship-to-shore radio as soon as he came to the jumping-off place—the edge of the continental shelf some 270 miles offshore where the depth of the water suddenly drops from 100 fathoms to over 1000, more than a mile deep, its furry line following the profile of the ocean bottom in exaggerated peaks and valleys, then suddenly yelping its deep-water alarm, the jagged line diving right off the bottom of the screen, a confused blip-blip and momentary blur of static, then dot dot dot, or rather dash dash dash, just like a heart monitor beeping its tinsel streak into a flat line.

That was it: the point of no return. He had taken out his array of pills, three months' worth—part of "making it look good," according to Sara, along with all the food and water and flare kits and other safety equipment—small pink tablets, big blue and white capsules, little round yellow ones, thin but heavy-duty maroon ones in case the others stop working, opened the amber vials one by one and emptied the pills over the side into the ocean in a fluttering stream like so much confetti, watching them dissolve into multicolored bubbles in the gurgling wake. Then he'd set the sails, steered the boat due east and looked to windward, waiting for nature take its course.

He's also pulled the outboard motor out of the well, momentarily toying with the idea of just heaving the damned thing overboard, but thinking he might need the added weight, has stowed it instead in the stern compartment after sealing up the engine well with the special insert they had made for that purpose. No more sloshing up of water in a following sea; Sara would appreciate that. Now the only machine still going is the knotmeter, ticking slowly in its measurement of distance over time, so he can use dead reckoning if need be to find out where he is. That too he will disconnect as soon as he knows he's where he wants to go. Then there will be no more mechanical aids, just him and the boat, the wind, the sky, and the sea.

Leaving the tiller for a moment—the boat is so well-balanced she can practically sail herself in wind like this—he gets his big sweater from down below, settles himself down in the sheltered angle of the cockpit next to the companionway where Sara always liked to sit, and resumes steering with his foot. The sun feels warm on his face. He watches the surface of the ocean rise and fall gently, like some huge creature breathing in its sleep. After a while he shuts his eyes, and listens to the murmuring voices of the dead.

It's hopeless, Sara thinks as she throws the covers back and gets out of bed. The children are still sleeping. After all it's not even 7 A.M. on a July morning; they'll be out for hours. Briefly she ponders the irony of parenthood; when they were babies they always woke up chirping at the crack of dawn, so that hers and Phil's idea of heaven was to sleep till 7 A.M. Now the children sleep almost until noon, and she wakes up at dawn. Sometimes she stays in bed, even though she finds it impossible to sleep, but she's been restless since Phil left, and if she lies in bed too long she gets anxious, wondering in spite of herself how he is, where he is, if he is in any pain, or cold, or sick, or frightened. She tries to resist these morbid imaginings, but it is hard, lying in bed alone with her thoughts running on. She wonders when it will be over.

Then she hears the phone ringing, hops out of bed and runs to answer it, wondering if this is it, the long-distance phone call early in the morning, the strange impersonal voice coming over the line with its bleak announcement (*"Hello, is this Mrs. Martha Gilead?"* Yes. *"This is Port Huron Hospital in Michigan calling. We're afraid we have bad news. They brought your husband in last night."* How bad is it? *"Pretty bad; he died ten minutes ago . . ."*), only this time the call will be for her.

But it's not the anonymous voice she has been dreading, it's Patience, her friend of the morning wake-up calls, who has called every day since Phil's departure, at first to ask if there is any word, then realizing from Sara's evasiveness that this is a dumb question—duh, excuse me, no phone lines in the sea, and anyway what's there to know until he gets to the other side, right?—has therefore tactfully stopped asking and now calls just to say hello, relay the latest college gossip, or simply talk. Sara is touched by this gesture, Patience's persistent mindless chit-chat making her feel somehow still connected, however passively for the time being, to the outside world, less isolated and alone. Sara isn't sure whether Patience has figured out what Phil is really up to, but she wouldn't put it past her.

They talk in whispers for several minutes, then Sara sets the phone back in its cradle, wondering if its ringing woke the children. No sound from either of the kids' rooms, no thud and shuffle of sleepy adolescent feet on their way to the bathroom. Already she misses the sound of Patience's voice over the wire, the sound of any voice. Her mind spins its wheels in the silence, no busy noises from other sources to give it traction. The silence and solitude she would have welcomed once now yawn before her with a monster's face, all dark throat and pointed teeth. But never mind, she tells herself, trying to ease herself into the habit of being alone. This too you will get used to.

She turns the television on to the early-morning news. When the satellite weather map comes on, she listens, eyes scanning the northeast corner of the map, the contours of the land reminding her of a person reclining casually on one elbow against the smooth expanse of ocean as though it were a beach, the other arm raised above his head as though to wave at someone, or to shield his eyes.

Nothing has changed. The air is clear for hundreds of miles, from the thrown-back, uproariously laughing fun-house profile of Michigan all the way east and out to sea. In fact, the forecast looks good indefinitely, the weatherman informs her. Fair weather, warm temperatures, no storms predicted for the foreseeable future. Even though she knows these things don't really matter, that it's out of her hands now and there is nothing she can do, she feels relieved. She wishes she could pick up the phone and call him, just to hear his voice again, to know he's safe, at least for the time being.

But there are no phone lines in the sea, and even though she feels herself connected, still listening, waiting to hear, she knows Phil is already far beyond her reach. Meanwhile, she stares at the satellite map as though if she could look closely enough, she'd see the tiny dot that is his boat on the big crumpled ocean, until it goes off the screen.

The only thing to do is keep busy, Sara thinks. She slips into a pair of jeans and a sweatshirt—it's fairly cool for July at the moment, that big high-pressure system keeping the temperature down—says, "Come on, zoo," to the dog and two cats standing in a graduated line at the top of the stairs, blocking her way as they gaze up at her expectantly, stiff as animal crackers. At her signal they take off like horses from a starting gate, jumping halfway down the stairway in one concerted leap, furry rears waggling the rest of the way in a confused thunder of twelve paws somehow hitting each tread separately. They sound like a rack of bowling pins rolling down the stairs.

Even this does not wake the children. She follows the animals into the kitchen, finds the cats hunched on the counter like vultures waiting for a carcass to ripen, the dog thrusting his stiletto nose at the crack in the door. She feeds the cats, puts the coffee on, then lets the dog out, keeping an eye on him from the garage doorway as he runs up and down the long driveway on squirrel patrol. A day like any other day, she thinks, then: who am I kidding? What a crock.

She watches the dog leaping up and down the line of trees edging the driveway, nose pointed upward, ears revolving like pointed radar dishes. He is chasing squirrels as they swing from branch to branch, taunting him from high up in the trees. She wonders what if anything goes on in his narrow head—this Bren of little brain—wonders if the dog really imagines that someday he'll catch one. Does he dream of running fast enough to scramble up a tree? She's seen him try. Is he waiting for one to miss a branch or have a heart attack, and drop down at his feet? Such faithfulness, such persistence in the face of forlorn hope, she thinks. Even though he is no Collie Cibber—*he* was one of *us*, this dog is one of *them*, i.e. the children—she has grown attached to this smallish, pointy-nosed dumb dog; there is something endearing about his loyalty to her, his willingness to please. She smiles, remembering Collie Cibber stalking seagulls on the beach, creeping toward them as carefully as a cat, closer and closer, until they exploded off the beach right in his face, and he stood there panting, watching them fly out of reach over the water with bright disappointed eyes. Again and again, never giving up, as if he too thought if he ran fast and far enough he might take off one day and fly. Old Collie Cibber, the dog of their youth. She shudders faintly; even after all these years she can still hear the sound of his old bones crunching that day she accidentally backed the car over him. A long time ago, seven years now, the year before Phil's second operation. As it turned out, she hadn't killed him; the dog died of old age a year or so later while Phil was recovering in intensive care. It still makes her sad to think that she wasn't there, but after all, he was only a dog. There are worse things. She takes a deep breath. The dog it was that died.

Her heart gives a sudden wallop of fear as she sees the dog streak down the long driveway toward the road, body like a bullet, hind legs churning practically in his ears. "Bren!" she screams, running out into the dooryard, afraid there'll be an accident, he will be hit and killed. The dog screeches to a halt in mid-gallop, wheels around and instantly runs back toward her, the sound of her voice a connection between them as effective as any leash. At least you won't run away, she thinks. Pretty soon the kids will be gone, then it'll be just you and me, buster; we'll be the ones who're left.

She opens the door and the dog trots in, the orange cat floats out as limber as a goldfish. The other one, dusty tortoise-shell like a roll of vacuum-cleaner lint, has vanished, probably hiding out in one of the odd places she prefers to sleep, so that Sara is always coming upon two yellow owl-eyes blinking at her where she least expects them, on the top shelf of one of the closets, the dirty clothes hamper, old cardboard boxes, dresser drawers. The cat has even gotten twirled in the dryer more than once and lived to tell the tale.

She fixes herself a cup of coffee, sits at the kitchen table drinking it. She stares at the phone, trying to get over the sensation that

Susan Kenney

he's just away, that there is still this connection between them, that any minute the phone will ring, she'll pick it up and it will be Phil calling to tell her he's all right. She's always like this with the telephone when anyone's away; the long, tense wait past the appointed time, the wringing of hands, dire imaginings, the ring like a lightning bolt, receiver snatched up, then the relief, oh, the relief of the familiar, wished-for voice coming over the line, so that she knows, whatever disaster may have happened, the caller's still alive.

So, even now with Phil so far away she feels the cord like a long telephone line stretching between them, knows she will feel his death, somehow, as a breaking of the cord. Then she will be alone: there will be no one in the world who loves her best. "Phil?" she murmurs to the air, wishing she could hear him answer just one more time. The dog thumps down at her feet with a groan.

"What?" he says, looking back over his shoulder into the shadowed cabin. It's only a reflex; he knows there's no one there, even though he thought he heard someone speak his name. For days now he has been ignoring the persistent sound of voices, chuckling in the wake, whispers from inside the cabin. Sometimes it sounds like the children giggling, his mother and father talking quietly, Sara carrying on about something, always just out of earshot, unintelligible.

Auditory and even visual hallucinations are common to solitary travelers; nearly all the solo voyage narratives he's read report them to a greater or lesser degree: Lindbergh's company of spirits behind him in the cramped cockpit of the *Spirit of St. Louis*, whispering directions and encouragement, murmuring secrets of the universe into his ear, their presence so convincing that it turned that intensely practical, mechanically-oriented man into a mystic; Manry and his pirates and assassins, Slocum and the pilot of the *Pinta* who steered him through a storm, conversing in broken Spanish which Slocum faithfully recorded in his log.

Chichester is vague on this point, his long catalogues of equipment and fascination with the technology of sailing possibly evasive. Yet he believed that messing about in boats, communion with the lonely sea and the sky (along with a change in diet and attitude and the persistent refusal of his wife to believe anything the doctors said), finally cured the lung cancer he was told he was dying of the year before he sailed alone across the Atlantic faster than anyone had ever done. Phil does not imagine there's any chance of that for him. Probably it wasn't cancer in the first place; a mistake in diagnosis more than likely, as Phil can testify. Anyway, it's clear Chichester was no mystic.

Lindbergh on the other hand felt that exhaustion and intense isolation accentuated by flying in dense fog breached some inner threshold of awareness and allowed him to communicate with the inhabitants of the immaterial world. Manry surmised his spectacular hallucinations were caused by the uppers he popped when he needed to stay awake for long periods; likewise Slocum thought his apparition was the result of a stomach upset caused by a surfeit of bad cheese and plums (or so the *Pinta* pilot informed him). Lewis, a physician by profession and thus more analytical of pathological phenomena, laid his own sensation of being often in the presence of others, in his case most often family members or friends, to wishful thinking combined with sensory deprivation, lack of sleep, and boredom, as for instance when he was becalmed for many days on his first solo transatlantic crossing. Still, he was grateful for the company, even if they were no help as crew.

Phil turns to face astern again, laces his hands behind his head, leans against the cabin bulkhead looking at where he's been, and thinks of some ghosts he'd like to conjure. Melville, perhaps, or Joseph Conrad? No, he suspects Melville would be too florid and long-winded, in love with the sound of his own voice, also a flatterer and sycophant; think of his letters to Hawthorne. Call me Ishmael; call me boring. Conrad, too; though no one has written better about the sea, according to contemporary reports in person he sported a thick, almost incomprehensible Slavic accent, and was a tedious and pedantic conversationalist. Too bad Captain Horatio Hornblower was only a figment of Forester's imagination.

Anyway, Lewis's theories aside, Phil knows he can't call up specific presences, only resist them. Most of the apparitions he's read about turn out perversely to be either people you'd never think to ask for, either alive or dead, or better yet, people you don't even know. Not friends, not family, not Sara, his parents or the kids; these are the voices whose timbre he resists, familiar shadows he refuses to see cast in the light, their presence too painful now that he has left them all behind.

The only thing to do is keep busy. The trouble is with weather like this, he thinks, feeling himself start to nod off again, is that there isn't much to do.

But the sun is high, and glancing at his watch, he sees it's almost noon, the best time for a sight. Rousing himself, he picks up the sextant, and half-sits, half-kneels in the companionway, bracing himself with one foot on the lower step, wedging the other knee in the opening. He rests his elbow on the top of the cabin, and begins the business of bringing down the sun.

Sailing is not so much a science as an art and thus demands complete attention, he thinks, angling the telescope toward the sun's bright disc. At least that's what he used to believe. He knows better now. All those variables he used to worry about, wind strength and direction, tide changes, rocks and shoals, so much to watch for, only matter when you're sailing close to shore. Out here it's a whole different story. He supposes the matters of discretion might still apply, whether to sail closer to the wind in order to gain distance at the expense of speed, or to lay off to gain the fastest point of sail, but as far as he's concerned now, this is all purely academic; they are only words. All he has to do right now is keep sailing out into the ocean and not come back. Rotating several shade glasses down to cut the glare, he squeezes the little pincers that hold the index arm in position and slides the arm along the notched silver crescent of the limb until he catches the pale disc of the sun in the center of the horizon glass. He rocks the sextant slightly to check the perpendicular, watches as the sun's image rolls back and forth across his line of sight like a marble in a spoon. He carefully angles the image down to the horizon, then letting go the releases, fixes the degree of altitude on the limb, twists the screw of the micrometer drum for the minutes, twiddles the vernier for the seconds, and quickly glances at the watch he's turned face to inside his wrist so he can get the exact time without losing the sight in the process. After all, if he's going to do this at all, he might as well do it right. At least then he'll know he's still headed in the right direction toward where he wants to go.

He puts down the sextant, picks up the *Almanac*, does his calculations and adds the information to the log entry. Day 7, 1200, Log 450, Lat. 41° 05′N, Long. 63° 20′W. Plotting his position on the chart, he sees that he is still some thirty miles inside Fishing Zone 4. Damn, he thinks; we must have gotten headed while I was sleeping. He's mildly disappointed by his lack of progress, but it's his own fault. He's really pressed it after putting in—somewhat self-indulgently he must admit—at Lindiscove that first night. Since then he's sailed all day and most of the nights, heaving to with the jib aback and the tiller lashed to leeward only a few hours at a time so he wouldn't lose much way. But after he crossed the shelf and dumped his pills he slacked off somewhat, thinking he might stroke out or have a fatal heart attack any time. It hasn't happened, his body resisting, stronger than he thought, and now he's having to think of other ways, like leaving the boat to self-steer while he goes sound asleep, hoping for a gale, a knockdown and blub-blub-blub before he knows what hit him. But he knows that wouldn't work either; left alone the boat simply will round up and keep on sailing. Even if he were to jump overboard the boat would just go on without him. She can always sail it herself.

So what the hell. It's a nice day, the air is warm, and they have lots of time. He smiles to himself, then nods. Why not? he thinks. What have we got to lose?

The kids have asked if they can have a yard sale, the way they have the other times Dad's been gone on an extended cruise. This is their only chance, they argue, knowing their father would never allow such goings-on, people pawing over their unwanted but still private possessions, the passing of money back and forth, all too undignified and crass. She can hear Phil now. Straight to the dump. Do not pass go. To the dump, to the dump. To the dumpdump-dump.

She has agreed more by default than otherwise, not saying that they could, but not coming up with anything else to do either, dogged by her own inertia, inattentive to what is going on around her, mired in the old habitual feeling of listening for the phone to ring, waiting, still on the line. So David and Linnie have spent the week collecting what they want to get rid of, nagging gently at her to furnish them with the *real* junk, of which they are convinced (their father's influence) she is the sole custodian.

Well, fine. It's almost two years exactly since the last big ream-out; today she'll clean out drawers and closets, maybe even the garage and workshop, see what she can find. If she can just get through the afternoon there's dinner to make and then the news to watch. And thus another day will pass, up and over, almost done.

The playroom has always doubled as Phil's dressing room, containing both his closet and his bureau. She stands in front of the big chest of drawers, looking at the various toilet articles lined up neatly across the top, the aftershave he stopped using when he grew his beard, lotion, stick deodorant, foot powder, all matching in their gilt-topped, marbleized containers from a fancy gift set. Why did he keep it all? And what did he take with him, anyway?

She opens the top drawer. It's full of folded underwear, socks balled up neatly in rows like eggs in a carton. Phil is the only tidy one in the whole family. She opens the next drawer. Alligator shirts in many colors, coiled-up belts, pajamas, a small brass box containing cuff links, the wedding ring he stopped wearing when he lost weight after the second operation. He had gained it back, but not in his fingers, and the huge ring could not be made smaller. She should have had the jeweler melt it down and make new rings for both of them after she lost the old one, she thinks, fingering the new, narrower ring Phil had had made for her for their anniversary last year. It's too late now, but she wishes she'd thought of it then, after she finally gave up hope of finding the other, even climbing and pawing through the piles and mounds of garbage at the dump looking for it the day after she discovered it was gone. She had found their trash, but not the ring. Phil tried to tell her it wasn't worth it, but she insisted anyway. At least it was worth a try.

She opens the third drawer, stares at the threadbare shirts, torn pajamas, moth-eaten sweaters, pitted corduroys he has steadfastly refused to replace. "Why spend the money? Not worth getting new ones, I'll never get a chance to wear them out." Another rolled-newspaper remark. I'll sell them, she thinks now. Or take them to the dump. That will fix you. You'll come back, find all your clothes are gone, have to buy all new ones. She smiles at the thought, the look of consternation on his face.

Then her cheeks start to tremble, and she feels the sting of tears. A dirty trick, if he were somehow to come back. And then there are the kids. She remembers how upset she was, after her father died, when her mother gave away all his things, his clothes, the new suitcase he'd been given for Father's Day that very week, worst of all the train set, even the houses Sara had put together for him. After that Sara had hidden away the things he made for her, the little chair and table for her marionettes, the other props, the china animals he used to buy each time he went away, afraid her mother, in her rage, would take them too. She had misjudged her mother though; crazy as she was for all those years, laying waste to all around her, so it seemed, but look at all she saved, the marionette theater for instance. It was Sara who got careless and left so much behind. But what is broken can be mended, what is missing can be found, what is lost can be recovered, and there's no such word as can't. What is gone can be replaced, Phil said, observing how she took to the new dog. But there are some things you just can't keep. Or replace.

Carefully she shuts the drawer. She stares at the things on the dresser a moment, then picks up the stick deodorant and unscrews the top. The stick, translucent as a piece of green sea glass, is worn down on one side, its surface rippled from being rubbed under his arms. She wonders why he didn't take it with him. So fastidious in his person, a shower every morning, the smell of him always so clean. Maybe he thought he wouldn't need it where he was going; on a solo voyage you're not coming back from who cares if you stink? The seagulls? She pushes up the waxen cylinder to see how much is left. Only half-used. The smell wafts up, Phil's smell, a combination of old oiled leather, shower steam, good clean sweat, and sex. Why not? she thinks. It will never keep. She lifts the stick up inside her loose sweatshirt, swabs it under her own arms, then screws the top back on tight and puts it back on top of the bureau, next to the gold pocket watch that used to belong to her father. Still ticking away. He must have wound it just before he left; it goes for eight days. The dial reads almost noon. She wonders if she should wake the kids.

She pokes her head into David's room, finds him stirring slightly, but still unconscious. His room is picked up, except for the boxes of unwanted items piled around the margin in expectation of the sale. Sara sighs. No longer awash with several weeks' accumulation of flotsam and jetsam, the children's rooms lack character now, their fantasy lives taking place elsewhere.

"Time to get up," she suggests. "It's noon. I thought you wanted to get ready for the yard sale." David groans and turns his face into the pillow.

They've also obviously been rummaging in the attic; there are boxes of old toys and other items covered with dust and insulation fluff stacked in the back hall between their rooms. In the presence of this impressive level of debris, she feels a sudden sympathy with Phil, the impulse to load it up and cart it to the dump sight unseen. She recognizes the appeal for him of the small birdhouse-like cabin of the boat, the compactness of drawers, the clever use of space, no clutter, not even the possibility of clutter, a place for everything and everything in its place. No wonder he hated to have her mess with it, pack it with more things; his monk's cell, his refuge, his retreat.

Linnie lies in her bed surrounded by pillows, stuffed animals, her floor littered with jars of cosmetics and various articles of bizarre but allegedly fashionable clothing. Other than this temporary clutter, the room is relatively neat. Only in sleep now, cheek rounded by being pressed against the pillow, does Linnie still resemble her baby self. Sara steps over the piles of clothes and leans over to kiss her on her forehead.

Linnie snorts, eyelids fluttering, and takes a deep breath. Her nostrils twitch; she loops her arms upward with a sleepy smile. "Dad? Is that you?"

"No," Sara says softly. "It's only me."

"How does it feel?" he asks.

"Fine," she answers, stopping slightly to peer under the boom, checking the set of the jib. The near feather is fluttering wildly. He pulls the jib sheet in. The telltales flutter, then lie flat against the sail as though they had been pasted on. She smiles at him as the boat leaps forward.

Phil blinks, and his vision clears the shadow from the tiller. She is not there. The long shaft nods slightly from side to side in a meager arc, its motion controlled by the twin loops of shock cord tied to cleats on either side. Sara, in cahoots with his mom and dad, as obsessed with safety and foolishly extravagant as they are, had tried to talk him into getting some sort of autopilot or self-steering mechanism, at least a tiller brake. He had refused, saying it wasn't worth the investment; his makeshift tiller jock worked fine, and in a pinch he could always use the old trick of tying it off with the genoa sheets. He wishes she would stop trying to stuff his boat with unnecessary gear. What does she think they did in the old days without all these gadgets? The Phoenicians could plot a course by the recognition of certain stars, notably Polaris, but early navigators relied mainly on what we now call dead reckoning or on visual contact with the shore. Yet in the sixth century St. Brendan crossed the Atlantic in a leather boat sewed up like a change purse, with nothing more than a wind rose (about as useful as sticking a wet finger up), and a cross-staff made like an upside-down sawhorse for taking sunsights, never mind a compass, or so the story goes. The Vikings hopped from island to island along the Stepping Stone route, thinking they'd hit Greenland when they were almost a thousand miles further west, fetched up on the coast of Maine. And—though he doesn't say this—where does she think he's going, anyway? What difference does it make?

She pops her head out of the companionway; all this time she has been rummaging in the cabin, stowing this and stowing that—the inflatable life raft that comes packed in what looks like an overnight case, a safety vest the size of a pack of cigarettes, the orange distress kit not much bigger than a cocktail shaker, with its pistol flare launcher, locater beacons and flying flares with little parachutes for God's sake—all part of her fascination with gadgetry, small things, miniature worlds. She never gets seasick, can stay down below indefinitely while the boat yaws and heaves and rolls and he, on deck, is puking over the side. He's only seen her green once, and that was with fear, not nausea.

"Probably none," she says, answering the question he didn't ask. "But you want to make it look good, so people won't figure out what you're up to. Right?"

He nods. She's got a point there. As always.

She shrugs, looking at him deadpan. "Besides, you never know."

He should have known she'd get her old pitch in somehow. He glares at her, about to reprove yet once more that old reality-bending optimism of hers, but her face, grinning now, round and rosy-cheeked and hopeful, framed in the brightwork of the companionway, suddenly goes as still and glossy as a picture under glass. He blinks again and she is gone, the companionway empty, the cabin silent.

Still, he has to admit she did have a point about making it look good, Phil thinks as he unlashes the tiller, sits down and absentmindedly steers the boat through waves that barely lift the bow, wash back against the hull with a lazy slosh. The romance of illusion. After all, isn't that what's gotten him this far? He's looked good for so long that no one could believe how sick he really was. Only Sara knows—has always known though she pretended not to—how bad things really are. The romance of illusion. In fact, since the effects of the chemo started wearing off, he's looked so goddamned presentable that even their closest friends assumed that he was cured, that this cruise was in celebration of his recovery. Hell, he can't even talk his own parents out of it, everyone so used to thinking of him as indestructible. Ah, but you've done so well. So they all cheered him on, giving him presents and advice, even offering to come with him. Of course he couldn't tell them he wasn't coming back.

How he's fooled them all these years, most of the time anyway, keeping on with his teaching, his life, his sailing, as though nothing were wrong. His one regret is that he hasn't done so many of the other things he once thought he wanted to or should: one puny book, a few articles, some paltry good works, but nothing that will last. It's taken all his energy just to keep on going, just to stay alive. Sara is the only one who knows this, and sometimes he's not even sure she understands.

So after all, it had been easier just to keep on preserving the illusion. There was the insurance to think of, particularly on the boat, invalidated if he didn't notify the company, pay an extra premium to take the boat offshore. Even then, they insisted he outfit the boat properly. So he had ended up going through the motions, letting Sara collect and stow the necessary safety equipment, food and supplies, the whole works.

Still, going through the motions turned out better than he thought. It was, after all, something he and Sara could do together, the last thing, in fact. He had moved onto the boat still sensing her disapproval, her refusal to accept, the suspicion that she regarded his sailing off into the sunset—or the sunrise, to be more exact—as a final act of cowardice. "You're not dead yet!" she'd screamed at one point. "Stop acting like it!"

But a few days later she had turned up, standing on the dock at the marina with her ditty bag and few days' worth of clothes. "The kids will be fine; Joyce is going to look in on them. Anyway, they're old enough," she'd said, her mouth trembling, when he'd asked her what she was doing here. "I just want to be as close to you as I can for as long as I can."

They had stayed together on the boat, working to make it shipshape, make things "look good" for the voyage, sleeping on board and, at last, making love in the tiny forward cabin.

Though it had been good, he had sensed her holding back, the old refusal to let go, and in his disappointment—after all, couldn't they make the best of what little time there was to be together?—had asked her finally what was wrong. "I'm afraid you'll die," she said. He stared at her in disbelief: surely her illusions didn't extend this far. Then he understood. "You mean while we're fucking?"

She nodded, huddled cross-legged in the V-berth, head bent, not looking at him: "I've been afraid for a long time. Your heart pounds so hard, I don't see how it can keep on going. I keep thinking it will burst."

In spite of himself he'd laughed. "Fucking in the fo'c'sle. There are worse ways to go."

"Not for me."

No, not for her. Still, they had had some good times. Then it was time for him to go, no farewell party, just Sara and the kids lined up on the dock at Indian Cove, waving goodbye. He had had to turn away from the sadness, the disappointment on her face. Bad luck, he'd told her, to watch a boat out of sight. He watched them file up the gangway, Linnie turning around one last time to wave, the small dot of her face barely visible. He'd forced himself to turn his own eyes seaward, not look back. And off he went.

So here he is. He wonders what to do, whether to wait a while longer, or just take matters into his own hands, open the seacocks and get the whole thing over with. Holding the tiller with his knee, he takes off his glasses, wipes his eyes clear, and looks at the reading on the log. The logline is hanging practically straight down off the stern, motionless, like a puncture in the skin of the ocean. He looks at his watch, 1700. Five P.M. He's come only fifteen miles in the last five hours. Still, he ought to be far enough out by now, unless he's been set more to the north than he counted on.

The boat has subsided into a random rolling motion, the rhythmic clank of rigging and flap and billow of sails indicating that the wind is about to die completely. The surface of the ocean behind him is as shiny and viscous-looking as an undulating pool of oil, the swells so long and flat now that they're barely noticeable. The seagulls squawk and jabber as they wheel around the cross-shaped mast like birds of prey. The sun is shining across the water at such a low angle the water looks colorless, transparent, almost white, the swells as motionless as sand dunes. On the other side of the sky the almost-full moon lies just above the horizon like a worn sand dollar washed upon a beach. The fair wind from the southwest that brought him this far on an easy beam reach once he got offshore has blown itself away, leaving only the ever-diminishing sea swells behind.

"Wouldn't you know?" he says aloud to no one in particular, flinging the tiller to one side in disgust. "You can't trust anybody.

Never give a sucker an even break!" In the absence of wind, the words echo strangely in his ears.

"*. . . All right*," *he says to Sara, and pushes the tiller across the coaming. The boat begins to swing around, then stalls, its sails flapping aimlessly, as limp and fragile as a closed eyelid. The water has lost its ruffled quality, and between them and the shore, the surface lies as flat and slippery-looking as a pool of oil. The boat coasts for a few feet, then settles back into the water like a roosting bird. The wind has simply blown itself away . . .*

"Well, how do you like that?" Phil says, his voice still echoing in his ears with the odd sense he's heard it all before. His head is pounding again, his stomach queasy; as he stares across the water a gray veil passes momentarily across his line of sight. Maybe this is it, he thinks. Maybe it's starting. He has the creepy sense there's someone with him, just out of sight, in the shadow the sail casts over the deck, or behind the mast.

But then his vision clears. Looking back over his shoulder, he sees the sea swells diminishing in the distance, the horizon flattening out. He squints across the sparkling water behind him, the rippled wake leaving a corridor of calm. A black speck appears, then disappears, on the still-heaving horizon. Oh, hell, not another boat. Just what he was afraid of, he's still not out far enough. He squints again; runs his gaze along the whole perimeter. Whatever it was is gone; an optical illusion perhaps, the last sun sight he took glinting a mote into his eye. Still, he can't take the chance. But it's all right. He'll just wait until after sunset, wait until it's dark.

Standing in the kitchen staring at the phone, Sara imagines this:

The phone rings. She snatches up the receiver. "Hello!"

A brief pause, as though the party were startled to be yelled at, then a polite, cultivated not-quite-British voice coming over the wire. "Mrs. Boyd? This is Dr. Ephraim Bierstadt calling."

She wipes a clammy hand across her jeans. The other one is wrapped so hard around the receiver the knuckles hurt. She tries to ease her fingers loose, then switches hands, her heart galloping. It's all right, she thinks to herself. What could this guy know?

"Mrs. Boyd? I'm sorry to call so near suppertime, but might I speak with Professor Boyd?"

"Uh, I'm sorry, he's not here," she answers automatically.

"I see. Can you tell me when he'll be back or where he might be reached?"

"I can't. He can't. I mean he won't," she stammers, tearing at her hair. Why is this man asking? Why is he calling now? "Be back, that is," she finishes stupidly. "He's gone."

"Oh, dear me." There is another brief silence, then the voice somber, even mournful. "I am so sorry to hear that. I feared I might be too late. My condolences . . ."

Of course he has misunderstood her, the expectation of Phil's demise too readily fulfilled perhaps, but nevertheless, strictly speaking not just yet. In the interest of accuracy she interrupts, "No, no, I didn't mean that. I mean he's gone away, on a trip. Sailing." Then thinks: Too late for what?

"Oh, how wonderful!" The voice exudes relief. "I dare *say*! When will he be back?"

"Ah," she equivocates, the words "he won't" suddenly sticking in her throat, superstition perhaps; to say it is to make it so. "I couldn't tell you. Was it important?" but she knows already, with the recognition through long familiarity of the bitter irony of fate; it is what they hoped for all along, the chance of the odd miracle.

"Hmm, rather," he drawls, the seconds ticking.

She imagines that she doesn't want to know, thinks she will hang up. She holds the phone a little way from her ear, still listening.

"Yes, well, will you tell him when he returns that we are in the process of developing a new treatment, or rather, a variation of the old which has showed some promising results, probably not a cure you understand, at least we can't say at this point, but nevertheless we thought it might be something we could give a try. After all, he's withstood so much, and he's still quite remarkably strong . . ."

Quietly she backs the phone further away from her ear, the voice still chirping like a cricket its cheery unintelligible message of hope come too late, reaches out her other hand and depresses the prongs with chilly fingers. The natter stops abruptly. She pries open her paralyzed fingers and hangs up.

But the phone does not ring; there is no call. She leaves the kitchen and goes into Phil's study. What else could I do, she thinks, standing by Phil's desk. She picks up the stack of plastic ID cards, half-a-dozen of them in various colors, one for every hospital, thinking she will just throw them out. It's too late now. He's made his choice not to go on, and she can hardly blame him. He has suffered so much, how could anyone ask him to do more? Yet she pictures a fleet of helicopters batting their way eastward toward the moon, rising over the ocean like sperm thrashing toward the egg; far below yet still visible, the small, white wavering triangle of sail.

She stares at the pile of X-rays she's pulled out of all the desk drawers, file cabinets, medical records, letters, lab reports, the works, thinking she'd get rid of them. Small bone-scans like a sinister deck of cards with Halloween skeletons dancing in the dark, big scintigrams with lightning bugs clustered here, here, and here, CAT scans like cafeteria trays; this small tapioca pudding your gallbladder, this loaf of bread your . . . oh, never mind. The only thing that's true is that it's suppertime.

Nevertheless, she shoves the X-rays, scintigrams, scans and IDs, the whole record of their lives since Phil first got sick all those years ago, back in the drawers where they came from, just in case.

Waves revolve in a circular motion. Agitated by the force of the wind blowing across the surface, the water resists the force, thus deflecting it downward, then up and around. The stronger the wind and the greater the distance over which it blows, the higher and steeper the waves. But the waves do not move forward appreciably, they merely revolve in a circular motion.

Although wave after wave gives the illusion of sequence, it is not the water moving, but the force moving through the water. Thus all the water in the ocean stays in one place, its only real motion a stationary breathing in and out with the tides. The water changes shape but not position. It is this circular motion that gives the sailor the illusion of moving forward in time and space. Think of the purely metaphorical use: waves of nausea, waves of terror. Waves in water too are metaphor, their forward motion no more than an illusion. Thus too life is an illusion of motion, of sequence. He, Phil, is not life; life is a force that moves through him. Thus it scarcely matters that it has been short and uneventful, soon to end. Life will go on without him after all.

A pity really, when he thinks of it. If it weren't for the other thing, he could do this; go across the ocean and come back safe. He knows so much more now, about sailing in particular. He used to wonder for instance, how wind blowing sideways into a sail could make a boat go forward. Now he knows that it is a combination more than simply a balance of conflicting forces, the wind blowing the boat to leeward, the force of the keel resisting, the two almost canceling each other out, but what little force of wind is left squeezing the boat ahead, until the motion of the wind sliding back along the parabola of sail creates a vacuum at the luff, and that too begins to suck the boat forward. This is the slot or funnel effect, proceeding from the center of effort at the belly of the sail along the luff; thus the boat leaps ahead, not merely pushed but also pulled along by the wind.

Of course all this is true only as long as you keep on moving. In order for a boat to move forward, for waves to revolve, you must have wind. But there is no wind, not even a hope of wind. The sails hang limp and ghostlike, not even a billow; the shrouds are silent, not a whisper of sound. Even the gulls have fled, quacking with boredom, a ragged line withdrawing westward with the sun. All around, the treacherous sea lies opaque and shiny as a mirror, flat and still as glass. Overhead the sky stretches brittle, colorless, and clear as a crystal bowl, air and water indistinguishable from one another, the seam of the horizon invisible. The sun dangles huge and faceless as the back of a gold pocket watch; Phil too feels suspended, motionless, as though he's trapped inside a huge glass lens, a drop, a tear. Suddenly it occurs to him, in the absolute stillness, that this is death. It has overtaken him without his notice. This silence, this lack of movement, this suspension of time and space is what death is.

Then the gold disc of the sun hits the invisible rim and bursts the surface of the ocean to fragments, iridescent rose, pink, red, silver, blue, slivers of a painting done on glass, that flash and stab bright streaks into his eyes, making them smart so that he has to squint and look away.

More rapidly than he thought possible the sun sinks downward, diminishing by half, pulling its rayed mosaic with it, now rubbed and faded like the worn bits of sea glass he and Sara used to collect as they walked along the shore, the sun sliding further until only a narrow chromium arc is left, shedding a small pool of pale yellow crescents catching light. Then this too vanishes, and all around the silvered surface tarnishes to charcoal, to pebble, then to ash. At his back he feels the chill, the long line of shadow flying across the water toward him, the dark. His heart thumps with terror. Oh, God, he thinks, I'm afraid.

Enough of this. Phil sheets the jib in tight and cleats the main, ties off the tiller amidships to keep the rudder from banging against the hull as they drift along in the swell. He checks the deck to see that everything is shipshape, then starts below to open the seacocks.

Sara stands in the kitchen glaring at the telephone on the wall, folded like a bat, sinister and lurking. She's had enough for today, ears pricked, body tensed, waiting for the goddamned thing to ring. What is she waiting for? There can be no good news.

But no news, on the other hand, is no news. She marches over and plucks the receiver off the hook and leaves it hanging. It begins to squeak in protest, shrill bleats that remind her of a heart monitor. The dog rushes into the room, toenails clicking, spots the receiver dangling near the floor, sniffs it, then cocks his head from side to side, trying to sort out the beeps. She covers her ears, briefly considers yanking the whole thing off the wall completely, throwing it out the window into the driveway, and running over it with the car; so much for the bad news.

But she knows this won't really help. Silly, anyway, to think that preventing the phone from ringing, refusing to answer can keep the worst from happening. No news is good news; if you don't hear about it, then it can't be so. This is nonsense, of course;

the bad news would still be out there humming on the wires, whether she picked up the phone or not. There is no safety. She puts the phone back on the hook.

As she opens the kitchen door to let the dog out, the narrow garage window opposite her momentarily takes on the rippled rose-streaked tinge of primitive stained glass as it reflects the sun going down across the way. She can hear David rummaging around somewhere in the garage, a hollow clunking noise as though someone were juggling Indian clubs, shortly resolved into the sustained rumble of a stack of wood falling over. All Phil's hard work.

"Hey," she says.

"Hey," comes the muffled reply, the disembodied voice for a moment disconcertingly like Phil's. A head pops up, flushed and dusty; David's. "Hi, Mom," he says breathlessly.

"It's getting dark. Don't you think it's time to quit? Tomorrow is another day."

He nods; Yeah sure, Mom, humoring her. Actually no reply. He disappears again. She hears the rustle of a heavy cardboard box being dragged over the concrete floor. "I'd rather stay here and work on the stuff for the yard sale a while longer, okay?"

"Yeah, sure," she answers. Rhythmic thumps from overhead, the floor vibrates and the window rattles: Linnie's stereo. Most of the garage is in shadow now, but she can see well enough to tell that number of boxes stacked along the walls is impressive. "You didn't go into my workshop, did you?" Sara asks, noticing that the door is open.

"No, I just looked, but can I?" David says hopefully. "There must be lots of stuff you don't want; you hardly ever go in there anymore. Everything's covered with dust."

"Hmmm," Sara replies absently, pacing along the tipsy row, the dog prancing at her heels. From what she can see poking out of boxes this is not just garage junk, but attic and closet too. She reaches down and swabs around in a large box apparently filled with nothing but wadded-up bunches of newsprint. "What's this," she asks. "Your crumpled newspaper collection?"

"Very funny," he says with the exaggerated nasal snideness that passes for teenaged irony, harmless enough. "What's that?" he shoots back, gesturing toward the open door of her workshop, the sheeted figures like so much covered furniture in a deserted house. "Your ghost collection?"

He doesn't mean it, she thinks, pressing her teeth together against the sharp obscenity that sweeps up toward her lips. He can't know how close to the truth his innocently smart-ass remark is. "Very funny," she says coolly, carefully mimicking his tone in an attempt to deflect the rising, irrational anger she feels; much more anger than is justified by the remark itself. It doesn't all belong on him. But some does, she thinks; he has to learn. "That was uncalled for," she says sternly. "Go inside."

"Aw, Mom . . ." he starts, as always the swift negotiator.

"Just go. I'm putting Dad's truck back in. You can do the rest tomorrow."

He shuffles reluctantly toward the door, thwarted, put upon, misjudged, while she walks out to the rusty old red truck, this too another of Phil's "wear-it-out" projects, slated for demolition in due course. She creaks open the door and hops up onto the sprung seat, cranks the ignition, revs the accelerator, clashes the shift lever into reverse and starts to back toward toward the garage.

"No, Mom! Wait!" Over the whine of reverse she barely hears David calling. What the fuck does the kid want now, more argument? She'll show him argument. She guns the engine louder, faster, twists the wheel, pops the clutch and backs up with the swift competence of righteous anger, thinking it's probably just the goddamned telephone, another nosy well-wisher calling to ask if there's any word. The mere idea makes her furious. She aims the truck toward its slot in the garage and zooms it in.

"Mom, stop!" David screams, and she sees him now, waving and gesticulating, in a slow-motion replay of that other time, but just too late as she hears the crunch and feels the thump of wheels, up and over . . .

Oh, Phil, oh Christ, not again, she thinks, slamming her foot on the brake and letting her head fall forward onto the cool crescent of the wheel in despair. Please not the dog. Not the goddamned dog.

———

"Phil."

Christ, who is it now? Phil thinks in annoyance, head down in the bilge reaching for the handle to the aft seacock. Can't they leave him alone? He squats back on his heels. A wave of nausea washes over him, stars spin before his eyes. Shit, now he'll have to go back on deck anyway before he pukes.

He sticks his head up through the companionway, peers at the darkening horizon. The sea is the rippled blue-black color of a mussel shell. Stars prick through the faded gray net of the night sky one by one, like the beginning of a show at some primeval planetarium. He can't see all of them. Someone's head is in the way.

"Hello there, Phil."

It's a man's voice, slightly nasal, on the high side, not one he recognizes. Cautiously he steps out of the companionway, staring at the figure sitting at the other end of the cockpit, leaning back against the coaming, legs crossed, baggy pants, a white shirt open at the collar, sleeves rolled up.

"Come on up," the figure says, then leans over, reaches down for something at his feet. There's a rattle, a slosh, a ripple of slicked-back, lightish hair, glimpse of a handsome profile, gleam of a silver martini shaker. "Got any glasses?" the figure says. "Mine got broken."

Phil shuts his eyes. Oh, God, he thinks. All those great souls floating around loose in the universe who could see me out—St. Augustine, Carl Jung, George Eliot, Thomas Merton, St. Brendan the navigator (my own personal choice), to name a few—and I end up with F. Scott Fitzgerald, drunk.

He starts forward, prepared at least to be polite. The man sits back, jiggling the shaker, and the light from the high, gibbous moon, almost as bright as daylight, catches his face. Phil looks again. No, not Scott. This is somebody he's never seen before, even in pictures. At least he doesn't think so. A man about his own age or even younger, forty or so, dark blond hair, round, slightly meaty face, creased forehead, broad straight nose, thin lips, on the stocky side, fairly good-looking but no movie star. Yet, something familiar about the cocked eyebrow, the witty, amused, slightly ironic smile. The man looks up at him, says in a jaunty voice, "Hey, son. Don't you know me?"

Phil sits down with a thump, staring, momentarily speechless. He clears his throat. It's him, of course it's him. "Sorry, uh . . . but you don't really look much like your photographs."

He nods tolerantly. "Studio shots. All dolled up. This is the real me."

"I guess I thought you would be older."

"No, I never got older. You stay the same, wherever you are at the time. Just the people who are left get older. But it doesn't matter; things really stay about the same. I'm still her father."

I should have known that, Phil thinks. Sara told me that all these years, when her father came to her in dreams, he never got any older. Now she is older than he was when he died. He had asked her if it seemed funny, but she said no, it didn't matter, things seemed right, really just the same. It made her feel relieved just to see him, better than all those other dreams where she was always looking and couldn't find him. He wonders if he too will come back to her in dreams.

"Why don't you get some glasses from down below and we'll have a drink and talk."

Phil hesitates. "Well, I was about to . . ."

He waves a hand dismissively. "Oh, I know. But that can wait. You've got lots of time. Besides, it's too light out anyway. The moon is up. Someone might see you. Let's just sit here a while."

He's right. It's much too light out. Phil gets some plastic cups from down below and sits across from him—should I call him Jim? James? Mr. Gilead? Dad? he wonders—while her father pours out the drinks and starts to talk.

Maybe it's the strength of the martinis, or the headache that he has all the time now, the pounding in his brain as though it were about to burst out of his head, the rapid fluttering of his heart against his chest, but he doesn't quite catch everything that's said. The face is familiar, but not the voice. Unexpectedly high and light, almost squeaky, like a record played a touch too fast, an odd mixture of tone and accent. He probably should have known her father had a western Pennsylvania twang, but somehow he always imagined him speaking in a cultured, upper-crust WASP cadence, yoicks and hoity-toity. That is what is lost first, he's heard, the sound of someone's voice. Even recorded, it can't be reproduced exactly. Like smells, too evanescent. Of course he never heard her father's voice, doesn't remember her even describing it. Not that this even is her father, really, come to that: it's just an hallucination. Why, he could be on his way down to the bottom this very instant, spinning down through miles of deep, cold water as silently as a leaf through air. He wonders when he'll get to the tunnel part, the dazzling light and beyond; if this man, whom he never knew, is to be his guide. On the whole, he thinks he might prefer good old Uncle Danny or the other old guy with the Christmas tree he vaguely remembers from before. Still, he's grateful for the company while he's waiting for the end.

"Do you have regrets?" Phil asks by way of conversation. "Dying so young? I mean, I wanted to do good in the world, but all I did was get sick and then go sailing."

"Oh, sure." Her father nods. "They weren't ready, Sara especially, the little kids so young. Hell, *I* wasn't ready. A lawyer, for cripes' sake, and I didn't even leave a will. Should have known better. It's not that we weren't warned. Just careless, I guess. But it was all so sudden. There wasn't even time to say goodbye."

Phil looks at the face in the moonlight. Yes, Sara does resemble him; a shadow passes, and he sees her face, pale, ghostlike, superimposed upon the other, smiling, laughing, but always the sadness around the eyes . . . He blinks it away. Well, his affairs are in order, the kids more or less grown up, Sara used to the idea of being on her own. He has given them all time to get ready, time to say goodbye. That's what he has bought them with his pain. Big fucking deal.

"You gave them that," her father is saying. "Even though it's still too soon. But then, I guess it always is."

Phil can't say anything. He knows that. But there's nothing he can do, not anymore. He has not, after all, as Sam suggested all those years ago—five years, nine months and fourteen day, to be exact—done nothing; he has done as much as he could for as long as he could. So what else is there except, in the words of the poet, "a quiet sleep and a sweet dream, when this long trick is over." Only the trick has been on him.

"That's true," her father says, as though he's heard him, which he no doubt has, since he's either a figment or a ghost. Phil's not even sure they've actually talked in words. Or even voices. "Still, you never know," her father says. He uncrosses his knees, staring off toward the western horizon, crosses his legs the other way. The light of the moon, now past its zenith, has bleached his hair and clothing so that he looks more like his photograph. "The thing that did me in they fix routinely now. Quadruple bypass, valve job, and Bob's your uncle; I could still be alive now. There are new treatments coming along all the time. For you, in a year, even six months, who knows?"

Christ, not another one, Phil thinks; I can see where Sara gets it. And suddenly in his voice Phil hears an echo, not just of Sara, but other voices edging over, like blurred images on a video screen, shadows beyond—"Perfect is the enemy of good," "the chance of the odd miracle," "one never knows when something might turn up." And the others whose live voices haunt him also, "I would do nothing, do nothing," "We have done everything for you that medical science has to offer at this point in time," "whatever can be done can be done here, done here, done here," a whole contradictory chorus of them now, saying "come back, too late, don't go, please stay, nothing something everything nothing . . ." and out of the water he seems to see pale phosphorescent fingers rising up, hands waving for his attention, clawing at the air to get to him, begging him, beckoning him back, waving him on.

He jumps up. "No!" he shouts to all the voices, the clutching, grasping, begging hands. His head throbs, across his chest he feels a searing pain. And all this time he thought he might be dead already, beyond the pain. "No more!" he shouts, whirls in the cockpit, ducks his head toward the companionway.

The moon in the western sky catches his eye, worn silver dollar slightly turned, not fully round, still bright, shining a glowing white path of pebbled light across the water so that the ocean swells, hardly more than ripples now, seem to stretch as motionless and frozen as snowdrifts across a winter field. He catches his breath, puts a hand against the hatch, studying the horizon in disbelief. A black speck is moving toward him, a waterbug, legs stroking, walking on water, stupid thing to come out this far, but no, as it looms bigger, he sees to his amazement it's a boat with oars, a figure rowing swiftly, small, determined face turning over the shoulder now and then to see how fast the distance is closing. "Oh God," he says over his shoulder to his companion, "Do you fucking believe this? She's coming after us, all the way out here, she's coming to rescue both of us!" He stares in amazement. "Doesn't she ever give up?"

The voice murmurs faintly, "She wanted to be there, you know. She couldn't just stand by and do nothing; she still thinks there might have been something more that she could do. She just wants to make sure that she did everything she could."

Her face, pale, turned toward him, round almost like the moon, he can see it now as she rows closer . . . *and she looks so pretty, sitting there with her cheeks reddened by the wind, hair all blown around in wisps, staring at him intently, earnestly, small and determined. "The tide is turning," she says. "That means there'll be wind."*

"Oh, God, Sara. It's too late. I can't." Turning to his companion, he cries, "Can't she just let me go?"

But there is no one there. He is alone, standing in the cockpit of his boat. All around the sea stretches white, limitless, empty, undisturbed.

It was not, after all, the dog. It was a box from the attic full of marionette props, including the little chair her father made her all those years ago. How could she have been so careless? She had screamed and cursed, hopped up and down, incoherent with grief and rage, while everyone scattered, the cats to their hiding places, the dog fleeing upstairs with Linnie, who had rushed down to see what happened, David off to his room, almost in tears. It was not really his fault. The dog, frisking by, had knocked the precariously balanced box down off the stack. David was on his way to put it with the other puppet stuff, next to the theater in her workshop, when she backed over it, crunching the box flat.

The pets and children are all asleep now, and the house is quiet. It's getting late, but Sara is sitting at the kitchen table with the pieces of the little chair in front of her, trying to glue it back together. It doesn't look too bad, considering; one side is still intact, the back broken only in two pieces. It's the seat that is the problem; old and brittle, the wood has splintered in several places, and can't be put back together without gaps.

She jumps as the phone rings right behind her ear; the chair topples over and the seat comes apart again. "Damn!" she yells, snatching the phone off the hook. "Hello!"

"You don't have to yell," her mother says in an injured tone. "I just called to see how you were doing. Is there any word?"

Oh, Christ, will it ever end? Anyway, her mother should know better. "No," she snaps. "And there isn't going to be any."

"You never know," her mother says in that ditsy know-it-all tone of hers that drives Sara nuts.

"Listen, Mom. He isn't coming back. Okay?"

"Oh." There is a pause while Sara's mother works it out. She may have been loony-tunes most of her life, Sara thinks, but she's not stupid. "Well," her mother says after a moment. "That's better really."

Sara can hardly believe her ears; Pollyanna the Glad Girl even after all these years? Shit. "Better than what?" she demands.

"Well, he's suffered so much. And better for you, too. This way you won't have to watch him die. I always thought, after your daddy died, that that's what saved me."

This is news, Sara thinks, standing there with the phone pressed to her ear, struck speechless by her mother once again. Even after all these years, her mother still hasn't lost the capacity to surprise her. But saved her from what?

"You know, his going suddenly like that, away from home. I knew something was going to happen, I could feel it, and I begged him not to go, but he said, 'Just two more leases to go and it'll be over, I'll be back.' And then the call came and I said how bad is it, and they said pretty bad, he died ten minutes ago, and you were writhing on the bed, sobbing, and all I could think was, 'I'm so glad I wasn't there.' I could never have watched him die. So it was better that way."

"Wouldn't it have been better if he'd lived?" Sara asks, then starts to say, maybe if you had been there, but imagining her mother with tears in her eyes, voice trembling, thinks no, that would be too cruel.

"No, not really," her mother says in a matter-of-fact voice. "He wouldn't have wanted to live that way."

"What way?"

"Suffering, maybe pain, always taking care. Imagine your father with no golf, no martinis, no rare steak? So it was better, for him, anyway. He would never have been the same, and he would have hated that." Her mother sighs. "That's the trouble. Nobody wants things to change. You keep wanting things—people—to stay the same. But everything changes. Even your own children get to be just people you used to know."

"Oh, Mom." Sara feels like crying, for her mother, for herself, for all the lonely years ahead, the ones behind. "Mom," she sniffs, wanting comfort, "you know that little chair that Daddy made me? It got broken."

"Well, never mind. You can mend it. You're good at that."

Sara nods. Her mother hasn't asked how badly. Tucking the phone into her neck, Sara sticks the pieces of the seat back together. The glue, with more time to set, now holds. What is broken can be mended.

"Okay, dearie," her mother says. "I won't keep you any longer. Just remember, your old mumsy's here if you need me. You sound tired; try to get some sleep."

"Thanks, Mom," Sara says, unable to think of anything more to say. What else is there? "Bye." She hangs up the phone, her mother's words a jumble in her head, echoes of childhood endearments, advice, feelings she's never heard her mother talk about before, too much to be taken in all at once. Yet in spite of everything—death, illness, insanity—she's still here. Somewhere along the way, she seems to have worked things out. Sara wishes she could say the same.

She looks at the little chair, propped up on the kitchen table.

It's a little wobbly, and the seat is pitted where the splinters don't all fit, but yes, it's mended. Holding it carefully, she opens the back door and goes out through the garage into her workshop, puts it with the other puppet things, near the stage where it belongs, where it will be—relatively speaking—safe.

She pauses, as she knew she would, by the covered figures, reaches over and pulls off a sheet. There, her father, reclining, an effigy, the folded, dead hands, the waxen lips, eyes closed, but not in sleep. He looks dead, and dead is what he is. Only in her dreams can she still find him; there is no changing that.

And Phil. She wonders if he too will come back to her in dreams. She draws the cover down, looks at the face, serene, the old perfection of his body, the line of chest and abdomen unmarred. Of course it isn't him. She should have known better. "Take a good look at me now," he said, "because I'm never going to be the same."

What is broken can be mended, but it will never be the same. She sees now why the figure doesn't, why it can't possibly look right; she has left out the scars, the pain, the lines of suffering, all part of him now. Not what he was, but what he has become. This has been his gift to them, time to get ready, time to to say goodbye, all bought with his suffering and his pain. She had demanded; he had given. "I'm the one who's going to be broken." How could she deny his scars, his suffering? How could she leave them out?

Stiffening her trembling fingers, with her thumbs she scoops the hollows a little deeper under the eyes, thins the cheeks slightly, carves with her little fingernail a small tight line here and here around the mouth, presses the lips together more firmly but still smiling, really very little changed, no weight lost to speak of, still strong. That too he gave them, the illusion of his indestructibility, business as usual, keep on looking good. Only the eyes grown cautious, warier, filmed over with terrible knowledge, grit from the grave.

Then with the nail of her index finger rippling the clay, dragging a V-shaped rumple behind it like a wake, she digs two long curved lines on either side of the big torso in the stiff clay, almost symmetrical, his belly like an uninflated basketball, one hundred eighty-four stitches all tied by hand, then molds the edges together carefully until they resemble raised and knotted bands of rope. Sweating, crumbs of clay sticking to her face, her hands, mixing with tears, she steps back, looks a moment, then covers both the figures, goes out and shuts the door.

But there is something more she has to do. Wiping her hands, her face, she goes upstairs to check on the children, the animals; all sleeping soundly. It's just past midnight, they will sleep till noon. She has lots of time; she can be there before dawn, back by eight. She leaves a note leaning against the toaster just in case, gets in the car and starts the long drive to the coast.

Toothpaste, toothbrush, dental floss, nail clippers. A lavender-colored stone rubbed smooth from the beach at Lindiscove, just the right size to fit into the hollow of his palm. Several pieces of sea glass also worn smooth, all different: cobalt blue, bottle green, amber yellow, pale violet, white, rose pink, dark brown. Three Bicentennial quarters, taped to a soggy card, the ink smeared, now unreadable; he sent back the baby rattle shaped like a telephone before he left, but here tucked in the lining, the lucky threepenny bits that turned up suspiciously year after year "just by chance" in Phil's portion of the plum pudding every time they had Christmas dinner at the house of certain friends. The green scapular his father gave him, blessed by the Pope, Mary, Mother of God encased in a waterproof plastic case, a sacramental credit card rimmed with green. The figure outlined in green with downcast eyes, shoulders lifted as if to shrug. The heart with a knife stuck through, dripping green blood.

No pills, not even a loose one stuck in a crease, to stave off the inevitable. All gone, sinking like so many bits of broken glass beneath the wake. How could he have been so stupid? Didn't he think that he might change his mind? Hell, that's why he did it, to make sure. But that was before he understood. All these years he thought it was Sara doing the running, refusing to face reality. Yet he's the one who's finally run away.

Panting, dizzy with effort, his heart pounding in his chest, Phil puts the Dopp kit aside and tries to catch his breath. The gray haze swings before his eyes like a curtain: the moon is waning, low in the sky, the sea like milk; soon it will be really dark, as good a time as any for the end. A faint breeze gropes across his face, fresh and cool, but from a different direction, northeast. The tide change, something about the movement of great masses of water, wind from another direction; right again. He sees her face, ruddy, hopeful, as she sits there almost primly, holding a wet finger up, certain of the wind.

It wasn't that she never gave up, he sees that now. She just went on anyway, without hope, wanting to be sure that she had done everything, that they all had done everything they could. That was what she needed to go on with; why she couldn't let go. If love could save, she would have saved him. It is this love that has tied her to him all along, the line between them, not her belief in the odd miracle, what he took to be her stubborn refusal to face facts. So his sailing off into the sunrise must have seemed not just an act of cowardice, but a refusal of her love. She had done what she could; the rest was up to him.

He wishes he could get back to her, but without the pills that's clearly impossible. He's fading fast; he can't even nod his head without the pain throbbing, hair standing on end, sweat pouring off him, his heart pumping so fast he knows the slightest exertion will bring the end. In his mind—or is it in the air, faint, whispering?—he hears "there's no such word as *can't*." He doesn't know whether to laugh or cry.

Mind working quickly now in a buzz of final possibility, it suddenly comes to him; all right, maybe I won't make it, but I can still let her know. He reaches for the orange distress kit, the one like a huge cocktail shaker filled with flying flares, rockets and parachutes, tucks it under his arm, and climbs carefully up the companionway into the night air. The moon is down, in a few hours the sun will be rising, but right now the sky is very dark, a good time to shoot the flares. If he can get help, attract a passing ship, who knows? Maybe he can still be rescued. It's pretty hopeless really; he's almost passing out, but at least she'll know when they find the boat that at the last he changed his mind, tried to get back to her. At least she'll know he kept on trying, right up to the end.

He takes a deep breath and with sweaty, trembling fingers twists the top off the round orange canister. A clatter as something falls out onto the sole of the cockpit. He looks down, sees four amber plastic vials of medication rolling at his feet.

Oh, no, he thinks, and starts to laugh. Where else? If I opened the distress kit, she knew it would mean I wanted to live no matter what. Oh, God, she knew, all the time she knew. *Just in case. You can't be too careful.* Still laughing, tears running down his cheeks, he pours himself a cup of water, counts out a dose of pink, of white and blue, gulps them down.

Pow! flashing lights like fireworks beam across the sky, falling like spent rockets; too late, he thinks, then realizes what he's looking at is not inside his skull; it's the aurora borealis, streamers and curtains of pale green, red, and peach, so close he can almost reach out and touch them, emanating from a single point behind and to the west, a huge arched stained glass window reflected in the sea. Magnetic north, not a fixed point but one that is constantly moving, roughly 20° south and west of true north. He takes this for his temporary compass mark; it will do until he can get a sight. He looks down through the companionway at the sextant, gleaming like a child's bright miniature rocking horse in its fine square box. The moon is down, the sun is not yet up, but there are still the stars to go by.

Before long, he feels the pounding in his head subside, heart slowing to a faded rhythm even with the slow washing of the waves. The aurora borealis has started to fade; he looks toward the east, sees a faint tinge of pink, a rim of liquid gold; the sun. A slight breeze gropes tentatively across his face, drying the dampness on his skin. Far off he sees the tiny ripples starting; sure enough, wind coming up from the opposite direction. He loosens the sails, watches as they flap to the lee, then swing back through the eye of the wind. The boat, almost but not quite dead in the water, ghosts forward slowly. It's not perfect, he thinks, but it will just have to do. It's not so bad, as long as we keep on moving.

Sailing is not so much a science as an art, Phil thinks, turning his head now toward the mainsail to check the luff, now toward the water to look for cat's-paws. There are so many variables, wind strength and direction, tide changes, rogue waves and rollers, tankers and whales, storms and calms. There is so much to watch for. And then there are matters of discretion, whether to sail closer to the wind to gain distance, sometimes at the expense of speed, or to lay off to gain the fastest point of sail. In sailing you don't always get exactly where you meant to go. He knows it is a journey fraught with peril. He knows that even now he may not get back, that it will not be easy. But then it never was.

Walking along on the beach at half-tide, not too chilly as long as she keeps on moving, Sara searches for bits of sea glass, pink, pale green, violet, cobalt blue, amber, brown, visible even in the pale light of early dawn. Rubbed smooth from their long journey in the sea, usually they look almost like pebbles, but this morning, washed by the falling tide, they are bright and fresh-looking as fragments of a stained-glass window. They have many of these at home, on windowsills, in jars, lamp bases, baskets, pockets of coats and jeans. Still one by one she picks them up, even a rare red piece, puts them in the pocket of her jacket, thinking perhaps she will make something of them later. As she walks, they click together like loose pieces of a child's kaleidoscope.

She pauses, looks out to sea. The sun is beginning to tinge the eastern sky with rosy light; she should be getting back, for the children. She stares out at the water, the lines of breakers rolling in one after another, blue-black, then silver, streaked with pink, then gold, regular as heartbeats, the faint breeze from the sea a cool breath on her cheeks. She wonders where Phil is now, how far he has gotten toward where he wants to go.

She remembers his face the last time she saw him, waving back at them over the stern of the boat as he sailed away, intent but smiling, determined, even gay. He looked so well that day, his cheeks ruddy, still so strong, sailing so good for him (*"You look wonderful, you know. Your color's better, not so chalky. This is good for you"*), that she wanted to call out to him, "Come back! There must be some mistake!"; remembers too as though it were yesterday that day he came upstairs, sat down next to her on the bed, put his hand on her leg under the covers, a look on his face that stopped her breath, so apologetic, so resigned, so sad she knew at once. "I didn't want to tell you on the phone. Nevins called. My test results are off."

He has done everything he could, and what he did was just. It has been a struggle, difficult and long, and he has been so brave. Too soon; yet there comes a time for letting go. There are no roads where he is going, no phone lines to the land of the dead. Still there is this cord between them, and she knows she will feel his death, when it comes, as a breaking of the cord. Then it will be over.

Staring out to sea, she feels the line stretch taut between them. It stretches and stretches, grows thin . . . but does not break.

Miles to the east the rising sun streaks the sky with color. Standing upright in the cockpit of the *Loon*, Phil watches as the sails shudder, shake, then fill with wind. The boat leaps forward. He takes hold of the tiller and turns toward home.

Author's Note

I would like to thank the following people for technical assistance—nautical, medical, and artistic—while I was writing this novel:

Chuck Lakin and Murray Campbell of Colby College for help with matters of navigation, meteorology, and phases of the moon; Patricia McIlvaine, M.D., Daniel Onion, M.D., Edgar O. Kline, D.O., Rodney Williams, M.D., Ronald Natale, M.D., Brahm Shapiro, M.D., Timothy Harrison, M.D., Heidi von Bergen, R.N., Jean Moses, R.N., Karen K. Mosher, Ph.D., for medical advice and information; Sam Banks, Ph.D., Joanne Trautmann Banks, Ph.D., Steven Bauer, M.F.A., Patricia Onion, Ph.D., John von Bergen, M.F.A., Andrew G. McIlvaine, M.B.A., Anne and James Kenney, for help with various other matters crucial to the conception and writing of the book.

I also want to thank Gerry Howard for his patience, sensitivity and forbearance in what must have been the most painless editing sessions a writer ever enjoyed.

To Maxine Groffsky, for constant help and encouragement in the role of agent and critic, but even more as good and faithful friend, for making both the sailing and the writing of it possible— thank you.

And to my husband Ed, who continues to inspire me with his grace and courage in storms and calms, rough winds and heavy seas, who always was and still remains the true sailor—more than thanks.

FOR THE BEST IN PAPERBACKS, LOOK FOR THE Ⓟ

In every corner of the world, on every subject under the sun, Penguin represents quality and variety—the very best in publishing today.

For complete information about books available from Penguin—including Pelicans, Puffins, Peregrines, and Penguin Classics—and how to order them, write to us at the appropriate address below. Please note that for copyright reasons the selection of books varies from country to country.

In the United Kingdom: For a complete list of books available from Penguin in the U.K., please write to *Dept E.P., Penguin Books Ltd, Harmondsworth, Middlesex, UB7 0DA.*

In the United States: For a complete list of books available from Penguin in the U.S., please write to *Dept BA, Penguin,* Box 999, Bergenfield, New Jersey 07621-0999.

In Canada: For a complete list of books available from Penguin in Canada, please write to *Penguin Books Canada Ltd, 2801 John Street, Markham, Ontario L3R 1B4.*

In Australia: For a complete list of books available from Penguin in Australia, please write to the *Marketing Department, Penguin Books Australia Ltd, P.O. Box 257, Ringwood, Victoria 3134.*

In New Zealand: For a complete list of books available from Penguin in New Zealand, please write to the *Marketing Department, Penguin Books (NZ) Ltd, Private Bag, Takapuna, Auckland 9.*

In India: For a complete list of books available from Penguin, please write to *Penguin Overseas Ltd, 706 Eros Apartments, 56 Nehru Place, New Delhi, 110019.*

In Holland: For a complete list of books available from Penguin in Holland, please write to *Penguin Books Nederland B.V., Postbus 195, NL–1380AD Weesp, Netherlands.*

In Germany: For a complete list of books available from Penguin, please write to *Penguin Books Ltd, Friedrichstrasse 10–12, D–6000 Frankfurt Main 1, Federal Republic of Germany.*

In Spain: For a complete list of books available from Penguin in Spain, please write to *Longman Penguin España, Calle San Nicolas 15, E–28013 Madrid, Spain.*

In Japan: For a complete list of books available from Penguin in Japan, please write to *Longman Penguin Japan Co Ltd, Yamaguchi Building, 2-12-9 Kanda Jimbocho, Chiyuoda-Ku, Tokyo 101, Japan.*

FOR THE BEST IN CONTEMPORARY AMERICAN FICTION ⓟ

☐ **WHITE NOISE**
Don DeLillo

The New Republic calls *White Noise* "a stunning performance from one of our most intelligent novelists." This masterpiece of the television age is the story of Jack Gladney, a professor of Hitler Studies in Middle America, whose life is suddenly disrupted by a lethal black chemical cloud.

            326 pages   *ISBN: 0-14-007702-2*   **$6.95**

☐ **IRONWEED**
William Kennedy

William Kennedy's Pulitzer Prize-winning novel is the story of Francis Phelan — ex-ball-player, part-time gravedigger, and full-time drunk.

            228 pages   *ISBN: 0-14-007020-6*   **$6.95**

☐ **LESS THAN ZERO**
Bret Easton Ellis

This phenomenal best-seller depicts in compelling detail a generation of rich, spoiled L.A. kids on a desperate search for the ultimate sensation.

            208 pages   *ISBN: 0-14-008894-6*   **$6.95**

☐ **THE LAST PICTURE SHOW**
Larry McMurtry

In a small town in Texas during the early 1950s, two boys act out a poignant drama of adolescence — the restless boredom, the bouts of beer-drinking, and the erotic fantasies.   *220 pages*   *ISBN: 0-14-005183-X*   **$5.95**

You can find all these books at your local bookstore, or use this handy coupon for ordering:

Penguin Books By Mail
Dept. BA Box 999
Bergenfield, NJ 07621-0999

Please send me the above title(s). I am enclosing ⸻
(please add sales tax if appropriate and $3.00 to cover postage and handling). Send check or money order—no CODs. Please allow four weeks for shipping. We cannot ship to post office boxes or addresses outside the USA. *Prices subject to change without notice.*

Ms./Mrs./Mr. ⸻

Address ⸻

City/State ⸻ Zip ⸻

Sales tax: CA: 6.5% NY: 8.25% NJ: 6% PA: 6% TN: 5.5%

FOR THE BEST IN CONTEMPORARY AMERICAN FICTION

☐ **THE WOMEN OF BREWSTER PLACE**
A Novel in Seven Stories
Gloria Naylor

Winner of the American Book Award, this is the story of seven survivors of an urban housing project — a blind alley feeding into a dead end. From a variety of backgrounds, they experience, fight against, and sometimes transcend the fate of black women in America today.

192 pages   ISBN: 0-14-006690-X **$5.95**

☐ **STONES FOR IBARRA**
Harriet Doerr

An American couple comes to the small Mexican village of Ibarra to reopen a copper mine, learning much about life and death from the deeply faithful villagers. *214 pages   ISBN: 0-14-007562-3* **$5.95**

☐ **WORLD'S END**
T. Coraghessan Boyle

"Boyle has emerged as one of the most inventive and verbally exuberant writers of his generation," writes *The New York Times*. Here he tells the story of Walter Van Brunt, who collides with early American history while searching for his lost father. *456 pages   ISBN: 0-14-009760-0* **$8.95**

☐ **THE WHISPER OF THE RIVER**
Ferrol Sams

The story of Porter Osborn, Jr., who, in 1938, leaves his rural Georgia home to face the world at Willingham University, *The Whisper of the River* is peppered with memorable characters and resonates with the details of place and time. Ferrol Sams's writing is regional fiction at its best.

528 pages   ISBN: 0-14-008387-1 **$6.95**

☐ **ENGLISH CREEK**
Ivan Doig

Drawing on the same heritage he celebrated in *This House of Sky*, Ivan Doig creates a rich and varied tapestry of northern Montana and of our country in the late 1930s. *338 pages   ISBN: 0-14-008442-8* **$6.95**

☐ **THE YEAR OF SILENCE**
Madison Smartt Bell

A penetrating look at the varied reactions to a young woman's suicide exactly one year later, *The Year of Silence* "captures vividly and poignantly the chancy dance of life." (*The New York Times Book Review*)

208 pages   ISBN: 0-14-011533-1 **$6.95**